"With humor and rare in
Christine Holden makes a
A Time for Us."—Rexanne Becnel

DON'T MISS THESE OTHER EXCITING TIME PASSAGES ROMANCES, NOW AVAILABLE FROM JOVE!

A Time
for Us

Christine Holden

JOVE BOOKS, NEW YORK

TIME PASSAGES is a registered trademark of
Berkley Publishing Corporation.

A TIME FOR US

A Jove Book / published by arrangement with
the authors

PRINTING HISTORY
Jove edition / September 1998

The Penguin Putnam Inc. World Wide Web site address is
http://www.penguinputnam.com

ISBN: 0-515-12375-7

A JOVE BOOK®
Jove Books are published by The Berkley Publishing Group,
a member of Penguin Putnam Inc.,
375 Hudson Street, New York, New York 10014.
JOVE and the "J" design are trademarks belonging to
Jove Publications, Inc.

PRINTED IN THE UNITED STATES OF AMERICA

10 9 8 7 6 5 4 3 2

In Memorium

Dedicated to the loving memory of my father, Paul Louis McKay, Sr. My prince, my hero, my love. We miss you.

And to Jason Albert Boettner, one of God's littlest angels, and our "my do" baby. He brought us profound joy.

Acknowledgments and Thanks

To Nicholas Edward Boettner, Jason's big brother, who still gives us profound joy.

To Edward B. Boettner, without whom none of this would have happened.

To A. Y. de la Villesbret, thanks for the conference and the confidence.

To Vincent D. Luckett, who cheered us with caviar and buoyed us with champagne.

To Jean Price and DeWanna Pace, for believing in us, encouraging our every endeavor, and challenging us every step of the way.

To *our* Trana Mae Simmons, critique partner extraordinaire and friend beyond measure. And Barney, the calm in each of our rough seas.

To Zoey Annalise Megahey, my daughter, the whirlwind, who delights everyone and fills them with happiness.

To my mom, Shirley Holden Ferdinand, the other half of this writing team, and the best mom any woman could ask for. I hope I do half the job with Zoey that you did with me.

And last but certainly not least, to Anthony Paul Megahey, my husband. Here's to blue skies and hot dives!

A TIME FOR US

Chapter 1

"FORSOOTH, MOTHER! 'TIS impossible!" As desperation warred with outrage inside her, Ailith deCotmer stared at her mother.

Meghanne shook her head with assurance. "Nay, 'tis not. Your father has worked long and hard on his new time device."

"But—"

" 'Twill be no more talk between us," Meghanne interrupted. "If we send you away, our liege will only find you."

"But you *will* send me away," Ailith insisted.

She lifted herself from her bed and walked to the narrow slit that served as her window. She looked out. The daily jousting amongst the Castle Guard was under way in the lists. The men's exercises were both intimidating and comforting. It relieved her to know how well protected they were. It frightened her to think that her liege wouldn't hesitate to use those same men against her or anyone else in the castle if the need arose.

Desperation nearly won, and though she fought against them, tears pooled in her eyes. Why had Preston Claybourne, the Earl of Radford, taken an interest in her, an astrologer's daughter?

"There's no guarantee 'twill be executed according to our hopes, Ailith."

Ignoring her mother's halfhearted attempt at reassurances, Ailith sniffled and swiped at an escaping tear. "Where will you send me?"

She didn't really want to know the answer, but she had to have some idea of the place and time that her parents wanted to catapult her into with that daft time machine her father was working on.

Meghanne shook her head. "I can't be certain where you will end up. Mayhap back in time, mayhap somewhere in the near future, but 'tis not a certainty that 'twill work. 'Tis certain your father's idea is beyond this present time."

Ailith swallowed convulsively. "If you do send me away, will I ever see you again?"

Knowing it highly probable that she might never see her mother again, Ailith tried to keep the question at bay when her father came up with his mad scheme. She had every right to an answer, however, although her mother did not have one. How could she, when not even Ailith herself knew what place and time she would be sent to—if the device was ever in proper working order? Anger at the lechery of men rushed to the surface. Ailith's blood pounded. Her mother remained silent, too overcome to do anything else.

"Y-you're not certain?" she whispered with dread.

Meghanne sighed. A sympathetic look marring her beloved features, she pulled Ailith into her ample embrace and stroked her daughter's hair.

Ailith clung to her mother. She never wanted to leave the safe haven of Meghanne's arms. But she had to, and very soon. Until he had married Lady Glenna, she may have harbored a secret hope that Lord Preston would take her to wife, but she had never thought he would ask her to become his leman.

If not for the love her parents showered upon her, Ailith would have questioned their motives about the time machine. It seemed as if they wanted to just cast her off into the unknown. But it was precisely their love that made them so determined to see her father's scheme through.

Her parents would do everything to protect her, even forfeit their own lives if necessary. Of this Ailith felt certain.

Through her tears, the faint smell of lilacs reached her. Her mother always rinsed her hair with lilac water from the earl. Nobles didn't gift their servants with expensive items. That continued kindness to her mother from Lord Preston should have made them suspicious. If and when she departed, would she ever smell that scent again?

"You must hasten, child. Lord Preston would not take kindly to waiting for an underling."

Ailith pulled away from her mother, shooting her eyebrows up in surprise. "Lord Preston awaits me?" she asked with trepidation.

"Aye, even as we speak, he awaits you in his solar."

"Oh, Mother!"

"Take courage, child. Methinks he prepares for battle. This war with France seems endless. Since Bolingbroke died and Prince Hal ascended the throne, it only gets worse."

"Would that an arrow aimed at Lord Preston's breast find its true mark," Ailith whispered with bitterness.

"Then would our plight be enhanced by our liege's death? Who then would become master of this keep? Do not make such an evil wish, Ailith," Meghanne chastised, "for *we* may well be the sufferers if such a thing came to pass."

Ailith lowered her head for a moment before fixing her gaze on Meghanne. "I-I'm sorry, Mother. I am merely distraught. I do not wish harm to befall His Lordship."

4

4 Christine Holden

"I know how it is with you, my child. But you must go now. You must not provoke his temper."

"Aye."

With a last tremulous smile to her mother, Ailith departed the small chamber she'd occupied since her ten and third year. Until a few weeks ago she thought they'd been luckier than most servants, she reminded herself as she started down the sharply curving stone stairway.

Her father, Galen, was favored by Lord Preston for his knowledge of the stars. As a result, Meghanne had been made chatelaine of Greyhawke, and she, Ailith, as rare as it may seem, was educated in all the basics of a highborn lady. She and her parents never questioned Lord Preston's motives for doing such an unlikely thing. Everything, however, had become clear to her at the tournament Lord Preston staged a month past. After paying an odd amount of attention to her for a fortnight, he'd made known his intentions for her on the last day of the festivities.

Wearing a gold-and-scarlet houppelande, Lord Preston had looked every bit the powerful noble. The sun glinted off his dark hair as he'd beckoned Ailith to his tent with a crook of his long finger.

Her heart constricting with pride at the sight of him, she'd gone to him with no hesitation. He wasted no time in telling her what he wanted.

Smiling silkily, he perused her from the pearl-and-gold embroidered caul covering her head to the green cotehardie covering her body. "Lovely Ailith. The time has come for you to assume the duties that I've prepared you for. You're ten and nine after all. Ripe for the taking."

Ailith widened her eyes. At first she'd thought she hadn't heard him correctly. "I beg your pardon, milord?"

His golden gaze held her green one. Even if his lustful expression had left doubt as to his intentions, his words wouldn't have. "It's time for you to become my leman."

She gasped and backed away.

"I've waited long enough for you and will wait no more to take you to my bed."

"Milord, nay! You can't be serious."

"I most certainly am serious, Ailith. You've known me long enough to know that I never jest. If I speak, it is to be taken seriously. . . ."

Anger swirled through Ailith as the rest of that awful conversation came to mind. She quickened her steps. It was as if she were trying to run from the past and escape the words that humiliated her and forever shattered her perception of the man she thought she loved.

Lord Preston had taken a sip of mulled wine and pinned her with a disdainful stare. "Although you would have made a fair wife, you have neither money, land, nor political ties. That's the reason I took Lady Glenna of Essex to wife instead. As well you know, this marriage has been sanctioned by King Hal. But I've always desired and admired *you*."

He'd looked at her belly, and Ailith squelched the urge to wrap her arms around her middle to shield it from view.

"If you bear children from our beddings, they will be well cared for. . . ."

Ailith halted at the entrance of the Great Hall. She must get her wayward temper under control before she reached Lord Preston's solar.

Except for a few servants replacing the stale rushes with fresh, primrose-scented ones on the floor, the chamber was nearly deserted. The hounds lay near the crackling hearth, keeping a watch on the goings-on. Despite the blazing coals, a chill remained in the air. Ailith barely felt it.

In spite of her attempts to calm herself, her thoughts persisted, and her anger didn't abate. She and her parents were under the strict protection of the Lord of Greyhawke. *Or,* she thought with loathing, *strictly at his mercy.* His kindness toward her and her parents was not at all due to his regard toward her father. After all, why would an earl show such interest in a lowborn servant girl without an underlying motive?

Realizing she would stand there until vespers stewing in her fury, Ailith rushed through the Great Hall. She waved at Neville, one of Preston's newly acquired knights, and continued on her way, ignoring the admiring look he threw her.

Ailith's thoughts continued to race dangerously. She would become the lowliest of servants; she would rot in the dungeon before she would become Lord Preston's leman. And she would tell him so! If Lady Glenna, his proper and lawful wife by his own choice—never mind the king's request—ever decided to come and live at Greyhawke Keep, Ailith would become no more than His Lordship's whore in the eyes of the other servants.

But 'twas rumored that Lady Glenna of Essex refused to leave her home and travel so far north because of an unprecedented fear of the roads. 'Twas also rumored that she was with child and did not want to leave her close proximity to London. The true reason mattered not to her, Ailith thought, directing her steps to another stairway which led to the solar entrance. She would *not* lie with a wedded man!

Standing before the heavy oaken portal, her spirits sank. The flames of her fury died as surely as if she had been doused in a chilly stream. Her silent wishes were hopeless. She was but a villein and he a powerful noble, who had favor with King Hal. She had no say whatsoever in the matter of her fate.

Raising her hand, she knocked upon the solid door.

''Enter.'' The voice beyond caressed the word.

Hating the sound, she stepped inside. Sunshine lit up the room, gleaming through the lone window, where Lord Preston stood looking out. Nearly all the windows were mere slits, but not this one, which was large and overlooked the bailey. Fine tapestries hung in strategic places on the walls, including over the hooded fireplace.

When Lord Preston turned to face her, her breath caught. In her distress she'd pushed all images of the man from her mind. She'd forgotten how magnificent he was and why he could easily command attention.

Wavy, black hair curled at the nape of his strong neck. His perfectly sculptured jaw defined his wide, sensuous mouth. He looked down his aquiline nose through golden eyes, heavily fringed with almost too long lashes. The barest of smiles played upon his lips as he studied her.

Not taking her attention from the lord of Greyhawke, Ailith walked fully into the solar. She'd been in his presence countless times before, but she didn't recall him being so tall or his shoulders so wide.

"You summoned me, milord?" she asked, her voice a mere whisper.

"Aye, Ailith," Lord Preston answered with irritation. " 'Twas some time ago. You have no chores to detain you, yet you delayed answering my summons. Why?"

He rested that golden gaze on her face briefly, then lowered it to her breasts and waist, continuing on to the flare of her hips.

Color once again stole into Ailith's cheeks; not from anger this time, but from the blush the heat of his perusal caused. Excitement kindled within her, and she damned him for sparking her untried senses. How could a simple gaze from this arrogant man so easily stir her?

"Why did you delay, Ailith?" he asked again.

"I beg your indulgence, milord." Not missing the sharpened edge in his voice, she couldn't raise her tone above a mere whisper. "I meant no disrespect." Shifting her weight, she folded her arms across her chest. "My delay c-comes from a w-womanly nature. I hope His Lordship can appreciate the reason for my detainment without further explanation."

Ailith hated lying, and in truth, the idea to plead her monthly had just occurred to her when Lord Preston boldly assessed her figure like the licentious lech he was rumored to be. Forsooth, her flux had just ended.

Sensing his delight at her unease, she dropped her arms to her sides and tossed her hair across her shoulders in defiance. She didn't want to give him any measure of satisfaction. Regaining her control, self-confidence filled her. "Why have you summoned me, milord?" she asked coolly.

Lord Preston laughed harshly. She raised her chin.

"I was fully prepared to *show* you why, sweetling." He towered before her. "Tell me, Ailith, are you really plagued by your monthly occurrence or are you just a clever liar?" he challenged in a silky voice.

Ailith gasped and spun away from him.

A huge, airy room, the solar was adjacent to her lord's bedchamber. Several chairs and benches stood in the room, one of which Ailith walked to and, without permission, sat down.

His mockery irritated her, his nearness riveted her, and her lie disturbed her. Heat flamed her skin. "I am offended by your charge, Lord Preston," she sharply retorted.

Lord Preston laughed, a great booming laughter that came from somewhere deep inside him. When mirth filled him as it did now, he seemed ten years younger, though in truth he had seen only three and thirty winters.

"Mayhap an apology is in order, Ailith, if the color staining your lovely cheeks is an indication of your honesty." In a thrice the smile departed his face, and his eyes narrowed. "Know this, lovely Ailith. You *will* become my leman. I will always treat you with the utmost kindness. And I promise any children you may bear me will be well cared for."

He paused and pinned her with an unreadable stare.

"Nature this day has only postponed the inevitable."

She remained motionless, trying to fathom her confusion. Since he hadn't taken her to wife, she wouldn't share his bed. He was a married man, and it would break her heart knowing she had to share him with someone else. He had been the subject of her maidenly dreams since he had moved her and her parents into the keep. For as long as she could remember she had heard tales of Preston's disdain for all womankind. Yet she had ignored all of those rumors because he had shown her nothing but the utmost kindness. His moods today veered sharply between intolerance and something she couldn't quite define. Desire, mayhap? His formidably compelling presence made her realize that if she didn't escape him soon, she would be privy to any requests he made of her.

The thought jolted her as though she had received a physical blow. How could her body betray what her heart whispered to her?

"Your father, and his father as well, have always had an honored place at Greyhawke for their loyal service," Lord Preston continued. "Your father's knowledge of the stars has always aided me in charting my courses in battle. Because of his service to me, you have been shown extra consideration."

Ailith shot to her feet. "Forsooth! I do not wish that kind of consideration thrust upon me, milord," she said, gritting her teeth. Boldly she went to stand before the large man.

Preston's black brows nearly touched as he looked down at her in surprise. "From your tone, sweetling, I gather you've been giving some thought to becoming my mistress." His gaze heated, and he dropped his voice to a husky whisper. "It would take little effort on my part to make you want me."

"You are a most attractive man, milord," she responded, rigid with anger at his smug assumption, "and most arrogant. But do save your efforts! Whatever my thoughts of you, I do not consider them an issue. The fact remains, Lord Preston, that I will *never* yield to you. I know in the end you will probably ravish my body, but you will never crush my resolve. After all, you are superior in strength to me." She threw the words at him like stones and flashed him a disdainful look.

His mouth thinned, and his jaw stiffened. Something infuriating and dangerous threatened to erupt from Lord Preston's control, which he seemed to be holding onto by sheer will. His furious look daunted her somewhat, and she swallowed, regretting her hasty words. But she refused to recall them or let him see how much he intimidated her. Glare for glare, she stood before him.

"Witch!" he growled in low tones. "You go too far! Your father is *not* indispensable. There are a score of star-

gazers out there ready to replace him. So tread carefully.
His position is not all that secure. In fact, his position depends on your cooperation. So do not forget from whence
you come. I can easily order you sent to the scullery."

"That is my every hope, milord," Ailith said defiantly.

"Oh, indeed? Then mayhap I should accommodate your
wishes. Then again, it's *my* wishes we're discussing."

He glowered at her. A black chill hung on the warning
edge of his words, but she laughed with contempt.

"With your propensity for self-indulgence, how can it
be otherwise?" she spat.

"You'd best hold your tongue or—"

"Do with me what you will, but I will *not* hold my
tongue!"

"Silence!" Lord Preston demanded. "Listen well,
wench. Your comeliness caught my attention. That I decided you would become my leman is to your advantage."

His furious look belied his low tone. The thin thread with
which he held onto his rising temper had nearly snapped.
But her own wrath refused to release her from its hold, and
she continued to provoke him.

"You are wedded to another!"

"Which matters naught to me!" he retorted. "You'd
best realize you have no say in this. You *will* curb your
sharp words and yield to my behest or you will get to know
what life is like in a dungeon!" he stormed, his temper
fully unleashed.

"Think you to frighten me with your threats?" Ailith's
emerald gaze clawed at him like the talons of one of his
prized falcons. "Life in a dungeon would be preferable to
the fate you intend me."

"You are a reckless wench," he told her. "Not many
men would stand before me with such defiance. But still I
will not allow it, not even from you. I care not for your
preference, and I will not let you prick my temper enough
to release you or do you harm. As much as you would like
to live out your days in my dungeon, I fear I must disappoint you. But make no mistake, you *will* surrender and

come to me with open arms. Or my dungeon *will* see its newest occupants in the persons of your parents! And I can promise you, if it ever comes to that, they will perish in there without ever seeing the light of day again!''

A small cry escaped Ailith's lips. She'd pushed her liege too far. Lord Preston Claybourne did not make idle threats. Now her pride had put her parents in dire jeopardy. She'd thought she would never go willingly to Lord Claybourne's bed. But the risk to her parents was too great. When next he summoned her, she would comply.

'' 'Twill be no need to imprison my parents, milord.'' Her words faltered, and she stiffened her bearing, holding her head at a haughty angle. ''I will yield to your wishes.''

''I'm to meet the king in the south of England near Dover,'' he explained. ''I do not know how long this campaign will last. Mayhap 'twill be several months. You will hold yourself in the highest virtue until my return.''

He reached for her then, pulling her roughly against his chest. Ailith's hands immediately went up as a barrier, pushing at him, but he held her fast. Lowering his head, he slanted his mouth over hers.

Ailith had no defense for his kiss. His lips covered hers. He probed the tender moistness of her mouth with his tongue, fencing with her own. She'd never known anything like it. A barrage of fiery sensations coursed through her. A low moan left her throat, but the passionate kisses Lord Preston was inflicting upon her caught it.

''M-milord,'' she whispered when he moved his lips away, her heart racing, her emotions roiling. ''P-please.''

Lord Preston raised his head and gave her an intense look. The pit of her belly clenched.

''Quite right,'' he said hoarsely. ''I must go.''

He set her apart from him, his golden eyes hot and mesmerizing.

''I will hasten my return, sweetling. I am of a mind that you can be as passionately pleasing as you can be passionately angry. I cannot wait to discover if I have judged you correctly.''

Chapter 2

AILITH HAD NO more contact with Lord Preston before his departure from Greyhawke, barely an hour after he'd summoned her to his solar.

Now, two days later, she sat on her bed in her small cramped bedchamber. Though the brazier gave off some warmth, the velvet mantle she wore helped to ward off the chill in the room. Meghanne sat in a chair across from her, stitching the hem of her houppelande.

Ailith pushed the distress she felt over her reaction to Lord Preston's kiss to the far recesses of her mind. So, too, did she dismiss the small worry she had for Lord Preston. He didn't need her to worry about him. He had Lady Glenna to do that. Besides, Ailith knew he would return to the castle safely. At one time Lord Preston had been her hero, and heroes just didn't die.

Her concern now was for her father and his secret time device, which he had erected in a little-known chamber in the castle. She feared her father was becoming addled. Thoughts of the device consumed all of his waking moments and even invaded his sleep, he'd said. Even if his device did work, how could he expect her to consent to its use on her?

" 'Tis the work of the devil.'' Her mother's voice cut into her thoughts. ''. . . and there's no guarantee 'twill be executed according to our hopes,'' Meghanne was saying.

Forsooth! Had not her mother already explained that to her? What was the purpose of doing so again? Wariness stole into her.

"And we do not know to which place you will be sent,'' Meghanne continued, thrusting her needle through the garment again.

"Mother, please,'' Ailith responded. With a sinking heart she realized that her mother shared her father's dream—or nightmare. She didn't want to discover which. "You must be careful of what you speak,'' she snapped, weary of her plight. " 'Twould not be prudent for word of father's device to find its way to the ears of His Lordship.''

'Twas her own fault her parents were so adamant about sending her away. She had vehemently voiced her objections of Lord Claybourne's intentions to her parents. Never had she dreamed they would try to rectify her situation in such a manner.

How could the Earl of Radford send Meghanne and Galen to the dungeons just to get compliance out of her? Galen? Her kindly father, who not only guided Lord Preston's courses in battle, but also lent him much wise advice?

Aye, her parents were furious with their liege, especially her mother. Her gentle, loving mother, who had taken Lord Preston under her wing and to all observers became more of a mother to him in the last few years than his very own lady mother had been in her entire miserable life. Meghanne also ran his household with the utmost efficiency because his lady wife refused to take her rightful place in the household.

Meghanne had resolved never to speak to Lord Preston again.

Bitterness ravaged Ailith. How could he betray their trust so? What did he hope to prove by making her his leman? 'Twas *his* fault she couldn't stop her parents from this scheme. And she was positive they, themselves, had not the faith in the device that they should. At least once a day Meghanne said 'twas no guarantee 'twould be executed according to their hopes. But today she'd sounded different when she'd repeated it for the second time in a quarter of an hour. Today 'twas also a catch in her voice. Ailith's suspicion increased.

"Mother?" she ventured. "Would I to consent to Father's plan, where will he send me?"

Resting her sewing on her lap, Meghanne looked at Ailith. "Your father cannot be certain of what place or time you'll end up. His hope is to catapult you somewhere into the future." She swallowed hard before continuing. " 'Tis certain your father's idea is far beyond this present time."

"*Far* beyond," Ailith agreed with a tinge of mockery. " 'Tis not comprehensible to me, Mother. Nor do I believe 'twill be to anyone else. We must not let this go farther than this chamber. We must take care never to mention Father's device to anyone. He could be branded a sorcerer."

"Then so be it, Ailith," Meghanne said in a resigned voice. "At the dark of the moon this eventide, when all are slumbering, we will go to your father's secret room and test his time device."

She stared, panic invading her. "Y-you will? H-how?"

Meghanne smiled gently. "Your father is going to strap one of the deerhounds onto his device and send him into the future."

"Will he bring him back?"

" 'Tis our hope."

Biting her lip, Ailith looked away. What would happen to the dog? And if they were successful with it, would they then demand to strap her in and send her away? Every nerve in her body stood on edge. She swallowed convulsively, rethinking her decision to become Lord Preston's mistress.

Never would she object to his attentions again. Thinking back on the kiss they shared, mayhap becoming his mistress had its rewards. *He* was certainly agreeable. 'Twas *she* who rejected *him*. Mayhap, too, she could convince her parents she'd had a change of heart. Then they would abandon their less than wise scheme to send her into the unknown. *As if it could really be accomplished.*

"I will come to your chamber tonight as soon as 'tis safe to do so."

"Aye, Mother," Ailith responded without spirit.

"Come, child, be of good cheer. Whatever your father decides, he will not act on that decision until after the Village Fair."

Ailith brightened and swung her gaze to her mother. "How could I have forgotten?"

"Aye, my daughter. On the morrow your father will pitch his tent in the square. And Lord Preston commanded Aida to accompany you to the fair. He left enough coin for you to make some purchases of your choice."

Unwanted warmth stole into Ailith. Even now, as despicable as he was, he still acted the part of her hero. Giving her coin to attend the fair was something he'd done since she and her parents had moved into the castle. "His Lordship is quite generous," she commented, glad that her warring emotions didn't creep into her voice.

"It seems so," Meghanne said dryly. "I must go now to attend my duties. I will see you at the evening meal."

"Aye, Mother."

Ailith watched Meghanne walk to the end of the long hall and descend the curving steps before going down to the inner bailey to observe the Castle Guard practice their skill with the sword.

Leading Agov, the deerhound, on a leash, Ailith followed her parents through the narrow, barely maneuverable passageway.

Galen deCotmer held the torchlight higher to illuminate the darkness ahead. "Not much farther."

They emerged into an opening just large enough to be called a room. When Galen lit the several torches that stood along the walls, Ailith saw that in addition to the contraption sitting in the center of the dank room, she and her parents filled the little space that was left.

"'Tis my life's work," Galen said with pride, placing his torchlight in a holder near the machine. He looked from Ailith to Meghanne then at his invention.

'Twas a simple-looking device. A cistern—though not recognizable as such—blended into the stone wall with a recessed hole above it for collecting rainwater. 'Twas a sluice gate at the very top with a long pole attached, which reached the bottom. That, in turn, was attached to a lever. Right beside the walled cistern stood a spoke-connected, circular frame, much like a wheel, fixed on its side and attached to a central hub, capable of turning on a central axle. The wheel had large spoon-shaped devices extending from the spoke beyond the frame. A chair was anchored to the center of all of this.

Galen turned his attention away from the machine and looked at his daughter. Disbelief and apprehension registered in her features.

"'Twill work, child," he said confidently. "Lord Preston has been fair to me, but 'tis where his fairness ends. 'Twould be better that it reached us all."

"Father." Ailith looked with curiosity at the invention before her. "I have every reason to believe . . . Nay, Agov!"

Hunching his back, Agov let out an angry growl. A large rat scurried across the floor. Ailith pulled back on the deerhound's leash. ". . . that Lord Preston will treat me with kindness," she continued, undisturbed by the rodent.

"And well he may," Galen said, his tone turning brusque. "But 'tis no justice in that brand of kindness. For if 'twas so, he would not force you to his bed."

"'Tis true he insists, Father, but I have decided to go willingly to him."

Galen stared, speechless.

"'Twas not so long ago that you wished him dead," Meghanne interjected. She studied Ailith as if she tried to see into the far recesses of her mind. "What has changed your mind, daughter?"

"If it's the device, Ailith," Galen began quietly, " 'tis perfectly safe. I will try it with Agov first."

"Nay, Father!" Ailith answered firmly. "I *truly* wish to stay."

Galen placed his fisted hands on his slim hips. "And accept your fate?" He shook his head. "Nay, Daughter. You are already ten and nine. Unless I can arrange a marriage between you and a farmer or merchant, which our liege has already forbidden, leman to our lord will be your final lot. You are fair of face, child, and therefore the gods will be kind to you." He softened his gaze. "Whatever your ultimate destiny is, I know 'twill not be as Lord Preston's mistress. The set of my mind is to send you away from this place." His final tone brooked no more argument.

"Aye, Father," Ailith mumbled in compliance to keep her father placated. But she would find a way to stay. She refused to get into that . . . that *thing*. Time device indeed!

"Now, we will strap Agov to the chair—" Galen began.

"H-how does it work?" Ailith interrupted with dread.

"Much like a treadmill, my child," Galen explained. "The power comes from the force of the water hitting the disks. The water's flow causes the wheel and the chair anchored to it to spin at a rapid pace. Fast enough to catapult a being into another time and place."

"I see." Ailith looked at her father, knowing the skepticism she felt came through in her gaze. When she first saw the machine, all she'd seen was a chair sitting atop a wheel from which extended several large spoon like devices. "How will you return Agov?"

" 'Twill be a simple matter to place the device in reverse of itself. That way the water flows onto it from the back side."

"Oh," Ailith said, not quite sure she understood what her father meant. Had her father become knotty-pated?

"Enough talk, Galen," Meghanne broke in. "We must

hasten now to try it. Someone may need us and discover us gone.''

"Aye, Meghanne. Will you hold my torch aloft?" He reached for the large dog as Meghanne complied. Straining against Agov's weight, Galen secured the hound to the chair. Agov meekly allowed himself to be strapped, then growled in protest at his inability to move. Galen patted his head. "Do not fear, Agov," he soothed. "You will feel no pain." He placed his hand on the lever.

"The cistern behind this wall is large. 'Tis my guess it holds enough water to bring Agov safely back. I must be careful to use only half at a time." Galen pressed slowly down on the lever, and the gate at the top of the cistern cracked slightly open. A stream of water trickled down.

From where she stood in the shadows, Ailith watched the satisfied look in her father's expression, his face aglow from the light of the torch. He seemed heartened by her mother's encouraging smile, and she hoped he could not discern the frown on her own face.

She took a step backward when her father pressed further and the water flowed faster, hitting the disks and causing the wheel to turn slowly. More pressure on the lever. More water force and the wheel spun faster. Finally he pressed the lever all the way down.

A wall of water crashed down on the trio, knocking them off balance onto the stone floor. The force extinguished the torchlight and thrust it from her mother's hand. Wood creaked, and metal groaned in protest as her father's invention splintered. Seeping into cracks and holes in the floor, the water ebbed swiftly. The torches along the walls still gave light to his shattered dream.

'Twas a sight to behold. Forsooth! Were it not for the stricken look on her father's face, Ailith would have collapsed in mirth—and relief. She hurriedly stood.

The time device lay in a crumpled heap of wood, metal, and screws. Agov had managed to free himself of his bonds and was now attempting to stand. Like a man with too much drink in him, the poor dog swayed and wobbled, going down on his belly, stretching his legs fore and aft of himself. Water beaded on his coat, and he reeked of the smell unique to a wet dog.

Meghanne sat sprawled on the stone floor, though Galen had risen to his feet.

Rats scampered to and fro, noisily protesting the unwanted watery invasion of their home. Everyone and everything was thoroughly soaked. Ailith swallowed a giggle.

"By the gods, I will not be defeated! I will perfect this!" Galen boomed his vow as he assisted Meghanne to her feet.

Stomping to the wall, he jerked a torchlight down from its hold and thrust it at Ailith.

"See to your mother. I will see to the hound."

"Aye, Father." Ailith barely kept her amusement and relief at bay, though she wore a straight face. She led the way back through the narrow passageway, where, once out, she and her mother each went their separate way to replace their wet garments.

Spotting Agov as he stumbled back to the Great Hall, Ailith halted. The blazing fire in the stone fireplace drew him. Going there, he shook his big body, spraying water everywhere. The flames hissed and crackled as droplets of moisture landed on the burning wood. Agov settled himself among the rushes, and Ailith started for her bedchamber, only now allowing her merriment to burst from her.

Chapter 3

THE NEXT MORNING a gentle shake coaxed Ailith out of a deep sleep.

"Wake up, child," Meghanne urged.

Ailith sighed. Stretching languorously, she fluttered her sleepy eyelids open. "Aye, Mother?"

"Will you sleep the day away? The sun is already midway in the sky."

Sitting up, Ailith threw the covers aside. "Forsooth! Why didn't you awaken me sooner? I would go with Father to the village to watch him pitch his tent."

" 'Tis not necessary. Your father left at sunup to visit a magician he knows, then he returned to the castle to work on his device. He was sorely disappointed last night."

"I know, and I'm sorry, Mother."

Meghanne cast her a skeptical glance.

"Truly I am," she murmured. And she was, but only for her father's blighted hope. "But mayhap Father should take a respite from such matters and enjoy the bazaar."

" 'Twas not a look of sorrow I saw on your face last eventide as we emerged from the passageway." Annoyance laced Meghanne's accusatory tone.

"Oh, Mother," Ailith began, "my heart goes out to Fa-

ther, for I know the work he has put into his invention. I
wish, however, I can make him, as well as you, understand
that I do not wish to leave.''

A knock on the door interrupted further discussion on
the matter, and Ailith felt grateful as Meghanne walked to
the door.

Ailith's sympathy for her father returned. Truly she was
sympathetic toward him. But not enough to feel guilty over
her elation at the failure of his invention. 'Twould be impossible for a body to survive a spin wilder than the one
poor Agov had experienced. Ailith feared the hapless dog
would be kilted out of balance for the rest of his life!

'' 'Tis Aida,'' Meghanne said as she pulled the door
open, ''come to attend you.''

Ailith swung her legs over the side of the bed. ''Hurry,
Aida. I have already missed much of the fair.''

Aida laughed. ''There is still much time left, Lady Ailith.''

''Lady Ailith?'' Ailith asked in surprise. ''Why do you
call me that? We have been friends since we were but
babes, Aida.''

Aida cleared her throat and dropped her gaze to the floor.
'' 'Tis the wish of His Lordship, my lady,'' she mumbled.

''And you will abide by that, daughter,'' Meghanne
prompted. Since no one knew of her parents' plans to hurtle
her through time, Ailith guessed her mother wanted her to
follow Lord Preston's wishes for the sake of discretion. Or
else why would Meghanne insist her compliance? She
frowned at her mother.

''Aye, my lady, please do not make it difficult,'' Aida
said. ''I do not care to incur our liege's wrath.''

''But he is not here . . .'' Ailith halted at the exasperated
looks on the two women's faces. ''Very well,'' she finished
in a light tone. ''You may even bow before me if the mood
assails you.''

''My lady, I pray thee, do not wander too far,'' Aida implored. ''There are men willing to do misdeeds to a maiden
alone.''

"Despair not, Aida!" Ailith exclaimed lightheartedly. "I will use good judgment. But I must see everything because I have not been to a bazaar in ten and two months. You may browse as you wish."

"Nay, my lady, I will walk with you. 'Twould be just our luck should Lord Preston return at this time and see you unattended. 'Twould not sit well with him."

"Nay, Aida, 'twould not," Ailith agreed. An unexplainable shiver coursed through her. A pair of terns screamed past them on their flight to some unknown destination. The roar of the distant surf could be heard above the din of merrymakers. A cloudless cobalt sky lent luster to the rolling hills, some covered with heather. The surrounding beauty was in direct contrast to her feelings. Yet she didn't wish to mar Aida's day because of her melancholia. "Fear not. Unless he has decided to turn his men around, he has barely made it to Dover yet."

"Lord Preston would surely be aggrieved should harm befall you," Aida continued as if Ailith hadn't spoken.

" 'Tis not my wish to cause him distress, Aida. Especially if the cause is from harm befalling my very own person." Despite her irritation with Lord Preston and her attempt at sarcasm, Ailith giggled. Distress to His Lordship without involving herself would suit her just fine. "Do come along."

Aida hurried her steps to catch up to Ailith.

"Mayhap, you can assist me in choosing some cloths for new houppelandes."

"Oh, my lady!" Aida exclaimed. "What an honor 'twould be to assist you in that happy task."

Laughing, Ailith stopped at a food merchant's stand to purchase some dried figs for munching. She passed some over to Aida.

Meandering through the crowd toward the tent of the cloth merchant, Ailith's thoughts settled on her parents. Guilt still pervaded her at her relief over her father's failed invention. But she feared her father would be discovered trying to rebuild his device. She had no doubt that it would fail again. How would she convince him of the lie that she wanted, nay anticipated, becoming Lord Preston's leman? When her compliance was due solely for Galen's and Meghanne's safety . . . and fright of her father's device?

If she became Preston's mistress, how would she guard her heart against him? But she must remember to appear happy at all times, despite the heaviness of her heart. She didn't want her parents to see through her deception.

Aida's voice snapped her out of her thoughts.

"Look, Lady Ailith, there's the cloth merchant's tent before us."

"Aye. Let's make haste to see what wares he offers."

Inside the tent, bolts upon bolts of the finest cloth money could buy were laid out on long trestle tables. Not entirely unused to the better things life had to offer due to Lord Preston's generosity, Ailith still widened her eyes at the sight of some of the material and the sheer volume of it. Glass-smooth satins, soft silks, transparent voiles, and lace as thin as gossamer were displayed.

"My lady!" Aida whispered in awe. "So much and so many colors. How will you ever choose what shade will be pleasing to His Lordship's eyes?"

Hearing that statement, the fat merchant's beady little eyes danced in his bald head as he rubbed his hands together.

"Aye, lady," he said in a craggy voice, "choosin' willa be a task. Might I assist ye?"

Ailith perceived the anticipation he felt at what might turn into a lucrative sale, but she laughed, trying to force gaiety into her tone, instead of the cynicism she felt at the Scot's avarice. She lifted a piece of silk from the display table. "This," she said with a firm nod of her head, "will become the gown I will wear when His Lordship returns. And that over there . . ."

She started toward the jewel-toned satin display when the sound of horses and armor changed the hum of bartering and noisy chatter to agonizing screams and unavailed pleas.

"My lady, we're being attacked!" Aida screamed. "We must hasten to flee this place!"

She grabbed Ailith's arm and steered her toward the tent's exit.

Ailith wrenched free, panting in terror. "Attacked?" Fear bubbled in her, and her stomach clenched. "But by whom?"

Peering outside, Aida cried, " 'Tis the outlaw, DeLepee Rouge! If we are found, the Red Sword's followers will make sport of us! Please, we must hide!"

"Aye, Aida." Ailith's heartbeat raced, and the muscles in her body tensed. "The cries grow louder. Oh, would we were still in the safety of Greyhawke! The Castle Guard will come and rout them."

" 'Tis a certainty, my lady. But by then we could be despoiled or worse. Please, we must go before they usurp this tent."

"Aye, lady," the merchant spoke up. "The wench speaks wisely. There is much danger both wit'in and wit'oot. I dinna wish tae perish inside a burnin' tent, for I ken they will surely torch it!"

Without another word he hurried through the opening, mayhap in hopes of finding a safe haven before the outlaws reached his tent.

"Oh, the cowardly swine!" Ailith sputtered, her temper flaring, for which she was grateful. She preferred her anger to her fear.

"We *must* leave, Lady Ailith," Aida insisted.

Ailith nodded. "Very well," she grumbled in complete control of her fear now. "I know that we must."

Taking her jewel-encrusted dagger from its place in her waistband, she cut a slit down the back of the tent, big enough for her and Aida to slip through.

Outside, nothing but forest faced them. A place rumored to be infested with murderers, rapists, wild animals, and the very outlaws they wanted to escape. Ailith wondered if they were going into a more dangerous situation. The sounds around them were loud and ominous.

"My lady, what can we do?" Aida cried in desperation. "Where can we hide?"

"Over here," a deep voice commanded.

Ailith and her friend turned toward the sound. A tall, black-haired, bearded man stood next to a black tent, which Ailith hadn't noticed before. Fear once again seeped into her core, and she damned herself and that emotion.

"W-what? I-I will not go in there." She tried to sound indignant rather than frightened. "We might as well stay here. They'll surely come to your tent, too," she added with a trace of wariness.

"They won't come in here," the man assured her. "They fear the black tent, calling it the Tent of Death. You will be safe inside, my Lady Ailith. I promise."

Unease and foreboding swept through her. Instinct told her to turn and flee as far away from this man as possible. She looked at him with suspicion. "W-who are you? And how . . . how do you know my name?"

"I am Brint Pfiester," the man answered without hesitation, "a magician and acquaintance of your father. Some years ago, when we were lads, Galen deCotmer saved me from attack by a rabid deerhound. In truth, he saved my life. Since from his own mouth he's confessed that you, his only child, are his love and indeed his very life, I now save his life by saving yours. You must trust that I mean you no harm."

Brint Pfiester spoke with a calmness that was almost mesmerizing. Despite the carnage going on mere yards behind them, he stood fearless, almost oblivious to it.

Ailith wondered at this. All too near them people were engaging in a struggle for their lives and possessions—people who seemed not to notice the black tent or the three individuals who stood before it.

Brint held his hand out to her. "Come, Ailith. We waste time. I am in your father's debt, and I promised to repay him."

"Hurry, my lady," Aida urged. "Hurry into the tent."

Ailith hesitated for the briefest of seconds before she and

Aida followed Brint inside the black tent, the sound of death still ringing in their ears. Inside, the tent was well lit by sconces. Her eyes widened in wonder, and she scanned the array of contents in the tent.

"Do not touch anything, my child," Brint warned, seeing her interest.

"Why not?" Ailith murmured.

"Because it could prove dangerous if 'tis not used properly," Brint answered.

Ailith's gaze flitted from tarot cards to jars marked with different names of tea and herb leaves, but riveted to a strange-looking object lying on the table. She could only describe it as an orb made of thick, rare and seemingly unbreakable glass with a silver handle attached to it. It was about the circumference of the bottom of an ale tankard and glowed with a fascinating light. She turned her attention to Brint.

"Be at ease, Brint Pfiester. I will not touch your table," she reassured him. "I hate this . . . this . . . this place!" she blurted suddenly.

Brint cocked an ebony brow at her, and Aida's lips trembled, her eyes misting.

"There's violence everywhere," Ailith continued, ignoring Brint's surprise and Aida's fear. "That's all I have ever known. Will I never know peace?"

As she spoke she thought of the clamor going on outside and of Lord Preston and his order for her to share his bed. If her liege had been here, the bold outlaws would never have attacked the village. Remembering his threat to imprison her parents for the rest of their lives if she didn't submit to him, Ailith decided, justified or not, Preston Claybourne was himself a violent man. And DeLepee Rouge would have found himself impaled on the end of His Lordship's sword.

"My lady, please!" Aida cried with concern before focusing on Brint. "Good master, my lady is weary. A place to rest her head, please, sir?"

Brint pointed to a small cot in the corner. "If she is of a mind to, she may rest there."

"Many thanks, master. My lady, please, do rest. I know Galen deCotmer is a brave man. For the sake of your safety he will join the Castle Guard to help vanquish the intruders."

Ailith realized Aida's encouraging words were meant to soothe Ailith as well as herself.

"Aye, Aida. My father will," she replied, brushing at a tear spilling onto her cheeks. "I am truly weary and grateful for the cot."

It was extremely hot inside the tent. The sun was still high in the sky, and if night still found them there, the coolness would bring relief—and more darkness. Because of the tent's extreme black color, no sunlight penetrated it. But, even with the sufficient light of the sconces, a foreboding air surrounded it. Ailith wondered if the atmosphere in there brought on her outburst.

Blinded now by tears, she started toward the cot and bumped into the table with the glowing orb on it. The strange object rolled toward the edge. Instinctively she reached for it, unconsciously bringing it with her to her place of rest. She settled her hand on a dial with strange writing and, with effort and nervous agitation, turned it.

She listened. As abruptly as the noise of battle began, it ceased. An unnatural silence shrouded the atmosphere.

"Oh, Father, mayhap you were right. If only your device had worked. For I truly wish now that I were somewhere in another time and place," she said with abstraction.

Dense mist suddenly enveloped her. Collapsing on the cot, she closed her eyes.

AUGUST 1998
NEW ORLEANS, LOUISIANA

"Joshua!"

The man whose name was being called didn't intend to

answer. Instead, he trudged grumpily along, cursing his medieval attire, which at the moment clung to him in the heat and humidity. He was sure more people had come than were invited to his Fifth Annual Medieval Faire.

What had begun as entertainment for the friends and family of the members of the medieval club he'd founded now had grown so big he'd had to borrow lawn space from his neighbor to set up two extra tents. He'd transformed the spacious front lawn of his home on the lakefront to an authentic replica of a medieval village fair.

All day he had been chivalrous and courtly, knightly and romantic. Usually he loved it, but right now he had too many damned problems. And he was glad his fair had come to a close. He wasn't sure which problem to put at the top of his list: Melissa, his parents—who were coming for an uninvited two-week visit with intentions of staying at his home—or his two antique shops, Kenley Galleries.

"Joshua!" the voice yelled with impatience.

Dammit, didn't that woman get the message? He'd ignored her call the first time, walking across the entire length of his spacious lawn through the dispersing crowd, hoping to discourage her unwanted attention. No such luck! He certainly didn't need a lecture from Melissa's friend on how a woman should be treated. Melissa Devereaux in particular. Knowing how Mellie wanted to be cared for, he just wasn't sure he was up to pampering her.

Joshua didn't want to confront Myra and have words with her, thus further being accused of maligning fair womanhood. Deciding discretion was the better part of valor, he quickened his pace.

"Dammit, Joshua Claybourne Kenley! Don't you take another step," came Myra's shrill little voice as she hurriedly caught up to him.

Stopping in his tracks, Joshua turned toward her. "I need some time alone, Myra," he told her with cool politeness. "If what you have to say is club business, talk to Stephen. You'll find him somewhere around here. If it's about Melissa and me, however, you're out of line—"

"Bingo, Joshua!" Myra interrupted, triumph in her tone and eyes. "I want to discuss Mellie."

"What went on between Melissa and me is none of your goddamn business. I will *not* discuss her with you. I suggest you get on with club business and leave me the hell alone!"

"What did you do?" Myra chastised in an annoyed voice. "Get up on the wrong side of your wigwam? You don't have to be so rude."

"It seems that's the only option you've given me," Joshua snarled. "Read my lips: I will *not* discuss Melissa with you! Stay the hell *out* of my affairs."

"Well, I never!" Myra huffed with indignation.

"Oh, yes, you have," Joshua sneered. "That's your problem. You *always*."

"Always? Well, I like that! I always *what*?"

"Interfere, little Myra, interfere."

Joshua stalked away from the aggravating little gnome. His long strides carried him quickly to his large tent, where he changed four times a day on two consecutive days, from modern-day man to medieval knight.

Pushing the flap aside, he stepped inside, glad that he had fended off Myra—for only the time being, he knew. He sighed, making a mental note to talk to Melissa about her pushy friend. It would help, however, if he could get Melissa to talk to *him* again. With a vicious curse, he began shedding his costume for the final time that day.

He shook his head, causing his long, wavy ebony hair to ripple against his neck. He'd allowed his hair to grow for the fair, and now that it was over, he couldn't wait to visit his barber. The long hair only added to his discomfort from the heat.

He could have gone inside his house, Kenley Manor, to cool off and freshen up in air-conditioned comfort, where most of his club members already were. But even with the throng of spectators still lurking outside, it seemed his tent was the only place where he could be alone at the moment.

Solitude beckoned him like a beacon. He needed to do some thinking.

He realized he'd have to apologize to Melissa. She hadn't taken too well his labeling of her as a spoiled, selfish snob. The argument had been a week ago, and he readily admitted to being at fault. He'd been tired and bothered with details concerning the medieval spectacle, his antique dealership on Magazine Street, and the one on Royal Street in the French Quarter.

Since Melissa had planned to be in the vicinity of his Magazine Street store, he'd asked her to pick up a vase from there and deliver it to his Royal Street store. She'd refused, telling him she wasn't in the delivery business, and that was what he paid his employees for. He'd lost his temper.

Giving it further thought now, he realized they were both right. That *was* what he paid his employees for; and Melissa *was* a spoiled, selfish snob. Nonetheless, he missed her and promised himself to try to set things right between them.

He sighed again and, fully nude now, paced the grassy length of space in the tent. A gasp alerted him that he wasn't alone. Turning to the sound, he grabbed his braes and held them in front of his privates, wondering if a child had wandered inside.

Not a person easily overcome by shock, he nearly fainted when his eyes fell on a woman who looked as if she really *was* from the Middle Ages. He knew every member of his medievalist club, and this person certainly wasn't one of them!

Hair unkempt and houppelande dirt-stained from crawling from the cloth merchant's tent, Ailith took a step back, resting her hand on her jewel-encrusted dagger. How had Lord Preston found her? Was it his intention to ravish her? Why was there such surprise in his golden orbs?

Her eyes widening and heart beating a rapid tattoo in fear and confusion, warmth filled her body at the sight of the magnificent form before her. Heat flaming her cheeks, Ailith stared, sure that Lord Preston had returned to rescue

her. But even through his surprise, he seemed quite displeased.

Should I demand he clothe himself? Nay, even unclothed,
he looks dangerous, and at the moment I do not wish to
provoke his temper.

"My lord has returned, to my great relief." Forcing her
eyes away from the striking beauty of his body, she rested
her gaze on his face.

Her voice trembled, her words foreign to Joshua. Not
only *foreign*, but *extinct*. Sweat beaded his brow. What was
that she said? What language was she speaking? It vaguely
penetrated his brain that he'd studied the language, but his
amazement prevented him from understanding her at the
moment.

Stunned, he stared into long-lashed green eyes. Her
blond hair reached just below her tiny waist. Though
smudged with dirt, her face was so lovely he almost forgot
to breathe.

"D-did your soldiers vanquish DeLepee Rouge, milord?"

When her liege didn't answer, Ailith stood stock still,
her hand still on the dagger. Her gaze, of its own accord,
once again wandered over the man before her. She frowned,
sensing something different, but unable to discern what.

Lord Preston was displeased, but his golden eyes had lost
their icy pierceness and instead burned with dissatisfaction.
His bare, hard-muscled chest, narrow hips, and perfectly
shaped legs almost caused her to go apoplectic. She studied
his hands, which held the braes and shielded his manhood,
before looking once again at his tanned, extremely handsome face. His hair, black as an onyx gemstone, fell in deep
waves down to his neck. Fire slaked though her limbs, and
she shuddered.

Forsooth!

When His Lordship rescued her, vapors must have overcome her because she had no idea how she came to be in
her liege's tent. She only knew if she stayed she would be
privy to his demands. He had an unwanted effect on her.

"Please, milord, give me leave to go to my parents to assure them of my safety," Ailith whispered.

Feeling damned foolish at the sight he must present, at the sound of her words, Joshua stared stupidly, then closed his eyes. A spectator caught up in the action had wandered in from the viewing stand. Or perhaps his fellow club members were playing a joke on him. But the angel with the dirty face would confess when he opened his eyes again.

Chapter 4

SLOWLY, CAUTIOUSLY, JOSHUA opened one eye, then the other. The beautiful, dirty-faced angel still stood before him. She had huddled herself against the rack filled with his medieval costumes and street clothes. For a moment, they stared at each other.

"Miss, you're trespassing," Joshua got out as he walked to where his jockey shorts were thrown across the top of the rack next to where his intruder stood.

What was Lord Preston saying? It wasn't their language, yet she thought it sounded familiar, like the King's English. But then, why didn't she understand him? Lord Preston had always demanded everyone speak the same language in his household. What was he trying to do now?

Uneasiness swirled through her. Something was amiss, but comprehension eluded her.

His Lordship quickly slipped a strange covering, much like a breech cloth, over his narrow hips, which bulged considerably in front as it concealed his loins. Ailith's eyes widened, and heat rushed to her cheeks as she forced her gaze from the sight. The arrogance of the Lord of Grey-hawke thoroughly offended her sensibilities!

Although His Lordship seemed determined to commit

one outrageous act after another, she must stop blushing, she commanded herself. She needed to get herself under control to match wits with her magnificent lord. But her gaze again roamed to his lower body. What was that attire shielding his manhood in such a blatant way? Her body heat rose, and her mouth went dry. She flicked her tongue over her lips.

Renewed resentment kindled within her. Even though she had decided to comply with his request to become his leman, she didn't welcome the effect he continually had upon her.

Lord Preston grinned as he slipped another strange garment over his hips, which covered the entire length of his long legs before pulling an odd-looking tunic over his wide chest.

"I get it," he said.

His voice was deep and pleasant instead of low and harsh as it had always been.

"You're supposed to be a medieval whore. Or are you a modern-day one, trying to entice me as you must believe the whores of the Middles Ages did?"

This time he really offended her sensibilities! She did not understand all of his words, but the word whore was plain enough! She refused to accept such an insult, even from the lord of the keep! Especially since 'twas he who wished to turn her into a whore.

She drew her dagger. "Nay, my lord," she hissed, deliberately disobeying his command to speak English, her anger making her bold. "I am not yet a whore! 'Tis you who seek to make me one. Take one step closer, and not even your threats on my parents' lives will save you from my dagger's point. You mock me, my lord, and you go too far!"

Joshua stopped in his tracks. *What* did she say? Recognition of an obsolete language struck him. Medieval French. *Langue d'oïl*? *What* did she say? He racked his mind for the language to connect her words. No, not *langue d'oïl*; not modern enough, but still medieval. She was *def-*

initely speaking medieval French. And she was damn good at it. He didn't have time for her little games, however.

He spoke in fluid French, not sure she understood his modern usage of the language. "Look, miss, I'll concede I'm impressed by your knowledge of the medieval language. If you're interested in joining the club, I suggest you call my office some time next week. I'll have to get one of my business cards from inside my house." He cast a wary eye at the knife in her hand. "I also suggest you put that thing away before someone gets hurt." He took a step toward her.

"Stay back!" she warned.

"Don't you think this game has gone on long enough?" Joshua snapped, feeling the first prick of his temper. "If you leave peacefully, I won't have you arrested."

Ailith comprehended his words, but not their meaning. "I-I do not understand, my lord," she began falteringly. " 'Tis not a game I play."

Why would he think she was playing a game? And now he demanded she leave? Why had he suddenly changed his mind about wanting her? Where was she? Where would she go? What trick was this? And his voice? She pondered again the more agreeable tone of voice he had suddenly acquired. Too, she wondered what medieval meant. And they were not from Middleages. Did he not remember they were from *Middlesbrough?* Her anxiety increased by a thrice.

Suddenly it dawned on her she no longer stood in the village square hiding in a black tent while a battle raged outside. But the sounds of battle had ceased just before she'd taken her nap. Hadn't they?

She glanced around frantically, searching for Aida, but only seeing . . . Lord Preston? Staring intently at the man, trembles assailed her. Though he was the mirror image of Lord Preston, suddenly she knew. She *knew*, and panic nearly overcame her. This . . . this man was *not* Preston Claybourne.

Sweat beaded her brow, and her heartbeat speeded. Could this stranger detect her fear?

Where was she?

Brint! The magician! He had warned her not to touch anything. She *hadn't* touched anything. She had gone straight to the cot to rest. Before that she had merely caught the glowing orb to prevent it from rolling off the edge of the table she'd bumped into.

The orb! Not only had she touched it, she'd picked it up and held it—and felt an odd sensation. A strange mist had surrounded her, then she'd drifted into a deep sleep.

And now . . .

Oh, God! With frightening clarity, she knew she was no longer in Middlesbrough. Was she still in her own time? She had a niggling feeling that she wasn't, because she'd never before seen garments such as the man who wasn't Lord Preston wore.

And were the Middle Ages what her time was referred to? Forsooth! Didn't everything have a beginning, middle, and ending? Was she now in the Beginning Ages or the Ending Ages?

Her parents! If she was not at Greyhawke when Lord Preston returned, he would imprison them. She must return. But how?

The orb. Somehow the orb had brought her here. But where was it? She had to find it so it could bring her back.

Frantically she looked around the tent. Then she spied it laying on the thing she'd awakened on; the thing that was suspended between two iron crossed poles. The swinging cot was as good a name as any, she decided. But the orb no longer glowed. What was wrong with it? Mayhap 'twas broken.

"No!" she whispered, desperate. She had to save her parents from Lord Preston's wrath.

Remembering that she had wished to be in another time and place, she rushed to the swinging cot and reached for the orb.

She squeezed her eyes shut. "I wish to be back in the black tent in Middlesbrough," she blurted.

Ailith allowed a few moments to pass before opening her eyes. Hysteria welled within her. No lumination emanated from the orb. It was still just a cold, dark object in her hand.

She shook the orb. Nothing. She shook it again, this time so hard her entire body shook with it. Nothing happened. Raising it to her ear, she listened, hoping maybe to hear some signal. After all, sounds came from the shells found by the sea, why couldn't they come from this piece of glass? But she heard nothing and she remained in the white tent with the peculiarly attired man, who was frowning at her as though she lacked wits.

Frustration swept through her. She clutched the orb to her breast, knowing she held her key to returning to her own time. Tears pooled in her eyes and rolled down her cheeks. Her vision blurred.

Joshua stared with incredulity at his beautiful intruder, who was now so obviously distraught. Despite his irritation at her invasion, he wanted to comfort her even as he wondered about the object she held in her hand. He took a step forward. She took a step backward.

"P-please, k-kind s-sir."

She halted and sniffled. Joshua realized how desperately she tried to keep the sobs out of her voice.

"W-where am I?"

Puzzlement filtered in him. Had she hit her head somewhere? Or had one of the horses run her over? He knew that assumption was ridiculous because he hadn't heard of such an accident, and if something like that *had* occurred, she would have lost more than just her memory.

Joshua took another step forward, hands held out in supplication. "I won't harm you, miss," he said in French. He rested his gaze on the—he narrowed his eyes in concentration—the orb she encircled in a tight fist. "May I see it?"

"Nay!" she cried. " 'Twill bring me back to Greyhawke Keep and to my parents! 'Tis mine!"

"Yes, it's yours, and this tent is mine, and you're trespassing," he snapped, this time in English.

The sympathy he felt for her evaporated, and he suddenly felt as if he were the subject of an outlandish prank. His patience reached the breaking point. If this was a joke, it was a bad one. Bad joke. Bad, *bad* joke.

Any minute now he expected his pals to rush into the tent yelling "Gotcha!" But no one came in, and the girl still held on to her knife with fake gems encrusted on the hilt, speaking an extinct language. He was through being impressed. If Stephen was behind this, he deserved his ass kicked. Yeah, a big-time ass kicking was definitely called for and would be gladly given.

Joshua grabbed the girl by her slender arm and ushered her through the tent flap. "Allow me to show you the way out, *my Lady*." Sarcasm dripped in his tone.

The girl gasped and stared at her surroundings in wide-eyed fright.

Wondering at her reaction, Joshua surveyed the area. Workers dressed in shorts and sleeveless T-shirts took down fair banners and dismantled tents. They were also collecting and folding the chairs where the spectators had sat. Nothing unusual was happening, but the sheer dread in the girl's emerald depths made him pause. Had she been in his tent hiding from someone?

"Has someone been harassing you, miss?"

She stared at him blankly.

Joshua decided to rephrase his question. "Were you hiding from someone?"

She nodded, but seemed hesitant to speak as she bent her head.

Sighing, Joshua gently crooked his finger beneath her chin and raised her gaze to him again. His blood stirred at the silky feel of her skin, but he tried to temper his reaction. "Don't be afraid. Tell me, and I'll take care of your problem." He regretted his curt mood earlier.

He would get some answers from her later about why she dressed and spoke the way she did. Maybe this had started out as a prank, but now it seemed serious. "Who are you hiding from?"

Licking her lips, she murmured, "DeLepee Rouge. T-the outlaw Lord Preston Claybourne, the Earl of Radford, has been chasing."

Joshua stiffened, affronted that she had so easily changed tactics on him by pretending fear to play him for a fool. What a good actress she was! Lord Preston Claybourne, the Earl of Radford indeed! Radford was his maternal ancestor, and though Joshua didn't hide his heritage, only his close associates knew what an illustrious family tree he had.

Still holding firmly to his unwanted guest, Joshua scanned the thinning crowd in hopes of spying Stephen. He caught no sign of his friend, but Myra sidled up to him. She was the last person he wanted to see. It was too much to hope that she wouldn't notice him leaving his tent with the girl. But Myra *would* notice. The meddling bitch would notice a flea on an elephant's ass a block away.

"Well, Joshua," Myra huffed, looking coldly at the girl. "I see why you wanted to be alone. Alone, all right! To cheat on Mellie. This will break her heart. How could you, you bastard!"

She trounced off, almost crashing into Stephen Edwards.

"Well, I beg your pardon to you, too," Stephen cracked with a tight smile as Myra stormed passed him. He glanced in Joshua's direction and stayed his gaze on the girl whom Joshua held around the waist.

The crease of annoyance brought on by his mutual dislike of Myra disappearing from his countenance, he lifted a sandy brow in question.

"Well, Sir Joshua, who is this scullery maid you have imprisoned in your arms?" he quipped, as always alive with mischief. "And is she the reason the little troll, Myra, is turning into the town crier? Oops! I mean the town snitch?"

Joshua glared at Stephen, his friend's amusement and appreciative sweep of the intruder snapping his hard-won patience. "This ends *now*, Stephen," he snarled. "Tell me what the hell's going on. Who is this girl?"

As if Stephen needed clarification about whom Joshua spoke, Joshua slightly thrust the girl forward, but refused to drop his hold from her.

Stephen regarded the girl critically, then transferred his gaze back to Joshua. "I've never seen her before in my life," he confessed. "Nor have I ever seen anyone so lovely. But I can assure you if I had met her first, she'd be on *my* arm, not yours."

Silently agreeing with Stephen's assessment of the girl's loveliness, Joshua shouted, "I mean it, Stephen! Knock it off!"

Stephen drew in a breath. "Get a grip, Josh," he said, all amusement gone from his tone. "I *don't* know the girl!"

Joshua stared dumbly at his friend. "You're serious, aren't you?"

"Yeah," Stephen answered. "What's the story?"

Frowning at her, Joshua moved his hand from her waist to her arm. "I found her in my tent."

Ailith flinched, her temples throbbing with anxiety, her grip on the orb tightening. Although she barely understood the form of English they were speaking, the two men were talking about her and had been since the blond man first halted in front of them. She slid a glance toward the man who resembled Lord Preston. Joshua was what the woman who reminded her of a magpie had called him.

God's teeth! Joshua was as magnificent as her despicable lord.

For a moment she forgot her predicament and even ignored the anger she felt vibrating from the steely grip of his fingers on her arm.

When metal hit metal and material snapped smartly, she glimpsed her surroundings. Peasants dressed in sleeveless jerkins and short braes were moving rapidly, nearly having cleared half the grounds of the tents and observer stands. She widened her eyes.

A clear, cloudless day, the heat in the place was stifling

and unlike any of the warmest days she ever endured in Middlesbrough. Green lawn stretched endlessly before her all the way to the hill that stood forty yards away and snaked around as far as the eye could see. Several trees sat on the ground, and sweet-smelling flowers, the likes of which Ailith had never seen, served as a beautiful backdrop for Joshua's keep.

Forsooth! It had really happened. She was in another time. All alone, and she would be hard-pressed to convince Joshua of her plight. Abruptly he released her and faced her.

"All right, miss, the show's over," Joshua said. "If you don't want to get arrested, you'd best be on your way."

He turned toward the man called Stephen, and they both began walking toward the house without another glance at Ailith.

Ailith stared at Joshua's broad back as he strode away, despair sluicing through her. She clutched the orb again and spoke aloud.

"I wish to return to my own time. I wish to return to Middlesbrough."

'Twas no use. The orb had somehow broken. Mayhap 'twas only usable once before its powers were weakened and the orb had to be destroyed.

When she felt the wetness on her cheeks, she realized she was crying and swiped her tears angrily away, refusing to let another one fall. She swallowed convulsively. Joshua and Stephen were only halfway across the lawn, having been momentarily halted by two of the peasant workers. She opened her mouth to call out to Joshua, but changed her mind. That was no use either. She barely understood him, and, likewise, he barely understood her.

Stephen said something to Joshua, and Joshua laughed, the sound, as it drifted back to her, warm and carefree. It occurred to her that Joshua laughed easily, unlike Lord Preston who rarely laughed or even smiled. As she watched Stephen and Joshua open the wide doors and disappear inside the huge keep, somehow she knew that Joshua's humors were nothing like Lord Preston's. The odd thought warmed her—and gave her the courage to force herself to move.

Joshua slammed the door closed as he and Stephen stepped into the welcoming coolness of his house and walked down the hallway toward the Great Hall, which ordinarily was his den. Even from this distance, the boisterous crowd could still be heard.

"Where did that female viper go?" he asked, thoroughly vexed.

He didn't like having to explain his actions to women. He didn't mind apologizing, if an explanation wasn't included. Simply saying "I'm sorry about what happened" was sufficient in his opinion. But given the circumstances now, how could he get away with that when even *he* didn't know what had happened?

And, he admitted to himself, it did *not* look good. He had already been naked when he discovered the girl in his tent. Shit!

But along with all of that came the overwhelming urge to go outside, haul the little troublemaker into the manor, and drag the truth from her. He sighed, honest enough to admit that he wanted to touch her again. His vexation increased. He had always, *always* been a one-woman man and he refused to allow some dirty-faced little con artist, whose breathtaking beauty would cause a man to forget which street he lived on—Stephen's assessment, not his own—to tempt him.

Despite how incompatible he and Melissa seemed, he was determined to make things work. If his mother wasn't correct in anything else, she was right when she said it was time for him to settle down and marry. He may not have dated more than one woman at a time, but he'd had his share of relationships.

Damn it. How frightened the girl had appeared. And young. And alarmingly alluring. He released a harsh curse. She could go to hell, and if she ever darkened his doorway again with her childish pranks, he would have her arrested.

"Myra is probably in your office, Josh, already in contact with Melissa," Stephen broke into Joshua's musings.

"What?"

"Myra. The female viper."

Joshua frowned. "Oh. Well. Actually the question was rhetorical."

They stepped into the den, where merrymakers roamed in inebriated blissfulness.

"Well, Lord Joshua! Thou hast returned," one of the male club members piped up at first glimpse of Joshua and Stephen.

"Three cheers for our esteemed leader!" a woman shouted.

"Hip, hip, hooray! Hip, hip, hooray! Hip, hip, hooray!" the club members, thirty in all, chorused, holding various drinks up in salute.

Placing his problems to the back of his mind for now, Joshua laughed. "Silence, you drunken serfs, else you shall be banished from my keep. I have not yet reached the point you have. You have obviously had a considerable head start in your consumption of spirits."

"Wine for His Lordship," Stephen commanded. "And for His Lordship's friend. We have some catching up to do!"

Ailith heard a burst of laughter as she crept down the corridor toward the sound. The strangely patterned tiles beneath her feet were cool and comforting. Forsooth, the entire passageway, where paintings graced the walls, was warm and welcoming. Much like Joshua's laughter, which, she reminded herself, was the reason she had come to the addlepated conclusion that she could somehow convince him to help her.

Reaching the entrance to the chamber where the revelry was commencing, she peeked in, doubts assailing her. She saw no evidence of tallows or rushlights, but yet the room was well lit. A Carona hung from the center of the ceiling,

glowing almost as her orb had, though by far more brilliant
as the light from the inside reflected against its crystal tiers.
She spied Joshua as he lounged upon a long, curving . . .

She searched her mind for what it most resembled. A
settle, that was the only thing she could think of. But this
settle wasn't wooden. It was soft-looking and inviting, and
it seemed able to seat ten people easily. A square, wooden
table sat in front of the settle and *glass*—Ailith gasped
softly upon seeing this—cups without handles filled with
what seemed to be cider and ale sat atop the table. Thick,
russet-colored woven fabric covered the floor. Ailith rushed
across the entryway, praying she hadn't been noticed.

Someone belched. A chorus of laughter followed, then a
reprimand by Joshua, and Ailith perceived the feigned
sternness of his voice.

The perpetrator, Stephen, muttered a contrite "Sorry, my
lord," along with another belch.

Ailith giggled, continuing down the passageway until she
reached the end. She stopped in her tracks. She found herself alone in a room with a magnificent curving stairway.
Unlike the dimly lit, narrow stone steps at Greyhawke
Keep, these were wide and made of the shiniest wood with
a long window at a small center landing. And there were
no sharp angles here. Instead, it spiraled around gently, almost gracefully.

Her gaze traveled to a table that stood in the center of
the chamber before going to the cushioned bench and the
black . . .

She tipped forward and studied the thing. It stood on
three legs, huge and imposing with a matching black stick
holding up its lid. White rectangular bars gleamed from it
and smaller black bars sat atop this. She stepped closer and,
securing her orb under one arm, pressed one of the white
bars.

The clear, sharp sound it made startled her, and she
jumped back as if she had been scalded by water splashing
from a kettle. But she realized it was some sort of musical
instrument; then she saw what looked like the letters *W-e-*

i-r-l-e-i-n-s written in gold in the middle of the panel directly above the keys, though she couldn't perceive the word's meaning.

She stood stock still, waiting for Lord Joshua or Stephen to come barreling down the passageway. When they didn't, she released the breath she had been holding. Another entrance portal stood in this room. Sunlight beckoned through its glass. Next, there were two double doors, which were closed, made mostly of glass and wood, and obviously connected to another passageway.

She took in her surroundings once again, frozen and stunned by the tableau. She stared down at the covering beneath the table.

God's eyes! What manner of place had she landed in? Who would lay a fine tapestry upon a floor and place a table upon it? The tapestry was red and white with fringes on each end. Intricate little flowers were woven into the material.

Lord Joshua should be ashamed of himself.

What manner of man was Lord Joshua to own such strange, beautiful furnishings for his keep? Who would use *glass* to drink out of? Or make portals that were made with glass? In her time, glass was not only rare, but expensive as well. How did the Carona shine so brightly without the use of tapers? Who would put tapestries on the floor? Didn't he know better? Mayhap he didn't have a lady wife and he *didn't* know any better.

A sense of survival along with a keen curiosity slowly seeped into her. Strange calmness settled into her now that she had overcome the shock and paralyzing fear that had gripped her earlier.

Hearing the sound of laughter and revelry coming from the direction of the Great Hall, she glanced up at the top of the stairs, then all around her again. She couldn't continue to stand there and not get discovered. Mayhap she could find a place for concealment abovestairs until she could think of a way to make Lord Joshua understand her plight.

Holding firmly to the orb, she skitted up the stairs as fast as she could. Luck was with her again. Apparently everyone chose to stay belowstairs at the moment. She looked askance at the flowered walls and ran her hand across the surface. Textured and pleasing to the touch. She frowned as her curiosity mounted again. What manner of keep was this? The walls were not made of stone, yet they appeared strong.

The sound of laughter and footsteps coming up the stairs snapped her out of her reverie. Mayhap she would speculate another time on the pretty walls.

Five closed doors stood in the corridor. Giving herself only a moment's hesitation, she rushed to the one nearest her. Noiselessly she turned the knob and, opening the door, slipped through the entryway, closing the portal just as quietly behind her.

Ailith drew in a breath. 'Twas a dream! Nothing in her wildest imaginings had prepared her for such luxury. With widened eyes, she took in the breadth of the bed and wondered how many people slept in it. Even Lord Preston's bed could not compare with this one. She walked across the burgundy fabric-covered floor to the bed and fingered the slate and burgundy covering. 'Twas a most glorious feeling. Even the material in the cloth merchant's tent wasn't this fine.

She looked across the chamber through an opened door. Inside stood what looked like a glass wall with something— she would have to go closer to discover what—behind it. That chamber was verde and white in color. The light streaming into that chamber was waning, making it difficult to see any more of the furnishings. She marveled at what must be the window hangings of the time she was in. The slate tapestries hanging from them had no crests, but they were nonetheless beautiful.

She wandered around the room searching for wall sconces or oil lamps, but found none. When the darkness settled in, how would they bring light into the room? 'Twould be interesting to find out.

Chapter 5

"JOSHUA, WAIT!" STEPHEN called.

Lord Joshua paused in the doorway, turning his attention to Stephen.

Ailith slipped unnoticed behind the door she'd opened. Fearing closing it shut would be too noisy, she left it partially ajar. She backed farther into the small chamber and became entangled in garments. God's teeth!

Instantly she threw aside several tunics that fell on her head. They were similar to the one Lord Joshua had donned earlier. She stilled herself and listened for the sound of footsteps rushing toward her. When none came, she released a frustrated breath. The thick fabric on the floor would shield any noise . . .

"What is it, Stephen?" Lord Joshua's agitated voice reached her ears.

"You look thoroughly annoyed."

Ailith bit down on her lip. The close proximity of their voices told her the two men stood within a stone's throw.

"I *am* annoyed," Lord Joshua responded. "I guess I'm not being a very good host. I've got too much on my mind to distract me."

"Well, if it's Melissa," Stephen said, "you know she'll get over her pique sooner or later."

"Oddly enough, it isn't Melissa I've been thinking of."

"Your parents, then?"

"No. I was thinking about that girl I found in my tent," he admitted. "She was extremely beautiful. God, her face was perfect."

"Yeah," Stephen agreed, his tone wistful. "I wonder who she was."

"*I* wonder where she went," Lord Joshua commented. "Maybe I should not have been so harsh with her. It was obvious she had an interest in the Middle Ages. She even spoke Medieval French."

Ailith frowned.

"Sounds like you're regretting running her off," Stephen said.

"Well, I could have given her my card. Maybe we could have had dinner sometime."

"Yeah. Right." A mixture of exasperation and sarcasm sounded in Stephen's voice. "You, the girl, and Melissa."

Lord Joshua laughed, then everything fell silent.

Ailith drew in several deep breaths to calm her racing pulse and agitated nerves. Instinct warned her that she was not yet alone. Quietly she stepped around several other peculiar garments.

Lord Joshua's attire hung all around her; some even sat upon rail-like white shelves next to what could only be footwear of the time she was in. Dozens upon dozens of ornamental belts hung over a metal holder. Ailith touched one and recognized the material as silk immediately instead of the leather of her time. Each end of these silk belts came down to a point. One end was wider than the other. Her intrigue increased.

Lord Joshua laughed.

She tiptoed to the door and peeked out. From her shelter in the garment chamber, Ailith widened her eyes in wonder, watching as Lord Joshua went to the table beside his bed. He reached his hand under the shaded device and brought instant light into the room. He repeated his actions on the other side of the bed.

Upon closer inspection, the shaded devices reminded her of the oil and wick lamps at Greyhawke. She sniffed. No acrimonious oil smells reached her nostrils, and she blinked in bafflement.

Stephen slid into a chair across the chamber, and Lord Joshua flung himself backward, spread-eagle across the bed, his handsome face taut with frustration.

"I guess my plans for Mellie and me spending some time together over here is shot to hell," he muttered.

"*Tsk, tsk,*" Stephen said in mild reprimand. "Don't sound so pessimistic, pal. It could still happen."

Lord Joshua glowered at Stephen, who shrugged.

"Well, it *could* have still happened," Stephen corrected, unaffected by the lord's look. "She was probably ready to forgive you for calling her a snob. But for exposing yourself in front of an exquisitely lovely little medieval urchin, she's going to make you suffer."

Lord Joshua sighed as Stephen continued.

"You know Myra the Mouth has gotten to her by now."

"Yes, I know," Lord Joshua snapped and laid his dark head against the pillow again. "And that's it until my parents leave. You know how they are about sex and sleeping together without a marriage license. Especially my mother. Shit!"

He groaned. An overwhelming urge to go to him nearly consumed Ailith.

"I *hate* it when they come here. Mother makes my feel like I'm nine years old again." His features twisted into a scowl. "She has exasperated me since I was a kid. I started locking my bedroom door at an early age to keep her from barging in anytime it pleased her. Even living alone I haven't abandoned that practice. Why do you think I have locks on the inside and outside of my bedroom door? To keep Mother from spying when I am not in here, and walking in on me unannounced when I am! Hell! I can't do what I want in my own home!"

"Of course you can," Stephen countered. "You can do anything you want in your own home, except have a woman in your bedroom." His mockery evident, he laughed heartily and clutched his chest. "And God forbid you have sex with her!"

Lord Joshua threw a pillow at Stephen, who ducked.

"Hey, now! Thee will have none of that, Lord Joshua," Stephen chastised. "Thou shall cease thy pillow throwing posthaste!"

"Then *thee* will shut *thy* damned mouth."

Stephen sallied with the pillow Lord Joshua had thrown at him, missing Lord Joshua by a few feet. Lord Joshua fired off another pillow. Precise and accurate, it hit Stephen's face before falling to the floor.

"Enough already, man!" Stephen huffed. "And I warn you, Joshua, don't mention our little pillow fight to anyone! Now, where was I?"

He paused, laying his finger against his cheek and rolling his eyes heavenward in intense concentration. Finally he pointed a finger at Lord Joshua.

"That's right! The fact that you must become a monk for the next two weeks. But knowing your parents, they could stay for two months. I don't envy your celibacy, pal. No, sirree bob!"

"Go to hell," Lord Joshua growled.

Mirth rippled through Ailith at the interchange, and she covered her mouth with her hand to hold in her laughter. Once the moment passed, she wondered why Lord Joshua would cede to anyone else's wishes, especially his mother's. Like Lord Preston, her perception of Lord Joshua was not that of a knotty-pated simpkin or a coward.

Mayhap, 'twas a reason for his attitude.

"Listen, Josh, why don't I make excuses for you and herd everyone out? This has been a long day, and I want to shed this costume." Stephen pulled at the sleeve of his houppelande.

Costume?

"Sounds good to me," Lord Joshua said. "Maybe if those clowns see you dressed in twentieth-century attire, they'll remember my living room isn't a Great Hall in a dank castle.''

Frantically Ailith searched her mind to remember which century she had been in before the orb had brought her through time. The year 1413 was in the fifteenth century! She had traveled five centuries into the future! God's ears! These were the Ending Ages, then. That thought didn't comfort her. She would have preferred to land in the Beginning Ages.

How would she ever return to her own time? And how had the orb brought her five hundred years into the future?

She leaned against the wall, the fear and despair she had tempered earlier again welling inside her.

''I only came up here to make a phone call to Melissa, but you're right. I am tired and can certainly use the solitude.''

''Right,'' Stephen agreed. ''I think I'll go to my apartment and crash too. I'll tell your house staff not to disturb you. G'night, Josh.''

''Thanks, Stephen. G'night.''

Ailith squinted through the crack on the hinged side of the door and saw Stephen stand, pad to the door, open it, and leave the room. She swung her gaze back to the other side of the garment room door, pushing it a little further ajar.

Her eyes grew as big as a beaker. Lord Joshua had gone into the other little chamber where he placed his hand on the wall, making light shine throughout. He stood before a round, marble basin, his back to her. A quick stream of water accompanied with loud splashes told her he was relieving himself.

The garment chamber suddenly grew warm as she felt heat creeping up her neck and into her cheeks. The thought flitted across her mind that he had to be awfully rich to own such an expensive-looking garderobe.

Lord Joshua went from the garderobe chamber to the entry door and turned the latch. Securing the bedchamber, Ailith surmised. She frowned as she wondered how much

protection this would offer. Why wasn't there a heavy bolt
across the door? She concluded that it must be awfully safe
in this time. Forsooth, Lord Joshua didn't even employ a
Castle Guard.

Lord Joshua returned to the garderobe room and slid the
glass to one side. He turned two golden handles. From her
vantage point, she saw a symbol on each one. What did
they mean? Suddenly a shower of water cascaded from . . .
from . . . from the metal thing, which reminded her of a
hunting horn, hanging in the center of a dark verde-tiled
wall.

She watched awestruck, barely able to contain herself.

His back to her, Lord Joshua peeled away his clothing.
Ailith stared, unable to turn away. A different kind of fascination assailed her. In a thrice she found herself viewing
the most magnificent form of humanity she had ever seen,
for the second time that day. Never mind that Lord Joshua
was the *only* naked man she had ever seen.

Long of leg, he had taut buttocks, a sinewy back, and
broad shoulders. As if on cue, he turned toward her. He
stretched his arms high above his head, accentuating his
flat stomach and the curly, black hair that led to his manhood, which drew her glance in spite of her intention to
look away.

The breath whooshed from her body. Heat curled like
warm molasses in the pit of her belly and spread throughout
her limbs. Her body felt afire, yet she shivered. There could
not possibly be another as beautiful as Lord Joshua—in his
time or her own!

But another did come to mind: Lord Preston. Though
she'd never seen her lord unclothed, Lord Joshua was indeed his mirror image with his tall frame, dark looks, and
golden eyes.

She shut her eyes for a moment, whispering to God
above that Lord Preston would bring no harm to her parents. Making the sign of the cross once her request was
complete, she decided it was best to put her parents' fate
to the back of her mind for now. Or else she would waste

away with worry and would never succeed in devising a plan to return to her own time.

Opening her eyes and releasing the breath she had been holding, she concentrated on what Lord Joshua was doing. He stood inside a dark verde receptacle, whose sides reached just above his ankles. A spray of water sluiced over his muscled body as he lathered himself with a soap she swore scented the entire bedchamber with an unfamiliar yet most pleasing smell. That done, he poured something on his hair from an odd-looking bottle and vigorously rubbed it through the long mass of strands. This lathered as the soap had, only this was frothier. Ailith decided that it could only have been liquid soap. Then he took down the metal water horn from its place on the wall and held it over his head, rinsing away the soap.

Placing the water horn back on the hook in the wall, he soaped himself again, this time with his hands. He turned around in the receptacle, which was catching the falling water.

Lord Joshua raised one muscled arm and soaped under it, then did the same with the other. Once again, Ailith somehow found her gaze riveted to his full front when he stopped moving about.

The man again bedazzling her, her tongue cleaved to the roof of her mouth. From the slick, wet hair on his head, down to the mat of ebony hair on his chest, to his . . . his . . . Ailith studied his manhood with rapt attention. Even in her inexperience, she felt he was remarkably splendid.

Lord Joshua stepped onto the floor and grabbed a towel and commenced with the task of drying himself. Then abruptly, she could barely see him. A whirring sound reached her ears, and her startled heart skipped a beat. Suddenly he returned into her range of vision again, in his hand an object that he held close to his head.

Ailith swallowed convulsively, her eyes bulging. 'Twas blowing his hair like a strong wind! This went on for several minutes before the machine stopped. She noted with incredulity that Lord Joshua's hair did not appear wet anymore.

She gasped low in her throat. Had the thing actually dried Lord Joshua's hair?

Without warning, a loud ringing noise filled the room. Ailith jerked as if shot with a crossbow and covered her ears, the sound piercing, frightening. Lord Joshua tromped to the direction of the racket and halted at the table beside the bed.

"Hello," he said and silenced himself. A smile of satisfaction lit his face. "Mellie, sweetheart! Why don't you come over and let me tell *and* show you how sorry I am that we quarreled?"

Ailith ignored Lord Joshua's silky tone when she saw that he was speaking into a . . . a . . . a very short ladle with two dippers? Lord Joshua picked up a little rectangular device and aimed it at the wall near the foot of the bed. When she heard music coming from the wall, she edged to the hinged side of the door. Her head swam with the wonder at what she saw.

Images of people moved in a huge box situated against the wall! Forsooth! The sound suddenly stopped, and the images began to change.

What sorcery was this? She slid back to the other side of the door, looking at the rectangular thing Lord Joshua held in his hand. Mayhap 'twas a magnetic compass like her father's but shaped differently. Lord Joshua kept pressing his thumb down on it, then he threw it onto the bed. Ailith ventured again to the other side of the door. The huge box was now silent and black!

Lord Joshua's voice drifted into her consciousness.

"Just stay put, Melissa!" he ordered in an angry tone. "Goddammit! Myra saw only what she wanted to see. I can explain everything. Since you won't come to me, I'll see *you* in thirty minutes."

He slammed the two-sided ladle back on the table, then headed toward Ailith's place of concealment.

Chapter 6

JOSHUA SWUNG THE door to his closet open. It was a huge closet; on one side dozens of slacks, jeans, and trousers of every description hung on a bar beneath another bar loaded with knits and polo shirts. On the other side hung bars similarly arranged with an impressive array of suits on them. Under the trouser rack sat two shoe racks, each one holding twenty pairs of shoes.

A faint scent of lilacs and sweat reached his nose. He frowned, wondering if someone had been in his closet earlier. At last year's faire his club members had invaded just about every nook of his house. Next year it might be a good idea to hold the spectacle at another location.

Turning his attention back to the matter at hand, he stroked his chin thoughtfully and studied the clothes for a moment before choosing a pair of blue beltless slacks and a gray polo shirt.

Seeing his wealth of clothing brought the beautiful little con artist to mind. He contemplated the reasons behind that. After all, he should have been elated that Melissa had finally called him and he could set everything straight between them. Instead, he felt like a total bastard for turning away the captivating intruder and a little guilty for owning so much when she had appeared so poor.

He reminded himself she had only been playing a role.
For what purpose was anyone's guess. If only he had asked
her name.

There was no use in regretting his actions now. Whoever
she was, she was long gone, and he would probably never
see her again.

Walking out of the closet, clothes in hand, he strode to
his bed and laid them down. Then he went to his chest of
drawers and opened them, pulling out a pair of jockey
shorts. After hurriedly dressing, he went back to his closet,
got a pair of black loafers and slipped his feet into them.
In the bathroom he combed his hair, and on the way out
of his bedroom he stopped at his chest of drawers again to
retrieve his keys and wallet.

He rushed down the steps, unable to replace the image
of a petite green-eyed urchin with the willowy, hazel-eyed
one of Melissa.

Ailith remained in her hiding place at the very back of the
clothes chamber, nearly smothered in garments, for several
minutes after Lord Joshua departed. Finally she breathed a
sigh of relief and wiped away the sweat that was beading
her brow. What would he have done to her had he discovered her?

She shuddered to think. Not yet ready to reveal herself
to him, she wouldn't have had a plausible explanation for
hiding in his garment chamber. Even in her time, trespassing was dealt with harshly. She wondered how she would
finally present herself to him. Deciding it was better to
worry about that later, she sat a while longer, assuring herself of her solitude.

Weariness nearly overcame her. She was dirty, hungry,
tired, and she needed to use the garderobe. She crawled
from her secret cover and stood, stepping cautiously into
Lord Joshua's bedchamber, still awestruck by her surroundings. Dashing across to the garderobe chamber, she in-
spected the water horn. Her feet squished in something and
she gazed down. Water stood in puddles on the floor.

Ailith scrutinized the glass enclosure. Mayhap 'twas there to keep the water from getting onto the floor.

Terribly uncomfortable with her need to relieve herself, she quickly sat on the marble garderobe. When she was finished, she released a contented sigh, then wondered how to eliminate the waste within.

"Lord Joshua did something," Ailith commented in a low voice as she studied the chest that seemed attached to the garderobe.

She pushed on its silver handle. Nothing happened.

"What did he do?"

She pulled the handle up. Still nothing. In frustration, she slapped the handle down. She released a startled cry when sheets of water ran down the sides of the garderobe, clearing it and replacing it with clean water. Rushing water whooshed in, and she jumped back.

Thoroughly enchanted with her discovery, she covered her mouth with her hands. A moment later she turned her attention back to the water horn Lord Joshua had used to bathe himself, inspecting it to the best of her ability. She, too, wanted to bathe herself.

How did it work? She pressed on the wall behind it. When nothing happened, she even turned the dial on the water horn. Nothing. She turned one of the knobs she had spied from her hiding spot—the one with the symbol *H* on it—and a rush of water spurted out.

Hot water touched her arm. Ailith almost released a scream, but squelched it in the back of her throat. Quickly she turned the dial off. So, the symbol *H* must be to warn everyone that the water was heated. Surely Lord Joshua did not stand under such a hot flow and not get scalded! With consternation, Ailith turned the other knob, this time finding the water *C*old! She turned it back off, wanting to scream in frustration.

She stood back, her breath coming in short pants. Mayhap if she turned both knobs at the same time, combining the hot with the cold, she would get a comfortable flow. She stepped forward to test her idea, but the same piercing ring she had heard earlier started again from the two-sided ladle laying on Lord Joshua's bed table. Startled, she hastened back to her hiding place.

Just as she pulled the door closed, leaving it ajar enough to see, she heard Lord Joshua's voice.

"Hi, this is Josh. Confess your sins at the sound of the tone."

A click followed, then a musical sounding note before another voice responded.

"Hello, dear. Why did I ever think I'd find you at home? Your father and I have decided we'll be in New Orleans by Wednesday. That should give you enough time to get over your Middle Ages party. We love you. Bye-bye."

Click, then silence.

Ailith crept to the side of the bed and stared at the talking box in awe, where the two-sided ladle was attached.

"What manner of sorcery is this?" she whispered.

She touched it gently, gliding her hands over the smooth, cool surface. The ceaseless questions about the magical things surrounding her thrummed through her mind. Her curiosity to learn about the objects made her anxious to confront Lord Joshua . . . Josh again.

She glanced back at the door Josh had gone through. Fingering her soiled garments, she peered into the garderobe chamber, then again toward the entrance door.

Dare she take that chance? Feeling grimey, she wanted and needed to take a bath. Or mayhap a water cascade. Josh had seemed to enjoy that. Aye, 'twould be pleasant to feel the water flow over her body.

Placing her indecision aside and without giving it further thought, Ailith walked to the garment chamber and discarded her clothes. Now completely nude, she scurried back out, stopping momentarily at Josh's odd chest and pulling out a drawer. Sifting through it, she didn't find what she wanted. From the next drawer she slid out, she lifted a long-sleeved tunic. She giggled, thoroughly enraptured in her odyssey, but sure the *tunic* was called something else since it had matching breeches.

Lifting out the tunic, she glimpsed the entry door one last time. She was going to the water cascade, but 'twould not do to have Josh find her in there, so she copied what she had seen Josh do and secured the lock on the door. If Josh returned 'twould give her enough time to get back to her hiding place while he unlocked his door. She hoped. Forsooth! How much time does it take to unlock a door?

She pushed that thought aside and headed for the glass enclosure, stepping into the verde receptacle. Placing a hand on each of the golden knobs, she turned them in unison and whispered, ''And the water will come out comfortably.''

When the water began cascading through her hair and over her shoulders, she laughed softly. She lathered her body as well as her hair with Josh's wonderful soap. And when she was finished, she twisted her hair, wringing out some of the excess water.

A drying towel hung on a rack. Retrieving the cloth, she marveled at its plushness and proceeded to dry herself with it, reveling in the feel of it against her skin. Finally, she wrapped her damp hair in it, then slipped into the tunic. The sleeves covered her hands, and the bottom fell past her buttocks, but intense satisfaction bubbled within her.

The garderobe floor now had double the amount of water on it, but she allowed only a brief consideration of it. Would Josh notice the difference when he returned? Ailith giggled. Or would he become confused? She shrugged in dismissal and scampered to the entry door, quietly unlocking it.

Bereft of her undergarments, she felt surprisingly carefree without them. The pull of hunger pangs in her belly again interrupted further contemplation on the matter. Realization dawned on her that she'd had nothing to eat since she'd shared her dried figs with Aida at the fair. How long ago had that been?

Although she tried not to think of her parents, her mind clouded with visions of the past. The urge to weep suddenly assailed her. *Would* she ever see her beloved parents again?

And just what *would* Lord Preston do to them when he discovered her gone?

She hurried across the plush floor, wriggling her toes as she did so, though she discerned no pleasure from it as she would have a while ago. Suddenly weighted down with grief, she returned to the garment room, her place of concealment. A shaft of light from the strange lamps filtered through the crack she left in the door. Behind the barriers of clothes lay her orb.

She halted, shocked. The orb was glowing dimly. Afraid to hope that her wish had been granted, she bent and retrieved it from the floor. Though almost undetectable, there was a glow!

Ailith drew in a deep, calming breath. She clutched the orb to her breast, amazed, shaken. As certain as she was that the orb was responsible for bringing her to this time and place, she was just as certain it would get her back to where she belonged. And somehow it had to do with the brightness of the orb's light. Why, then, wouldn't it glow brighter and take her back to her own time?

"I wish to go home!" she whispered fervently, grasping the orb so firmly her fingers began to hurt.

She waited, but nothing happened. Not even a dim glow could be detected now. She swallowed a sob and sank dejectedly down into the farthest corner, ready to dissolve into a heap of self-pity. Suddenly the entrance door to the bedchamber swung opened.

"Lordy! That man sure is messy."

The feminine voice drifted back to Ailith in a huff as she sat in her hiding place.

"Loquisha, girlfriend, come look at this here mess!"

Soft footsteps seemed to follow the sound of the voice.

"Shawanda," another female voice said, "Mr. Josh ain't never made that big a mess before. A body could swim in that puddle. I'm sure sorry we ain't had done left yet when Mr. Josh come down. If we ain't had to clean so many glasses that his club members done left, he never would have had the chance to ask us to clean his room."

"Every time him and Miss Devereaux gets on the outs, that man goes off the deep end," Shawanda said.

"You thinks he loves her, girlfriend?" Loquisha asked.

Shawanda harumphed. "Who knows 'bout Mr. Josh, chile. Miss Melissa ain't one of the best catches, I swear. And with all o' his money, he can do better."

Ailith sidled within viewing range of the voices and fell back on her haunches in surprise. These women reminded her of the Saracens with their swarthy skin, but one of their skin tones was slightly darker, reminding her of rich mahogany. Thick plaits seemed to grow out of her scalp, hanging past the woman's shoulders, while the other one had hair that was shiny and curly. Both were short, but while one was stout, the other was slender.

Ailith settled back in her hiding spot. A short burst of silence ensued, followed by a rustling of movements, then the sound of drawers being pushed closed. 'Twould be the drawer in the chest she'd left open, Ailith figured out, thinking it best not to return to her viewing spot for now.

"Well, I'm tired, Loquisha," Shawanda muttered. Her skin reminded Ailith of honey. "This has been a long day. I'm 'bout ready to go home."

"Me, too, girl," Loquisha responded.

"Well, you two ladies did a great job as usual."

Ailith's hearing perked at the sound of the cheerful male voice.

"Connor, you come to inspect?" Shawanda snapped.

Connor released a long suffering sigh. "Don't go get on your high horse, Shawanda," he said good-naturedly. "I've come to thank you and try to give you the bonus the boss left for you two ladies."

"Really? A bonus?" Loquisha chimed in.

Ailith smiled at the glee in the woman's voice. If she could put her mind to it, she could figure out *everything* that they were saying. As it was, she understood some of what was being said.

"Mr. Josh appreciated the help, ladies," Connor said.

"Especially staying on to finish the cleanup. You two deserve a bonus, I think."

A bonus, Ailith thought and frowned in concentration. That's what you get when you finish a job. And apparently 'twas something *pleasant* to get. She wondered what you got if the job didn't get finished. Would Josh demand harsh punishments as Lord Preston did?

"Ladies, Mr. and Mrs. Kenley are supposed to arrive tomorrow, so go home and get over the fair," Connor encouraged. "You want to be able to start fresh in the morning. Everything seems in order in here."

Ailith perceived movement in the room, then all light disappeared when someone closed the door to her hiding place. Soon afterward, she heard another door closing. Silence cloaked the room like a heavy mantle.

Ailith remained without moving for long moments before finally stirring to open the door once again. A sudden flash of weak light appeared, startling her and stopping her from her original intent.

'Twas coming from the orb.

"Oh!" Her gasp came unconsciously, loudly. "I wish to go back to my own time!" she blurted, trying to seize the opportunity before the globe dimmed. She shut her eyes as tightly as she could, but when she opened them again, she still remained in her place of concealment in the garment chamber.

Her spirits sank as desolation swept through her. She was lost and alone, with no idea where she was, and no one to turn to. Her thoughts would not settle enough for her to think of a plan to confront Josh and convince him to help her. Though there was still a dim glow about the orb, it had obviously ceased to work, and she was very probably stuck five hundred years into the future for the rest of her life. And her parents would be stuck in Lord Preston's dungeon for the rest of theirs.

Dropping the orb beside her, she brushed away an unwanted tear and huddled herself to the very back of the wall. Her stomach grumbled again, but her sudden fatigue overcame even the discomfort of her hunger. Mayhap if she rested, she could then figure out what to do when she awakened.

Drawing her knees up to her chest, she sighed and closed her eyes. Just as she calmed down enough to attempt to sleep, the garment chamber door was once again swung open without warning.

Chapter 7

"IT LOOKS LIKE we're never goin' to git out o' here," Shawanda grumbled in complaint as she hung a pair of slacks on the trouser bar. "Are you sure this is it for the night, Connor?"

"Quit your griping," Connor admonished. "I just wanted to make sure everything was done. There's no telling what kind of mood our esteemed boss will be in when he gets home. Don't want to give him a reason to fuss."

"Especially if he's out with his Mellie," Shawanda cracked. "I wonder what that woman does to him."

"Well, that's not our problem," Connor returned. "I intend to go out and get drunk and maybe get something else, too, if you get my drift." He winked at her. "Care to join me? My treat."

"The drink I'll take." Shawanda placed her hands on her slim hips and shook her head, causing her curls to bob up and down. "Just don't expect me to be the 'something else' you intend to get."

"You and me?" Connor responded with mock indignation. "Don't be ridiculous! We have nothing in common."

"What do you mean, nothing in common?" Shawanda uttered, truly indignant. "You're not trying to tell me I'm too black for you, are you?"

"Now you're being silly," Connor declared. "Your color has nothing to do with it."

"Oh, no?" Suspicion crept into her tone. "Then what's your problem?"

"You're a Baptist," he responded. "And I—" he pointed to himself as if to emphasize his point—"am a strict Catholic. I could never get involved with a Baptist girl! My mother would kill me! If she were still alive, that is."

He smiled at the girl who stood before him eyeing him narrowly before she burst out laughing.

"All right. I'll have *one* drink with you, Connor. Just make sure the something else you get out there is something you can *live* with."

Connor hugged her around her shoulders as they started toward the entrance door, leaving the closet door wide open.

"So you do care?" Connor murmured. "Do you really think I'd let lust jeopardize my life . . . ?"

Shawanda and Connor departed before Ailith could hear the girl's response. After a while she wondered if she was now alone in the keep. Deciding if she wasn't totally alone, everyone who remained was at least bedded down by now, she once again left her hiding place. Creeping to the door, she opened it slowly and peeked up and down the hall. There was no one in sight and not a sound to be heard. Cautiously, soundlessly, she tiptoed to the stairs, halted and listened again.

She glanced behind her, toward the closed doors, then stretched her neck trying to look belowstairs and beyond. No movement. Nothing. Boldly, she continued down the steps, stopping at the bottom. Forsooth, 'twould be disastrous if Shawanda and Connor were still around.

With a shiver of satisfaction, Ailith concluded that she was beginning to comprehend more words. She understood Catholic and several other words. And she was quite sure she understood that Josh and his . . . his . . . what . . . leman? Is that what women who are kept by men in this

time were called? Well . . . his lady. Josh and his lady were
not getting along. That thought sent intense pleasure
through her, and she couldn't comprehend why.

Walking warily through the long passageway and past
the chamber she had glimpsed earlier, she saw a light glowing from a lamp similar to the one next to Josh's bed. This
one sat on a table next to the circular, cushioned settle.
Ailith wanted to examine the lamp and sit on the settle. Or
the matching chair. Or even the woven floor. Either place
appeared equally comfortable. But she didn't dare. If she
was really alone at the moment, she did not know how long
she would remain so. Her priority now was to find something to eat.

Which chamber housed the kitchens? Was the kitchen
situated belowstairs? Was there another stairway that led to
another floor beneath this one? Ailith doubted it as she
wandered down another corridor. Would she recognize the
kitchens as such if she saw them?

She came to a room that housed a large, rectangular table
surrounded by twelve chairs. A huge, exquisitely ornate
chest with doors and drawers on the front stood against one
wall. On top sat a beautiful vase, which seemed awfully
familiar to her.

Where would she get such a knotty-pated notion from?
Yet the thought persisted that she had seen it before. The
delicate vase was sided by two silver candelabras. She
paused only momentarily to admire their beauty before going into the next room.

Ailith stopped and gawked. This room was saved from
complete darkness by a light coming from the wall. 'Twas
sheer magic!

Oh, would that her father were here to see all of these
wonders! Her heart constricted at the thought of what must
be happening to her parents at the moment.

Glancing around, she knew she was in the right place.
The aromas wafting through her nostrils were as tempting
as anything she'd ever smelled before. 'Twas a huge bowl
of fruit on the cupboard . . . At least, she thought 'twas a

cupboard. Shelves with doors hung along the walls. Everything was shiny and black and white and glass.

The storeroom was made of . . . of glass! Ailith studied
the glass door and the food behind it. 'Twas not large
enough to be called a storeroom. Mayhap a glass enclosed
alcove? Well, whatever 'twas called, she knew without a
doubt 'twas not a storeroom. Mayhap 'twas simply called
a food keeper.

She attempted to slide the door across in the same fashion she had in the garderobe chamber for her water cascade.
But this door did not budge. Perplexed, she observed it a
few seconds and, using the handle on the end, pulled down
on it. The door flew open. A blast of cold air hit her in the
face, and she jumped back.

"Oh! How can this be?" she marveled aloud. "How is
the cold air contained when 'tisn't even cold?"

For the first time since her arrival, she realized the inside
of the keep was cooler than she remembered it being outside. *What* magical place was she in?

She scanned the contents of the food keeper. She wished
for a dish of *chawdon*, but didn't spy any swan meat. Mayhap there was some *blamanger* or some *hoggepot*? But she
didn't find any. She did see chicken in a sack—a *see-
though* sack, as was most everything else in this food
keeper. Ailith frowned to herself as she identified foods
familiar to her.

There was a roasted hunch of meat, which appeared to
be beef. Then there was the chicken. And onions, lemons,
leeks, and numerous other foodstuffs. She saw no evidence
of wild boar, pheasant, capon, vulture, or eels and wondered how long it had been since Josh had last hunted and
fished.

Grabbing the sack containing the chicken and ripping it
open, she tore off a leg and began to munch on that. She
found a similar, but smaller sack with a vegetable, which
at first she thought were turnips. Upon initial bite of them,
she knew they were not. These vegetables had been cut into
chunks and were wonderfully browned and tasty. Then

there was bread; bread like she had never tasted before. Created with garlic, parsley, and butter, it had been baked until 'twas crusty and brown.

Ailith washed down her food with a big tankard of milk. The milk tasted slightly different in this time, but 'twas the only container she had been able to open. Her gaze roamed over the fruit on the table. 'Twould not be prudent to take some to her hiding place. Their sweet fragrances would surely give her away.

She went to the shelves on the walls with the closed doors, and opened one at a time. She discovered what could only be trenchers, cups, containers, and goblets of the time in the first three shelves she opened. The other shelves contained more food. There was food in paper and glass containers, which held hard round sweet treats made from some kind of flour. Some of the sweet treats even had nuts and dark chunks in them. 'Twould help to have some on hand were she not able to get belowstairs again undetected.

The paper . . . sacks . . . ? . . . were sealed, so she did not bother with them.

Thinking it unwise wasting time to find something to put her precious hoard in, she simply took the entire sweet-filled jar from the shelf to bring with her abovestairs. She gazed about with eagerness.

She had bathed. She had eaten. But most important, she had remained undetected. And now she was exhausted.

Taking her jar, she began her journey through the magnificent keep, down its passageways, finally coming to the spiraling staircase. Scampering up, just as she reached Josh's bedchamber, she heard his deep voice call out to the man named Connor.

Chapter 8

FOR THE NEXT three days Ailith played her cat-and-mouse game, enjoying the intrigue of outwitting the occupants of the house.

'Twas most exciting! She giggled to herself, recalling the tongue-lashing Josh had given Connor at finding the food keeper . . .

She searched her mind for the *other* name, the one Josh had used. Aye! The *refrigerator*. That was the word she'd learned the night Josh had almost caught her below . . . Nay . . . No . . . *Down*stairs.

The kitchen devices were called *appliances*. She knew that because Josh had also stipulated to Connor that all the appliances in the kitchen, especially the refrigerator, should remain closed at all times if they were equipped with doors!

She'd left the refrigerator door open, as well as all the shelf and cabinet doors. Connor tried to convince Josh that an out . . . a . . . a *burglar* had invaded his domicile.

Ailith held her hands to her mouth to keep from laughing out loud. Josh had accused Connor of being drunk enough to have done the deed himself. What burglar, he'd barked, would eat chicken and *potatoes*, then leave their *storage bags* strewn across the counter?

She had even learned that there had been some of her favorite foods at Josh's Medieval Faire, but what hadn't been eaten at the revelry after the spectacle was over had been thrown out. Though Ailith had nearly gone apoplectic about the waste, *that* had seemed to be the one thing Josh had been pleased about.

"Who, on ordinary occasions, would eat some of that shit anyway?" Josh had snorted. "I certainly don't have an everyday appetite for rede rose, sambocade, garbage, tansy cake, pigge in sauge and all of our other medieval authenticities."

"Actually the Red Rose Pudding and Elderflower Cheese Pie was quite tasty," Connor replied. "I also enjoyed the *Monchelet*. You know? The lamb stew?"

"Whatever."

Not long after, Josh had dismissed Connor, and Ailith had released a pent-up sigh of relief that the man hadn't gotten into an abundance of trouble over her actions.

Since then she bided her time until she knew she was alone in the house. Neither the same time every day, nor was it as long as the first day. She was unable to take a water cascade again, and she barely had time to sneak down for more food. Or use the garde . . . the *toilet*.

Every day she'd tried to get the orb to glow enough to bring her back home. As it happened on the first day, a dim light glowed from it at times, but for the most part it remained dark and cold. When she wasn't trying to figure out how to return to Middlesbrough, she was thinking of a way to reveal herself and ask Josh to help her. With her limited knowledge of his language, it would prove most difficult. So she ordered herself to remain hidden for a while longer and ignored her increasing restlessness as best she could.

She'd learned the meanings of many new words in the past several days while hidden in the garment . . . the *closet*. The huge image box was called a *television*. And the talking box attached to the two-sided ladle was called a *telephone* and *answering machine*.

The verde water receptacle was a *shower stall*. When she learned that, she'd felt a little embarrassed that she hadn't known what it was. There were tubs for bathing in her times, but they didn't resemble that one. Still, it should have been obvious. Then the water horn was called a *shower*. And the machine that Josh used to dry his hair was called a *hair dryer*.

'Twas fascinating and exciting, these new and wondrous discoveries. Unbeknownst to Josh, she watched television when he did, laughing at the antics of a man named David Letterman. Though she didn't understand his jests, especially those about the man named President, she found his animal tricks amusing.

It didn't take her long to realize that *president* referred to the ruler of the place she was in, though she still didn't know *what* place she was in.

Sometimes David Letterman spoke of the President's Cabinet. At first she wondered about the differences between the President's cabinet and Josh's. Was the President's bigger? Did it have more shelves, mayhap?

But her question was answered on the *nightly news*. The *Cabinet* gave counsel to the President, much like King Hal's advisers.

She loved to hear Josh laugh his friendly, carefree laugh, the one that made her feel warm all over and speeded up her pulse. But at the moment 'twas not a happy sound he was making. He stood in his bedchamber. A ferocious scowl hardened his features as he scolded the black girl Ailith now recognized as Shawanda. Ailith wondered why Shawanda was called black. Her skin color certainly was not black. 'Twas more light brown than black.

". . . and what in the hell have you done with my pajama top, Shawanda?"

Ailith listened, concentrating on the words that were being spoken.

Vexation creased Shawanda's expression. "What are you talking 'bout, Mr. Josh?" she huffed back.

"The bottoms to my green silk pajamas are here, but the

top is missing," Josh snapped. "Have you any idea where it is?"

Shawanda glared at him. "Do I look like I'm panting for your pajama top? I sure hope you ain't accusing me of taking it. Won't do for me to work where I ain't trusted. Mr. Joshua, I ain't got any use for your things," she continued in indignant outrage. "*I* like my clothes a little more frilly. And in case you ain't noticed, Connor's been acting mighty strange. Maybe you should check *his* room."

Josh sighed, giving her a contrite look. "I *didn't* accuse you, Shawanda," he muttered. "And I'm sorry if I gave you that impression. I've been preoccupied of late. I'm sure the top will turn up." He smiled at her, his eyes glowing with warmth.

Ailith wondered how Shawanda didn't melt at his feet under such devastating charm.

"My parents will be here in less than an hour. See that their room is in order. If you and Connor need help while they're here, ask your cousin Loquisha to give you a hand."

Shawanda returned his smile. "Connor has already told her to come back," she replied. "He thought your parents were coming in day before yesterday. Anyway, Loquisha and I both thank you for that generous bonus."

"No problem. You two deserved it. Listen, Shawanda, I may need you to stay on late this evening. I don't know what my parents' plans are." Josh gritted his teeth. "I *never* know what their plans are!"

Shawanda laughed. " 'Bout once a year you get like this, Mr. J., when your parents come for their annual visit." She raised her eyebrows and suggested, "Why don't *you* go visit them next year?"

Josh grimaced. "I tried that once, but they still came here. I had to put up with them *twice* in one year. Visiting my folks is ten times worse than them visiting me." He chuckled. "So that's a bad suggestion, Shawanda."

She shrugged. "I'm going downstairs to give Connor a hand. Loquisha should get here any minute. I know you want some privacy to get ready for your parents' arrival, Mr. J. I'll just see you later.''

With that, Shawanda left Josh alone. Although Josh was the master of the ke . . . *manor*, the liberties his workers took with him never ceased to amaze Ailith. They had absolutely no fear of him.

She kind of liked that.

Ailith watched Josh repeat the routine she'd become familiar with in the past three days. He turned the latch on the door before disrobing. She closed her eyes and bit down on her lip, trying to temper the clenching in her belly at the sight of him.

'Twas almost too much to bear. Shame and guilt over watching his magnificent form without his knowledge accompanied strange yearnings toward the man himself. She tried to avert her eyes, but of their own accord they always remained riveted to his body. He was too beautiful for words.

And the heat! Forsooth! 'Twas all she could do to control the flusters and sensations coursing through her body at the nearness of him when he came into the closet and nearly overwhelmed her with his fresh, clean scent. The mere sound of his voice lurched her heart into excitement.

Even when Lord Preston had commanded most of her thoughts, she hadn't felt the compelling pull that Josh caused within her. Aye, Lord Preston may have been her hero, but Josh was her dream.

Guiltily she continued to spy upon Josh, again wondering why he always left the shower door open when he showered. She also wondered when *she* would ever be able to shower again. She felt so dirty at the moment.

While Josh was blow drying his hair—now cut a lot shorter, almost in the Norman fashion—the telephone rang. In the full glory of his nakedness, he traipsed to the phone.

"Hello, Mother!"

Josh rolled his eyes heavenward.

"Yes. Yes!"

He dropped onto the bed.

"Well, I can certainly come pick you up," he said.

Ailith detected the resentment in his tone.

"All right, then. . . . Melissa? Of course she'll be here. . . . Yes, I'll expect you in the next half hour. See you then. Bye."

Ailith watched Josh slam down the receiver and thrust his hands through his hair.

"Shit!" he snarled.

Pressing a button, he caused a loud tone to sound off. He dialed a *telephone number* and walked away from the phone to begin dressing.

"Hello?"

A voice Ailith recognized as Stephen's came over the— what was that Shawanda had called it? The speaker phone? Yes—speakerphone.

"Stephen, where the hell are you?" Josh asked.

"At home, which should be obvious since I answered my telephone."

"Stephen," Josh began, warning clear in his voice.

"Now, if you mean what am I *about* to do, then I'm on my way to pick up Mellie and her dwarfish friend."

"Good. I guess I can tolerate Myra for Melissa's sake."

Clad in jockeys and black socks, Josh started toward the closet. Eyes widening in alarm, Ailith scrambled as noiselessly as possible to her shelter behind the score of suits and jackets.

"My parents are en route here. So get the hell over here as soon as possible," Josh ordered, raising his voice while he stood in the closet.

"Right," Stephen hollered back. "I'll expect a calming drink for all my trouble, Josh. Any one of those two women could cause a man to become an alcoholic."

From his tone, Ailith surmised Stephen was only half jesting.

Josh laughed. "That's only if you're a weak man, Stephen. Just quit your griping and deliver the hags to my doorstep."

"See you in a little bit," came the unenthused reply, then a buzzing sound.

Josh padded over to the telephone and pressed another button, bringing silence back into the room.

Dressed and groomed, Josh unlatched and opened his door. In a matter of minutes Loquisha scurried in and began tidying up the bathroom, setting things in order.

"You might as well take them shower doors down, Mr. Joshua," she grumbled flippantly. "They ain't doing no good where they is, 'cause you certainly don't seem to know what they's there for."

She sauntered out of the room before Josh could respond to her. Ailith heard him growl something in return, however. Just as he started out of the room, she felt a sneeze coming on. She pinched her nose to ward it off, but not before a partial sound escaped.

Josh paused abruptly. An alert frown crossed his handsome brow. He stared at his closet, listening intently. After a moment he shrugged and continued on through the door, leaving it wide open.

Breathing in a sigh of relief that he hadn't found her, Ailith placed a hand over her heart, in an effort to stop its racing. God's breath! If she didn't reveal herself or return home soon, she would be found dead of an apoplectic fit caused by all of these near discoveries.

Calmed once again, she glared at the door he'd left open. What did that man have against closing doors? She couldn't leave her hiding place now, because she could easily be seen wandering around in Josh's room! *Shit!* And she couldn't close the door. If Josh returned right away, he would know something was amiss. Though he hadn't investigated, she knew her sneeze had made him suspicious; a closed door would give him reason to search.

With a sigh of resignation, Ailith settled herself in the relative security of the closet. Sometime later, just as she relaxed, the sounds of pleasant voices drifted up to her. God's mercy! This had to be her restitution for spying on

Josh daily. But listening more closely, she realized the sounds were downstairs at the front door.

She inhaled a sharp breath and inched to the edge of the closet door to listen.

"Hello, Joshua."

Ailith recognized the voice as belonging to the irritating little magpie.

"Myra."

That was Josh, whose voice was rigidly polite.

"Lead me to the spirits," came Stephen's taut voice.

Thinking a celebration was about to commence, Ailith brightened. Although she couldn't join in, she would enjoy hearing the sounds of revelry. Most of the time, there *was* always someone other than herself in the house, but she still felt terribly alone and lonely.

Equally, when she and Josh were alone in the bedroom, she had to remain quiet and undetected, which only served to sharpen her despair.

As the night wore on, she heard new voices and much laughter. With her customary boldness—her mother had complained constantly about it—she left her hiding place and went to sit in the opened doorway of Josh's bedroom. Quickly she learned to connect the names to the new voices she heard.

Frances was the name of Josh's mother. Her voice was soft, her words usually drawled out. Josh's father, Jonathan, had a blustery tone. Someone named Kayla was in attendance also, and her speech was husky and authoritative. Myra's pitch was sharp, nasal. And Melissa's voice was cool and condescending, especially when Stephen spoke to her.

Ailith laughed when Josh and Stephen did. She rallied behind Stephen when he and Myra argued. She poked her tongue at the sound of Melissa's voice. And she tapped her toes to songs that Stephen put in something called a *CD player*. Each time he changed *compact discs*—Ailith continued to marvel at her new discoveries—he said the name of the minstrel in that charmingly mocking way of his.

Soon Ailith learned—from Stephen—that they were *singers*, not minstrels, and she giggled. She, along with everyone else, listened to Ray Charles, Elvis Presley, U2, Dr. Hook, Elton John, and *Dr.* John.

"And now, ladies and gentlemen, we have 'Love in an Elevator' by Aerosmith," Stephen announced.

By the mischievous sound of his voice, Ailith imagined his cobalt eyes were twinkling.

When the music blasted through, Josh snarled, "Goddammit, turn that crap off!"

"Really, Joshua honey," Melissa spoke, her tone smug. "You can't expect any better from him. He's an assh—"

"Drop it, Mellie!" Josh imparted flatly.

Ailith wondered what she'd been about to say.

"Melissa, dear, you should be ashamed of yourself!" Frances muttered with disapproval.

"I should be," Melissa responded.

"But we all know you're not," Stephen bit out.

"Enough!" Josh ordered.

Ailith questioned why he would allow things to get so out of hand.

"And now, Stephen," Josh began again, "we're going to listen to music that will allow you to think clearly. Amadeus and Debussy."

"Aww, come on, man!" Stephen declared. "This is a celebration, not a funeral!"

Ailith was soon inclined to agree with Stephen's perception. 'Twas easy to listen to, and she would have enjoyed it at another time, mayhap at supper. For a celebration, however, she preferred Stephen's music.

Pleasure at having "met" everyone in attendance swirled through her, even as hunger assailed her. The tantalizing aromas of the night's fare did nothing to quell the rumblings in her belly, so she decided to return to her hiding place to munch on the last of the sweet treats she'd pilfered from the kitchen. Tonight, 'twas unsatisfactory to her taste buds, though they satisfied her hunger for the time being.

Boldly she went to the bathroom to get a drink of water,

absently carrying the cookie jar with her as she munched on one of the sweet treats. Placing the jar on the counter, she started to retrieve a small glass, but paused and listened intently.

She heard footsteps coming up the stairs! Though thirsty, she decided against getting the water and, placing the glass where she found it, hurried to conceal herself, forgetting the jar.

"Damn it, Mother!"

Ailith heard Josh's exasperated voice as he came through the doorway.

"There are no women's clothes in there!"

The sound drew closer to the closet, finally halting right before the opened doorway.

"Even if there were, I am a twenty-nine-year-old mature adult. A grown man! I would think you would have noticed that by now!"

"Why, Joshua, whatever are you talking about, dear?" Frances asked demurely.

Josh laughed without humor, then released a defeated sigh and went to sit on the chair next to the window.

"I'm sure you don't know. Just look around to your heart's content. But if it will save you some searching, Melissa is not living here."

Frances smiled sweetly. "I never thought that, dear. Even if you two are living together, I know you can refrain from your regular routine while I'm in residence. After all, you know how I feel about that sort of thing."

"Of course, Mother. I'll just set aside *all* of my physical needs while you are 'in residence.' "

"Don't be angry, darling," Frances soothed. "I know how lusty the Kenley men are. You are not only a descendant of the Kenleys, but also of the Claybournes, the most libidinous lot of all, especially that Preston, that poor, unfortunate man!"

Ailith's heart slammed against her chest. Josh was a descendant of her lord? No wonder he hadn't believed her when she'd mentioned the outlaw DeLepee Rouge that

Lord Preston was chasing! And *what* did Frances mean
when she said that poor, unfortunate man?

"It's not you I'm worried about, Joshua dear. It's the
poor girls that bother me. You're such a handsome, charming devil, they'll gladly do your bidding without benefit of
marriage, not considering what harm they will cause their
own reputation," Frances said, thoroughly horrified.

"Mother, please!" Josh asserted. "This is 1998, not
1898!"

"Yes, dear, I know. August 21, 1998 to be precise. But
I wish you would get serious with someone. We have a
long, illustrious family line to continue. And we simply
can't have any more illegitimacy staining our proud heritage. Once was enough."

Josh snorted. "As if *they* didn't stain our heritage with
illegitimacy regularly."

"Cynicism doesn't become you, dear," Frances pointed
out. "Come. Let's rejoin the others. Can't have Melissa
running up here to this bachelor's bedroom in search of
you."

Josh shook his head and gave a short laugh. "You won't
quit, will you? How long are you intending to stay, anyway?"

"It all depends on your father's whims, dear. Anywhere
from three weeks to three months." As she started for the
entrance door, she said, "Oh, did I mention we decided to
stay at least three weeks, instead of our customary two?"

"Shit!" Josh groaned.

His tone was just loud enough for Ailith to discern before
he followed his mother and exited the room, this time closing the door.

Ailith rested her head on her drawn-up knees. Her orb
had brought her 585 years into the future? Maybe if she
had gone precisely 500 years forward or even 600 years,
the orb would still work. And Josh was a Claybourne? Of
course, he had to be. That explained why he was Lord
Preston's replica.

She recalled Frances's words concerning Lord Preston.

Had he met with some unfortunate end? He constantly left to go on marches and raids. Indeed, would he be dead when she returned, if that's what Frances was hinting at? For some strange reason, her voice had been filled with compassion and not sorrow.

Unable to sort out her confusion, Ailith yawned and decided to push the matter aside for the moment. Feeling tired, she snuggled closer to the back wall and before long dozed off into a deep sleep. When she awakened, she had no idea of the time. It was still the same night; she knew by the shaft of light shining through the crack in the door from the lamp that had been on earlier and was still on. She listened intently from her little corner. She heard not a sound, not even the gentle snores that sometimes emanated from Josh when he bedded down for the night.

Ailith scooted to the door and peeked out. She was still alone. Suddenly remembering the jar she'd left in the bathroom and thankful that Josh hadn't gone in there, she crept to the entrance door and placed her ear against it to listen for sounds in the hall. None came forth. Pulse pounding and throat dry, she hesitated only a brief moment longer before hurrying to the bathroom to remove the evidence of her presence.

As soon as she stepped inside the room, she heard the bedroom door being thrown open, then closing again. She knew it could only be Josh when the latch was clicked into place.

Chapter 9

TRAPPED! WITH NO place to hide.

Stunned and wide-eyed, Ailith watched Josh empty his pockets, then place their contents on the top of his chest of drawers. Afterward, he sat on the side of the bed and took off his shoes before removing his necktie and unbuttoning his shirt.

He absently looked into the bathroom, and his gaze fell immediately on her. His mouth dropped open in sheer shock. He started to speak, but Frances's voice, along with her knock on the door, prevented him from doing so.

Ailith gasped, as startled as Josh, wishing for quick and immediate death. Standing before him with exposed legs and indecent clothing, humiliation, fast and unrelenting, crept from the tips of her toes to the top of her head, and its heat scalded her.

"Joshua, dear?" Frances called. "Are you asleep yet?" The knob turned, but because Joshua had locked the door, it didn't budge.

Open-mouthed, Joshua blinked owl-eyed at the little beauty who had invaded most of his thoughts these past three and a half days and who now stood in his bathroom wearing his pajama top!

My pajama top! And to think I've lamented the fact that I wouldn't ever see her again.

Slow fury percolated in him. He pushed aside the tiny sparks of longing and eagerness that flared within him. Noting her shining hair and scrubbed skin, his jaw clenched, and he narrowed his eyes. Her gaze widened.

"Joshua!"

His mother's voice cut into his stunned senses before his brain could form any words for him to sputter to the intruder.

"Joshua!"

"Er . . . yes, Mother?" Joshua called. "Just a minute."

Quickly he slammed the bathroom door shut, but not before catching a glimpse of the scarlet blush on the girl's face.

"I'm sorry, Mother," Joshua said as he unlocked and opened the door. "I was in the bathroom. What can I do for you?"

"I wanted to thank you for a lovely evening and tell you good night."

"Well, it was my pleasure, Mother," he replied automatically. He wanted to get this interview over with quickly so he could confront the girl. "I'm glad you enjoyed it."

"You're not still annoyed with me, are you, Joshua? I know I'm an impossible prude, but I still believe in old-fashioned values."

"Of course I'm not annoyed, Mother. I respect your right to your opinion. Even if you have imposed it in *my* house."

Joshua laughed good-naturedly, a far pretense from what he was experiencing at the moment. His roles in the Medieval Faires he'd hosted had taught him how to act and cover up the true nature of his feelings, even to the extent of schooling his features to register nothing at all. He wanted his mother gone so he could wring the girl's scrawny neck.

"I'm glad you understand, darling," Frances drawled. "Good night, Joshua."

Though above average in height for a woman, his mother still had to stand on tiptoe to kiss him.

"Good night, Mother."

With that, Frances turned and departed. Joshua closed his door once again. After turning the key in the deadbolt lock, he slid the latch securely in place as well, then stalked to his bathroom and threw open that door. He must remind Connor that his key would be required to gain entrance into Joshua's bedroom until after his mother left.

The girl stood against the shower door, an oversized bath towel draped in front of her and pooling at her feet. Her long blond hair floated over her shoulders and down the length of her back, cradling her exquisitely beautiful face like a soft cloud.

For a moment Joshua merely stared, swallowing hard. What a vision she was! And the fear shining in her emerald depths stopped him from berating her right away as he had intended to do.

He cleared his throat in an effort to calm himself. It barely worked. "So we meet again," he said, his voice silky, a clear warning to all who knew him that he was furious beneath his staid exterior. "Medieval maiden," he added for emphasis when she remained silent.

The thought that she had somehow managed to get inside his house undetected galled and surprised him. Why and how had she done it?

Perhaps she was some kind of misguided groupie, although he'd never thought of himself as a groupie magnet. After all, he was conservative by nature—definitely *not* groupie material—and fame didn't trail him in the rock-star or actor sense. True, he was well known locally and in certain national and international circles due to Kenley Galleries and his Medieval Faires, but that didn't qualify him for celebrity status by a long shot. So *what* was her story?

The girl had yet to speak. His anger boiled over.

"First of all, miss, you're *still* trespassing," he snarled. "Perhaps I neglected to make that clear enough to you last Sunday. So let's start over."

Joshua treaded with menace toward her. She deftly stepped away from the shower door and scampered back toward the wall. He paused, not liking her fear.

"You can begin by telling me your name," he told her, not entirely unkindly.

The girl merely stared.

"Your name, miss!" Joshua repeated, somewhat impatiently.

For a moment she remained silent before squeaking, "I-I am called Ailith."

"Ailith?" Joshua raised his brows in skepticism. "Rather an unusual name. But at least we're making progress. Now, tell me, Ailith, why are you in my bathroom wearing my pajama top?"

'Twas not hard to comprehend Josh's words. The nearly four days she'd remained undetected in Josh's house gave her a quick course in this time's language and lifestyle.

Although he'd made his statement in a calm manner, Ailith detected an edge to his voice. She stepped farther back.

"I-I had no other place to go." She hated the timidity in her tone. "I had nothing else to wear when I took a-a water shower in your gard . . . your bathroom. . . ."

Joshua detected an accent, an *English* accent. Why hadn't he noticed it before? Because the first time he heard her speak she'd been speaking Medieval French. Was this yet another role she had affected?

He strode forward, not stopping until he stood directly in front of her. Big mistake. If she had been breathtaking from the short distance that separated them, she was heartstopping up close. And vulnerable. And young. And alluring. "Where are you from, Ailith?" he asked gently.

Somehow she managed to answer, "F-from Middlesbrough."

Ailith's pulse beat frantically, Josh's nearness devastating to her senses. If Josh's appeal and handsome looks had been magnetic from afar, they were overwhelming near her.

Josh's voice cut into her thoughts.

"And where is Middlesbrough?"

" 'Tis in England," she answered.

Josh laughed without a shred of amusement.

"You're a long way from home. How did you get here?"

Ailith glanced away from Joshua. She still held the towel in front of her, her back against the wall.

"I-I don't know how I came to be here," she finally whispered.

"What?" Joshua asked with incredulity.

When she looked up at him again, the grief and despair in her beautiful eyes tore at his heart, quelling the last of his anger.

"I . . ." she began in a trembling voice, but stopped.

Tears pooled in her eyes and started rolling down her smooth cheeks, spiking her long, dark lashes.

A sob of misery escaped Ailith's throat, and she felt the wistful urge to fall into Josh's arms. She really had no explanation of how she got here, and she suddenly feared he would turn her out. What would she do then?

"I . . . don't . . . know . . . how . . . I . . . came . . . to . . . be . . . here," she repeated brokenly.

Joshua shook his head in pity and, taking her by the arm, guided her into his bedroom and to the nearest chair. "Sit down, Ailith. There's nothing to be frightened of," he soothed, tempering his almost uncontrollable urge to draw her into his embrace and comfort her. "Are you telling me you have amnesia?"

Confusion creased Ailith's brow. "Amnesia?" she sniffled.

"A memory loss," Josh explained. "Well, maybe, a partial one. You did remember your name. Can you remember anything else about yourself?"

"I . . . Nay . . . um . . . No," Ailith lied.

She drew in a deep breath to calm herself. A faintly woodsy smell from his skin, coupled with Josh's usual freshness, invaded her nostrils. She bowed her head, regretting her disavowal.

Since she hadn't suffered a memory loss, she remembered everything about herself. But would Josh believe the truth? Could she chance telling him? Nay . . . No—she must remember the words in this time were said differently from her time, although their meanings paralleled in many cases.

She couldn't risk Josh turning her away, so she decided to let him believe the falsehood. He seemed to have softened at her misfortune. 'Twould . . . *That would* certainly be to her advantage.

"Do you even know how you came to be in this country?" Josh asked, concern lacing his husky voice.

"N-no, I do not," Ailith answered in a quavering tone.

Dread swept through her. She was 585 years in the future *and* in another country? But of course. Why hadn't she recognized Josh's strange speech? Recalling that she had noted everyone's voice patterns earlier, she realized they all spoke in a relaxed, almost lazy, manner. "W-what country is this?"

"America," Josh answered. "The United States."

Sweet Mary! Where had she been sent? Trembles assailed her. She had never, *ever* heard of a country called America The United States! Without warning, her tears started once more. She felt doomed never to see her parents again.

"Ailith, it's all right," Joshua murmured. He patted her arm in a consoling gesture. "We'll get to the bottom of this. Tell me how long you've been inside my house."

"I came in behind you and your friend Stephen Sunday last," she answered, swiping away her tears.

Appreciating her boldness, Joshua stared at her. "You've been in here all that time?" he asked with a grin.

Meeting Josh's twinkling golden eyes, Ailith's heart fluttered, his look captivating, disarming.

"Yes," she replied, her mouth curving upward shyly.

Joshua groaned softly. Her tentative smile and liquid gaze, shining with innocence, called forward his protective instincts, which up until this point he hadn't known existed.

Maybe that was because the women he was used to dealing with would scoff at such antiquated ideas.

"Well, Miss Ailith . . . What's your last name?"

" 'Tis . . . I-I mean *it is* deCotmer. Ailith deCotmer," she answered.

Her lilting voice struck a vibrant chord within Joshua. "Miss deCotmer, you must tell me everything you've done since you've been inside my house without my knowledge," he teased, wanting to put her at ease, drinking in her nearness.

After she had occupied most of his thoughts these last days and now that he was over his shock and anger, a strange contentment filled him. He inhaled sharply, telling himself the feeling was only his imagination.

He had Melissa, and Ailith deCotmer had a family, who even now was probably searching for her.

"And, now, my bold little angel, why don't you begin relating your adventure in my house?" he asked when she remained silent.

Ailith giggled at Josh's light tone. Warmth stole into her, and she relaxed, the magnitude of her problem suddenly not as frightening. She proceeded to tell him about the first time she used his toilet, his shower, and the first time she set foot in his kitchen.

Joshua listened with curious interest. Extinct words sprinkled her speech, but when she'd realize what she said, she corrected herself, using the modern replacement.

From her explanation it sounded as though she'd never been in a modern home before, let alone a modern kitchen. Impossible, of course, unless she was from a Third World country, and she had already said she was English. Definitely *not* Third World.

Was she really an amnesia victim? Or was she a very clever con artist? And what the hell was this obsession she had with medieval times? He was fascinated with the Middles Ages also, but Ailith deCotmer was taking *her* fascination to the extreme. At times, he swore she took on a medieval persona. For now, he would give her the benefit of the doubt and allow that she was an amnesia victim.

If she really was playacting, Joshua knew she couldn't keep it up indefinitely. Even Olivier wasn't that good. And he considered Sir Lawrence to be one of the finest actors of all time.

Joshua was sure if she wasn't suffering from memory loss, then there had to be a motive behind her bold subterfuge. Either way, he would find out what.

"So you hid and slept in my clothes closet?" he asked for confirmation.

"Aye," Ailith answered in distraction as she adjusted her towel, slipping it from her top and securing it over her legs.

Joshua swallowed hard. He cursed the spurt of desire he felt as he imagined her top falling away as well. When she continued, her words garnered his full attention.

"I even ate in there."

"You *ate* in my clothes closet?" he asked, slightly annoyed. "Ailith, this is New Orleans." He thrust his fingers through his hair. "Eating inside clothes closets is not a way to keep down the cockroach population!"

Ailith didn't understand everything Josh said, but she caught the irritation in his voice and knew he was displeased at her for eating in his closet. "I'm sorry," she whispered. "It won't happen again." She frowned. Josh had said New Orleans. When she'd first asked him what country she was in he'd told her America The United States. God's eyes! Where exactly *was* she? Mayhap . . . *Per*haps Josh would clarify that later.

"Forget it." Josh walked away from her and went to sit on his bed.

She felt bereft of his presence, but decided against following him.

"When did you last eat?"

"A few hours ago," she answered. "I ate the last six cookies left in the jar."

Josh laughed, and Ailith's heart began thumping so frantically she knew Josh could hear its beating.

"You brought the entire jar of cookies up here?"

"Yes."

"Smart girl. But still, you must be famished." Joshua stood. "Let's go downstairs, and I'll fix you some leftovers from tonight's dinner. Then we can discuss how to get you some help. Your family must be worried sick over you."

At the mention of *her* family, he suddenly remembered *his*, who were in the house. His mother. He could never explain Ailith's presence in his bedroom to her. Even the explanation Ailith had given *him* was farfetched. No, he would have to keep her hidden until his parents departed.

"Shit!" he snarled. "On second thought, Ailith, you stay here, out of sight, until I return. I'll bring you a plate of food. But in the meantime, I don't want anyone else to know you're here."

"I understand, Josh," Ailith told him.

"Why doesn't it surprise me that you know my name," he murmured.

"I heard you say it on your answering machine," she clarified. "And I also heard Stephen say it."

He understood then why she called him "Josh," and laughed. "I see. If you're comfortable with Josh, that's fine, but feel free to call me Joshua."

She nodded. "As I was saying, since we are not wedded, your mother would not approve of us sharing this room. While you are gone, may I bathe?"

There was that strange choice of words again. She said "wedded," instead of "married." Joshua looked at her, unsuccessfully trying to dispel the image of how she must appear with bathwater beading her flushed skin.

"I really must insist you stay hidden until I get back. You can bathe then. And we need to talk more. You must tell me what else you overheard while in your place of concealment. I'll be right back." With that, Joshua strode from the room and used his key to lock the door from the outside.

As soon as Joshua left, Ailith hastened back to her hiding place as he'd directed her to do, though she left the door open. Her breath came in short pants, and her pulse pounded in her temples.

Mayhap . . . Perhaps 'twould . . . it would . . . Perhaps, it would not be difficult to tell Joshua about the orb, and Lord Preston, and Brint Pfiester, and also about her parents, and her friend Aida. Oh, she so wanted to find a way out of her dilemma. He believed she had a memory loss, after all. And she knew Joshua was correct. Her parents must be worried sick about her, even as they were subjected to Lord Preston's wrath.

From the *clock* on Joshua's bedtable, she knew about ten minutes had passed before he reentered the bedroom.

"Ailith?"

"Yes, Joshua."

"Come out, come out, wherever you are," he called in a teasing manner.

Ailith came out of her hiding place just as Joshua set a tray of food down on one of the bed tables.

"Everything had been put away, but I managed to slice some roast for a sandwich. I also heated up a bowl of oyster and artichoke soup. And I hope you like dessert. There's a slice of lemon doberge. To wash everything down, you have a glass of cold milk. Does that meet with your approval, my lady?"

Ailith smiled in appreciation. "You're very kind, sir," she responded, gazing hungrily at the tray.

"Don't be shy, Ailith. Go ahead and chow down," Joshua urged.

Ailith looked in question at him.

"Eat. Go ahead and *eat*," Joshua clarified, amusement curving his mouth.

"Oh." Ailith laughed nervously and reached for the spoon and bowl of soup. "Thank you."

Each delicious mouthful she took made Ailith sigh with relished satisfaction.

Joshua watched in pleasure as she put away every morsel of food in record time.

"Well," he said as he watched her drink the last drop

of milk. "You certainly *were* hungry. Would you like another sand—"

The knock on his door interrupted him in midsentence.

"Joshua, dear!"

His mother's voice floated through the door, grating on his aplomb.

"Are you talking to someone in there?"

"Yes, Mother," Joshua called back. "I'm on the telephone," he said, smugly applauding his quick wit—just as the telephone started to ring.

Chapter 10

"Shit!"

"Joshua!!" Frances huffed. "Are you using obscenities in there?"

Joshua scowled at the closed door. "Slide under the bed, Ailith," he whispered.

"But—"

"Go!" he ordered.

"Y-yes," Ailith responded meekly. The bed was low, but given her size, she slipped under without a problem.

The phone kept ringing.

"How can you be on the telephone when it's ringing?" Frances shouted.

Joshua stomped to the door and opened it, then hurried to answer the telephone.

Frances sailed in, her silk bedrobe in disarray as if she had donned it hastily, her hair partially braided.

He would either have to get thicker walls or he would have to move his parents' bedroom farther away from his own.

Hands on hips, she stopped in the center of the room, her gaze sharp, assessing, taking in everything.

Joshua banged the receiver back on the hook. "What can

I do for you, Mother?'' he asked resentfully.

''I . . . Did I interrupt anything, son?'' She threw him a wan smile. ''I really didn't mean to. You didn't have to hang up on *my* account.''

Joshua thrust his hands through his hair. Why, of late, did it appear women were giving him so much trouble? He sighed. ''I didn't hang up on your account, Mother,'' he snapped. ''It was a wrong number.'' *Just what I needed.* ''I had just hung up when you knocked at the door and the phone rang again,'' he told her, hating the lame lie. He could have at least come up with a better one.

''I see,'' Frances muttered, setting her jaw in determination. She surveyed the room again, her glance falling on the tray where the empty dishes sat.

Stern recrimination crossed her face, so briefly Joshua swore he imagined it.

''Dear, you must have a tapeworm,'' she drawled. ''I can't believe you ate again after the big meal you put away at dinner.''

He shrugged in dismissal of her skeptical look and, acquiring a hint of her patronizing tone, said, ''Habit, I guess, Mother. I usually snack while I watch TV, regardless of what I have for dinner.''

Giving a pointed glance at the darkened television, Frances merely smiled again and marched to the closet. ''I've noticed you don't close your closet door, dear. Why is that?'' She walked fully in, shoving garments aside, enabling the back wall to come into view. Finding nothing, she cleared her throat, came back into the bedroom, and closed the door.

''Subtle,'' Joshua growled, looking at her in exasperation. ''Real subtle, Mommie dearest. Would I be foolish enough to hide someone while you're here?''

Frances remained silent for a moment, before she relented. ''Forgive me, Joshua. I really didn't come in here to spy on you. You see, I was going downstairs for some ice when I thought I heard a woman's voice in here. Which, when one thinks about it, is not *my* concern anyway.''

She was going down for ice, eh? Sure, and Ailith really was from the Middle Ages! His mother's disheveled appearance attested to her lie. But he wouldn't press the issue. He wanted her out of his room.

"It's all right, Mother," he told her. "You can't help the way you are. I blame Grandmother Claybourne for that. With your major prudish ways, I'm amazed you and Dad were able to procreate." He held out his hands, the gesture almost one of supplication. "But here I am. Pam and I are living proof that you overcame the Claybourne Sex Doctrine." Narrowing his eyes, he dropped his hands back to his sides. "Or was it the Sex*less* Doctrine?"

"Oh, you're so clever, aren't you?" Frances said with an easy drawl. "The only part of my mother's . . . *doctrine* that stuck was the part about sex before marriage. Remember, I'm a descendant of the hot-blooded Claybournes and your father is descended from the notorious Kenleys. It was God's will that we only had you and your sister."

Joshua already knew the effect his lascivious ancestors had on his parents' sex life. Or, more to the point, his mother's *ideas* about sex, which, to his chagrin, hindered his personal life whenever she visited. Hell, it amazed him that he hadn't grown up with any hang-ups. He frowned.

Frances laughed at Joshua's obvious irritation.

"Darling," she soothed, "your mother is entirely normal in every respect, with the exception of that one quirk, of course. I'll try to stay my distance from your room, dear. But please indulge me if I get a little curious and barge in again. It won't be easy, though, since you're still in the habit of locking your door." She walked to the night table and picked up the tray. "I'll just take this down with me. Good night, dear."

"Good night, Mother," Joshua grumbled as she sailed out the already opened door.

He closed and latched the door and for a few minutes stood motionless and quiet, wanting to be assured that Frances wouldn't storm his room again. Then he went to the night table with the TV remote on it and flicked on the television. Sound blasted through, loud enough to make any other voices in the room indistinguishable.

Joshua bent low to look under the bed. "Ailith?" he called. "You may come out now."

Ailith dragged herself out and stood. Hair in disarray, her face was pink from the effort of getting out from under the bed. Her green gaze settled on Joshua, sending a signal to his private parts, though her look bore artlessness and innocence. He swallowed hard at the lovely picture she presented.

He drew in a deep, steadying breath. "I'm sorry about the interruption, Ailith. But I'm afraid you'll have to get used to Mother's interference in my life." As soon as the words were out, Joshua wished to recall them. Not only because they were untrue, but because he didn't like the longing and the regret the statement caused.

He cleared his throat. "I mean, until we can sneak you out of this room without her finding out you've set up housekeeping in it."

Try as he might, he couldn't deny how badly he wanted his mother and Ailith to meet. He felt Frances would take an immediate liking to Ailith, unlike her feelings for Melissa.

Shit! *Had* he taken leave of his senses? What was this unaccustomed longing? Sheer madness, he knew.

Ailith wouldn't have to get used to Frances, because Ailith wouldn't be in his life for very long. She had a family somewhere out there, and she would go back to them as soon as her memory returned. And he would continue his relationship with Melissa, who was as conservative as he was himself and who would have had a stroke at the mere thought of stowing away in a stranger's closet, no matter how desperate she was.

Joshua raised his hand and brought it to Ailith's hair, needing to see if the strands felt as silky as they looked. They were, but after a few caresses he ceased and stepped away from her.

Ailith laughed nervously, his gentle touches stoking the

fire burning within her. *He's so tall*, she thought in awe of him. Her cheeks flamed hotter, and she wondered why she blushed.

Joshua smiled down at Ailith, her blush as it went from pink to red not lost on him. Pleased that he had that effect upon her, he deepened his grin. "Oh . . . er . . . if you would still like to take a bath you're more than welcome."

"Thank you," Ailith responded, rather breathlessly. "A bath would be nice."

"Come, then. Let me show you where the tub is."

Joshua led her to the bathroom, where he slid a panel back from the wall revealing another room twice the size of the shower room. He pointed to a marble tub.

"I don't know if you're familiar with this, Ailith, but this is a whirlpool."

"A whirlpool?"

"Yes. When in use, the water is in a perpetual whirling motion. You'll find it very relaxing." He leaned over and started the water going.

"Oh!" Ailith gasped.

Amazement lit her eyes as she stared at the device facing the tub.

"You have another garde . . . toilet in here."

Joshua chuckled. "Not exactly. That's called a bidet," he explained. "Just leave that be for now. When you get out of here, I'll let one of the ladies explain its use to you. In the meantime, you can adjust the water in the whirlpool to the temperature you like." He showed her which faucet did what.

"I know what the symbols *H* and *C* are for, but thank you."

Joshua started for the door, but halted at her call.

"Joshua?"

"Yes?"

"May I borrow something else to wear?"

Joshua smiled. "Perhaps another pajama top?"

"Bottoms, too, maybe?"

"Bottoms, too," he responded with his endearing laugh.

He left her, but returned within moments, a pair of his pajamas in his hands. "I hope these meet with your approval." He held up the gray silk sleepwear for her inspection.

"Yes," Ailith responded shyly. "Thank you again."

Joshua handed her the pajamas and left her to her privacy.

After putting on his own nightclothes, Joshua lay across his bed, pondering the situation. He knew *nothing* about the girl other than what she had told him about herself, which wasn't very much. He did know that she was the loveliest creature he'd ever seen. Even his tall, willowy, hazel-eyed Mellie couldn't compare, and Melissa was considered a beautiful woman, which was part of her problem. Melissa *knew* she was beautiful and expected to be placed upon a pedestal and treated with kid gloves. It didn't matter that *she* seldom, if at all, handled anyone with such care.

But Ailith? Slight-statured, petite Ailith . . . Did she really have amnesia? *God, she's a looker.* He chastised himself for his wayward thoughts. He had always reprimanded Stephen for such adolescent ramblings, and now Ailith had come and reduced him to Stephen's mentality.

Ailith . . .

He hoped she was enjoying her bath. Maybe he should have put some of Melissa's bath oil in Ailith's bathwater. No, Ailith shouldn't smell the way Melissa did. Ailith deserved a scent all her own—something unique and rare. Maybe he would visit a French Quarter perfumery and have them create a scent for her.

What the hell was he thinking! He wouldn't allow himself to be taken in by an exquisite face. The girl could be the biggest con artist of the twentieth century. But if she was, what was her motive? Joshua leaned back against the pillows and flipped his thumb over the remote control, rapidly flicking through channels.

A thought suddenly struck him. Where would Ailith sleep? Could he allow her to sleep on the floor or in a chair?

He certainly wasn't going to relinquish his bed to her. Maybe if she promised to keep her distance he would offer her one side of the bed.

Ailith came out of the bathroom just as that particular thought floated through his mind. He groaned at the stunningly adorable image she presented wearing his pajamas, which hung loosely on her small body. Her pale blond hair cascaded down her shoulders like a golden cloak. *He* would need a steel barrier between them to keep from touching *her* if he laid next to her.

He looked at her and smiled. "Well, I trust you enjoyed your bath, Ailith," he said, admiring her pinkened skin as he perused her from head to toe.

"Very much," Ailith answered, not knowing where to go or what to do even if she got there. "Thank you."

Though more than sufficiently covered, she felt naked before Joshua. Her face heated, and she had to squelch an odd urge to giggle. For the past sennight, her face had continually heated, and she didn't think her circumstances would get better anytime soon.

In her time, a woman was strictly forbidden to wear male garments. Besides that, Joshua was wearing a similar pair of pajamas in a different color. The memory of Joshua sauntering around in his naked glory flashed through her mind. Guilt pervaded her for the clandestine viewings of him, and she stood next to the bed trying to focus her thoughts and emotions on the situation at hand.

"Is something making you uncomfortable, Ailith?" Joshua asked, amused at the ridiculous predicament facing them.

"Nay . . . No," Ailith blurted, too late to stop herself from using the familiar wording of her time.

A frown creased Joshua's brow, and his face clouded with suspicion.

"Middlesbrough must be quaint indeed," he remarked, rather sarcastically.

"I . . . Well . . ." Ailith faltered, not knowing what to say, but taking umbrage at his derisiveness. "I don't quite remember how I spoke in Middlesbrough, Joshua!'' she scoffed. ''Nay or no, however, they mean the same, as well you know. I hope my answer was sufficient.'' She glared at him before flouncing to the chair across from the bed and sitting down.

Joshua laughed, his admiration for her deepening. ''I didn't mean to sound so abrasive, Ailith,'' he said. ''But I've noticed your choice of words and have found them strange for this day and age. You shouldn't blame me for being skeptical. After all, you've been living in my home for the past three days without my knowledge.''

''I know.'' Ailith hesitated. Now was her chance to tell Joshua everything. But she couldn't yet. She couldn't be sure if he would think she was a madwoman, so she said, ''I had no choice. I'm sorry.''

Joshua drew in a breath. ''It's all right, Ailith. We'll get to the bottom of this. For the time being, I'll accept that you're telling me the truth and trust that you're not a female serial killer.'' He laughed, looking for her reaction to his statement.

Ailith gave him a blank look, wondering if the confusion she felt showed on her face. Joshua spoke of female serial killers and of getting to the bottom of . . . what?

''You're certainly very kind allowing me to stay here, Joshua. For that I'm grateful. And I am not a female serial killer.'' *Whatever that is*, she added silently. ''And . . . and I want to get to the *bottom* of this, too,'' she said with a yawn.

''And so you should,'' Joshua responded, bemused at her hesitant response. ''But not tonight. How long has it been since you slept in a bed, Ailith?''

The question startled him as much as it seemed to have Ailith. Hadn't he already concluded that her sleeping next to him would be sheer torture if he couldn't touch her?

Ailith looked at him in surprise. She hadn't thought of where she would sleep, other than where she had been sleeping for the past three days. Exactly how long *had* it been since she'd slept in a bed? Was it only three nights ago? Nay . . . No, 'twas . . . it was four nights ago. Four nights ago in Lord Preston's keep.

But Joshua would never believe that. She bowed her head. "I-I don't recall," she whispered.

"It must have been uncomfortable on the floor. Sleeping in a chair is just as bad." How would he ever make it through the night? "My bed is roomy enough to accommodate two people quite easily. . . ."

Joshua paused at the repelled look on her face.

"Did I say something wrong?" he uttered, aggravated.

He looks for all the world like Lord Preston, and now he's sounding like him. Like Lord Preston, he's trying to get me into his bed. Well, I would rather sleep in the dungeon with the rats before I'd sleep with Joshua Kenley!

Her temper flared. "If you know not what is wrong about two people who are unwedded to each other sleeping together, then, my lord, my telling you won't make a difference!" she sneered. "I *will not* sleep with you, Lord Preston!"

Ailith gasped. Too late she realized this man was not the Earl of Radford. Her mother always warned her her wayward tongue would get her into great trouble.

He's Joshua! Joshua Kenley!

Suspended between two vastly different worlds, she wondered where her place was in either. Could she return to her own time and be happy, having sampled the luxuries, conveniences, and safety of this one? If she stayed here, would she be able to survive in this time, not knowing exactly what was needed *to* survive here? But she had to go back for the sake of her parents.

She constantly confused her time and the time she was now in. Mayhap if Joshua didn't look so much like Lord Preston, it wouldn't be so perplexing.

Did Joshua even have a dungeon?

"Drop the act, lady!" Joshua barked. "This is the nineties. Sex and marriage don't always go hand in hand. Not that you don't already know that, sleeping in strange men's bedrooms. For the record, I was being polite! I had no intention of touching you. But given your attitude, I don't give a damn where you sleep!''

'Tis so hard pretending. The language is the hardest. So similar, yet so different. Oh, would that he only continued to believe she had a memory loss—amnesia.

"I . . . Joshua, I didn't mean to make you angry. I sometimes get confused and think that I belong in another time. I-I didn't mean to imply that you would . . . would . . .''

Ailith's gaze met Joshua's angry scowl.

Animation no longer lit Ailith's face. She seemed withdrawn, worried, and terribly unhappy. But she suffered from more than just a memory loss if she believed she belonged in another time. Though he wondered why she kept speaking of Preston Claybourne, Joshua's anger dissipated and he breathed in deeply, trying to push aside his doubts about her sincerity.

"It's okay, Ailith," he said, his tone reassuring, gentle. "Maybe what ails you is more serious than we think.'' For a moment, he studied her as she stood at the foot of the bed, facing him. "Are you sure my mother didn't hire you to test my willpower and patience?'' he asked, only half teasing.

Ailith smiled. "I have not yet met your mother.''

"I'm only joking with you.'' His gaze lingered on her face. "Come lie down, Ailith. You need to rest in a bed. I promise I won't touch you. Not on purpose, that is.''

Ailith frowned. "What do you mean?''

"I mean if I touch you, it will be done accidently during sleep,'' Joshua answered.

"Oh!''

"Well?''

"Well, what?''

"Are you coming to bed or not?''

"Yes.''

Ailith went to the opposite side of the bed from where Joshua lay. She stared at him for a few seconds before getting into bed herself and turning her back to him.

Joshua chuckled softly. "That'll work, too. Good night,

Ailith.'' He turned off the light next to his bed, then flicked off the television set.

Quiet settled between them. The only sounds now penetrating Joshua's mind were ''house sounds''—the whirring of the central air, the creaking of a wall, the ticking of the second-hand clock with the lighted dial, and the steady breathing of the angel, who had fascinated him from the moment he saw her, but who now lay in his bed out of reach.

Turning his back to Ailith also, Joshua settled himself for sleep, the house sounds now soporific, lulling him into slumberous bliss. . . .

''Good night, Joshua.''

Ailith's soft voice floated to him, and he cursed his generosity, wanting nothing more than to turn to her and take her into his arms.

Ailith sighed. She heard Joshua chuckle in response and she smiled, relaxing. She had allowed several minutes to pass before responding to Joshua's polite wishes because she'd wanted to get her frantic pulse under control. Now feeling Joshua meant to keep his word about not touching her, she was able to breathe easier.

Snuggling deeper into the soft bed, she stared at the draperies, wondering if the wicked heat coursing through her was only her imagination.

No. Without a doubt, she knew Joshua's nearness caused it.

Chapter 11

WHEN AILITH AWAKENED, she stretched content-
edly. Awareness of where she was dawned on her, and she
sat up in the big bed. Not seeing Joshua and thinking he'd
left before she'd awakened, disappointment welled within
her. Then she noticed the bathroom door closed and
breathed a sigh of relief.

She settled back against the pillow, anticipating seeing
Joshua.

Five minutes later, Joshua came out of the bathroom with
a towel draped around his neck. He looked in her direction
and returned the smile she gave him.

"Well, good morning, Ailith." Barefoot and bare-
chested, he wore only green trousers. "I hope you're rested.
You slept like a log. If that is any indication, then you are
indeed well rested."

Remembering she had slept beside him, Ailith blushed
and lowered her gaze. "I slept very well," she murmured.
"Thank you."

"I'm glad," Joshua declared softly.

Smiling at the rosy color of her face, he rubbed the towel
vigorously over his still-damp hair. Because he'd wanted
to look at Ailith again, he did not blow dry his hair. Morning or night, she was breathtaking.

Seeing Joshua's intense look and not knowing what to do, Ailith threw aside the covers and climbed from the bed. "I-I was surprised when I awoke and found the bathroom door closed, Joshua," she blurted without thinking as she scampered toward the bathroom. "After all, I have not seen you do it befo—"

She stopped in mid-sentence when she saw Joshua's face turn red as a beet, just then realizing what she'd let slip.

"Oh!" She rushed to close herself in the bathroom.

"Stop!"

Joshua boomed the word so loud Ailith was sure the rafters of the house shook. She froze in the doorway and turned to face him. He glared at her with twin orbs of angry fire, his face contorted with rage. Fear filtered in her, and she shrank back.

Joshua pointed to a chair across the room, nearly choking on his fury. "Sit!" he ordered.

Seeing his withering stare, Ailith's knees weakened, and she slinked to the chair and sat. "I-I . . ." she stammered.

"Goddammit it, lady!" Joshua yelled, feeling the veins in his neck and throat bulge against his skin. "What the hell kind of a pervert are you? Are you some kind of peeping Tom? Tess? Is that how you get your jollies?"

Ailith shook her head in denial, thinking that was the safest course, since she didn't understand all of Joshua's terminology. Harsher curses fell from his mouth, and his eyes reproached her, burned her.

"I-I didn't mean to watch," she mumbled in her own defense. "I . . . The door . . . both doors were left opened."

His nostrils flared. "Both doors?" he sneered.

Ailith nodded with vigor. "Y-yes. The closet door and the bathroom door. I-I couldn't h-help b-but s-see you."

"Yes, you could have!" he snarled. "You didn't have to *look*."

He narrowed his eyes at her and suddenly he didn't appear quite as wrathful. Ailith relaxed somewhat.

"What exactly did you see?" he asked in a softened tone.

Recalling exactly what she *did* see, heat overtook her. "I-I saw you! I . . . Joshua, please forgive me," she whispered. "Don't throw me out. I . . ." She bowed her head, staring down at her folded hands where they rested in her lap. "I'm sorry."

Joshua stood over her. He closed his eyes and breathed in deeply, willing his calm demeanor to return. He had never in his life been as enraged as he was moments ago. When he looked at Ailith again, her head remained lowered, and he could see only the top of her golden hair. Though he couldn't tell, he was sure she was crying. His heart tripped. For a moment he felt sorry for her. That only lasted a moment. No matter how he fought to regain control, he was still very angry.

"I ought to have you arrested, Miss deCotmer. Don't misunderstand me. I am not a prude, not by a long shot. The fact that you viewed me in the buff doesn't bother me. What's disturbing is you did it secretly." He paused in remembrance, then continued. "I think our first meeting found me undressed. Did you like what you saw so much then that you had to have another peek?"

Ailith bounded from her chair, all regret gone. "How dare you!" she gritted out, suddenly seething with anger and humiliation.

"How dare me? How dare *you*! Lady, you're way out of line," Joshua said with contempt. "I wanted to make love to you last night. I have never lain beside a woman for the first time and not touched her. But I had made a promise to you. And now in the cold light of day, seeing what a devious trick you are, I'm glad I didn't. You *will* come clean *now*, Ailith, or you will regret ever sneaking into my house!"

Not comprehending most of his words, Ailith was still sure he insulted her in some way. His sneer told her that. He wanted her to *come clean*! What did that mean? She'd bathed last evening. She definitely wasn't dirty.

"I mean it, Ailith! I want you to tell me the truth about why you're here."

Ailith's glare lashed him as surely as his father's belt used to.

"I don't think you're ready for the truth, Joshua," she imparted flatly, bristling as she realized he hadn't been referring to her personal cleanliness. *Come clean, indeed!*

"Try me," Joshua countered harshly.

Ailith stared at his taut features, her own ire increasing to a dangerous level. How dare he mock her! What would he say if she revealed her secret to him? Would he still stare at her with such accusation or would he finally believe her?

Cursing the arrogance of men, Ailith stalked to the closet and retrieved her orb. "This," she pealed when she stood before him again, "is how I got here!" She poked Joshua in his middle with the orb.

Perplexity replaced Joshua's anger for a moment. "That?" He pointed to it. "What is that thing? What the hell are you talking about?"

"It's an orb, Joshua. Somehow it brought me to your time."

The look of total disbelief on Joshua's features urged Ailith to explain further.

"I am the daughter of Galen and Meghanne deCotmer. My father is an astrologer. He has favor with Lord Preston Claybourne, Earl of Radford, Master of Greyhawke Keep, where we make our home in—"

"*Stop!*" Joshua stormed, his face turning a mottled red. "What kind of a damned fool do you take me for, Ailith? First you tried to make me believe you suffered from amnesia, now this outrageous, preposterous tale—"

"*You're* the one who said I had amnesia!"

"How is it you didn't correct me?"

"I was afraid you would turn me out. I can't leave your house. 'Tis . . . it is the place the orb brought me, and I must be here in order to return to my own time."

Joshua barreled to his bed and sat on the side, pinning Ailith with a stare.

"So I'm supposed to believe you're from some distant era? Tell me, Ailith, what year are we talking about?"

"F-fourteen thirteen," Ailith answered, faltering under his scrutiny.

Joshua whistled, then laughed harshly. "You're nothing if not a good actress and a superb liar. I applaud your imagination."

Ailith's chin rose in indignation. "You don't believe me?"

"Not so far, miss," Joshua said, anger creeping into his tone again. "I don't believe in ghosts, Ailith. *Or* time travel. Even in this age of technology, people don't live to be over five hundred years old, and technically you've been dead for centuries. Nothing I've studied about the fifteenth century ever mentioned time travel. They did not have the know-how! Try again, Miss Slick!"

Despite the rage roiling within her, Ailith tried to affect an air of calmness. It was imperative that Joshua allow her to stay and *her* anger only seemed to inflame *his* more.

"I'm sorry if you don't believe me, Joshua, but I have told you the truth," she said in a serene tone.

"Tell me," Joshua began as he stood and walked to his closet. He didn't speak again until he came out, fastening the buttons on the shirt he had slipped on. "How is it someone from a different time and place, especially an era as uncivilized as the Middle Ages, is so thoroughly familiar with so many modern facilities? You seem quite at ease with everything from the television to the bathroom," he drawled, in complete control of his anger now.

Joshua's silky voice disarmed her almost more than his rage had. She drew in a breath, clasping the orb tighter.

"I know you won't believe this either, but I watched and listened. And remembered. I watched television when you watched it. I overheard your servants talk. And I overheard you talk on your telephone. . . ."

Joshua raised an ebony brow. "You expect me to believe that you are a fifteenth-century maiden—and I use the term loosely—ignorant of all things modern. But you have been able to learn in three days all about TV's and phones and electric lights and whatever the hell else in this house I've taken for granted. You're telling me you learned about that in three days?''

Even as he considered that all those things were second nature to him, he mocked her with his tone.

"Yes," Ailith answered, her voice as challenging as her look. "I expect you to believe me because I have yet to lie to you!"

For a second, Joshua looked at her with incredulity. "What did you say about Preston Claybourne?" he asked in amazement, ignoring her reply. "You alluded to him the first day I met you."

"Why, er, Lord Preston is my liege," Ailith answered in confusion. "W-why do you want to know?"

"I am a descendant of Lord Claybourne on my mother's side, and what you said about him just registered."

Though she already knew that bit of information, Ailith responded, "A descendant?" She frowned. "What do you mean over five hundred years old?" she asked, Joshua's earlier words just dawning on her.

With an abruptness that startled her, Joshua burst out laughing.

"What's so funny?" Ailith asked with suspicion.

"I suppose *we* are," Joshua answered. "There seems to be some sort of delayed action in our brain cells. Or perhaps we're going too fast. Somewhere in our conversation you mentioned Preston Claybourne. *That* just registered to me. *You* tell me how you came to know of my ancestor, and *I'll* tell you what I meant by over five hundred years old."

Ailith knew Joshua wouldn't believe her, no matter what she said.

"I believe I read about the Master of Greyhawke Keep in my studies in England." She sighed, a stab of loneliness piercing her. If only he would believe her, she wouldn't feel so bereft. "I-I am sorry, Joshua. I'm rather confused."

"I'm afraid I have to agree with you, Ailith. You're either very confused or very clever." Joshua regarded her in question. "Which is it?"

Clever? Ailith thought. *If only I were clever enough to explain this thing that defies definition or reason.* If *she* couldn't understand it, how could she explain it to Joshua and make him believe her? Trembling slightly, she tried to shake off her dispiriting thoughts, but didn't succeed. She gave Joshua a melancholy glint.

"I-I wish I *were* clever enough to unweave this disorder in my mind. I keep wishing I could go to sleep and wake up in my own home."

Tears, which had been lurking behind her eyes, slipped down her cheeks. It surprised her to feel Joshua's fingertips lift her chin and, with his other hand, dry her tears with a handkerchief.

"Don't cry, Ailith," Joshua croaked, taking her into his arms. "I've been unnecessarily harsh with you. Whatever the problem is, we'll get to the bottom of it."

Ailith reveled in the comfort of his nearness and his arms, even as her misery nearly overwhelmed her. "If only it were that simple, Joshua," she whispered.

"I'll make it simple," he murmured. "No more tears, Ailith."

He gently pushed her away from him and stared at her for a moment before succumbing to an urge to kiss her. Sweeping her into his arms again and then off her feet, he brought his mouth slowly to hers. After a series of tender kisses, he coaxed her lips apart and eased his tongue into her warm recesses.

Ailith sighed at the contact of Joshua's lips upon her own. She moaned, and another kiss came to mind, the one that had left her dignity in shreds.

Lord Preston! She shoved against his chest. *No! This is Joshua. . . . Joshua!*

The sensations spiraling through her were so similar, yet so . . . so different. So gentle. So right.

This was not a display of possession, an act to show who

was in control. This was something sweet, intoxicating, and she wondered if she would ever recover. But if this went too far, what would she do when she returned to her own time? She thought it wise to end this gentle torture.

Feeling Ailith's hands splayed and pushing against him, Joshua released her and set her back on her feet. "I am sorry, Ailith. I shouldn't have done that." He stepped away from her to complete the task of dressing.

Ailith didn't respond. Instead, she sank back down into the chair, trying to regain control of her emotions. Her heart hammered, her knees felt weak, and heat burned every part of her body.

Joshua felt puzzled. All along he thought Ailith was being coy, acting out a misguided fantasy, out to con him in some way. He certainly didn't think she was innocent of anything. Innocent was not a label he would have hung on her—not until he kissed her. He had never before kissed someone so inexperienced. So innocent. Innocent, and sweet, and stirring.

Joshua stared at Ailith, and she raised her green gaze to him. She looked utterly helpless, exquisitely gorgeous, and unlawfully young.

That's it! She looks like jailbait! The little bitch is trying to ruin my reputation.

His stare turned to a murderous scowl.

Seeing the look, Ailith flinched. "Have I offended you, Joshua?" she asked, wondering if her kiss had displeased him.

"How old are you?" Joshua snarled.

"I-I am ten and nine. I-I-I mean I am nineteen years old," Ailith answered in confusion.

Joshua released a big gulp of air.

Get a grip, butthole! She's legal. Although I haven't touched her, a lot of good that would have done me if she wasn't. I slept in the same bed with her. Ten and nine, huh? Poor baby is seriously confused!

"Ailith," he began. "I need to know your clothes size. You know, dresses, jeans, or slacks, whatever it is you prefer to wear. And undergarments, lingerie, things like that.''

Ailith stared at him, a little bewildered.

''Sweetheart, before you can leave this room you must be properly attired.''

''A-are you turning me out?'' Ailith asked nervously.

''No, Ailith,'' Joshua replied gently. ''I must find a way to sneak you out of this room to get you some help. You need to see a doctor, a psychiatrist. Then I need to sneak you back in again.'' He smiled at her.

Ailith returned his smile with a shy one of her own. She wanted to protest. She didn't need a doctor. Her protests, however, would be useless. What she needed was to find a way to make the orb work again. She wished she could make Joshua believe her. Without his help, she would never get back to her own time. And she had to. Her parents were in danger of imprisonment, or worse once Lord Preston returned from his campaign.

She had to get back before Preston's return! She would think of a new way to approach Joshua. If she got him to believe her, she knew he would help her. But how could she make what happened to her credible and acceptable to him? Somehow she would think of a way.

She had to. Her beloved parents depended on it. Her sanity depended on it.

''I don't remember my clothes size,'' she lied. She should have said she didn't *know* her clothes size.

Within moments Joshua had retrieved a garment tape from his bureau and began measuring her. He turned her this way and that, almost caressing her with his touch. Ailith's consternation increased. As much as she wanted to return to her parents, she wasn't sure now that she wanted to leave Joshua.

She released a troubled sigh and wondered whether there could ever be a happy ending to the predicament in which she found herself.

Chapter 12

"GOOD MORNING, DEAR," Frances chirped to her son, who strolled into the kitchen carrying a tray, loaded with the remains of breakfast.

Joshua set the tray down on the counter. "Good morning, Mother."

"Well." Frances turned from her task of readying coffee for brewing to look at him. "I don't know whether to feel hurt or insulted that you've chosen not to have breakfast with your father and me."

"You shouldn't feel either, Mother. It's nothing unusual. I often eat in my room while I get a head start on my work for the day. I really thought I was being considerate of you and Dad. After all, I don't always eat breakfast the same time every day."

"Oh. I see. That's how it is." Frances eyed the tray again, then returned to her chore. "It looks as if you had enough on that tray to feed an army. If the amount of dishes is any indication, dear."

Joshua glared obliquely at his mother. Taking the pitcher of milk from the tray, he put it in the refrigerator. "I read or heard somewhere, Mother, that males keep growing until the age of thirty. If that's true, then I'm still a growing boy. A *hungry*, growing boy."

Frances laughed. "Heaven forbid you turn into a whale by the time you *do* stop growing, darling."

"Never fear, Mrs. Kenley," Joshua murmured. "That won't happen. I exercise regularly."

"I know, dear. I'm only joking. Oh, do talk to Connor," she continued, by way of changing the subject.

"Connor?" Joshua frowned. "About what?"

"Well, you know how he is." Frances looked toward the doorway. "He wanted to make the coffee, and I insisted on doing it myself. He's in a pique now and probably pouting somewhere."

Joshua grinned. "I can't believe Connor isn't used to your bossiness by now."

"I'll ignore that, dear," Frances remarked with a good-natured chuckle. "Just tell him he doesn't make coffee to suit my tastebuds. I am not here to take over his duties. Just his way of making coffee."

Joshua smiled indulgently. "I'll be sure to pass along the message, Mother. I hope you don't mind fending for yourself for a couple of days. I gave Shawanda a few days off. Something about her cousin coming in from Chicago," he lied. "Connor's here, of course, and Loquisha is not at all reliable without Shawanda around to ride herd on her. So she's off for a few days, too."

"I'm quite capable of taking care of your father and me. Don't worry, dear," Frances said sweetly. "Tell Connor he needn't bother preparing anything for dinner."

The sound of his mother's voice a little *too* sugary for his comfort, suspicion suddenly gnawed at Joshua, and he stared at her, trying to fathom her motives.

Shit! What is she up to now?

Would his carefully laid plans be torn asunder?

A day had passed since the scene in his bedroom with Ailith. Once he'd secured her measurements, he'd gone downstairs to his office to telephone Stephen. After telling him about discovering Ailith and the fact that she had amnesia and no clothes, they'd spent all yesterday afternoon shopping for her. One of their destinations had been Victoria's Secret for lingerie. There they'd found they were not as sophisticated as they'd thought.

Viewing one particularly enticing outfit on display, Joshua wrote down a list of the purchases he wanted to make, left them with the saleswoman, and told her he'd be in later to pick them up. Then he and Stephen had made a quick retreat, embarrassed and red-faced.

"Lingerie is fine as long as it's already in a woman's wardrobe," Stephen muttered. "Or better yet, on her body, but it's daunting to *see* it as items in the store."

"I'm inclined to agree," Joshua snorted. "Rather intimidating."

Like two guilty little boys caught with their fingers in the cookie jar, they had finally laughed with merriment at their artlessness and went their separate ways. Joshua, anxious to get back to Ailith, had exacted a promise from Stephen to pick up the purchases and bring them to Kenley Manor this morning.

Once home, and knowing his parents were going to be in and out most of the day until late evening, Joshua had dealt with the presence of Shawanda and Loquisha by giving them two days off. By then, he hoped, a doctor would have seen to Ailith.

Connor, like Stephen, Joshua felt, could be trusted. And although he had the utmost faith in Shawanda's integrity, he realized if too many people knew his secret, it would cease to be a secret.

Thinking of the night he'd spent lying next to his beautiful English amnesiac, Joshua groaned. Every organ in and *on* his body sprang to life, especially when he recalled the sweet and stirring kiss they'd shared. He'd lain awake for hours. Guessing at Ailith's inexperience, the things he had wanted to do to her would have probably restored her memory instantly. Somehow that thought saddened him. If her memory returned, would she recall a man in her life?

"Joshua!"

His mother's annoyed voice burst into his reverie.

"You're not listening to me, dear."

Joshua drew in a breath, striving for patience. "I'm sorry, Mother. What did you say?"

"I was saying I'm going to make reservations at Brennan's for us for dinner tonight. Perhaps, Melissa, Stephen, and the flight attendant." She paused in concentration. "Kayla! That's her name. Perhaps they would like to join us?"

His suspicion increased. For the most part, Frances didn't seek out Mellie's company. Their mutual dislike for each other generally made for miserable evenings. But maybe he was reading too much into his mother's motives. She had, after all, promised to try and be more tolerant of Melissa for his sake, and so far things were going smoothly. That was possibly due to the fact that Melissa and his mother had only been in each other's presence on one occasion since his parents had arrived. Even if Mellie and his mother had been the best of friends, however, he wouldn't have gone.

No way am I leaving Ailith alone.

"Thanks, Mother, but I have to decline." A glimmer of hope that he and Ailith would have time alone filled him. "I am committed to some work I must do."

"Oh, well. Maybe some other time." Frances passed him a cup of just-brewed coffee, then swept to the breakfast nook where the counter was located and sat, patting the stool next to her.

Joining his mother at the counter with his coffee, Joshua gave her a charming smile. "I hope you're not disappointed, Mrs. Kenley," he said and took a sip from his coffee.

"Oh, good heavens, no!" Frances exclaimed. "I only hope you're not." She threw him a calculating grin. "We're meeting the Walkers after dinner at their home for a drink. Just thought you'd enjoy seeing them. Cassidy will be there. I hear she's quite a little beauty."

I'll bet she couldn't touch Ailith, Joshua found himself thinking.

He shook his head in amused disbelief. "Surely you

wouldn't expect me to make a pass at Cassidy with Melissa in tow, would you, Mother?'' he asked with a sly grin.

Frances took a delicate swallow from her cup before she answered, ignoring the ringing of the doorbell. ''Only with the utmost discretion.''

''Mother, I thought you liked Melissa!'' Joshua goaded.

''I don't mean to offend, dear, but Melissa is quite a bitch,'' Frances drawled casually as the doorbell sounded again. ''I should think you would have recognized that by now.''

Joshua's astonishment at his mother's language turned to laughter, and she joined in as she stood and went to answer the door after the bell rang for a third time without Connor responding.

Moments later Joshua heard his mother's mutter, ''You're here early this morning, Stephen. But I think you missed breakfast. Joshua ate in his room.''

The sound of their voices drew closer as they walked back to the kitchen.

''I didn't come to eat, Mrs. Kenley,'' Stephen replied.

Frances glided back to her seat as Stephen paused in the doorway.

''Josh, shouldn't you be getting ready to hit the salt mines?''

''Don't mind me, Stephen,'' Joshua answered. ''I just took some time to have a little tête-à-tête with my mommie dearest.''

Stephen chuckled. ''Well, quality time with Mumsy is always recommended. But now it's time to go to work.''

''May I, Mommie?'' Joshua asked with laughter in his tone.

Frances shook her head. ''As if my denial would stop you from your goal,'' she responded in a chipper voice. ''Whatever it is.''

''As if,'' Joshua imparted.

Frances chortled as she stood. ''Have fun, boys. I offered to buy you two dinner tonight, but since Joshua declined, you're on your own.''

"What!" Stephen demanded as they all departed the kitchen and started toward the stairway. "How dare you take it upon yourself to decline an invitation for me, Joshua!"

Joshua shrugged.

"Well, you can still come, Stephen dear," Frances declared. "We've been invited to the Walkers afterward." She sighed wistfully. "Cassidy Walker is visiting her parents. She was always such a charming little thing." She began her ascent up the stairs.

Stephen snorted as he and Joshua followed Frances. "No, thank you, Mrs. K. I'm afraid I have to pass on it, too. I don't mind that Joshua answered for me. We really will be quite busy for the next few days," he said, reaching Joshua's bedroom.

"Of course, dear. You boys behave yourselves today," she imparted, passing them to get to her own bedroom. "Your father and I have our day planned, darling, so I probably won't see you again until tonight since you're so busy. See you later." Reaching her door, she opened it and disappeared into the room.

"Whew!"

Joshua opened his own door, and he and Stephen nearly fell into his room in their haste to get inside and escape.

Stephen shut the door and secured the lock. "I love your mother, Joshua, but if she were *my* mother I would limit her visits to once every five years."

"If she were *your* mother, her visits wouldn't bother me in the least!" Joshua retorted, going to the partially opened closet. "Ailith?" he called in a low voice. "It's safe to come out now."

Ailith untangled herself from the garments and stepped into the bedroom, wearing Joshua's bathrobe. Having seen Joshua earlier, she directed her heartstopping smile to Stephen as she stopped next to Joshua.

Immediately, Joshua pushed the annoyance of his mother aside.

"Good morning, Stephen!" Ailith exclaimed. "It is good to see you again."

Stephen returned her smile with one of his own and took her hand into his. Bringing it to his lips, he kissed it.

"It's even better to see you, Ailith," he told her.

Joshua narrowed his eyes at Stephen, unaccustomed jealousy surfacing. Knowing his friend's weakness for beautiful women and how easily he charmed them into his bed, Joshua didn't like the gleam he saw in Stephen's eyes when he looked at Ailith—especially since Stephen had expressed an interest in Ailith at their first meeting. Joshua grabbed Ailith's hand and led her to a chair.

"You may sit down, Ailith," he murmured. "You needn't hide anymore. I'll have Connor bring your things in from Stephen's car." He turned his gentle regard from Ailith and gave Stephen a hard stare. "You did bring them?" he asked, his tone testy.

Stephen gave him an oblique look and answered him in a like manner. "Yes," he replied, then burst out laughing. "I, my friend, would never risk your ire or our friendship over a woman." He swallowed and threw Ailith one last appreciative glance. "Besides, from the look on both your faces, I believe I'm a tad late in the affection department."

"You don't know what the hell you're talking about!" Joshua snapped. He stomped to the telephone and snatched up the receiver.

At Joshua's annoyance, Stephen's laughter deepened. "*Au contraire*. I'm never wrong."

Joshua only glared at him as he spoke over the phone to Connor.

Ailith sat listening to the two men, her own annoyance simmering. She had learned enough about this time to know that women had certain rights and, judging by Shawanda's attitude, could demand the same respect afforded men. Ailith had come to admire the housekeeper's ready replies to offending remarks, intentional or not. Connor and Joshua usually apologized to Shawanda, always assuring her their remarks were not meant as insults. And Shawanda never lost her temper. Even her most scathing words were uttered with sugary sweetness. May—Perhaps there was a reason for that. As long as Shawanda didn't lose her temper, they seemed more responsive and ready to make amends.

So how would Shawanda respond to Joshua's and Stephen's indifference to her presence?

Ailith sighed loudly, drawing the two men's attention to her. "Joshua, Stephen," she piped up. "It's been decided I have a memory loss, *not* a loss of wits. Please refrain from your present mode of conversing without regard to my presence as though I were indeed knotty-pated or without hearing."

Her haughty gaze flitted from one man to the other as they looked at her in utter surprise.

Joshua recovered first. He gently placed the receiver back on its cradle and gave her a sheepish smile. "You are absolutely correct, Ailith. We were callous in our regard to your feelings. No insult was intended, but I apologize if I *have* offended you."

"Likewise," Stephen chimed in. "Sometimes, Ailith, I can be a total ass. I apologize." He looked at Joshua. "To both of you, for that matter."

Ailith smiled in satisfaction. "I accept both your apologies," she replied quite pleasantly.

Imitating Ailith, Stephen batted his eyelashes at Joshua. "What about you, Josh? Do you accept my apology also?"

"Blow it out your ear, Stephen!" Joshua sneered and went to answer the door in response to the knock.

Despite herself, Ailith laughed, branding Stephen as a mischievous rogue who delighted in provoking Joshua.

"It's Connor, Mr. Josh," they heard through the door.

Joshua quickly ushered the man inside, before relocking the door.

Viewing Connor closely for the first time as he laid several large packages on the bed, Ailith realized he wasn't much older than Joshua and Stephen. Perhaps his white-blond hair was what misled her. Overhearing some of Connor's conversations with Shawanda, Ailith knew mischief filled him as much as it did Joshua and Stephen.

Connor surveyed the room, his glance falling momentarily on Ailith, then going to rest on Joshua.

"Will there be anything else, Mr. J.?" he asked, unflapped.

"Just your complete discretion, Connor," Joshua warned.

A wicked grin split Connor's face, and he winked at Ailith.

"Why, whatever do you mean, sir?"

Joshua glowered at him.

"Watch out, Con!" Stephen smirked. "Ole Josh here ain't in a playing mood. Wink at her again, man, and your boss just may throw you out the window."

At Stephen's teasing tone, and knowing he had an ally, Connor's grin split wider.

"I see nothing out of the ordinary, sir, so why would you need my complete discretion? Mr. Stephen is always up here. That's not unusual."

His gaze again fell on Ailith, who now sat as still as stone.

"I see you've bought a brand-new toy. A very beautiful *adult*-sized doll. May I comment on the lifelike quality of her, Mr. J? I assure you she's nothing like the rubber woman I keep in my room. Guess I'll have to keep Mrs. Kenley outta here. Wouldn't want her to discover her son's pastime."

"Good man!" Stephen said. "One after my own heart."

Joshua slapped Connor on the back, walking to the door with him. "So you'll have no problem keeping my mother away from this room, Connor? Or making sure she doesn't find the key to the lock?"

"It would give me the greatest pleasure to outwit Mrs. Kenley, sir," Connor responded with glee. "Believe me, she won't cross the sill of your door."

Stephen snorted in disbelief, and Joshua raised a skeptical brow.

"Just trust me," Connor replied. "Now what about Sha-wanda and Loquisha?"

Joshua sighed. "I trust them. You know that. But for the time being, I would prefer things to remain as they are. Keeping a secret can be burdensome."

"Very good, Mr. J. I'll handle it, sir," Connor assured him as he stepped into the hall.

Joshua reclosed and locked the door after Connor's departure, then turned to face Ailith.

"There are five boxes." He pointed to the packages Connor had placed on the bed. "One box has lingerie. In another, there are a couple dresses, and two skirt-and-blouse sets. Another has jeans and shorts. The others have a slack set in one and socks and pantyhose in the last."

Ailith gave Joshua an intense gaze, trying hard to follow and understand what he said. She'd seen jeans on television.

She smiled. "501 Blues?" she asked. "Like on TV?"

Joshua sent her such an admiring, heated look, her belly clenched. His eyes conveyed a private message, entrancing and mesmerizing, one she didn't quite understand, but with the memory of his kiss still fresh in her mind, one she could easily recognize.

Stephen cleared his throat, but didn't quite break the moment.

Finally Joshua said huskily, "No, angel, not 501 Blues, but similar."

Ailith felt herself pinken and tried to focus on what else he'd said. *Lingerie. What could that be?* She'd seen so many kinds of clothing and their uses on television that she really couldn't place all of the names. She'd even seen attire made just for the breasts. Intensely aware of Joshua's bracing presence, she tried to remember what the breast attire was called. *Cross Your Heart? Nay. No. It was called a bra. Aye! Yes. Cross Your Heart Bra. What a strange name for a garment.*

Ailith considered the matter further. Perhaps it wasn't strange, after all, considering the bra's use.

"Ailith?"

Joshua's concerned voice cut into her musings.

"Are you all right?"

"Yes, Joshua," Ailith answered, going to inspect the boxes on the bed. She glanced down at them, then looked up at Joshua.

"Open them," he instructed. "Stephen and I will go downstairs to give you some time to get dressed and go over your things. Lock the door when we leave. Don't want Mother bursting in on you," he said with a grin.

"Yes," Ailith said, "I will. And thank you for the new garm . . . clothes, Joshua."

"My pleasure."

Joshua opened the door and cautiously peeked out. He motioned to Stephen that all was clear, and they stepped out into the hallway.

Ailith hastened to lock the door and started to walk away when she heard Stephen's cheerful voice.

"How neat Ailith will look . . ."

She wondered what *neat* meant.

". . . without shoes on her lovely little feet."

"*Shit!*" Joshua boomed.

Going to dress herself, Ailith giggled when Frances's indignant voice reached her.

"Joshua! Are you using obscenities out there?"

Chapter 13

AILITH STOOD WITH rapt attention for the critical inspection Joshua and Stephen did of her. Pride at her accomplishment filled her. She had managed to figure out how most of the clothing worked. A bra *had* been in the lingerie box, but it had much less material than the ones advertised on television.

She would figure out the use of some of the other things in the box later. Gazing at Joshua, she smiled expectantly into his golden eyes.

Joshua smiled back. Ailith continued to fascinate him. He had been out of her presence for nearly an hour, wanting to be assured that she would be decent when he returned, but the entire conversation had been about her.

Now Joshua watched Ailith, admiring the fit of the tight black jeans and bright red blouse she wore. Her freshly washed hair shone with pale highlights, and her scrubbed skin brought to mind a delicious peaches and cream dessert. His glance traveled down to her bare feet, and he frowned.

Perplexed, Ailith studied Joshua. She thought he was pleased with her appearance, but the irritation in his eyes told her otherwise.

"Is anything amiss . . . wrong, Joshua?" *I'll get this confounded language right eventually.*

He laughed, slightly embarrassed. "Yes, Ailith," he said. "Your shoes are a-missing."

"In his haste to clothe you," Stephen put in, "he forgot to buy you footwear."

"Which will be rectified as soon as possible," Joshua returned.

"Oh!" Ailith looked down at her feet, then back at Joshua who wore a chagrined expression. "I-I . . . Yes, I do need shoes, don't I?" she managed, flustered.

Joshua nodded and, with a gesture as automatic as breathing, took her into his arms, hugging her close to his chest. How right she felt in his arms. What would he ever do when she regained her memory and rejoined her family? How could he let her go? Those unbidden thoughts jolted him, and his arms tightened around her.

Ailith trembled slightly, Joshua's touch throwing her off kilter. Though his embrace was gentle, she felt the strength of his arms. Wrapping her own around his waist, she returned his hug, reveling in the nearness of him. She had to return to her own time to save her parents, but how would she be able to leave Joshua?

Stephen cleared his throat. "Is this an exclusive club, or can I get in on the action?"

Joshua and Ailith broke apart. When she smiled shyly, Joshua winked at her, then he turned to Stephen.

"Exclusive," he said. "Now, check to see if the coast is clear. We're going shoe shopping."

The coast *was* clear. Joshua was certain that his mother, showering or otherwise occupied in her bedroom to prepare for the day, would be indisposed for some time to come. His father didn't interfere in his affairs, so Joshua was not in the least concerned that his father would discover them sneaking out of his room. If Jonathan did, he would look the other way.

Carefully and quietly, holding Ailith's delicate hand, Joshua led the way outside to his BMW, which was parked in the front driveway.

Ailith's eyes grew as wide as saucers, awe and fear shining in them.

Joshua frowned at her reaction.

Pulling back on his hand, she looked up at him. "Pray tell, what kind of war weapon is that?"

Stephen eyed her suspiciously. "What the hell did she say, Josh?"

"You heard her as well as I did, Stevie," Joshua answered, surprised. "You've got ears." He turned his attention to Ailith. "War weapon? Are you serious? Are you talking about my *car*, Ailith?"

She stared at him, her face clouding with despair, then glanced at the car again.

Oh, God! It's a car! What's a car?

Ailith vaguely recalled seeing a similar thing on television. A car? She searched her mind, the shock receding. Aye, of course she'd seen a car on TV before. What made her call it a war weapon?

Mayhap it was because she hadn't expected real people to own a *car*. To her, watching TV was the same as viewing a stage performance of her time. She had seen cars in some of the numerous short skits that came on between the longer shows—all of which she considered the make-believe world of this time. Even then, she hadn't been sure of a car's use.

She studied it closely for a few moments. It seemed so frightening up close . . . so big and immobile.

On TV it had been moving. What made it move? Was it as safe as it appeared on TV?

"I-I have no memory of . . . of a car," she stammered in bewilderment. Her new discovery unnerved her. She smiled timidly at Joshua. "I-I don't know why I called it a war weapon."

Joshua exchanged a quick, confused look with Stephen before shaking his head and responding to Ailith. "Your amnesia is strange indeed." Alarms sounded loudly in his brain. He recalled the research he had done, years ago, when a high school classmate lost his memory. "You can remember your name, your *parents'* names, your home-town, but nothing else. Usually amnesia victims forget their personal history, but never what's in the world around them. How can you not recognize a car?''

Ailith drew in a steadying breath. Confusion evident in her tone, she said, ''I-I don't know. I-it's coming back to me now,'' she lied. ''I realize that's a car.''

Please, God, don't let him ask me what a car is for!

Stephen opened the door on the passenger side. ''Hurry, Josh,'' he demanded. ''You can discuss this in the car. Frances could be lurking behind a curtain in one of the upstairs windows.''

With a laugh, Joshua urged Ailith to get inside the car and sit. Just before he closed the door he caught the fright-ened look on her face. For a moment he wondered if her story about the orb was the truth. No! he decided quickly. Time travel didn't exist. Walking around to the driver's side, he stopped to talk to Stephen.

Inside, Ailith sat very still. She willed herself to relax. Slowly the comfort of the luxurious seat seeped into her brain, and she took in the strange apparatuses before her. What was the wheel for? She stopped her speculation long enough to bring her attention to Joshua when he looked into the car.

''Are you all right?''

''Yes,'' she replied. ''Thank you.''

''Good.'' Joshua turned back to Stephen. ''Listen, pal of mine—''

''Forget it, Joshua!'' Stephen protested. ''Whenever you begin with 'pal of mine,' I know you're going to talk me into something I don't want to do. Something that usually involves Melissa. So save your breath. The answer is no!''

''Stephen. Come on—''

''No!'' Stephen gritted. ''If you need to do something for Mellie, then do it. *I* will take Ailith shoe shopping.''

''No, you won't!'' Joshua snarled. ''You heard how Ail-ith sounded. I can't expose her just yet to Mellie. Pick

Emily up from the airport for me,'' he implored. ''I'll owe you one.''

''You'll owe me *big*!'' Stephen snapped. ''You know Melissa and I have this great mutual hate for each other. And I can tolerate Queen Emily about as much as I do Myra. Why, all of sudden, are all of Melissa's friends swarming the city?'' He paused in his tirade. ''But I agree with you,'' he said with a sigh. ''Ailith doesn't need to be around those three hags at the moment. Melissa would insist you deposit Ailith at the nearest loony bin. Ailith's a great-looking girl, Josh, and would make most women green with envy.''

Joshua got behind the wheel as Stephen bent down and stared at Ailith through the car window.

''Get a grip on your libido, lech. Just do as I ask. Emily's plane is due to land in an hour.'' He glanced at his watch. ''Melissa asked me to pick up her friend because she had a meeting this morning.''

Stephen winced, then let out a sound curse. ''You do this on purpose, Joshua,'' he accused. ''I'm always the one stuck with running Melissa and her vipers around. She's *your* girlfriend. We all don't have to suffer because of your misfortune. Emily, for God's sake!''

His friend had nothing against the British in general, but Emily Chesna personified most people's perceptions of cold, pompous English snobs, which was the reason for Stephen's present display. Joshua pushed aside the truth of Stephen's statement that Stephen was always left to drive Melissa around when it came to her chores. It suddenly struck him that he was only in Melissa's presence when absolutely necessary. That was either when she demanded he escort her out—usually once or twice a week—or to satisfy his sexual needs. Exactly what kind of relationship did he and Melissa have?

''What am I expected to do with the arrogant Miss QE1, once I have her in my clutches?'' Stephen grumbled.

Joshua pushed aside his thoughts and took an envelope from his car's sun visor, then passed it to Stephen. ''Melissa's house keys are in there. Just give the envelope to Queen Emily and deposit her at Mellie's house, and your task is done.''

"Happy days! Where will you be?'' Stephen inquired. "Canal Place? New Orleans Centre? Riverwalk?''

"Probably none of those places,'' Joshua replied. "Ailith and I will spend the day across the lake. She's been cooped up too long indoors. We'll buy some shoes in Covington. Anyway, Stephen, make that appointment with Dr. Griegs for Ailith whenever you can today. You know I can't trust my secretary with this.''

Stephen sighed. "Sure thing, Josh.'' He walked to his Lexus, which was parked next to Joshua's BMW.

"Buzz me on the car phone if you need to,'' Joshua called.

Without responding, Stephen slammed his door closed and started his engine.

When Joshua backed out of the driveway, he blew his horn at Stephen, who followed behind him.

Now awed by the thing called a car, Ailith sat rigid. She looked with uncertainty at Joshua. He smiled at her.

"Fasten your seat belt, Ailith,'' he instructed. "I don't let anyone ride with me without that safety device hooked up.''

My what? This seat has a belt?

Ailith observed Joshua in his seat. The thing wasn't a belt! Joshua was harnessed in his seat like a donkey to a cart. Is *that* what he wanted her to do? Harness herself in?

"Ailith,'' Joshua said with impatience, "grab the retractor and pull the tab across your chest, then insert it into the buckle.''

She looked at him blankly, not understanding him one whit.

"Do it *now!*''

"I would,'' Ailith snapped back, "if I knew where it was! This is the first time I've been in your car, Joshua. Please have the courtesy to show me what to do!''

Blasted man! She'd never *seen* a car, let alone ridden in one. If he had the decency to believe her story, there wouldn't be all of these problems.

Joshua coasted the car to a stop on the shoulder of the road. Frustration assailed him. He had to remember that she was sick and needed his help. Demanding her to do ordinary, everyday things would only hinder her recovery.

He flicked the hazard lights on, then leaned across his seat to reach around Ailith for her seat belt.

"Let me help you, Ailith," he croaked.

He accidently brushed against her breasts, and desire stirred within him.

Ailith stiffened to ward off the quivers in her middle as Joshua fastened her seat belt. His nearness confounding her to no end, she focused her attention outside.

They had stopped in front of a modest-sized house. A huge, sprawling tree sat in the yard, surrounded by bright flowers. Strange, colorful wheeled devices rested on the porch. From their small size, she decided the things were for children. Playthings, perhaps?

All of this faced a street and a wide field. She noted the sign with the letters *P-o-n-t-c-h-a-r-t-r-a-i-n B-l-v-d.*, and deduced it must have been the name of the street.

Puffs of snowy clouds flitted across the sky, and Joshua's woodsy-fresh scent filtered into her nostrils. She turned to him and realized he was staring at her.

"T-thank you, Joshua," she whispered. "I . . . Just be patient with me a little longer. I'm sure everything will come back to me in time."

In time. In my time. But your time, Joshua, is so inspiring. This travel conveyance. This car is amazing.

"Of course, Ailith," Joshua murmured.

He gave her cheek a whisper-soft caress before moving the car again.

Ailith took in her passing surroundings, enthralled at so many cars and other kinds of travel conveyances on the road. When Joshua pulled beside a very large, elongated . . . car . . . ? . . . with a score of windows where people could be seen looking out, she drew in an excited breath.

Joshua glanced at her oddly.

"That's called a bus. In case you can't recognize it."

The inkling of doubt he'd felt earlier assailed him again. There was not a trace of guile on her face, just pure innocence, of which she probably wasn't even aware.

Who was she? Her memory loss only had her annoyingly inconvenienced, not frighteningly out of touch. But *he'd* said she had amnesia. *She* said she was from another time.

Bullshit! With all the technology available here in the twentieth century, no one had yet found a way to breach the time barrier to the past or the future.

Joshua gave Ailith a sideward glance. Her face enraptured, her green eyes sparkled like emeralds, shining like a child's first glimpse of a circus. He almost believed she was from another time then. But he knew the Middle Ages didn't have the know-how to build a pair of skates, let alone a time device.

No, she was just an amnesia victim with a total loss of memory. Joshua shook his head. Not total, he corrected himself. She did remember her name and her parents.

He pulled up to the toll booth, which led to the Causeway, the twenty-four-mile-long bridge over Lake Pontchartrain that connected the north and south shores. He chanced another look in Ailith's direction.

She was breathing deeply and rapidly now, ringing her hands together and staring in front of her, where the lake and the bridge stretched on forever, with seemingly no end in sight.

Joshua turned his attention back to the toll taker and paid the fee, then started the half-hour ride across the bridge.

"Are you all right, Ailith?" he asked with concern.

"Yes," she quickly replied, clutching the sides of her leather seat as if they were her lifeline.

She was riding in a car on a stone bridge over water. Miles and miles of water. How safe was this journey? But this was Joshua's time. The nineteen nineties. Safe enough. Right? She had no way of knowing.

"God's eyes!" She gasped aloud.

Joshua frowned, then raised a brow, but decided not to comment on her terminology and instead asked, "Is something wrong, Ailith?"

Ailith laughed nervously. "No, Joshua. I-I am just amazed at all the water."

"Well, it's not that deep. Only about fifteen feet."

Ailith smiled, her unease evident. "How many fifteen-foot people do you know?"

Joshua laughed. "I take it you can't swim?"

"No," came the timid reply.

"Then I'll have to teach you."

"W-what sea is this?"

"It's not a sea," he replied. "This is Lake Pontchartrain." He paused, wishing he could offer her more comfort. "Be at ease, Ailith. You're safe enough on this bridge. Just think of me as your knight in shining armor, ready and willing to rescue you from danger."

Ailith smiled, and at the wistful look crossing her beautiful face, Joshua wondered what was going through her mind.

A knight in shining armor indeed, Ailith thought ruefully. Even in her time, such a knight was rare. Preston had been hers, but his armor had tarnished. Could she expect something more from Joshua? She wanted to.

"All right," she said finally, the tension in her body evaporating. "I'll think of you as my champion knight."

Joshua smiled at her. Was there another woman—an actress or model—as exquisitely beautiful as Ailith? He conceded to himself there was no lack of female beauty around, but none stood out as Ailith did. There was something so different about her.

Taking glimpses at her as he drove, she looked almost ethereal.

Ethereal? Ha! The little con artist is as far from ethereal as heaven is from hell. Joshua narrowed his eyes at her. *Little bitch.* He fixed his eyes on the road again. *She was playing him for a fool! No one could be as innocently provocative.* He sucked in a ragged breath. *Get a grip, Kenley!*

Any fool can see something's not right with this girl. Give her the benefit of the doubt before you condemn her further.

He glanced back at Ailith and found her beaming a smile his way, which he returned. Joshua hoped she *wasn't* a con artist. She was just too beautiful to go to anybody's jail. But what if she really did have amnesia and later recalled that she was married? He consoled himself that she was only nineteen. Marriageable age, yet still young enough *not* to be married.

She affected an air of serenity. "Are we coming to the end of the bridge, Joshua?"

"No, it's more than another mile or so, Ailith," Joshua answered. "We'll go to the mall when we get off to do some shoe shopping. Then we'll have lunch and maybe take in an early movie. Would you like that?"

Ailith laughed shakily. "Oh, would I!" she responded with enthusiasm, though her feeling didn't quite match the sound. *What, pray tell, is an early movie?*

"Good."

Joshua soon left the bridge behind and continued on for two blocks before turning right and stopping at a traffic light.

Another one, Ailith thought. She watched the cars on the cross street move parallel to Joshua's car, then the red light changed to green, and she smiled to herself as the other cars stopped. *Now it's our turn.*

She sat as calmly as possible, but at certain times her excitement at this magical place surfaced. Oh, would her father were here! *Did I say would? Watch your language Ailith deCotmer. The word is if.* If Father were here, what would he think of such wonders?

Joshua drove into the parking lot of the Covington Mall. "Here we are, loony medieval lady," he teased. Catching a glimpse of her little pink toes, a carefree feeling stole into him. "Well, as pretty as your feet are, we can't let you walk barefoot through the mall by yourself."

Ailith sat there, unconcerned that she had no shoes, seemingly oblivious to the fact that some people, himself included, considered it the height of indecency to traipse about in such a manner. But suddenly he didn't give a damn. He untied his shoes, slipped his feet out of them, then took off his socks, tossing everything on the backseat.

"There. Now we're even."

He laughed and crossed his leg over the seat to wiggle his toes over her feet.

"Oh, Joshua!" Ailith laughed, thoroughly enjoying their playful moment, Joshua's intoxicating nearness almost undoing her.

"Let's just hope mall security doesn't see us and throw us out."

Getting out of the car, Joshua found the concrete already warm from the midmorning sun. His mood buoyant, expectant, he strode around to Ailith's side and opened the door, taking her hand as she cautiously stepped out.

"The ground is hot, isn't it?" she asked.

He judged the distance from his car to the mall entrance, then scooped her up in his arms, deciding the walk would be too far for her to bear comfortably. And he didn't want her to suffer any discomfort whatsoever.

Half expecting her to protest, it pleased him when she merely gasped in surprise, then laughed in pleasure. He returned her merriment.

If he would have swept Melissa off her feet in public, she would have murdered him. Hell, she would have blasted him if he would do such a thing in private. And until now, he'd always sworn he was content with a self-sufficient woman. But he found he enjoyed Ailith accepting his help without accusing him of maligning the strides women had made. And Ailith herself was quite self-sufficient.

Ailith wrapped her arms around Joshua's neck, feeling very vulnerable to his attention. If she didn't feel such foreboding for her parents, this man of the nineteen nineties could easily captivate her. Closing her eyes, she buried her face in his wide chest. Feeling the rumblings from his laughter, Ailith knew she didn't want to leave Joshua Ken-

Chapter 14

Aɪʟɪᴛʜ's sᴇɴsᴇs ᴄᴏɴᴛɪɴᴜᴇᴅ to be astounded with one wondrous sight after another and for the most part she had no definition or words for what she saw. Every now and then Joshua volunteered bits of information to her, but more often than not he didn't, and she refused to ask.

This *mall*—as Joshua called it—took her breath away. It was as strong as Greyhawke Keep, but much airier and brighter. It also went on forever. She discerned no bad smells or any rushes on the floor.

Serfs and peasants—

Ailith studied the passers-by. Was there a master of the mall? These people, dressed in various odd garments, seemed as carefree as the wind, almost as if they were masters of their *own* fate.

Children scooted by, their parents tagging behind, keeping a wary eye on them. Groups of young men or women sauntered along, laughing uproariously at times. Couples rambled about, stopping to peek into the windows of certain shops.

No, none of these people were peasants or serfs. They were just . . . people. Her new discovery jolted her, but pleased her all the same. The easygoing lifestyle of the inhabitants of this time period enthralled her even as she again wondered if she possessed the skills necessary to survive here.

She would lay those thoughts aside to ponder later. For now, it contented her to hold firmly to Joshua's arm as they strolled through the mall.

They'd gone immediately to the cobbler's ... the shoe merchant ... where Joshua bought her eight pairs of shoes, including *sneakers*, boots, and high heels. Though she accepted all the purchases graciously, she wondered at the safety of wearing shoes with such spiked heels. She remained silent, however, and decided to wear the sneakers. They felt so comfortable while she tested them.

Afterward they took her purchases and went to another shoe merchant's shop that fashioned only men's footwear. Since Joshua was barefoot, he made a purchase of a pair of sneakers similar to the ones she wore. Then they went back into the mall to explore.

Suddenly she dug her nails into Joshua's arm. "Look at that, Joshua!" she whispered in awe, hardly able to contain her excitement. "What in the name of Saint Peter is that?"

She pointed to a cart centered between the footpaths which had a device with a glass dome. Inside the dome, puffs of little white balls danced in the air.

Joshua looked at Ailith in sheer amazement. How could she not recognize a popcorn machine? Since they'd entered the mall, he'd been furtively observing her. Always her expression was nothing *less* than awestruck.

Despite her amnesia, something should have struck a chord of familiarity, but Ailith seemed to view everything as if for the first time. Everything she touched appeared to be a new and dazzling discovery. From her shining eyes, he knew she was enraptured by it all.

Did she really have amnesia? She'd repeatedly told him that *he* was the one who insisted she had amnesia. *She* insisted, however, that she'd come from a distant time.

Dear Lord, could she be telling the truth? No, goddammit! Joshua refused to accept that. That sort of thing was scientifically impossible, and even the thought should have been too preposterous to entertain.

Yet there was something surreal about her. She was exquisite and soft and innocent and ... and brand-new. Innocent not only in virtue, he believed, but innocent to this world. *His* world.

No! his mind rejected. She might have still been a virgin, but she was *not* innocent.

Forcing the troubling thoughts from his mind, he looked at her.

"Aren't there malls with popcorn machines in Middlesbrough?" he asked testily.

For a moment Ailith gaped at him, and some of her pleasure seemed to evaporate.

"Why ... I ... Yes, I suppose there are," she stammered. "I'm *sure* there are, Joshua. I-I just don't remember."

She gave him a brilliant smile then. His heart almost forgot to beat.

Regretting his curtness, Joshua drew in a breath. "Well," he croaked, "why don't we buy a couple bags of popcorn and see if you can recall the taste?"

He walked up to the cart and placed the huge shopping bag of shoes down. After viewing the menu and choosing from a variety, he ordered two bags of hot, buttered popcorn. Paying the vendor, Joshua passed one bag over to Ailith.

"Try it," he encouraged.

With one hand, he picked up the bag again and held the popcorn with the other. Then he watched as Ailith placed the treat into her mouth and began chewing noisily.

"Umm," she said. "Popcorn is very good."

"Yes, it is," Joshua agreed. He raised his bag, which was brimming over, to his mouth and sucked some in.

Ailith laughed, and Joshua joined her.

"The packages are occupying my other hand," he explained as they began strolling through the mall again.

"So I can see," Ailith chimed in, taking the snack from

him. "Allow me to feed you, my lord. I-I mean Joshua."

"My pleasure, Ailith," Joshua replied casually. He didn't allow her to notice that he realized what she'd let slip. The glorious blush staining her lovely cheeks gave her away.

"Pluck a kernel in there." He opened his mouth.

Though her face flamed, Ailith laughed and did as Joshua asked. Relieved that he hadn't commented on her choice of words, she relaxed again.

A little later, when Joshua took her to the movies, she could hardly contain herself and watched the images with rapt attention. She noted the differences between movies and television. There was no remote control to change the channels, and this screen made a TV's look minuscule by comparison. So enraptured was she by the moving pictures that she barely noticed when Joshua left her side.

But she did notice his return a few minutes later because he carried a cardboard tray loaded with delightful treats.

She picked up an oblong-shaped bread, slit on one side and stuffed with a sausage.

"Those are hot dogs," he explained. "You have chili and mustard with onions for toppings."

Ailith took a bite and closed her eyes at the delicious taste, deciding *hot dogs* would become her favorite food.

Once she finished her first treat, Joshua introduced her to another.

"Try some nachos," he coaxed as he bit into one. "These are topped with melted cheese and jalapeño peppers."

She smiled and popped one into her mouth. The chip crunched around as she chewed it, and when she bit into the pepper, her eyes watered at the almost too spicy flavor. As she became used to the heat of the jalapeño, she realized *nachos* outranked hot dogs for her favorite food.

"We'll save the other goodies for later," Joshua said, picking up his hot dog and finishing it off in record time.

"I'll be fine, Joshua," Ailith said, reaching for a bag of potato chips.

Joshua looked at Ailith with skepticism. He didn't want her to become ill, but he hadn't been able to resist buying a variety of snacks. When he'd gone to the concession stand, he'd thought of Ailith's delight at tasting popcorn, and that had swayed him. But now, watching her, he wasn't sure if he'd used sound judgment.

He soon realized his unease wasn't misplaced. Throughout the long movie, Joshua attempted to deter Ailith from the many new treats—Snickers and Milky Way candy bars, Skittles, Coca Cola, and more buttered popcorn—but Ailith insisted she sample each one with increasing fervor, thoroughly enjoying everything she ate.

By the end of the picture, she swore she would never recover. The variety of foods roiled around in her belly, and nausea nearly overtook her. As they headed to Joshua's car, she leaned her head on his shoulder, her sickness making her weak.

Finally, gratefully, Joshua was opening his car door and securing her to the seat, then slamming the door shut and going to the other side to slide in.

"Rest your head on the headrest, sweetheart."

Through her dizziness, Joshua's voice floated back to her, and she did as he had suggested, closing her eyes in an attempt to ward off the rising tide of pain in her middle.

Joshua looked at Ailith as he started the car. Apparently the headrest hadn't offered her any comfort, because she now huddled against the door in a heap of misery, looking quite green around the gills. Even through her sickness he sensed her embarrassment. He felt quite guilty about having bought so much for her and then not insisting she restrain herself. But he wasn't her father, and telling her in no uncertain terms that she *couldn't* have any more of the snacks would have been treating her like a naughty child. Now he wanted to put her at ease. "Poor baby," he said as he drove out of the parking lot. "Poor, poor little piglet overate. I'll give you a remedy for that when we get home." Although he was smiling, his remarks reflected his sympathy.

"Blow it out your ear, Joshua!"

For a moment Joshua looked at Ailith in surprise. Then he smiled to himself, realizing he'd said that exact same thing to Stephen this morning. Shaking his head and promising to be more careful with what he said, he hoped they would make it home without Ailith losing the contents of her stomach all over herself.

Home. He looked at his watch. Shit! His parents had probably returned to prepare for their evening with the Walkers, which meant it was too early to go home. Or was it?

He would call home from his car phone to find out if his parents had left.

"Is the coast clear, Connor?" Joshua asked once he had him on the telephone.

"No, Mr. J., it isn't," Connor answered. "Your parents are still here. It's only four o'clock, sir, and I don't think they're planning to leave until six."

"Damn the luck." Joshua sighed and glanced at Ailith, who again sat with her eyes closed. "All right, Connor. I'll call you in an hour. With half an hour's traveling time back home, that gives me an hour and a half."

"You could go to one of your stores for a half hour, sir."

"Yeah. Well, we'll see," Joshua imparted. "Call me if my parents leave before six."

"Very good, Mr. J."

"Thank you, Connor," Joshua muttered and hung up.

Sensing Ailith's extreme distress, he peeked in her direction and found her holding her hand over her mouth. Spying a Walgreen's Drugstore, he pulled off the highway and into its parking lot.

"Ailith," he said softly, leaning over to her.

Ailith moaned a response.

"I'm so sorry you feel so ill, sweetheart. Sit here until I get back. I'm going into the drugstore to see what the pharmacist has to offer for your upset stomach."

Ailith merely nodded.

Joshua got out of the car and locked the door behind him, hastening toward the store entrance.

Ailith had never felt so sick before and wondered what remedy people in Joshua's time used for her affliction. In her time, rosemary and woodsage potion would have helped, along with her mother's love and gentle touch.

Until she had started to feel so sick, she had never enjoyed herself as much as she had today. She'd been so filled with pleasure that she'd thoroughly pushed her parents and her dilemma out of her head.

If only she could throw up, she thought as everything surfaced with a vengeance in her mind. The illness, coupled with abrupt images of the black tent, Aida, Brint Pfiester, Lord Preston, and her parents, made her feel suddenly trapped, and she began to breath rapidly. She fiddled with the door handle, trying to get out. When she failed, she banged on the window and released a frustrated sob.

A man walked up to the car just as she saw Joshua walking out of the drugstore carrying a plastic bag. Though she knew the man was speaking, she couldn't understand his words, but clearly understood Joshua's.

"Hey, buddy, get away from that car. What are you doing to my wife?"

Wife? Wife!

I'm not Joshua's wife.

For now, she was too upset to speculate further on his meaning. She realized the man had responded to Joshua's snarling words, but she hadn't listened to his reply. The man walked away, and Joshua hurried to his side of the car, opening the door and slipping in.

He stared at her for a few seconds, then a frown creased his brow. "Ailith, honey, what's wrong?" he asked in worried tones.

"I want to go home, Joshua," she responded in her own language, too upset to remember the words she had learned. "I can't bear it any longer." The words rolled from her tongue fast and furious. "I know not what sin I have committed that I must be punished so."

Joshua unbuckled Ailith's seat belt and drew her into his arms, feeling the trembles racking her body.

"Shhh," he soothed. "You're not being punished, my heart. You just ate too much junk food and—"

"Nay!" she cried and attempted to wiggle out of his embrace. " 'Tis not the food I am referring to! My unsettled stomach 'tis inconsequential compared to my misery when I think of my parents. I know not what has become of them. I know not what will become of me if I am forced to stay back in this time. Every new wonder I experience, every new food I taste, every new habit I learn makes me yearn to stay here in 1998. Even as I long to remain, I pray to return to my own time because my parents need me there; because this place frightens and amazes me; and because I don't know if I can adjust enough to survive."

Joshua remained speechless, too stunned to speak at first. He caressed and slid his hands up and down her back. Slowly, gradually, her sobs subsided, and her body stilled. She had been babbling, but the significance of her choice of extinct English and French words as well as their meaning gave him pause. Yet he had understood her as she jumped between the languages.

Obviously she had multiple personalities, a medieval one included.

He was a man who reasoned things out, and if there was no logical explanation for something, his scientific way of thinking denied any other possible theories. As it did now with Ailith. The only conclusion his mind allowed him to accept was that she was either a con artist, an amnesiac, or a person with a personality disorder. If she had more evidence than just a mere orb with a dim glow—suggesting the batteries inside it needed changing—then he might have believed her. But still, he would help her. He hoped Stephen had made the appointment with the psychiatrist. She needed help and quickly.

Joshua pushed her a little apart from him. "Ailith, how's your stomach?"

"Still upset," she whispered.

"You're going to be all right," he reassured her, hating the defeat he heard in her voice. "I've bought you something to make you feel better." He smiled at her, gazing into her eyes, which shone like the brightest emeralds from the tears pooling in them. "All right?"

"Aye," she responded wearily.

His heart shattered, and a strange, intense feeling rose within him. One that he had never experienced before. One that he didn't care to name now.

He began emptying his bag. "I've got spring water, paper cups, Alka-Seltzer, Pepto-Bismol, Emeril, Maalox, and ice-cold 7UP. Take your pick," he encouraged. "The sooner you take something, the sooner you'll feel better."

Ailith looked first at Joshua and then at the items between them on the car seat, not knowing which to choose. "I . . . Please pick one for me," she implored.

"Of course," Joshua replied. "I've always found Alka Seltzer works best for me, followed by a nice, cold 7UP. I'll fix one of each for you."

He went about the task of preparing the *Alka Seltzer* for her and handed it over to her once he was finished. Aware of his scrutiny, she drank the fizzling water, then frowned in disgust.

"Argh!"

Joshua grinned at her. "I take it you don't care for the taste."

"You take it correctly," she said.

He opened a can of 7UP for her and handed it over.

With a wary glance his way, she raised the can to her mouth and drank deeply, then drew in a breath, the bubbles tickling her tongue and watering her eyes.

"Easy, Ailith. Drink slowly. We want to ease your upset, not worsen it."

Ailith started to respond when a huge belch escaped her lips. She flushed with embarrassment.

"Oh!" she piped up.

Joshua burst out laughing. "That's what you needed. How do you feel now?"

Ailith contemplated her nausea for a moment, then smiled. "Better," she replied in amazement. "Much better. Your remedy works fast indeed."

"You probably won't feel one hundred percent better until you eliminate all that junk you ate. But these things will hold you until we get home." Joshua looked at his watch. Four forty-five. Between the visit to the drugstore and the time spent parked, three quarters of an hour had passed.

"Will the motion of the car bring your nausea back, or do you want to stay here a little while longer, Ailith?" Joshua asked as he cleared the space between them of the drugstore items.

"I won't mind if we leave now," Ailith replied softly.

"We'll leave as soon as you finish your 7UP," Joshua answered. "Take your time." He smiled at her and sighed.

He thought of bringing her home and letting her occupy one of the bedrooms openly as his houseguest. No. He nixed the idea immediately, and it wasn't because of Mellie, or his mother for that matter. It was because of Ailith.

Who indeed was she? If she really did have amnesia, she didn't need to be exposed to Frances or Mellie. They would run roughshod over Ailith with their overbearing personalities. That also held true if she suffered from a personality disorder. Though he steadfastly refused to deal with any other possibility for her odd behavior, the thought niggled at his conscience that she may have been telling the truth.

Why would he refuse even to consider that she had been jetted here from another era? He had already decided why. So why would he continually question his beliefs when he'd never done so before?

The idea of time travel was too . . . too unthinkable, too uncanny.

Some of Ailith's words floated through his mind. Ten and nine, she said was her age, but that was her *other* personality coming through. Normal people just didn't say things like that anymore.

She's a beautiful, nineteen-year-old girl who desperately needs help.

Ailith's sweet voice brought him out of his disturbing thoughts.

"7UP is quite delightful to the tastebuds, Joshua. Almost too tasty to be medicinal."

Joshua swallowed hard, the odd urge to laugh at the unreal insanity of this situation nearly overtaking him. God! She had never tasted 7UP before, and she thought it was medicine!

Maybe he needed to seek out his friend Gene Callenberg, an antiquarian/historian as well as a professor, who helped him discern the authenticity of some of the antiques Joshua acquired for his shops. But before he did that, he would demand it of himself either to accept Ailith's story or leave Gene out of this puzzle.

"Are you finished drinking your 7UP, Ailith?" he asked, not bothering to tell her that it was soda pop. He couldn't bare to see her blank look, then her look of astonishment as she tried to hide her ignorance of her environment.

"Aye . . . yes, I'm through." It dawned on Ailith that she had lapsed into her own language in her panic to get out of the car. Weary and tired, she didn't care to speculate on Joshua's reaction. If he was suspicious or displeased he would let her know soon enough. At the moment she still felt rather ill and wanted to return to his house to lie down. "I am ready to leave, thank you."

Unease swept through her as Joshua started the car and left the drugstore behind. They drove at a seemingly slower pace than they had before they got to the mall. Mayhap, she reasoned, it was just her imagination.

She felt Joshua's eyes on her and chanced a glance at him. The intenseness of his expression startled her. Whatever he was thinking even made him frown. His eyes fell on the clock in its place on the . . . shelf . . . panel . . . whatever . . . she was too miserable to attempt to name it.

Why didn't she just ask Joshua the name of the place that held all those . . . those instruments? She knew why.

Because his suspicions of her, whatever they were, were roused enough.

Joshua smiled at Ailith. "Are you still feeling better?" he asked.

"About the same," she replied.

He again looked at his watch, then glimpsed the clock on the dashpanel. They synchronized. "I think it's time we went home."

She merely smiled shyly at him.

Joshua groaned inwardly. Suddenly he didn't care about her background, even if she turned out to be a little crook. An almost overpowering urge to kiss her breathless pervaded him. There was something so damned vulnerable about her that all he wanted to do was caress and protect her.

He coasted to a stop at a traffic light. "I'm sorry you got sick, Ailith," he murmured. "It was really my fault that you did. I should not have bought all that food. Forgive me?" he asked, his voice gentle.

"Of course," she replied softly. "I had fun. Everything was enthralling. The stroll through the mall, the popcorn, the shoe purchases, the movies, even the junk food." She laughed. "I can't blame you for my avariciousness. That was solely my doing. Next time I'll know better."

The ringing of the car phone prevented Joshua from responding. "Hello?" he said after picking it up.

"Mr. J.? Connor here."

"I'm on my way home, Connor." The traffic light turned green, and he started forward again. "Is the coast clear?"

"That's the reason for my call, sir," Connor answered. "Your parents left no more than five minutes ago. And your mother said she would see me in the morning."

"They left almost an hour earlier than they'd planned," Joshua commented.

"Are you complaining, sir?"

Connor sounded incredulous.

Joshua laughed. "What do you think? Thanks for the tip, Connor. I'll be home between now and six. If any shift in my parents' plans find them back at the house call me to let me know.''

"Will do, Mr. J. Will that be all, sir?'' Connor inquired.

"Have you heard from Stephen or Melissa?''

"Not a word, sir.''

"Good. See you soon, Connor.''

With that, Joshua placed the phone back on the cradle and turned his regard to Ailith once again. Sadness seemed to cloud her face. Her gaze met his, and she gave him a wistful smile before turning to look out the window.

He realized she didn't want to speak anymore, and somehow he was to blame. Had she decided not to forgive him for overfeeding her, after all? But such pettiness seemed so out of character for her.

Ailith watched as the Causeway and Lake Pontchartrain came into view once again. Mariners dotted the water as the sun gleamed off of the various small vessels as well as the lake itself. Gulls skimmed the waves, then took flight once again. When she stared hard enough, she even discerned schools of fish swimming. All of this beauty only deepened her misery.

She assumed Joshua must have wondered why she had stopped talking. But what was there for her to say? He had Melissa. She had allowed herself to become so enraptured of him that she'd forgotten that fact.

Because she had felt he and Melissa were not getting along, Ailith had pushed her to the back of her mind. Men of this time were the same as they were back in hers. Lady Glenna and Lord Preston had not gotten along, so Lord Preston had decided to make Ailith his leman but refused to give up his lawful wife. She'd thought Joshua to be different. But he had held her in his arms to comfort her and had called her sweetheart. And, by all that was holy, she refused to wonder why he had told that man she was his wife. Yet he would return to Melissa and place Ailith in the aft of his thoughts until it suited him to do otherwise.

Joshua was all that she had, and still she didn't really have him, even though she was totally dependent upon him.

He hadn't believed her story that she was catapulted here
from another time, and more than likely he never would.
And she didn't know enough about his time to fill a water
goblet. This day at the mall had made that fact more than
clear to her.

But even with that daunting knowledge, Ailith contemplated leaving the relative safety of Kenley Manor and going out into Joshua's world on her own. Riding back home
with a tense silence between them, Ailith concluded *someone* out there would believe her story.

She merely had to find the courage to venture out and
discover who.

Chapter 15

AILITH SAT LOOKING out of the window in Joshua's bedroom at the placid waters of the lake. Streaks of lightning arced across the slate-gray sky, lighting it up every now and then.

Tonight Joshua was hosting another dinner party, this one for Melissa's friend Emily. And tonight Ailith would leave.

She didn't know why she felt so bereft. After all, she knew Joshua and Melissa belonged together. They had been together before she arrived. Still, Ailith wished Joshua belonged to her.

Staying any longer at Kenley Manor would only add to her hurt and confusion. Besides, Joshua's parents had decided to move to New Orleans and would reside at Kenley Manor until the *condo* they'd purchased was ready.

Upon passing this news to her, Joshua had thrust his fingers through his beautiful, dark hair.

"Shit, you can't win them all," he'd grouched, then decided to accept his fate.

On several occasions Frances had nearly discovered Ailith. Ailith felt sure if she stayed any longer, not only would she cause friction between Joshua and Melissa, but also him and his mother. Yes, it was past time she departed.

It had taken her three weeks to decide to leave Joshua and Kenley Manor behind as she had vowed while riding home from Covington Mall. Perhaps that was due to how wonderful he'd been to her when they'd returned home and most concerned for her well-being. He had tended her with the same care her mother used when Ailith was ill.

She had thrown up and suffered other elimination maladies as well. Even now she blushed in remembrance. But Joshua had soothed away her embarrassment, then had washed her face, helped her to disrobe and tucked her into bed. Once there, he'd lain beside her, holding her in his arms.

When she recalled how unhappy he'd looked the next morning, she frowned. She knew he had gotten out of bed before full light had arrived that day and taken a shower. Afterward, the telephone had rang, and though she hadn't been fully awake, she'd heard him remark to the person with whom he was holding the conversation that not even the cold shower had helped.

She still didn't have any notion of what that meant. Since that day, she had fallen asleep alone in the bed. Usually Joshua sat in his chair to watch television or otherwise occupied himself on the telephone or with other chores. She always woke up alone in bed, although she knew Joshua slept in it. Occasionally she'd awaken during the night and find him asleep on the far end.

She would never figure out Joshua and his strange moods.

In contrast to his change toward her at night, their days were joyfully enchanting. They reveled in outwitting the occupants of the house. Two weeks ago Melissa had accompanied her friend Emily to New York for some unexplained reason, so they didn't have *her* to contend with.

Maybe Ailith hadn't left yet because she hadn't had the chance.

This past Monday Joshua had taken her and Stephen to lunch at a bistro on Royal Street near Kenley Gallery of

Antiques, then they'd gone to the Audubon Zoo. While there, they'd run into a member of Joshua's medievalist club.

Stephen had been the one to explain Ailith's presence by claiming she was a distant cousin of his, who was visiting New Orleans for the first time, while Joshua had stood by silently, not correcting Stephen's statement.

Pain as sharp as an arrow had pierced Ailith's breast, and at first she'd wondered about Joshua's acceptance of the falsehood. But of course Joshua would deny knowing her. When she was at his house, he kept her behind lock and key after all.

Each day the three of them went somewhere—the Aquarium of the Americas, the New Orleans Museum of Art, cruising on the Natchez, touring a plantation—where she continued to be entranced by things she glimpsed for the first time. She no longer had control over her reaction to most of what she saw. She was usually awestruck and couldn't hide that fact.

After the first day she no longer wondered why Stephen accompanied them everywhere. She realized he was a decoy in the event of incidents such as the one at the zoo.

At times Joshua seemed delighted with her responses to her discoveries. Other times he would frown in confusion, bewildering her in the process. Through it all, she knew Joshua continued to be amazed at her sense of wonder.

While they were out or when they played their game of hide-and-seek, his kindness overwhelmed her. Even with Stephen there—and his reasons for being there—Joshua would constantly find reasons to touch her, causing all kinds of tinglings to course through her. Sometimes he brushed an errant lock of hair from her face or held her around her waist to steady her as she attempted to walk in her spiked heels. He held her hand, took her arm, hugged her around her shoulders. Whatever it was he did, she loved the feel of his hands on her—and her resentment for him increased by a thrice.

But the physical contact always ended when they returned home, although he'd taken her for several midnight strolls around his *neighborhood*, laughing the first time she'd called it a village.

What caused him to change so toward her? She knew he enjoyed being out with her, and she sensed his contentment of the past weeks.

Ailith shifted in her seat. The rain had started hesitantly, and the gloom of the moment matched her mood.

She couldn't understand Joshua. She told herself she didn't *want* to understand him. Yet, despite everything, it devastated her to think that he vacillated between hot and cold where she was concerned.

The rain began to come down steadily, and Ailith moved from her place by the window to sit on the bed. She pushed herself against the headboard and stretched out her legs. Taking the remote off the nightstand, she fiddled with it a few seconds before aiming it at the television. It was time for her favorite *soap opera*. For the next hour she would let John and Marlena's troubles replace hers.

Ailith always kept the sound from the television just loud enough to hear. There was nothing Joshua could do about his parents for the time being but outwit them.

She smiled at Joshua's craftiness, because outwit them he did. When the room was being cleaned, either he or Connor always remained in the bedroom, and Ailith would conceal herself either under the bed or in her former hiding spot, the closet.

Not having much interest in the scene on TV at the moment, Ailith recalled Loquisha's complaints and began to giggle.

"No one person should dirty that many towels, Mr. Josh," she'd grumbled, scoffing at the sometimes six or seven towels he used per day.

After Loquisha had left the room, Joshua had commented, "She would have had conniptions if she had to do Ailith's laundry, too!"

The job of doing her laundry was given to Connor, who had once slyly remarked to Joshua what a novel and titillating experience it would be to discover some of Victoria's Secrets and swish them around in Woolite. Joshua had merely laughed, but Ailith frowned, failing to get the humor.

She brought her full attention back to the program. The sound of a key in the lock alerted Ailith that either Joshua or Connor was coming in and distracted her once more from the TV.

"It's only me," Joshua said in low tones after he'd closed the door behind him. "What's going on with John and Marlena?"

Ailith ignored Joshua's mocking tone. "Marlena's possessed, and John's going to exorcise her."

Joshua rolled his eyes to the ceiling, then gave her an indulgent look. "Poor baby. You really must be bored." He plopped down in a chair. "I promise you we'll remedy that real soon."

Ailith flipped off the television and moved to sit on the side of the bed. "But I *like Days of Our Lives*," she protested.

"Well." Joshua crossed his ankle over his knee and laced his fingers behind his head. "You have to admit those soaps do stretch the imagination a bit."

Ailith threw Joshua a penetrating look. "And how do you propose to remedy it?"

Joshua's gaze was no less piercing. "Dr. Griegs is back at work, fully recovered from his unexpected surgery. You've been rescheduled to see him next week."

Stephen had followed Joshua's orders and made the appointment with the utmost haste, demanding that the psychiatrist see Ailith within the week. He'd finagled an appointment for the following week, but the day before the scheduled time, Dr. Griegs's secretary had called and said the doctor had fallen ill and would have to reschedule due to surgery to correct the problem. Now, three weeks later, Ailith had a new appointment. The only drawback to that was she was in no need of a doctor.

She stood from the bed and walked to the chair Joshua sat in, stopping in front of him.

"I'm not ill, Joshua," Ailith said in a poignant whisper.

Though she would be far away from Kenley Manor by next week, a large part of her still wanted to convince Joshua she was telling the truth about the orb. "I'm lost."

The sound of her voice touched Joshua to his core. In an instant he was out of his chair and gathering her in his arms.

"Ailith, don't," he said, his voice hoarse with yearning. "You're *not* lost. You already know you live somewhere in Middlesbrough. We know that's in England. Dr. Griegs will help you remember exactly where in Middlesbrough you live."

"Oh, Joshua! Why won't you believe me?" Ailith implored. "I am a maiden from *1413 Middlesbrough*. Somehow the orb brought me to your time. And to you," she added softly.

Joshua held her closer, yet looked down at her with misgivings. Dispiriting thoughts warred with and invaded his senses. No! She didn't say what he thought he heard her say, what she'd insisted upon all along. He couldn't bear to think, let alone imagine, Ailith being born into such a cruel era.

The thought jolted him. Had he decided to accept her story? He couldn't honestly answer that at the moment because he hadn't given it much thought over the past weeks. His most important agenda had been keeping his sanity during the long nights next to Ailith, though he crawled into bed hours after her to make sure she had fallen asleep.

He had resolved to keep his distance from her, yet in the daytime he couldn't get enough of her company, even if it had been shared with Stephen most of the time. But Stephen's presence had been necessary, Joshua insisted to himself.

A disapproving voice questioned him, what for? Why was it necessary to have Stephen with them? Certainly not for Mellie. He hadn't been intimate with Melissa in nearly two months—long before Ailith's appearance—and he was beginning to wonder if they still *had* a relationship.

Was it for Ailith's well-being? Was it because she seemed so ignorant of everyday, ordinary things? And what if she really was from the fifteenth century? If given a choice, would she stay with him or would she return to her own time?

He looked at her and found her regarding him with misty eyes. When, he wondered, had she lost the future and began reaching back for the past? And why? If she had an affinity for the past, why couldn't it have been a more civilized era? But he knew she hadn't had any choice in the era she had been born into. And if she was telling the truth, apparently she hadn't had a choice in the era she had been jettisoned into.

He glanced at her lips, moist and slightly trembling, inviting his kiss. As he lowered his mouth to hers, an irrelevant thought fleeted through his brain. Despite his disdain for the barbarianism of the Middle Ages, *he* was president *and* founder of a medievalist club.

The contact of her quivering lips burned his own with a sweet fire and shut down all thought. His heart pounding, he deepened the kiss and explored further, teasing, grazing her tongue with his.

Ailith stood on tiptoe, straining against Joshua's muscular frame, knowing if she were successful with her plans to leave, this would be the last kiss she would ever share with Joshua.

Strange feelings ripped through her being. This, *this* was what she wanted from him along with all of the kindness he'd already shown her. And if only she knew her parents were safe, if only there were no Melissa, she would gladly stay with Joshua forever if he asked.

Joshua skimmed his mouth over her face, lavishing kisses on her cheeks, her eyes. He blew in her ear, then nibbled at the lobe. He slid his tongue over her throat before finding her lips again. Tremors of excitement surged through her body, and she shuddered with powerful need.

"Ailith," Joshua croaked, reluctantly pulling his mouth away from hers. His body burned, and his loins ached. She swayed in his arms, and he held her tight, steadying her, as shaken as she appeared to be by their kiss. For a long moment he gazed into her emerald eyes, caressing her back and shoulders in silence, before releasing her. They stood facing each other, electricity crackling between them, the web of desire that he had spun dangerously weakening his resolve.

"Ailith," he said finally. "Please forgive me. I-I don't want to take advantage of you simply because we share this bedroom in secret."

She remained silent for a second, staring at him with an unfathomable expression on her face. "But you won't—"

"I'm not so sure," Joshua interrupted. He rubbed his hand over his eyes, then thrust it through his hair. "I'm very much attracted to you. So much so that I can barely lie next to you without becoming aroused." He snorted. "I've taken enough cold showers during the past weeks to attest to that."

"I see." Ailith walked to the window, glimpsed out, then turned back to him. "I understand," she told him, her voice toneless. "After all, there is Melissa."

Joshua laughed, low and harsh. "Melissa and I are hardly on speaking terms at the moment," he replied.

Alertness replaced Ailith's unreadable expression. "Oh," she murmured. "Then you must really be looking forward to your dinner tonight."

Grinning at the sarcasm in her tone, Joshua shook his head. "Perhaps watching the soaps has its points after all," he said.

Ailith eyed him suspiciously, and her still-swollen lips reminded him of the almost uncontrollable passion that had flared between them minutes ago.

"What do you mean?"

"The soaps have taught you how to respond sarcastically," Joshua observed, "but appropriately."

The way Joshua was smiling at her nearly stole her breath away and her irritation fled. She returned his smile.

"Actually," she began, "my lessons came from Loquisha and Shawanda. I marvel at what they get away with saying to you and Connor."

Joshua's grin widened. "Loquisha and Shawanda are two of a kind and cut from the same cloth. Although they can be quite annoying sometimes with their sarcasm, they can also be quite right with their grievances. Besides, I like them. But," he continued in a more sobering tone, "getting back to us . . . I've always considered myself a man possessed of the highest integrity *and* respect where women are concerned."

He sighed, and undisguised heat turned his eyes to liquid gold, making her knees weak.

"Ailith, I want you, yes. I know there's lust there. I am only a man, after all. But my feelings for you go beyond mere lust," he confessed.

Her heart soared at the knowledge. God! The longer she stayed in Joshua's presence, the more difficult her decision to leave became.

"And for that reason I won't allow my feelings to cloud my judgment," Joshua continued. "There's a lot that has to be sorted out about you. Until I get some satisfactory answers, there will be no more weak moments between us." He abruptly turned and went toward the bathroom. "For the record, Ailith, Melissa has nothing to do with the way I feel about you." He stepped inside the bathroom and closed the door.

Returning to the bed and sitting back against the headboard, Ailith pondered Joshua's last remarks. *Melissa has nothing to do with the way I feel about you.*

How was she supposed to know how to interpret that?

She snatched up the remote and flicked on the television again. Another soap had replaced her favorite one. Only slightly disappointed at having missed the *Days* ending, she looked abstractly at the images on the screen.

What did Joshua mean? How *did* Joshua feel about her? Did his intentions toward her match Preston Claybourne's

intentions toward her? Did Joshua have in mind to make
her his leman and Melissa his wife?

Just as she hadn't wanted to be second in her liege's life,
she didn't want to be second in Joshua's life. Suddenly she
wondered what *her* feelings were toward Joshua. Why
would she even contemplate giving everything up for
Joshua? Only a few short weeks ago her emotions had been
in an upheaval over Lord Preston's kiss. Was she a wanton
who deserved no better than what she was getting? Was
Lord Preston a mere girlhood love, or was Joshua a substitute for her liege?

Guilt immediately washed through her. How could she
even think to compare her magnificent, gentle Joshua to the
arrogant, overbearing Preston? The two men were nothing
alike.

It seemed in Joshua's time, unlike her own, women *did*
have a say in choosing their own destiny. She would never
be first in Joshua's life, so she would choose to be out of
it completely.

Whatever the true extent of her feelings for Joshua, she
couldn't recall feeling the unbearable jealousy toward Lady
Glenna that she did for Melissa.

She sighed just as Joshua came out of the bathroom
wearing a bathrobe with a towel draped around his neck.
Turning off the television once again, she gave him a shy
smile, his sudden presence embarrassing her in the wake of
her confusing thoughts.

Joshua smiled back at her. "Soaps over?"

"Yes," Ailith answered without elaborating.

Joshua came toward her. "Well, since you'll be up here
alone tonight, would you like me to rent a couple of movies
for you?"

Watch movies without Joshua?

Ailith recalled the enjoyment she felt on the couple of
occasions he had rented movies for them to watch in the
early evenings. And how the magic of the microwave oven
popped popcorn for them in two and a half minutes. Even

if she was staying there to watch it, she did *not* want a bloody movie!

"Thank you, no," Ailith answered, her tone aloof. "There's always something interesting on cable to watch."

Feeling a frown contorting his face, Joshua stared at her. The confusion he felt over her annoyed him almost to distraction. And now . . . ? Did he detect a note of *coolness* in her tone? How dare she have the nerve to be cool toward him. After all, he had shone her nothing but kindness, hadn't he? Even after she'd tried to convince him to believe that cockamamie story she'd concocted, he'd helped her.

He gave her a frozen smile, but tempered his simmering rage. When he spoke, his voice was as restrained as hers. "All right. Perhaps I can get you some magazines," he offered. "Maybe you'd like something to read if you're bored watching TV?"

Ailith threw him a look scathing enough to burn him to cinders.

"Did I say something wrong, Ailith?" Joshua asked with ire, not liking her censorious look.

Ailith didn't answer Joshua right away. She barely understood the images in some of the magazines, let alone the words there. In her time she considered herself quite an educated maiden, and perhaps there she was. But unfortunately in Joshua's time, she was no better than a lackwit.

She got off the bed and walked to the window. She watched the falling rain a few seconds and abruptly realized Joshua didn't know she couldn't read the words of his time with complete comprehension.

"No, Joshua, you said nothing wrong." With a sigh she turned to gaze at him. "I did not mean to sound cross. I . . ."

She stopped, swallowing back the despair that threatened to choke her with heartsickening oppression.

At the pained look on Ailith's lovely countenance, Joshua's anger dissolved. Walking to where she stood, he lifted her chin with his hand. The mask of sadness on her face made his heart twist. He drew her into his arms and pressed her head against his chest with one hand, caressing her around the waist and back with the other.

"I can't stand seeing you so unhappy, Ailith," he said in a husky voice. "I didn't mean to hurt your feelings. I'm sorry."

She felt so right in his arms. He desperately wanted to have sex—

No! Sex was for casual acquaintances. Brief encounters. Just having sex with Ailith would never do. He wanted to make love to her—slow, passionate, ultra-sweet love. He wanted her to belong to him.

Ailith slipped her slender arms around his waist, and his control nearly shattered. Yet he dare not kiss her again. Amnesiac, con artist, medieval time traveler, or whatever she was, he wouldn't be able to control his desire for her if he tasted her sweetness again. His loins sprang to life. To discipline his raging passion, he needed to push her away and get out of there.

But he continued to hold her close to him, steeling himself against his roiling emotions. He sensed that *her* emotional state was too fragile for him to abandon her so abruptly, so he held her. Without saying a word, he knew he was giving her a measure of comfort.

She was an enigma to him, a fascinating puzzle, but with Dr. Griegs's help, maybe they would find out who she was. And if, after fitting all the pieces together, Joshua found she wasn't married . . .

His thoughts skidded to a halt. He would not think beyond the present moment. He wrapped his arms fully around her.

"I don't want to force you to do anything you don't want to do, Ailith," he said gently. "I won't let anyone in here, so feel free to do whatever you want to."

Ailith raised her head and gazed into sober golden eyes. Her heart lurched. She wanted that worried look to be in consideration for her feelings, for her well-being, not for his own peace of mind.

Pushing herself out of his strong arms, she smiled tremulously. "I'll be all right," she lied. She would never be all right again. Not without Joshua. "Television is new to me, Joshua. In truth, I find it quite interesting."

She wished he would believe that her ascension to his time had made everything new to her, but he didn't want to believe that. He was more comfortable believing she suffered from amnesia.

Joshua regretted the loss of Ailith's softness in his arms. He regretted also that she still appeared so emotionally confused. "Television can be interesting sometimes," he agreed, "but it depends on what's on." He walked away from her to go to his closet. After a while he came out clad in dark blue trousers and minus the bathrobe and towel.

"I'll come back up here as soon as time permits. In the meantime, before anyone gets here, I'll have Connor bring you a tray of food from tonight's menu," he said as he continued to dress.

"I'd like that."

Ailith brightened at the prospect of some culinary delight. It would be prudent to leave on a full stomach, and she'd decided days ago what she liked best about Joshua's time was the food. Well, she amended, food was up there with everything else.

Knowing Joshua was going to lock her in when he left, an idea struck her. "Might I have a bottle of champagne, too?"

During the next hours, she would think of a way to convince Joshua to let her listen in on the dinner party. But, instead of sitting on the landing as she would tell Joshua she was going to do, she was going to leave.

Proceeding to knot his tie, Joshua said with a laugh, "You most certainly may have some champagne." He unknotted, then redid the tie to his satisfaction. "There's some chilling in the refrigerator as we speak. I'll have Connor put a bottle in a champagne bucket and bring it up with your food tray."

"H-how will I open it?" Ailith wondered if her plans

were already going awry. "I guess Connor can do it," she mumbled dejectedly.

"I'll come up personally and open it for you," Joshua assured her. He slipped on his suit coat. "My parents are out at the moment, Ailith. Connor is here, and so are Shawanda and Loquisha."

"But *you're* leaving," Ailith observed.

Drawing in a breath, Joshua threaded his hand through his hair. "Yes. I have to," he explained. "I have two important meetings to attend. I'm sorry, but my presence at both of them is a necessity."

Ailith nodded and smiled bravely. "I understand," she responded in a small voice.

"I'll probably have Melissa and Emily with me when I return."

"Of course."

He held her gaze to his own until the wounded look he saw there forced him to look away. How could he explain his relationship with Melissa? When had he decided anyone, Ailith included, deserved an explanation for his actions?

"I'll come up to open the champagne as soon as I can after I get back home."

"Thank you."

Her solicitude suddenly infuriating, Joshua forced a smile. "I'll see you later, Ailith."

He contemplated her for a moment before exiting the room and locking her in.

Chapter 16

DESPITE THE WEIGHT of despair caused by her impending departure, Ailith thoroughly enjoyed her meal of veal and oyster sauce, shrimp dijon, warm three-pepper salad and brabant potatoes. The strawberries and chocolate mousse dessert would have made her simply ecstatic on an ordinary occasion. Tonight it was merely sustenance to get her through the coming hours.

After eating, she bathed and stretched out on the bed in her pj's. The closer it came for her to leave, the more uncertain she became. Indeed, she hadn't even thought of where she would go. She didn't know how to barter for goods or what currency notes to use to pay for them. Not that she even had any coin.

The key turned in the lock, and she sat up in bed as Joshua opened the door and stepped inside the room.

Raising a finger to his lips in a gesture for her to remain quiet, he relocked the door.

Ailith jumped off the bed and went to stand before him, ignoring the quickening of her blood caused by Joshua's magnetic presence.

"Were you followed up here?" she whispered conspiratorially.

Joshua laughed softly, sensing Ailith's enjoyment of the cat-and-mouse game they played against the rest of the household. "Not at the moment," he whispered back to her. "But I can't be sure that someone won't come up." He looked around in puzzlement, cursing under his breath at her devastating appeal. "Where's the champagne?"

"In the bathroom on the counter," Ailith answered.

He wondered at her glum-faced expression, but decided not to comment. Hoping to alleviate her pensiveness, he gave her a silly smile and raised his eyebrows up and down. "So!" he teased. "Ve vill toast in zee bassroom. Vot iss zee significanze of zat?"

Ailith bowed her head, but not before he was sure he'd caught a glimmer of tears in her eyes. Just as he would have comforted her, she raised her gaze—dry now—to his and gave him a cheerful smile. The change occurred so quickly he wondered if he had imagined her sadness.

"Ask Connor about the champagne," she said. "He put it in the bathroom."

Joshua nodded, noting Ailith's intense survey of him. "Maybe I will."

As he walked to the bathroom with Ailith right behind him, he wondered how he would leave her to rejoin his dinner party.

With a sigh he lifted the bottle out of the bucket and gave it a vigorous shake. "Watch this."

He pushed up on the cork, exerting pressure with his thumb, and it shot out with a loud "pop." Champagne spewed from the bottle. Quickly he reached for a glass to catch the bubbly wine, and Ailith's squeal of delight warmed him.

Filling their glasses, he momentarily held her gaze with his own. Then he smiled and raised his glass. "To your health, Ailith," he croaked.

"Likewise," Ailith returned softly.

Joshua drained his glass in two quick gulps. "I'd better get back down," he said with regret, "before someone comes looking for me. Will you be all right?"

"O-of course," Ailith answered, disappointed he was leaving her so soon.

She wanted him to stay with her; she wanted him to say he believed her and that he needed her. But, of course, he would do none of those things. He had Melissa.

Joshua stared at her a moment. "I'll see you later," he said, walking out of the bathroom. Going to the door, he placed his hand on the knob.

"Joshua!" Ailith called, remembering she needed to have the door unlocked.

Not opening the door, he turned and regarded her curiously. "Yes, Ailith?"

"Um . . . m-may I join the party?"

His questioning look deepened. "I'm afraid that's impossible," he answered. "You know the reasons."

That hadn't been what she wanted to say. "I-I d-don't mean *really* join you," she explained nervously. "If you left the door open, I could walk very quietly to the stairs and sit on the upper step and *listen* to the party. . . ."

Joshua remained silent for long moments. "I'm sorry," he said finally. "But I can't allow that. Someone might discover you."

"Oh, no, Joshua, I'll be as quiet as I was the last time," she promised, wondering if he detected the near desperation in her tone.

Narrowing his eyes, he asked, "What last time?"

"Well . . . um . . . the first night your parents got here."

Joshua's glare urged her to explain.

"That's how I got to 'meet' everyone. I familiarized myself with the sound of their voices."

"You nervy little sneak," Joshua said with a tinge of amusement. "Maybe I should pay a little more attention to what goes on inside my house. You've really made yourself at home."

"And I do appreciate your hospitality, Joshua Kenley," she whispered, her warring emotions wreaking havoc on her already faltering resolve. She scrutinized him a second time, wanting to imprint his handsome features in her mind.

"So," she said, in control once again. "Do I have your permission?"

Joshua pondered her question momentarily. "It's against my better judgement, Ailith, but yes. You do have my permission to spy on me and my guests this evening."

Ailith suddenly wished he had said no and left her, locking her inside the room. But she smiled and said, "Thank you, Joshua. I promise I'll be as quiet as possible."

"Fine. Still I need your promise that you'll be careful enough not to get found out. I shudder to think what chaos would ensue if you are. Besides, I am getting used to having you all to myself."

He gave her a killer smile and opened the door. After peeking out and discovering no one about, he exited the room, leaving the door unlocked and Ailith's fate in her own hands.

Chapter 17

"JOSHUA, AS USUAL, you're the exemplary host and perfect gentleman."

Emily's accented voice grated on Joshua's already frayed nerves. He wanted this night over with and Melissa and her entourage gone. He hoped he'd made the right decision in giving Ailith permission to come out of their bedroom. But he sensed Ailith needed him in some way, and he wanted nothing more than to go to her and discuss what was bothering her. Besides, he much preferred her company to that of his guests.

Everyone had moved from the dining room to the living room, and now they lounged around in various seats, sipping various drinks.

"I do feel I must reciprocate."

Emily was still dominating the conversation, as she had the entire miserable evening.

Thrusting his fingers through his hair, Joshua gave her a blank look.

"I must reciprocate your hospitality," Emily clarified. "I would like to host a breakfast for you."

Joshua gave her a little laugh. "Your sense of propriety is commendable, Emily," he said, barely civilized, "but a breakfast really isn't necessary."

"Joshua! What in the name of God has come over you?" Melissa asked sharply. "You can't refuse Emily. That would be the pinnacle of rudeness."

He glanced at Melissa narrowly. Ignoring her chastisement, he searched his mind for any feelings beyond friendship that he had for her. He found he had no great desire there. The realization that he'd never actually had any struck him, and he wondered why he'd dated her for as long as he had.

Certainly her beauty had drawn him. But was he really that shallow? After all the times he'd accused Stephen of such juvenile behavior, was he no better?

The answer lay in the woman herself. Melissa was shallow, drawn to him because of his money and distinguished name, not because she held any great passion for him.

"Joshua!"

Melissa's voice broke into his musings.

"Are you even listening to us?"

He contemplated her willowy body. Childbearing, he knew, was distasteful to her because she didn't want to ruin her figure, nor did she want the responsibility. But when he'd assured her that he would hire a personal trainer for her if she wanted one and a nanny for any baby she bore him after they were married, she had snapped her consent and demanded the subject be changed.

He realized not only that he didn't love her, but that also he had begun to question whether he really *liked* her. And why had he even considered marrying someone whose views on matrimony and parenthood didn't match his own?

His mother's voice finally brought his full attention back to the conversation.

"I think a typical English breakfast sounds scrumptious. Do count me in, Emily."

Joshua glared at his mother. "I hardly ever have time for breakfast, Mother. I think I discussed this matter with you once before. Mornings at the galleries are my busiest time." He turned his regard to Emily. "I do appreciate the offer, but I'm afraid I'll have to decline."

"Oh, Joshua, don't be such a killjoy," Melissa admonished in exasperation. "Surely you have enough competent help to take over for a few hours while you have a break."

"Which, in my opinion, he very badly needs," Frances put in. "He has been awfully busy of late. He hasn't even had time to socialize with his father and me."

Melissa threw his mother a tight smile.

"Well, we do feel for you, Frances," she intoned.

"Leave the boy alone, Frances," his father piped up. "If he's busy, he's busy. Men sometimes have more to do than sit around at teatime, dangling our pinky in the air."

Stephen laughed. "Now, Jonathan, watch your language. We men are outnumbered here by one. You could get us all labeled as sexist pigs."

Myra scowled at Stephen, giving her fat face a troll-like appearance. Her wide eyes narrowed to mere slits, and her short-cut, curly, almost frizzy hair seemed to stand on end.

"Well, does that mean you'll come to breakfast?" she asked, challenge in her tone.

Stephen shrugged. "Don't know. What does a typical English breakfast consist of?" He turned a brittle smile to Emily. "English muffins? Fish? Or is it kippers?"

"All those things," Melissa huffed. "Em and I will do it on Saturday. Then Joshua will be able to attend." She threw Joshua a smug look. "His workload is light on weekends."

"Count me out," Stephen said.

"Why?" Emily asked.

"Because in America we don't eat Moby Dick for breakfast," Stephen replied.

"Right," Myra scoffed. "But we eat Miss Piggy. All that bacon, ham, and pork sausage to clog the arteries. At least fish is healthier. I think you owe Emily an apology, cretin!"

Though Stephen shot Myra a venomous stare, Frances's urgent tone stopped him from replying.

"Oh, dear! Oh, dear!" Frances chimed.

Joshua knew she was attempting to defuel a potentially ugly situation.

"I'm sure Stephen was only joking, Myra. There's no need to take offense, dear."

Not in the mood to placate Melissa and her friends, Joshua said, "Don't mind Myra, Stephen. She's the way she is because she has nothing of interest to occupy her time. You really can't fault her."

Stephen glared at Myra. "You're wrong, Josh," he snarled. "She's a pushy, meddling, little troll and badly in need of a life!"

Melissa and Emily gasped in indignation.

Surprised laughter escaped Joshua, although on many occasions he'd described her in almost the exact terms.

"Stephen!" Frances declared in horror.

"You bastard," Myra chirped.

"Of course, I mean no harm," Stephen continued, his voice inflected with cordiality and mockery. "Just as I'm sure you were merely joking when you deemed me a cretin."

Myra had the good grace to blush.

"Some of us are quick-witted enough to get to the point every time." Stephen grinned satanically. "While others remain virgins, never lucky enough to get the point at all."

With a murderous glare in Joshua's direction, Melissa stood and stormed from the room, going into the entrance hall and stopping at the foot of the stairs.

"Joshua!" she yelled in a savage tone. "I would like very much to speak to you in private!"

Just then, she glanced up.

Frozen in her spot since Melissa had appeared in the hall without warning, Ailith gasped now.

Melissa's shrill scream echoed through the house. The grating sound mobilized Ailith into action. Not waiting to see if Melissa's scream brought the entire bunch into the hall, she scooted up the few steps she had climbed down.

Emily's voice, definitely different from the others with the same accented sounds as her own, had halted her journey to the laundry room when Ailith had heard it, and she'd realized immediately that the owner was Emily from London. She'd vaguely wondered what London was like in this day and age. Although she'd never been to London in her own time, she knew it was in her home country of England. Were there similarities between America the United States and England?

Ailith damned the curiosity that had made her stay and listen for Joshua's answer to Emily's invitation to breakfast as well as the ensuing argument that had kept her rooted to her spot.

She didn't stop running until she reached the service steps. Hurrying down them, she rushed toward the laundry room to retrieve her jeans and go out into Joshua's world.

In moments not only did Joshua and the rest of the dinner guests surround Melissa, but so did the three servants, who had been busy in the kitchen.

"What in the world is the matter with you?" Joshua asked, trying to keep his worst fear in check.

Did she see Ailith?

"I-I . . ." Anger vibrated Melissa's entire body. "You bastard!" she hissed. "There was a woman on the stairs. What is she doing here, Joshua?"

"Was she a little blond strumpet, Mellie?" Myra squealed at the top of her lungs.

"Yes!" Melissa shrieked. "Wearing something that looked like a silk bathrobe. Who is she, Joshua?"

"Melissa, dear, you must be mistaken," Frances drawled. "I've been here for nearly a month and I can assure you the only females in this house are myself and, during the day, Joshua's two housekeepers. I don't know what you saw, but it certainly wasn't another woman."

Joshua flashed his mother a grateful look and noticed a flicker of uncertainty in Melissa's eyes. He glared at Myra, vowing if she opened her vicious little mouth again, he'd feed her small, stout ass to the sharks at the aquarium.

This is not the way he wanted things to end between him

and Mellie. Their relationship was over, but she deserved some measure of respect.

Melissa looked at Joshua, waiting for an explanation, but he remained silent.

"I know what I saw, Mrs. Kenley," she finally insisted. "There was a girl on the stairs."

Connor stepped forward, his eyes wide. "You saw it, too?"

"There," Melissa said triumphantly. "You see? I never make mistakes. Connor saw her, too!"

Joshua and Stephen exchanged incredulous glances. To think Joshua trusted his butler, who was about to give his secret away.

Connor smiled. "Now do you believe me, Mr. J.? Just because you've never seen the apparition doesn't mean it doesn't exist."

"Wait a minute!" Loquisha exclaimed. "Apparition? Like in ghost?"

Connor nodded. "Yeah, but she's harmless. Sometimes she doesn't appear for weeks."

Loquisha turned on her heels, heading toward the kitchen. "Bye!" she said over her shoulder.

"Girl, hold on a minute," Shawanda urged. "Loquisha, come back here!"

"You pigs stick together," Myra huffed to Connor, then, softening her glare, turned her attention to Melissa. "There are no ghosts here, Mellie. I'll just bet it's the same woman I saw Joshua with at the fair!"

Melissa glanced contemptuously at Joshua. "I demand to go up to your bedroom," she sneered.

"Not in front of his parents, Melissa," Stephen jibed. "Try to have the decency to keep your amorous intentions in check."

"Oh, I *do* despise you," Melissa hissed.

"Come on, Melissa." Joshua roughly grabbed her arm and started up the stairs. "Be my guest!" he growled.

Anger and exasperation taking hold of him, he no longer gave a damn about sparing Melissa's feelings. Indeed, as he headed toward his bedroom, the weight caused by his subterfuge lifted.

His main concern now was for Ailith. What would this commotion do to her already fragile mental condition? Would yet another personality emerge? Whatever the results, he vowed to see her through it.

With everyone following and still holding on to Melissa's arm, he reached the upstairs hall. "Shall I aid you in your search, or can you do it alone?" he taunted resentfully.

"I'll help you, Mel!" Myra volunteered.

"You'll keep your instigating little gnome ass right where you are, Myra!" Joshua told her in a calm but deadly voice. "This is Melissa's show, and she has my permission to search every room up here."

"I sure hope she finds a live body, Mr. J.," Shawanda snapped. " 'Cause if she don't, we'll never get Loquisha back here."

Joshua frowned at Shawanda, but didn't answer, watching as Connor gently pulled her behind him.

When Melissa began her search, there was a glimmer of doubt on her face. Having taken note of Joshua's scowls and testy tones, no one said anything more. Even his mother hesitated to speak at that juncture. She knew him. It was prudent to remain silent.

Looking in his room first, Joshua knew Melissa must have been nearly blinded by anger because she didn't notice the cleverly disguised feminine clothes hanging in his closet.

His consternation increased, however, while she searched the five bedrooms with a fine tooth comb and didn't discover Ailith. When they returned to the hallway, the pounding in Joshua's head threatened to blow off the top.

Where is she? Why did I consent to let her sit on the staircase?

Melissa's apologetic voice vaguely penetrated his brain.

"Oh, Joshua! How could I have made such a fool of

myself? I'm so embarrassed for my shrewish outburst."
She laid her hand on his arm.

"So what else is new, Melissa?" Joshua snapped. Ailith
had to be somewhere in this house. He had to find her.

"I don't blame you for being angry, darling," Melissa
cooed.

She seemed unaffected when he moved her hand away.

"And I apologize. Maybe I-I just *thought* I saw someone.
I-I'm a little reluctant to concede that Connor was right
about ghosts. I don't believe in ghosts."

"Well, I don't think the ghost cares whether you believe
or not," Connor rebutted, starting down the stairs, dragging
Shawanda with him. "It's probably quite contented with
your reaction to its discovery. Um . . . *her* discovery."
Reaching the bottom step, he released Shawanda's hand.
Looking up, he called, "Mr. J., shall I serve the liqueurs
now?"

"No, Connor." Joshua walked down the stairs, his entourage hot on his heels. "At the risk of losing my rating
as an exemplary host, I think any attempt to save this evening would be ludicrous."

"I'm inclined to agree with you, son," Jonathan said,
looking somewhat relieved. "Who's up for a romp through
the French Quarter?"

"I vote we go to a club," Myra suggested. "Maybe in
the Warehouse District."

Mellie turned her humbled expression to Joshua. "Darling, Em and I would love to go. Please join us."

Joshua ignored Melissa, stopping short of throwing
everyone out to find Ailith. "Mother?"

"Fine, dear," Frances replied. "We're easy. We'll just
join the rest of the crowd."

"Good. Have fun," Joshua said. "I'm going to sit this
one out." He directed his glance to Emily. "Emily, as
usual, it's been . . . an experience seeing you again." He
turned to Stephen. "I need to discuss something with you."

"Certainly" came the quick reply.

Joshua saw the worry he felt for Ailith reflected in his

friend's eyes. He began climbing the stairs. Without turning, he said, "Tell Connor to get up here, will you?"

Aware that everyone there knew just how far to push him and knowing they realized he'd reached his limit, his abrupt departure finally ended the evening.

He entered his bedroom, going straight to the bed, though Melissa had already looked under it. "Ailith, are you there?" he called. No answer came. Still, he stooped to look under the bed. Nothing. He straightened himself.

He knew she wasn't in the closet. He'd made that discovery along with Melissa. But he walked to it anyway and searched inside. She wasn't in there, though her clothes remained hidden under his own on the hangers.

Joshua yanked off the top to the shoe box where she'd placed her orb. It remained there . . . glowing dimly. He probed it for a place to put batteries. He found none.

He shook it, as he'd seen Ailith do the first day she'd arrived. He brought it to his ear and listened for . . . for— he wasn't sure what.

After exhausting all other possibilities that ran through his mind, he could settle on only one conclusion. Ailith had been telling him the truth.

"Shit!"

Had she left him and gone back to 1413 Middlesbrough?

"No!" he cried, dropping the thing back into the box and hurrying out of the closet. "She's in this house."

If she had left, the orb would have gone with her.

Stephen and Connor rushed into the room.

"Josh, she isn't in here," Stephen informed him.

"I can see that, Stephen," came the harsh reply.

"No, Mr. J.," Connor added with worry. "Not just *this room*. She isn't in the house!"

"What are you? Supermen? You haven't had time to search this entire house."

"Josh, while we were busy arguing her existence with Melissa, Ailith must have sneaked down the back stairs," Stephen explained.

"H-how do you know?"

Chapter 18

AILITH LEANED AGAINST the building, lifted one slippered foot off the ground, and winced. Her feet hurt. How far had she walked? More to the point, where was she?

While everyone had been busy with the commotion up front, after Melissa's scream, Ailith had sneaked down the service steps and finally went to the laundry room. Connor had been too busy preparing for the dinner party to bring her laundered jeans upstairs. After exchanging clothes, she'd realized she hadn't brought her sneakers down with her—she had intended to go upstairs and change—but she'd shrugged and crept from the room. On her way out she'd almost run into Loquisha and had to duck behind the island in the kitchen, hoping that wasn't Loquisha's destination. It hadn't been—the back door had. Soon Ailith had heard a car speeding away.

Afterward she'd noiselessly opened the same door Loquisha had exited, stepped into the warm night air, and began running. When she'd put a safe distance between herself and the manor, she'd slowed down. Breathing rapidly, she walked then, without looking back. When she finally did stop, she found herself on a practically deserted but sufficiently lighted street and spied the building on which she was now leaning.

Turning to face the window of the building, she saw a puppy on display, asleep in a cage. Not having seen any other breed of dog except the deerhounds of Greyhawke Keep, she wondered what kind this one was. It looked like a little ball of white fur. The thought brought a smile to her lips, and she tapped on the glass. When the puppy raised its head slowly and stretched lazily, her smile widened. Ailith tapped louder, and the puppy became alert as it fully awakened and began wagging its tail happily. She laughed aloud.

"What a beautiful creature you are," she murmured. "I wish Joshua could see you. I know he'd like you as much as I do."

Joshua. She missed him already. Seeing the puppy brought to mind how much she liked experiencing new things with Joshua. What dreadful mistake had she made in leaving? This had to be done, she chastised herself, determined not to have any regrets.

She paused abruptly and surveyed her surroundings. Many shops lined both sides of the streets, though most of them seemed to be bolted for the night, but not all. There was a shop, or perhaps it was a tavern, where people came and went. She studied the goings-on for a few minutes. No one came out carrying any purchases. At one point two men staggered out, one leaning on the other for support.

Yes, it was definitely a tavern.

Grinning at the spectacle, Ailith walked away from the window and the adorable puppy, who was still wiggling and wagging its tail. She glanced back. "I must leave you now, little one. Mayhap . . . Perhaps Joshua will get to see you one day."

Without surveying for oncoming cars, Ailith stepped off the curb and into the street. She couldn't say which frightened her more, the screeching sound of the tires as the car slid to a halt just a few feet from her or the loud honking of the horn. Fear nearly stealing her breath away and eyes widening, she froze and covered her ears with her hands. The glare of the bright light on the car's front momentarily blinded her.

A man jumped out of the car. "What the hell's wrong with you, miss, walking in front of a moving automobile? Are you drunk or something? You scared the living shit out of me! Go ahead and cross and get the hell *out* of the street!"

The angry driver finally got back into his car and slammed the door.

Feeling his eyes boring into her, Ailith forced herself forward, reaching the safety of the median on shaky legs. Once again she heard the screech of tires when the car whizzed passed her, the wheels spinning at high speed.

Taking huge gulps of air to calm herself, she wondered what she was doing out here all alone. If she didn't have the foresight to be frightened before leaving Kenley Manor, she was certainly frightened now.

Anger at herself for foolishly venturing so far from the manor and Joshua surfaced. How could she survive in his world without his protection? But how could she go back there, even if she knew the way back?

She did *not* want to be the cause of trouble between Joshua and Melissa *or* his mother, for that matter. Melissa was his . . . his love, which was the reason Ailith had left. That, and because the thought of Joshua loving Melissa cut Ailith to the core.

Melissa was at his side tonight, however, and regardless of how much time Ailith and Joshua spent together, they did so from necessity, not choice. And they did it in secret.

Frances trusted Joshua to respect her request of not having women in his bedroom while she visited. Melissa trusted him not to betray their relationship. He hadn't, Ailith reminded herself, but would Melissa believe that?

Ailith still felt she needed to protect Joshua from her presence at Kenley Manor, but she knew no one outside of his home besides Stephen and she didn't know where he resided. That meant she had no other place to go but back to Kenley Manor.

She couldn't believe she had contemplated leaving him without his knowledge and a plan of survival. Surely when she explained her decision, he would find her some other place to stay. If she could find her way back to the manor, she knew Connor would hide her until it was safe to sneak back into Joshua's bedroom once again. She needed to get home. Home.

"Joshua's home," she said aloud, somewhat calmer. It sounded so right. She would try to retrace her steps . . .

"Are you all right?"

Ailith looked up into the face of a very handsome man, whose skin was a tawny brown like Shawanda's. He must be of African descent, she thought irrelevantly. During the times she had gone out, she'd seen many African-Americans and had marveled at their diverse complexions.

"Miss?" the man questioned, a frown crossing his face.

Ailith nodded.

"Are you hurt, lady? Lost?" came the next questions.

Wondering if she could trust him, Ailith stared.

"Are you ill?"

"Ill?" Ailith shook her head. "Nay . . . No!"

The stranger narrowed his eyes. "Nay? You're not from here, are you? Are you French? But who says 'nay' in France? Or in any language?"

She regarded him blankly. She'd said nay again. She could only attribute that to shaky nerves.

"Look, miss," he said, "I'd like to help you, but I don't know how. You obviously don't understand English. Come with me. I'll find a telephone and call the police."

He reached his hand out to her.

Wondering if she should trust him, she hesitated a moment, then turned and fled. Running without thought to her well-being, pure luck brought her safely across the street to the other side. Out of harm's way of oncoming traffic, she heard the man calling after her to wait, he wasn't going to hurt her. But she couldn't be sure of that, so she ran farther away from him, as fast as her legs could carry her.

Finally stopping under a light on a corner, she rested against a narrow post, gasping for breath. Thoroughly confused now as to her whereabouts, she remained quiet for a moment until her breathing returned to normal. Leaning back, she heard a loud snarl.

Oh, God! What now?

Close to tears, she raised her head to see a huge dog, one the size of a small pony, baring its teeth at her. A cold knot formed in her stomach, and her blood tingled with fear. Just as she opened her mouth to scream, sure that the monster was about to attack, a voice commanded the beast to return.

Snapping her mouth shut, Ailith felt tears sliding down her cheeks. Swiping at them angrily, she wondered what would happen next or what her next move should be.

She needed to reach Joshua but didn't know how to, and frustration at her inability to do so surfaced. Not realizing she stood at a bus stop, it surprised her when the vehicle pulled to a halt beside the curb. Hesitating for a moment, she boarded the bus and quickly sat down.

"The fare is one dollar and twenty-five cents, miss," the operator told her as he moved the bus forward. "Please put it in the fare machine."

Ailith stared at him through the rearview mirror, her eyes brimming with tears.

He glanced up and smiled at her.

"I'll just bet you haven't got the fare," he said kindly.

Ailith shook her head.

"That's okay, little lady. Who'll know you didn't pay? You're my only passenger."

His grin widened, and she returned it, contemplating the man's ebony color and thinking that he must have been an African-American also.

"I end my route at the lake, miss. Are you going that far?"

A light went off in her mind. Joshua lived by the lake! Relief spiraled through her.

"Cat got your tongue?" the man asked. "Well, I'm sorry, but I can't let you ride any farther than that for free."

"Oh! I-I'm sorry," Ailith said apologetically. "You've been very kind. Thank you."

"My pleasure."

For the rest of the ride, nothing more was said. It gave her a chance to realize that Joshua would have discovered her gone by now. If Melissa had had her way, he would have discovered it long ago. After all, Ailith had to have been away from the manor for hours. She hoped she hadn't caused Joshua any undue worry. Or was he worried at all? Maybe he was so concerned with placating Melissa and whatever her reaction had been to spotting Ailith, that he had hardly noticed Ailith's departure.

She sighed. She would discover the answer soon enough.

A little later the operator reached his destination and beckoned her off his bus.

"Thank you," she murmured once again.

"You're mighty welcome, miss," came the response. "Hurry and get to where you're going," he advised her when she started walking away from him. "It's after midnight and mighty dangerous for a lady alone."

She nodded, and the doors closed behind her as the driver started the bus forward once again. She watched as he made a U-turn at an intersection and headed back in the direction from which he'd just come.

She glanced around and found the scenery familiar thanks to Joshua's midnight strolls with her. Sure she was near his manor, she started walking.

All along Lakeshore Drive lights lined the street. Cars with silhouetted figures inside were parked here and there. People. She wasn't entirely alone, but she was hot and tired. Positive she was heading in the right direction, she moved faster.

Eyeing her surroundings, she was still unable to see the house because the levee was too high, and she needed to get over to the other side. Turning her path in that direction, she started climbing. Within a few minutes, she reached the top, breathing heavily and noticing too late that a man with long, dirty blond hair was up there.

"Hey, baby, you lost?" He stood a few feet from her, urinating. When he completed his task, he didn't bother to cover himself.

Even from where she'd frozen in her tracks, the stench of ale . . . beer and offending body odors reached her nostrils.

The man spat on the ground.

Ailith started off, running in the direction of the house, his evil laugh floating back to her.

"Come back here, bitch! I've got something for you!"

Hair flying wildly, she didn't look back and didn't dare stop. Heart hammering like a soldering bolt and tears streaking her eyes, she saw blue lights flashing in the near distance.

Without warning, her pursuer dived, grabbing her around her legs and knocking her off balance. Fighting with feet, legs, arms, and hands, she broke free, rolling down the embankment, and with all the breath she could manage, let out a bloodcurdling scream. She hit the concrete at the bottom of the levee, and blackness swirled over her as the wind was knocked out of her.

In his frantic effort to find Ailith, Joshua called the police. After he, Stephen, and Connor drove around, looking unsuccessfully for her, he felt there was no other choice. Convincing them she had amnesia and that she was wandering around alone, the cops responded to his call. But Joshua decided to scour the levee just once more. If he didn't have any luck this time, he would use his car again to search for her.

He spotted her when she first started running away from the man. Joshua had been too far away to help her, however.

When he saw the man knock her down, he couldn't believe the man would be so bold with the flashing lights of police units so near, and there had been no definition for the rage that swept through him. Always a fast runner, he jumped on the man before his dirty hands could touch Ailith again.

Determined not to let the would-be-rapist escape, Joshua held the slightly built man's scruffy neck in the crook of his arm. Wanting to check Ailith for injuries, he dragged the man to where she lay.

Reaching her and cursing furiously, he slammed her attacker as hard as he could against the pavement, putting one knee in his groin—his *exposed* groin. The pervert howled in pain. Turning to minister to Ailith, Joshua pressed harder and ignored the man's cries.

By now Stephen had arrived with four police officers. Wanting to beat the scum within an inch of his life, Joshua instead brought all his weight to bear on the knee that was pressed to the man's groin and thrust into the soft tissue with all the rage in him.

The attacker opened his mouth to scream, but no sound came out. His eyes rolled back, and he relaxed, sinking into oblivion.

Joshua moved away and turned his full attention to Ailith.

Ailith stirred and moaned.

"Ailith. Ailith, sweetheart, can you hear me?"

Joshua's worried voice came to her in a fog. It was Joshua, wasn't it?

"Ailith?"

The voice became clearer. *Joshua.* She fluttered her eyelashes, then opened her eyes.

"Joshua! Oh, Joshua!"

She struggled to sit, then clung to him, bursting into tears, reveling in the feel of him.

Joshua held on to her as tightly as he felt he could without crushing her bones. "Thank God I found you in time," he croaked. He caressed and rubbed her back and shoulders, then gently pushed her a little apart from him so he could look into her eyes. He knotted his face into a frown. "Are you all right?"

"Y-yes, I th-think so. I just had the wind knocked out of me. I was so frightened."

"Why the hell did you go out all alone, Ailith?"

Joshua's eyes glowed golden, reflecting his agitation at her foolery.

"I-I am an intruder here, Joshua," she whispered, miserable and exhausted. "I do not want to come between you and Melissa."

"Josh," Stephen interrupted. "The cops have arrested the scumbag. They need a brief statement from you two."

"Thanks, Stephen." Joshua turned to Ailith, filled with worry and emotion. "This won't take long."

It didn't. A burly policeman, his light blue shirt and dark blue trousers crisp and tidy, quickly scribbled Ailith and Joshua's stories on the paper in his clipboard. "If we need anything more from you we'll be in touch." With that he hurried back to the cruiser and got in on the passenger side. Minutes later, the car sped away.

Stephen looked at Joshua. "Is she all right?"

"I hope so."

"Can she walk?"

"Can you, Ailith?" Joshua asked with concern.

"I think so, Joshua," Ailith answered. "Please help me up."

Joshua and Stephen each reached for one of her arms.

"You'd better get her home before your mother gets back, Josh," Stephen suggested.

Joshua grumbled a reply, then looked at Ailith. She really did seem fine, but he couldn't be sure. She could be in shock. After all, she had just gone through a harrowing experience. He took her hand and started for the house, breathing a sigh of relief that he'd found her.

Chapter 19

STEPHEN STOOD IN Joshua's bedroom after bringing Ailith a shot of brandy. "If you're sure you don't need me anymore, Josh, I'll take my leave," he said, watching Ailith as she sipped her drink.

Joshua nodded. "I've got it covered. Thanks for your help, pal."

"Good. I'll let myself out."

After Stephen departed, Joshua turned to Ailith, his face masked with undefinable emotions.

"Are you sure you're all right, Ailith?"

"I'm a bit shaken, Joshua, but I'll recover," she reassured him with a cautious smile. Taking another swallow of her drink, Ailith shifted in her seat. When he continued to give her a penetrating stare, she said, "I'm fine. Really."

"I'm glad." Moments passed before his next question came. "Do you mind telling me what you meant by those remarks you made over by the levee?" he asked, his irritation and disapproval finally evident.

Ailith raised her eyebrows, surprised at his testy tone. "W-what remarks?"

"About Melissa. About you being an intruder here," he snapped, more harshly than the situation called for.

"Well, I *am* an intruder," Ailith reiterated. "For my sake you've been dishonest with your parents and . . . and your Melissa."

A slight smiled creased Joshua's face. "And have you been dishonest with me, Ailith?" he asked, caressing the words.

"No," came the single, whispered reply.

Joshua gazed at her and swallowed hard. Her hair, shimmering with golden highlights, floated like fine silk around her shoulders and back. And her face—there was nothing or no one he could think of to compare it to. She was uniquely beautiful, and strong, and brave.

She had done what she had to to survive in this time, but because he hadn't been able to fit everything into a neat little puzzle, he had almost lost her. He cleared his throat.

"When I discovered you were missing, I searched for your orb."

Surprise again stole into her features. "Y-you believe me?"

"I don't know what to believe."

He walked away from where Ailith sat with her back against the headboard, and went to the closet. After retrieving the orb and bringing it to the bed, Joshua laid it next to her, then took her small hand in his. "Tell me again about the orb," he said. "Tell me about yourself."

"Oh, Joshua! You *do* believe me," Ailith blurted with incredulity.

"I didn't say that, sweetheart. I merely want to hear your entire story. You never did tell me everything."

Joshua listened with rapt attention as Ailith began relating her tale about the life she was abruptly wrenched from. She went back to when her father's grandfather had found favor with the Earls of Radford and how that favor continued to this day . . . that day.

Joshua smiled with tenderness at her.

"Because their astrological charting and predictions invariably proved correct," she continued, "my father's grandfather and father and their families lived in relative comfort under their liege's protection.''

"Well, what about you and your parents?'' Joshua asked, fully caught up in the story.

Ailith bowed her head. "In my ten and third year, Lord Preston ordered my parents and me to leave our home in the village and reside at the keep—''

"Didn't your grandfather and his father before him reside at the keep?''

"Yes. But not their families. And residency there was only on occasions.''

"Whenever the mighty lord of the keep needed them?''

"Yes,'' Ailith confirmed. "They had their own chambers. Sometimes for as long as two months.''

"I see,'' Joshua murmured, giving her hand a gentle squeeze. "Go on, love. You and your parents were ordered to live at the keep. Then what?''

Love? Go on, love?

Ailith drew in a ragged breath, unnerved by the sudden jolt of need and longing she felt as well as the charged atmosphere.

"Um . . . well, um . . .'' She frowned and cleared her throat. "H-he made my mother chatelaine. M-my father became his chief astrologer.''

Joshua pinned her to his look. "And you?''

The question sounded somewhat challenging to her.

She shrugged. "I was given my own private quarters, a tiny cramped chamber tucked away abovestairs, just off the great solar. Lord Preston also decreed that I be educated in the manner of a highborn lady.''

"In all my studies, that just didn't happen, Ailith. The twain never met, so to speak. Oh, the lords of the keep dallied with lowborn maidens. They took lemans, concubines, and whores to their beds.''

Ailith gasped, but Joshua continued as if he hadn't heard.

"But they didn't give a pittance about their education.''

Ailith attempted to snatch her hand out of his, but he refused to relinquish his hold.

"Are you calling me a liar, Joshua?"

"No," Joshua told her. "But I think you should get all your historical facts right before you go any farther with your story!"

This time succeeding in yanking her hand away, she jumped from her place on the bed and turned to glare at him. "You . . . you sexiest pig!" she sputtered. "I thought you believed me."

"Sexiest?" Amusement lit his voice at the altered word, thinking she meant sexist. "Sexiest? Why did you call me that?"

"I don't know. I heard Stephen say that earlier," she admitted. "I had to call you something. What you think you know about my time, Joshua, you only *read* about," she continued with righteous indignation. "I've *lived* it. You can't possibly know everything about it. I resent your insinuation. Lord Preston Claybourne saw to my education. Whether his intentions in doing so then was to show kindness, I do not know. I know his intention now is to force me to become his leman."

Joshua rose from his place on the bed and reached the door in three long strides. "I need a drink," he said over his shoulder. "I'll be right back."

He returned before he was missed, carrying a filled ice bucket, a glass, and a bottle of Scotch.

"Would you like a drink?"

"No," Ailith answered. "I've already had champagne and brandy."

"Did you drink all the champagne?"

"Oh, no! I couldn't possibly."

After pouring his drink, Joshua's gaze melded with hers.

"Have you any idea what is going on in my mind right now?" he asked hoarsely. "Everything in me is telling me what you have described is impossible. Physically. Scientifically. Technologically. Dammit! It's impossible, Ailith. Yet you're here, and instinct is telling me you are indeed from another time. How? How? It's not logical. It's not rational. It's not possible!"

"Oh, Joshua, you believe me! You do." Still holding his gaze, Ailith went to stand before him. "Why else would you be so upset? Even you have to know that some things can't be explained. It's called phenomena. I saw it on TV."

Joshua groaned. "But I did explain you, didn't I? I said you have amnesia."

Ailith fluttered her long eyelashes teasingly. With a provocative swing of her slender hips, she crawled back on the bed.

"You were wrong, Joshua," she said demurely.

Joshua stood over her, holding his glass of Scotch on the rocks. "Convince me," he said, then settled in the chair facing her.

She gave him an enigmatic smile before going on with her story. She told him how Preston Claybourne had summoned her to his bedchamber with intentions of making her his then and there.

When she saw Joshua bristle, she wondered at his reaction, but continued her story without commenting.

Telling him how she had thwarted her liege's plans by pleading her monthly, her voice faltered when she related his threats to her parents. At this news she noticed Joshua's jaw tense. But when she related the story of her father's invention they both laughed.

Finally she told him of the bazaar and the outlaw, DeLepee Rouge—the Red Sword—and of her friend Aida; of Brint Pfiester and the black tent.

"Oh, Joshua," she lamented, "what will . . . what *has* become of my parents and Aida? Lord Preston won't take kindly to my absence."

Having stayed a distance from Ailith for as long as possible to better gauge her reactions, at her sudden despair he decided to go to her. He went to sit on the side of the bed, putting his glass on the night table. He slid his hand down the sleek silkiness of her hair, then took her in his arms.

"Ailith, I don't like to think of myself as narrow-minded and one-dimensional, but the unexplained has always been hard for me to accept. It has to be logical to fit into my pattern of reasoning.''

He kissed the top of her head, and Ailith rested it against his chest.

''Are you telling me you believe me?''

''Yes, I guess I am. As impossible as it seems.''

''What changed your mind?''

''You.''

''How?''

Joshua sighed. ''There were too many things you didn't know. Had never heard of. Had never seen before.''

As he looked down at her, Ailith raised her head and regarded him in question.

''Your face, darling,'' he finally explained. ''It was more telling than any story you could have told. The awe and wonder came through in everything new and different that you saw.''

''But . . . but—''

''Yes, I denied it. I didn't want it to be so. And in all honesty, it's still hard to comprehend.''

''When did you come to accept the truth?''

''Tonight,'' Joshua answered. ''When I thought you had left me and found your way back to your own time. When I thought I'd lost you forever.'' He caressed her smooth cheek. ''I once apologized for kissing you, precious heart, but never again, for I can't apologize for loving you.''

Joshua's head dipped, his mouth finding her own, her gasp absorbed by his sweet, demanding kiss.

He loved her! *Joshua loves me!* Holding that thought close to her heart, Ailith gave herself fully to his kiss, relishing the feel of his mouth on her own. Stirring her senses, his tongue twined, mated, and teased, making her tremble in his embrace.

He briefly left her mouth.

''My God,'' he whispered against her lips. ''You're so innocent.''

His meaning was multifaceted. He knew how new she was to this world and that she had not fully experienced the pleasures of a lover's touch. Until now he'd not thought of the infamous double standard. But the idea of Ailith being a virgin gave him a certain satisfaction. Melissa certainly hadn't been when they'd first made love, and it hadn't bothered him in the least. After all, neither was he.

When Ailith moaned in pleasure as he left kisses along her cheek and nibbled at her ear, he placed all thoughts of double standards and Melissa aside and focused entirely on Ailith. Kissing her wildly, he pushed her gently on her back across the bed.

With unfamiliar need, Ailith returned Joshua's kisses, arching her body to meet his. When she felt his hands caressing her breasts, shivers racked her, and she couldn't prevent a loud moan from escaping her lips.

Instantly Joshua stilled and looked down into her face.

"Joshua," she murmured, needing him, knowing instinctively only he could quench the fire burning within her.

"Yes, baby," he whispered. "I know."

He captured her mouth again with a passionate kiss nearly rendering her witless. When the kiss finally ended, he was as breathless as she was.

"Ailith," Joshua said hoarsely, "I intend to tell my parents about you. How much, I don't know. And not right away. Besides, I don't think they've returned yet. My mother would have been knocking at the door had she heard your moan. And I would not have liked that. I want you all to myself tonight."

With passion dulling her brain, it was difficult for Ailith to follow most of the conversation. She heard herself ask, "W-what moan?"

Joshua laughed. "Never mind, sweetheart. Make all the noise you want. I expect you will anyway before the night is over."

He sat up, pulling her with him and drawing her into his arms. Though he knew what her answer would be to his next question, he still wanted to hear it from her lips.

"Have you ever been with a man, Ailith?"

"Never."

Joshua released a breath and crushed her to him, her unhesitant, one-word reply a powerful aphrodisiac. The evidence of his arousal bulged in his pants. Never had he wanted a woman so badly. That thought crossed his mind just as another hit him—he'd never been so desperately in love before either. He frowned and wondered when it had happened.

Deciding to ponder the depth of his feelings later, he confessed, "Ailith, I've fallen head over heels in love with you."

"Oh, Joshua, I love you, too," Ailith returned. "But this is not right. Melissa—"

"Was never that important to me," Joshua finished. "We were never compatible. Mostly, however, I was never in love with her."

"What about your mother?"

"Mother wasn't in love with her either," he teased.

Ailith giggled. "You know what I mean."

"I do, darling. And you don't have to worry about Mother. You're going to be her daughter-in-law. She'll love you."

"Is that some kind of proposal? I do hope so." Ailith smiled mischievously. "Otherwise, you're being rather presumptuous."

"I stand corrected, my love," Joshua said sheepishly. "That *was* presumptuous of me. Allow me to remedy it. Ailith deCotmer, I love you as I've loved no other woman. And I want you in my life for as long as I live. Will you marry me?"

Tears rushed to Ailith's eyes. She had dreamed of this moment for the past several weeks, never imagining it would actually come to fruition. "Oh, Joshua," she whispered. "Yes. Yes, I'll marry you. Need you ask?"

Joshua chuckled. "It seems I had to." He fell silent for a moment and contemplated her face. "I love you, you geriatric brat, and I want to make love to you."

He began unbuttoning her blouse, and Ailith sucked in

a breath as his probing hands caressed the flesh he uncovered.

"Geriatric brat?"

"Face it, love," Joshua said as he unfastened her bra and exposed her proud, firm breasts. He licked the tip of one, peaking her buds. She gasped.

"You have the face of an angel and the body of Venus. . . ."

He slid her jeans down her hips, kissing her navel, before sliding her denims down to her ankles. He pulled them over her feet and threw them aside.

"But," he continued, "you're six hundred years old." His gaze worshipped her naked body. "And, I might add, remarkably well preserved," he rasped.

He brought her hands to his top shirt button. They trembled as she fumbled with the first one. He covered her hands with his.

"It's all right, darling. We have the rest of the night."

He unbuttoned the first button, and together they finished undressing him.

Ailith's tiny hands roamed over the curly, dark mat of hair on his broad chest. Her smooth touch explored further, skimming over his stomach, wreaking havoc with his hard-won control. He had wanted her for so long, but he must not let his driving need shatter his composure. He gulped a sharp intake of breath.

"You are so beautiful," Ailith whispered.

He saw the hesitation to explore further in her eyes. She looked at his arousal, seeming spellbound by it.

"Oh!"

"It'll be all right, sweetheart." He nibbled at her lips.

Ailith slipped her arms around his neck, parting her lips for his kiss. Deep and stirring, the maelstrom of desire nearly engulfed her.

Joshua's hands were all over her body, sending delicious tingles to the core of her. She nearly buckled off the bed when he brought one of his fingers to the heart of her venus mound. He took one of her breasts into his mouth and circled the other with his fingertip. The blood in her veins turned to liquid fire, and when Joshua's lips found hers again, he kissed her deeply. A down-spiraling undertow caught her, whirling and spinning, drowning her in heat and desire.

His finger entered her and gently stroked in and out. Lost in a riptide of emotion and inflamed even more, she arched her head back and moaned softly. His touch was a heady wine, robbing her of her senses.

Joshua pressed the length of his body over hers and gave her kisses as though each one were his last. He touched and caressed her, inciting his senses, sending his control over the precipice. His aching maleness came in contact with her femininity. Gently he slipped into her almost unbearably hot, tight center.

Caught by surprise, Ailith gasped in pain, then clenched her teeth.

Joshua kissed her brow. "My sweet, my darling, I love you. Let me bring the feeling back."

He barely moved, the pleasure of being inside her indescribable. He slid his hand down between them and began massaging her hardened bud.

Ailith arched her body to meet his, feelings of fire and magic racing through her again.

Joshua gritted his teeth and began moving slowly against her. Nothing in his memory could have prepared him for the exquisite rapture he felt being inside her. She moaned again, heightening his already raging desire. He buried himself deeper, then withdrew before sliding into her moistness again, his moves deliberately slow and provocative.

Ailith's body burned, aching for succor. Seeming to know what she needed, he moved faster, and faster still, until he brought them both to a climax so powerful their world careened with the intensity of it.

When Ailith felt Joshua's arm encircling her like steel bands, she clung to him just as tightly. They remained joined together for long moments until their breathing returned to normal.

After a while Joshua withdrew from her. He rolled over, bringing her with him.

"I love you," he said fiercely. "And you were wonderful. Are you all right?"

He wrapped his fingers in her slightly dampened hair and caressed his cheek with it.

"*You* were wonderful," Ailith responded. She snuggled closer to him. "I do love you so. And yes, I am very all right. Will I wake with you lying next to me in the morning, Joshua?"

"Next to you?" Joshua laughed softly. "Don't be surprised if you find me *inside* you."

Ailith giggled. "Maybe I should keep watch and make sure that's where I'll find you." She yawned.

"Think you can stay awake for that?" Joshua asked with amused skepticism.

"Umm," came the sleepy reply.

Joshua reached over and turned off the lamp. "I'll just kiss you awake."

Ailith didn't respond, and he realized she had already fallen asleep. A dim glow drew his attention to the carpet. He frowned when he saw the orb and realized it had fallen off the end of the bed. Too drowsily content to give more than a moment's consideration as to why the orb had lit up, he settled deeper into the bed, pulled Ailith closer, and promised himself that when he awakened in the morning he would find a way to make the orb work again.

Chapter 20

WITH HER LEGS locked around his hips, Joshua held on to Ailith's bottom, driving himself deep inside her. She moaned senselessly as his thrusts became faster.

She clung to him, feeling waves of pure bliss, not caring, not feeling the water that rained down on them from the showerhead. She felt Joshua shudder and groan when he gave one final thrust, shattering her with its force. Weak and breathless, she rested her head on his shoulder, her legs still wrapped around his hips.

Still inside her, Joshua maneuvered them from under the shower spray, holding on to her. Slowly he withdrew from her, then set her on her feet.

"All right, my love goddess?"

"Well, I have nothing to compare you to, but *you're* no less a love god," Ailith responded softly.

"Take my word, darling, there's none better than I," he said in a teasing tone. "There's no need for comparisons. Make sure you remember that."

Ailith laughed. "Yes, my lord."

She gently pushed Joshua back under the spray. Retrieving the washcloth that had fallen to the floor, she began washing over his chest with it.

Joshua grinned happily, enjoying to the fullest the attention she was giving him. "Will you ever get enough?"

She soaped, and indeed fondled, his privates.

"Why, whatever do you mean?" she asked.

Joshua laughed at her picture of innocence and serenity. "You little medieval witch. That's what sidetracked our shower in the first place."

"Do not blame it all on me, Joshua. *Your* kisses started it."

"So soon after waking up, almost finding me inside you."

Ailith giggled. "I wasn't asleep."

Joshua pulled her against him. "You're irresistible, precious. And I'm learning more and more that you're a brat. Did Galen and Meghanne spoil you?"

At the mention of her parents, their predicament and her need to return to her own time came to mind, and Ailith's gay mood fled. Without another word she stepped from the shower. Taking a huge towel from the bathroom shelf, she wrapped it around herself, then took a smaller towel and vigorously rubbed it over her hair, catching the excess water from it. Afterward, she walked from the bathroom.

Draped in his own towel, Joshua followed her.

"Ailith, I'm sorry, darling. That was insensitive of me."

"Oh, Joshua," Ailith cried. "I wonder if I will ever see my parents again. Are they still alive? Can I return and save them? I miss them so."

Joshua drew her into his strong arms.

"Don't cry, sweetheart," he whispered. "We'll find a way to make the orb work, I promise. And when we do, you and I will go together to get your parents and bring them into the future with us."

Ailith's breath caught. "Y-you mean it?" she whispered, afraid to believe her hearing.

"I mean it," came the husky reply.

Ailith pushed herself out of his embrace. "What happened to the orb?" she asked with apprehension, remembering they had it last night.

"Stay calm, darling. It rolled off the side of the bed, and I was sidetracked this morning from picking it up." He walked to where he'd seen it last night and retrieved it. "Here it is."

Rushing to his side, Ailith lost her modest cover.

Looking at her, Joshua groaned. "You did that on purpose," he accused.

"I didn't realize the towel fell away," Ailith explained.

Not bothering to recover herself, she reached for the orb, which Joshua lifted just out of her reach.

She threw him a speculative stare.

"Let's get something straight, my lady," Joshua told her in a no-nonsense voice. "If I am to study this orb, I must have complete concentration. No distractions such as the temptation you've just presented me with."

"You don't think . . . ?" Ailith began in mock horror, her voice trailing off as she got the towel off the floor and shielded herself once again.

Joshua chuckled and sat in the chair. Ailith settled herself across from him on the bed.

He studied the orb intensely. It had a tarnished, silver handle with an attached globe, encircled by a dial with strange markings on it. The markings were barely discernible, because the dial was also tarnished and the dial itself seemed unable to turn.

Aladdin's lamp came to Joshua's mind, and he rubbed his thumb on the handle. Half expecting a genie to pop up from nowhere, he smiled sheepishly at Ailith, wondering if she knew what he was thinking, or even if she'd heard of Aladdin and his lamp.

He looked at the markings again. What he could see of them appeared familiar. He narrowed his eyes in concentration. Finally it dawned on him what they were. Arabic. Arabic symbols. He was sure of it. He knew Hindu-Arabic numerals had been brought to Europe around 1100, but they hadn't yet come into general use in Ailith's time. Not for thirty-five or forty more years, somewhere between 1448 and 1453.

One mystery solved—that of the origin of the markings—
but another one added to the puzzle. Where had Brint Pfiester found this in the year 1413?

Joshua realized there were no ready answers he could
form and decided to take the orb to Gene Callenberg to
have it translated. He frowned. He supposed he should have
it cleaned first.

"Is there anything wrong, Joshua?" Ailith asked, apparently taking note of his frown.

He stood up. "No, love," he answered. "Have you seen
the markings on the orb?"

Ailith nodded. "Yes, I have. What do they mean?"

Joshua shrugged. "I don't know. That's why I'm going
to take it with me and have them translated."

Excitement lit Ailith's lovely eyes as she rose from the
bed and stepped into his embrace.

"I'm so excited," she murmured.

The sound of her animated voice sent waves of intense
emotion through him.

"Will we be able to get back to the time I left?" she
continued. "Will it be dangerous? Suppose we end up
someplace else?"

Tightening his arms around her, Joshua laughed. "Your
questions are pertinent, and we will need firm answers before we attempt to breach the time barrier. But I promise
you we'll find answers."

Joshua fell quiet, reveling in the moment. How had Ailith
stolen into his heart as she had? When had he let his guard
down? He had been in constant turmoil because he'd had
Melissa, and he didn't want to cheat on her. He had never
done so, and he hadn't wanted to this time.

Yet, technically he had. Although he had decided it was
over between him and Mellie, she knew nothing of his decision.

Guilt dampened his happiness. Melissa deserved better,
no matter how her actions of the past several months indicated that *she* no longer wanted the relationship.

He released Ailith and stepped away from her. "Ailith,

I'm going to call Melissa today and ask what would be a good time to stop by her place. I need to inform her about my impending marriage to you and I want to do it in person. I also think I should explain the circumstances of how I met and fell in love with you.''

Ailith bristled, and Joshua noted the sudden uneasiness clouding her face.

"I see," she replied with a staid calm. For a moment, she merely stared at him. "I agree Melissa should know of our upcoming marriage, Joshua," she began finally, her voice cool and clear. "It is, after all, the decent thing to do. Letting her learn about it after the fact would be rather mean-spirited. But the events leading to us falling in love are irrelevant." She crossed her arms and raised her chin. "Indeed, they are of no concern to Melissa Devereux."

"Melissa knowing all the facts would soften the blow from the news of our engagement," Joshua told her without inflection. "Besides, Mellie knows practically all of my moves. She would have discovered if I was openly dating someone else." He smiled, hoping to alleviate Ailith's hostility. "I swear, Myra is equipped with radar. *She* would have found out and informed Mellie."

Ailith gave him a withering glare.

"What are you going to say to *Mellie*?" she snarled, the insecurity she always felt when she compared herself to Melissa resurfacing. "That you're in love with a maiden from 1413?"

Joshua narrowed his eyes at her. "Damn it, of course I'm not going to tell Mellie that you're from another era!" he snapped. "I'm going to tell her that I think you have amnesia, which is the reason I've kept you sequestered in this room."

"If you can't tell her the bloody truth, Joshua, then don't tell her anything about me!" Ailith stormed, knowing Melissa wouldn't believe she came from another time.

"I will tell her what I deem necessary," he gritted out. "Why the hell can't you understand my reasons for believ-

ing Mel deserves *some* explanation? She doesn't deserve a
quick good-bye at the watercooler.''

Not quite comprehending his last statement, Ailith turned
her back to him. ''Why can't *you* understand and accept
my reasoning that Melissa not be told any more than is
pertinent?'' she replied distantly, wondering what his real
reasons were.

Joshua drew in a deep breath. ''And just what are your
reasons, Ailith?'' he asked more calmly.

Ailith didn't respond. How could she? How could she
explain the way her belly clenched at the thought of him
going to Melissa? That her reaction to his intentions was
due more to unease and insecurity than anything else? What
would he think if Ailith told him she thought Melissa was
in love with him, and if he spent any time with her she
would convince him that *he* loved her, too?

''Ailith?''

She swallowed, her fears and uncertainties about everything making her head pound.

''I have to get dressed so I can go and make a living for
us,'' Joshua said, then walked to the closet without another
word.

For most of the day Ailith's thoughts remained dull and
disquieting. She attempted to view the situation from first
Joshua's point of view and then Melissa's.

Joshua was an honorable man and only wanted to do
what he felt was best. And Melissa deserved some sort of
explanation as to the whys and whats concerning the
breakup. But to Ailith's way of thinking, Joshua need not
say anything about her to Melissa. The less *Mel* knew about
her, the less she could persuade Joshua that Ailith was
wrong for him.

Each time Ailith remembered Joshua referring to Melissa
as Mel or Mellie, alarm tingled along her spine. She wondered how long he would be away from the house. Usually
he would have returned home at lunchtime, but today he
hadn't.

The ringing of the phone startled her out of her wandering thoughts. Joshua's answering machine picked up the message.

"Ailith, darling," the voice said. "This is Joshua. Pick up the receiver."

"Oh!" Despite her irritation, at the sound of his voice, her heart leaped. She lifted the receiver from the cradle of the phone and placed it to her ear as she had seen Joshua do. "Joshua?" she said with uncertainty.

Joshua smiled. "Yes, darling." He knew this was the first time she'd ever spoken over the telephone, and he could only imagine her chagrin. "Can you hear me all right, sweetheart?"

"Yes," Ailith told him. "I can hear you fine. Oh, Joshua, I *love* the future," she gushed. "Back in my time it took hours for a message to reach someone if the distance was short, and days, sometimes weeks, if it was long. And then if there was a reply—"

"Ailith," Joshua interrupted with a laugh, the turmoil he'd felt the entire day over their disagreement dissipating. "Baby, you're babbling. Stop and listen to me a minute."

"Oh, Joshua, I'm sorry. I didn't realize. It's just that I'm so glad to hear your voice. I was just wondering how long you would be away when the phone rang."

"Darling, you're doing it again. Now may I speak?"

"Yes."

"Good. Listen. I didn't have any luck with the orb today, but I did have it cleaned. It's quite an exquisite piece of work, a beautiful object."

"What do you mean you didn't have any luck?" Ailith asked, her voice registering her disappointment.

"My friend, Professor Gene Callenberg, is out of town for a few days," Joshua explained. "If anyone can interpret the markings, he can. We're not stopped, darling, just slowed down," he said in a reassuring voice when she remained quiet, knowing she wouldn't be at peace until she went back to her time and rescued her parents. "We still have a date with your past . . . your present . . . Hell, Ailith, what the devil is it?''

Ailith chuckled, and he sensed she forced it out.

"When will you be home?"

"Later. I still have things to do around here," he clarified quickly.

She cleared her throat. "H-have you contacted Melissa?"

"I've tried to," he said honestly. "But I've been unsuccessful."

"I see."

Joshua made a mental note to sit Ailith down and have a talk with her. He wondered why she was so adamant about him not telling Mellie about her.

"Ailith, I'm going to tell my parents about you tomorrow," he said, not wanting the pleasant telephone conversation to turn into another argument. "I had planned on doing so tonight, but Stephen has insisted he meet my six-hundred-year-old fiancée."

"You told him?" Ailith gasped.

"Yes."

"And he believed you?"

"Had to convince him, but eventually he did. He has also insisted on making the trip back with us."

"I don't know what to say, Joshua," Ailith responded in a teary voice.

"Don't you dare cry, Ailith deCotmer, when I'm not there to comfort you," Joshua admonished. "I can see having Stephen over tonight was a bad idea. I'll try to keep my hands to myself while he's there."

Ailith remained silent for a moment before she chirped, "Well, I'll plead a headache. Maybe he'll leave early."

Joshua chuckled. "What a wonderfully devious modern woman you've become. So quickly, too. I love you, sweetheart. I'll see you around seven."

"I love you, too," Ailith whispered in a ragged voice. Again she quieted. Finally she murmured, "I'll be waiting for you."

Tenderness welled within him, but hearing the vulnerability in her voice, he didn't respond to her statement. She needed time to adjust to their changed relationship.

"When you hang up, baby, place the receiver back the way it was. Okay?"

"Okay."

"So long till later, darling."

"So long."

After placing the receiver back on the cradle, Ailith laid across the bed, thinking what a magical place Joshua's time was. She'd sent her very own voice miles across town to him, and he'd heard her. *Her voice.* How many more new discoveries could she stand? She smiled. Joshua's beloved voice had reached her miles away also.

For the time being she wouldn't dwell on their opposing views concerning Melissa, and she couldn't wait to see him.

When she yawned, she realized she'd been up late last night. The events came back to her. If Joshua hadn't been there for her when she needed him, she wondered what would have happened to her. Would that man have killed her? Were people just as barbaric in Joshua's world as they were in hers? Somehow she felt Joshua's time was infinitely more safe.

Joshua. He was there to protect her. He loved *her*. She had to cling to that belief because he was her world and she loved him with her whole being.

Her eyelids drooped. She'd take a nap and wake up refreshed when Joshua got home. *Before* he got home, she told herself.

How lucky she was that it was Joshua's house—his tent—that she had been sent to from her own time. But most fortunate of all was that she had been sent to Joshua.

Chapter 21

AILITH SAT ACROSS from Joshua at the table in the breakfast nook, nervously rubbing her hands together as they awaited Frances to put in an appearance. In an effort to calm herself, Ailith thought back to last night's dinner.

Among other tasty dishes, lobster had been served. Having never tasted the shellfish before, she wondered how she had lived without it. Her father had always eaten with great relish, and visions of Galen tasting the delicious dish now came to mind. She smiled. Once she had heard Shawanda describing a new garment to Loquisha, saying it was to die for. That's what Galen would have thought of lobster—it was to die for!

When she was back in her own time, she had lived close to the North Sea. Why hadn't Lord Preston ever featured lobster at supper?

Ailith's musings drifted to Stephen, who had at first expressed his disbelief, then wonder at her orbit through time. Her heart had pounded when he'd suggested Joshua charter a plane for him and Ailith to fly to Las Vegas and marry. To her disappointment, Joshua had declined, saying he wanted Ailith to have the wedding every woman dreamed of. She had been happily surprised to discover Joshua had a younger sister, one Pamela Michelle Kenley-Wetherford.

Pam practiced law with her husband at his law firm in Chicago. Ailith learned that Brighton Wetherford III had inherited the firm from his father, and that Stephen and Joshua took pleasure in trashing the man whom Stephen referred to as Blockhead Weatherboard the turd.

When she'd turned to Joshua for an explanation, he'd told her Brighton was a jerk who had an exalted opinion of himself and expected everyone else to share his sentiments.

"We pull a fast one on him every chance we get," Stephen had added.

Ailith thought she'd learned to understand Joshua's English enough to follow a conversation, but she realized she hadn't. It was just as confusing as ever. She had been prevented from asking for a definition, however, when Connor had carted in their food.

After dinner, two glasses of white wine, a glass of sauterne, and two glasses of champagne, Ailith had lain on the bed and groggily listened to the plans Joshua and Stephen were making to return to her time.

"With what we've learned from the history we've studied and what Ailith has actually lived, we'll get a pretty good perception of what we'll be facing," Stephen had murmured with excitement.

Though she'd tried, she'd barely been able to follow their conversation. When Joshua finally joined her on the bed and began undressing her, she'd had no idea of the time. Now, dressed in a white V-neck summer sweater accentuated with a gold chain necklace and tan slacks, time crept by. She shifted in her seat. Where was Frances? Did she always take so long in coming to the breakfast table?

Joshua smiled at her. "You look lovely, darling. There's no need to be nervous. Mother's not an ogre. Although sometimes it may appear that way."

Chewing on her lip, Ailith regarded him. "B-but won't she be angry with you?" she stammered finally. "F-for going against her wishes?"

Joshua lifted his inky brows in question. "What wishes?"

"You went against her wishes and kept me inside your bedcha . . . bedroom," Ailith answered, her apprehension bringing out signs of her origin.

Joshua laughed. "We'll just have to see what her reaction will be, won't we?"

He wasn't quite sure what his mother's reaction would be, but he dared not tell that to Ailith. For the length of time Frances usually visited, he didn't mind giving in to her unreasonable demands. After all, two weeks wasn't a long time. If he had to, he put a rein on his libido or visited Melissa at her place. For the sake of his mother's eccentric sensibilities, he really hadn't had a problem—not then.

But not even for his mother's appeasement—if she needed appeasement—would he consent to put Ailith in another bedroom.

A frown creased his brow.

"Why are you frowning, Joshua?" Ailith's voice quivered.

Joshua's gaze roamed over her, but he smiled. "I was just thinking how lost I'd be without you."

Ailith gave him a shy look, but became distracted when Connor walked into the adjacent kitchen.

"Mr. Josh, I didn't realize you had come down already," he said.

He turned a curious look to her.

"Good morning, Miss Ailith. Mr. J., Mrs. Kenley will be down any moment, sir. Thought you should know."

"Thank you, Connor, I know," Joshua replied. He reached across the table to give Ailith of reassuring squeeze of the hand. "We're waiting for her."

Connor smiled. "Does this mean explanations are forthcoming, and Loquisha may perhaps return to work?"

Joshua laughed. "Perhaps."

"Thank God! Shall I brew some coffee, Mr. J.?"

Joshua shook his head. "You know how my mother feels about your coffee, Connor. Tell you what. Why don't you break out the machine and make cappuccino? That way everyone will be happy. Mother loves it,'' he stressed.

Connor shrugged. ''Very well, Mr. J., if you insist.''

''I insist.''

''Did I hear the word cappuccino?'' Frances asked, gliding into the kitchen with Jonathan in tow.

''Good morning, Mother, Dad.'' Joshua didn't rise from his chair.

He glanced at Ailith, and she gave him a timid smile.

''Good morning, dear . . .'' Frances began, but stopped when her gaze fell on Ailith.

As his mother walked to the table, Joshua stood. ''Mother, I'd like you and Dad to meet Ailith deCotmer. Ailith, these are my parents, Frances and Jonathan.''

Ailith rose and went to where Joshua's parents stood.

''H-how do you do?' she said with an outstretched hand. ''It's a pleasure to meet you, Mr. and Mrs. Kenley.''

''Why, what a beautiful little flower you are,'' Frances responded warmly, shaking the proffered hand. ''Call me Frances, dear.'' She looked at Joshua, her eyes gleaming. ''Could this be your ghost, dear?'' she asked with a sly smile.

Joshua gawked in surprise at her. ''You knew?''

''I'm not entirely a fool, darling,'' Frances answered mildly. ''I suspected you were hiding something. I never dreamed that something would be someone so lovely.''

''W-what gave me away?'' Joshua asked sheepishly.

Frances laughed. ''All those trays of food Connor brought up. There was enough on them to feed a regiment. And the extra bath towels your housekeepers complained about.''

Joshua snorted. ''I thought I was being so clever. Why didn't you say something?''

''I realized I shouldn't dictate to you in your own home, dear.'' Frances released a dramatic sigh. ''Besides, your father forbade me to interfere.''

''Good for you, Dad,'' Joshua told his father, who was assisting Connor with the cappuccino.

"Your mother can be pushy sometimes, son," Jonathan chortled, not raising his eyes from his task. "I like visiting with you and I didn't want you to ban us from coming back."

"Never, Dad. You're always welcome here. And until your new place is ready, you can stay as long as you need to."

"Thank you, Josh," Jonathan replied.

"Mother," Joshua continued, a trace of annoyance entering his voice, "I can't believe you didn't tell me you knew. I hid Ailith for over a month when she could have been free to have the run of the house."

"I'm sorry, darling," Frances murmured, her expression innocent. "I didn't know you were hiding her from me. I thought you were hiding her from Melissa."

"Mother, you're amazing," Joshua growled. Indignation sharpened his tone. "You still got your way by remaining silent."

"Don't be angry, Joshua. I didn't do it out of meanness," Frances declared. "I could never see what *you* saw in Melissa Devereaux. When I discovered you had a young woman in your room, I hoped something would come out of that." Her look turned fond. "Forgive me, darling. You, too, Ailith. I didn't mean to turn you into a virtual prisoner."

Joshua regarded Ailith a second. "What do you think, sweetheart, are you up for forgiving her?"

Ailith laughed. "Yes, of course."

Frances hugged her warmly and urged her to sit down.

No one said a word as Connor began serving the cappuccino. Everyone seated again, he inquired of their preference for breakfast, then went into the kitchen to prepare it.

Frances was the first to speak again. "Well, when's the wedding?"

"Mother!" Joshua scoffed.

"Well, dear, just because I accepted what you did doesn't mean I approve," she replied rather scathingly.

Noting his mother's only concern at the moment seemed to be matrimony, Joshua sighed deeply. If she didn't ask, he wouldn't volunteer unsolicited information about Ailith. He didn't know how he would respond if she did began to question Ailith's background. Or how *she* would respond if told the truth. His mother was unpredictable and rather unflappable in most situations. After getting over her initial shock, he suspected she would insist on going back in time with them.

"Joshua," Jonathan broke in, "Ailith is a lovely girl, son. And you must care for her if you hid her inside your bedroom to be with her—although it does seem ridiculous for a grown man to do." He cast a disapproving glare at Frances before continuing. "My point, however, is she deserves better. Any fool can see that she loves you."

Joshua looked at Ailith and burst out laughing. "Darling, you must learn to keep your face blank whenever you're around my parents. Otherwise you won't be able to keep any secrets."

A blush stole into Ailith's lovely countenance, and he winked at her.

"Mother, Dad, I want Pamela to meet Ailith and attend the wedding, so an immediate wedding is not on the horizon," he said adamantly.

"Harumph!" Frances muttered, a lethal challenge entering her eyes.

Connor entered the suddenly tense room and began serving breakfast. For long minutes after he departed, everyone concentrated on their meal.

Joshua prepared himself for battle, knowing his mother only remained quiet to get her thoughts in order in an effort to force him to her will.

"Dear, as soon as Pam is free and able to travel to New Orleans, I'll throw the wedding of the century for Ailith."

Joshua smiled without humor, but didn't respond, preferring instead to chew a piece of tender ham.

Frances set her utensils aside with a loud clatter, having

barely touched her meal. She turned a narrow-eyed glint to Joshua.

"Until that time, however, I think it's morally right for you and Ailith to *be* man and wife, if you insist on living *as* man and wife."

Joshua groaned. Why was it he was sharp with everything and everyone except his mother? She always won. It wasn't that he didn't want to marry Ailith. There was nothing he wanted more in this life, but he wanted to do it on his and Ailith's terms.

Lifting a piece of toast from his plate, he lightly smeared a dab of margarine on the bread. Taking a bite, he turned his attention to Ailith but addressed his mother. "Ultimately, Mother, the choice is Ailith's," he said in a steely voice.

"As if you have really given this child a choice," Frances gritted out, indicating Ailith with a wave of her hand.

"Enough, Frances," Jonathan commanded.

"Hush, Jonathan! I have stayed out of this long enough."

Softening her gaze, she regarded Ailith, who was staring at her with widened eyes.

"Dear, since the choice is yours, when would you like to marry my son?"

Ailith shifted in her seat, her hesitation to answer obvious.

"Tell me, Ailith," Joshua said softly.

"As soon as we can be married," she responded.

Joshua nodded.

"You will start plans immediately for a civil wedding to take place in three days between you and Ailith," Frances commanded.

"I-is this what *you* want, Joshua?" Ailith whispered, lowering her gaze.

At the thought of Ailith becoming his wife, eagerness welled within Joshua. When he didn't respond right away, she looked up, and when he caught the rush of pink again staining her cheeks, he knew the intimate message he'd wanted to convey had gotten through to her.

"Of course, Ailith. I want nothing more than to make you my wife."

The smile Ailith bestowed upon him made his heartbeat quicken, and he felt like a giddy schoolboy in the throes of experiencing his first love.

"Good. That's settled."

His mother's voice broke the mood. She grabbed Ailith's hand and pulled her from the chair.

"Let's leave the men alone so we can become better acquainted."

With that pronouncement, Frances led Ailith from the room and toward the staircase.

Joshua glared at his mother's retreating back.

"Look at it this way, Mr. J.," Connor said, grinning humorously from his place in the kitchen. "Loquisha's return is on the horizon. She'll be delighted to learn that Miss Ailith is a real live person."

"Don't let your mother prick your temper, son," Jonathan interjected. "When all is said and done, *you* will end up the winner. You'll have Ailith. Although you've respected your mother's wishes, you must remember this is *your* home. If you prefer to live out of wedlock with your Ailith, that's entirely your affair."

Joshua stood up. "Thanks, Dad," he grumbled. "Too bad Mother doesn't share your views."

Jonathan got up from his seat and followed Joshua into the hall. "She loves you, son. I know she'll abide by any final decision you make." He gave Joshua an encouraging smile. "Now, you'd better retrieve Ailith from your mother before she has her thoroughly confused."

Joshua sighed. "You read my thoughts, Dad. Ailith is a maiden in distress in Mother's clutches."

Chapter 22

EVERYTHING WAS HAPPENING so fast. Ailith was to become Joshua's wife in just one more day! But until the event happened, she didn't believe the marriage would take place.

That morning, she and Joshua had had another bitter disagreement concerning Melissa. He had finally contacted her and, after dinner, left to go to her place.

When Joshua returned, would he still want to marry Ailith?

She hadn't told him Melissa threatened her security with Joshua. How could she? He had said he loved her, and perhaps that should have been enough. And it would have been, except he'd known Melissa so much longer than he'd known Ailith. Together, Joshua and Melissa had acquired a history. How could she compete with . . . history?

Ailith laughed softly. She'd been sitting in the den since Joshua departed, flipping through several medieval history books, trying to grasp their meaning, but unable to because of her rioting emotions.

For the one hundredth time she wondered why she felt so threatened by Melissa. Whatever history Melissa and Joshua had together, she knew it was nothing in comparison to the living history Ailith had to offer him. They would go back to *her* time. For Joshua, that would be the ultimate experience in history, she knew.

Though able to read some things in the books, she found the letters were shaped differently from the ones in her time. When pictures accompanied captions, their meanings became immediately clear. The accuracy of the drawings amazed her. One drawing actually looked like the village surrounding the keep she lived in. She wanted to learn everything about Joshua's time, and it seemed Joshua wanted to learn everything about her time.

Bored, Ailith put the book down. The house was very quiet. The Kenleys were out for the evening, and Connor had retired to his room. She felt all alone, although she knew she wasn't. All she had to do was call Connor's name, and he would respond immediately.

But it wasn't Connor she wanted. She wanted Joshua. *He's* the one who'd abandoned her for Melissa. She glanced at the wristwatch Joshua had given her. Eleven-fifteen. How long does it take to tell someone it's over?

Tired of sitting alone in the den, she went upstairs to the bedroom and changed into her nightclothes. Sitting back on the bed, she flipped on the television. Letterman was on.

She tried to concentrate on her favorite program, but her thoughts wouldn't let her. What were Joshua and Melissa doing at that moment? Deciding she didn't want to know, she wouldn't speculate.

After Joshua had departed this morning, Frances had come into the bedroom bearing a book containing the family history of the Claybournes and Kenleys, which she had filled a long time ago. When Joshua had returned home this evening, he'd merely flipped through it, saying his mother brought the book with her every year, though he hadn't looked at it in years. He'd laid it on the night table, which was where it sat now.

Ailith reached for it. It was bound in dark blue linen with the title *A History of the Claybourne and Kenley Lines* written in gold script. Opening the cover and turning the vellumed pages, she scanned the contents, finally coming to information concerning Greyhawke Keep during her liege's lifetime.

Lord Preston Claybourne became impotent in 1429, caused by wounds sustained at Orleans. His lady wife, Glenna of Essex, had already borne him seven sons and two daughters. On July 31, 1414, Preston became the father of an illegitimate son by his young leman, who was reported to be the true object of his affections. She died in childbed. Preston expired in 1437, but by many reports he never overcame his lost love.

The words jumped out at Ailith and she threw the book aside. She had died bearing Preston's son? But how could that be?

What great harm had been committed when she'd accidentally traveled forward in time? Had she somehow altered history? It was possible that the woman Frances had referred to was someone else instead of Ailith. She searched her mind, trying to recall a woman whom Preston held in great esteem. There were none besides herself, and even that was questionable. After all, if he held her in such great esteem he wouldn't have wanted to force her to his bed.

Apparently, however, she had yielded to him. What was the significance of Frances recording Preston's illegitimate child? Had he achieved extraordinary accomplishments?

Ailith picked up the book again and turned to the page she had been reading. The remaining passages gave information on Preston's legitimate children and the fate of Lady Glenna, but nothing on her son or who would've been her son had she not zenithed through time. She flipped to the next page.

Held in high esteem by Preston, Aimon, the illegitimate son, was knighted in 1435. No other information was given.

With a sigh, Ailith laid the book back on the table, making a mental note to question Frances the first chance available. At least now she knew what Frances had meant when she referred to Preston as "that poor unfortunate dear." He had become impotent.

Thinking it useless to worry anymore about the situation until she knew more of the story, she allowed her thoughts to wander to Aida. She wished Aida was with her, because she missed her companionship. They'd always been as close as sisters. Thinking of how Lord Preston had altered that bond by turning that friendship into a servant-mistress relationship, Ailith frowned. If Aida were here, she would ease Ailith's troubled mind about Melissa.

"So would Meghanne," Ailith whispered aloud. How she missed her parents!

She'd been away from them more than a month, and she feared what might have happened to them. Her hope was that Lord Preston was still out on campaign with King Henry.

After reading about the king who had just recently ascended the throne with the death of Bolingbroke, she hoped Lord Preston would be out as long as the war lasted. From what she could grasp in one history book, *that* war lasted one hundred years, not due to end until 1453.

That thought amused her. Forty years should be time enough to get her parents and Aida and bring them back to live in the future with her and Joshua before Lord Preston's return. But, of course, he had died long before the war's end.

She eyed the book again but refused to retrieve it. Suppose she discovered Aimon really was her son? Would she then feel obligated to stay in her own time when she returned with Joshua?

Joshua. David Letterman was signing off, which meant it was 11:30. She sighed. She *wouldn't* wonder where Joshua was. Indeed, she wouldn't think about it.

Turning off the TV, she yawned. Stretching out on the bed in the semidarkened room, she wondered, despite herself, if Joshua would come and tell her it was over between them. That it was all a mistake. That he loved Melissa instead.

Oh, she wished he would come home!

She needed to discuss her discovery with him and what

it boded. She needed to know that Melissa hadn't stolen him back again. But most of all she needed his presence.

Though she didn't want to watch television anymore, she decided she would stay awake and await his return.

Ailith stirred, the ringing in her ears consistent. She stretched, forcing herself to wakefulness. When the ringing stopped, her sleepy regard fell on Joshua, who had picked up the receiver, stopping the noisy jangling of the telephone. By the time her thoughts were focused, he'd hung up again.

"Good morning, darling." He leaned over to kiss her on the lips.

"Good morning?" Ailith asked, surprised. She squinted at him. "It's morning?"

Joshua climbed out of bed. "Midmorning to be exact," he said. "Get up, woman. We're going out for coffee and *beignets*."

Scooting out of bed, Ailith stopped before him. "I-I thought to wait for your return last evening, Joshua, but I must have fallen asleep," she explained, searching his face.

Holding her face between his hands, Joshua kissed her deeply.

"You slept like an angel," he told her when the kiss ended. "I didn't have the heart to awaken you, sweetheart. Besides, it was way after two o'clock when I got in."

He dropped his hands to her waist and pulled her closer to him.

"After two o'clock?" Ailith replied, her body stiffening in his arms. "I see. You and Melissa must surely have had a lot to talk about."

Joshua held her tighter as she tried to push herself out of his embrace.

"Oh, so you're still piqued about last night."

"Let go of me, Joshua!" she demanded. His indifference to her pain hurt and angered her.

"Never!"

Joshua laughed and, lifting her from the floor, swung her around.

"Darling, Melissa and I talked for less than a half hour. She understood that our relationship had reached a point where it could not go forward anymore. Mostly, however, she understood that we did not love each other."

"Th-then she wasn't angry?"

"Um . . . not anymore." Joshua chuckled. "She did call me a sneaky, lascivious pig for keeping you hidden in here for nearly a month."

"Oh!" Ailith cried with indignation.

"When she learned how old you are, she called me a lecherous, dirty old man."

Joshua set Ailith on her feet.

"She said I was pond scum."

"Oh, Joshua, I'm so sorry. She really was very angry."

"She isn't angry anymore, darling," Joshua assured her. Tenderness softened his golden eyes. "She just had to vent her anger. She finally realized I didn't have to tell her about you. She knew I didn't wish to humiliate her. We're on speaking terms, Ailith. Melissa and I make better friends than we do lovers. I wish her the best."

Ailith flung her arms around his neck. "Forgive me, Joshua. I had all kinds of thoughts about you and Melissa going through my head. None of them were pleasant."

Joshua kissed the top of her head, and Ailith leaned her head against his chest. "That's understandable, my love, especially under the circumstances."

"What kept you out so late, Joshua?" she asked softly, her joy that Joshua really did love her almost overwhelming.

"I stopped at the New Tipitina's for a quick drink and ran into Stephen. We each had two drinks and decided to leave when someone sat at our table, delaying our departure. Professor Callenberg—"

A jolt of anticipation shivered through her. "Professor Callenberg?"

"Yes. *Antiquarian* Professor Gene Callenberg. Remember, I mentioned him to you a couple of days ago? He's an expert in ancient and medieval history. He's also a scholar in alphabets and numbers, interpreting ancient letters and numbers into modern comprehensibility.''

Ailith gasped. ''What did he say about the orb?''

Joshua sighed. ''I didn't have it with me, Ailith,'' he answered, ''but he's anxious to see it. I'm sure he'll have something encouraging for us when he does see it.''

''Will you take it to him today?'' Ailith asked, unable to keep the excitement out of her voice.

Until she spoke to Frances about the family history, she wouldn't mention what she'd read to Joshua. She didn't want to alarm him as she herself had been last night. Now, after a night's rest and with the assurance that her wedding to Joshua would take place, she was better able to put things in perspective. ''Does he know about me?''

''No, he doesn't know about you,'' Joshua answered. ''And I'll bring the orb to him after our wedding. Right now, we're to meet Stephen at Café du Monde in the Quarter for some *beignets* and *café au lait*. The three of us are going to go out and play today.''

Ailith clapped her hands together. ''Oh, how wonderful!''

''Hurry and get dressed, darling. I want to introduce you to more of my city.''

Ailith threw her arms around his neck and kissed him hard on the mouth.

''Keep this up,'' Joshua growled, ''and you and N'awlins will have to wait for that introduction.''

''N'awlins perhaps could wait,'' Ailith responded with a laugh, ''but it would be rude to keep Stephen waiting.'' Smiling coyly, she glided to the bathroom.

Chapter 23

LATER THAT NIGHT Ailith politely listened as Frances planned a wedding supper for her and Joshua. Although she didn't protest, she vowed to herself she would take complete charge of her own wedding ceremony. She liked Joshua's mother, but realized when she and Joshua settled in together, she would have to take command of her own affairs. Otherwise, Frances would run her life as well as her home.

Ailith understood that she still didn't know enough about Joshua's time to plan anything at the moment, but she would acquire Joshua's assistance if it became necessary. Besides, she would watch and listen and learn from Frances, assuming the know-how from her in planning the church ceremony whenever it took place.

Up to now, the evening had been quite pleasant. She, Joshua, and Stephen had dined at Bacco's after an enchanting day in the Quarter. Directly upon their return to Kenley Manor, Frances had phoned her daughter, Pamela, and introduced Ailith to her via long distance.

Pam sounded friendly and bubbly, and Ailith knew she would like Joshua's sister when they met in person. She enjoyed talking to her over the telephone, though she vowed she'd needed an instruction book to follow the conversation.

Pamela said things like Darwin's Theory of Evolution to Ailith, swearing that a certain lawyer she knew had only evolved to cretin stage.

Ailith had laughed at that remark only because Pamela laughed first. In actuality, she'd had no idea what it meant.

During the course of the conversation, it was decided that Pamela would stand as Ailith's matron-of-honor whenever the church ceremony took place. Though it had been Frances's suggestion, Ailith and Pamela readily accepted, agreeing that it was a splendid idea.

In ending the conversation Pamela had wished her the best of everything and said she looked forward to meeting her.

Frances's voice burst Ailith's thoughts.

"Tomorrow, Ailith dear, you and I will go to Canal Place and visit Saks Fifth Avenue. I'm sure you can find something appropriate to wear for your wedding."

Ailith looked curiously at Frances. "Saks Fifth Avenue?"

"Saks is one of my favorite stores."

Frances eyed her intended daughter-in-law critically. She wondered if perhaps she was being a little too forward. She had a feeling that beneath Ailith's lovely, fragile exterior, lay a casing of Pittsburgh steel. She kind of liked that.

"But whatever suits you," she continued, "is fine with me, dear. We can always go to the New Orleans Centre. There are some fine stores there, including Lord & Taylor's and Macy's."

"I . . . Thank you, Frances," Ailith faltered. "Since I am not familiar with the stores, I-I think I'll trust your judgment *this* time."

Ailith finished with a dazzling smile, which Frances returned with a knowing one of her own. Ailith's last remarks confirmed her earlier thoughts. Her soon-to-be daughter-in-law had a backbone of steel.

Joshua hadn't missed Ailith's response to his mother either, and he and Stephen shared satisfied smiles. Joshua was proud of her and happy for himself. Where his mother was concerned, he realized he was somewhat of a wuss. Ailith would not only stand up to Frances for herself, but also for him. His tiny, fragile, delicately beautiful wife-to-be would protect him from the big, bad Mama Bear.

It was ridiculous, but he figured his mother had cowered him all these years. He'd never given much thought to what she would have done if he had gone against her wishes. As it turned out, he did go against her, and she did exactly nothing. Well, he had ended up agreeing to marry Ailith earlier than he'd planned. Still, that was *his* wish also.

Well, Mumsy, Ailith is your match. She'll never let you intimidate me again.

Joshua realized how incredibly wimpish his thoughts were. Bringing his regard to Ailith, he caught her gaze and gave her a wide, silly grin.

"At last"—he smirked, getting up—"I have an ally."

Frances raised a brow in skepticism. "We'll see, darling," she responded smoothly, catching his meaning.

Joshua threw his mother a challenging look. Like her, he felt Ailith had a natural tendency to assert her will. As he got to know her, more and more of that trait came out in her. "Anyone for a nightcap?"

"I'll have a sherry, dear," Frances said.

"So will I," Jonathan piped up.

"And champagne for the rest of us," Stephen, who had been unusually quiet, said.

"Frances, might I suggest we retire with our sherry to our bedroom?" Jonathan put in. "Leave the young people to themselves."

"Oh, of course, Jon," Frances answered without hesitation. "I was going to suggest that. Tomorrow, after all, will be a long busy day."

Joshua handed his parents their drinks. "Well, if you insist, Mother."

"We both insist," Frances stressed, then turned to Ailith. "Good night, dear. Don't stay up too late," she advised and took a sip of her drink. "You don't want to have circles under your beautiful eyes for your wedding." She nodded her head in Joshua's and Stephen's direction. "Good night, boys." With that, she and Jonathan exited the room.

Pleasurable excitement filled Ailith. She was going to become Joshua's wife, not his leman. His *wife*.

Her delectation soared even higher when, as they drank the champagne, the conversation turned to their intended trip back to her time.

She wondered if they would truly be able to go back. If they did, would Lord Preston be at the keep? Her concern peaked. The danger to Joshua and Stephen would be very real. Perhaps, also, to herself.

Lord Preston had demanded that she keep herself in the highest virtue. Knowing she had not done so, in fact would already be married to another upon her return, caused unease to sweep through her.

Maybe she shouldn't marry Joshua until after she discovered if she was Aimon's mother. But to her way of thinking, history was already altered. For Aimon to have been born in July, she would have had to become pregnant in October 1413; when she left, it had already been the fifteenth of September. Yet she'd been gone for little over a month, and in this time it was just now September twenty-seventh.

What was the significance of that? She wasn't sure. She only knew she had to get back to save her parents.

But where would they land if they went back? At the keep? In the village? Would they be in *immediate* danger? Perhaps if Lord Preston was still engaged in warfare, they would have a chance. Thinking of seeing her parents again, a sparkle of elation returned.

She wouldn't allow thoughts of Lord Preston to daunt her. Once she had outwitted him; she would simply have to do it again. She'd pleaded her monthly . . .

Her thoughts crashed to a halt. In truth, her monthly flux had just ended the day her liege had summoned her to his solar. Awareness that the time for her next flow was now due dawned on her. Actually her flux was several days late. She'd lain with Joshua three days straight and she didn't even have her usual symptoms.

Then that meant . . . Holy angels of God! It was unthinkable! Did she have Joshua's babe inside her?

Would he still go back in time with her if he knew? She wasn't entirely certain herself, so she wouldn't mention it to him. But what other reason could there be for the delay? Her monthly flux had never been even a day late!

Of course, if their departure from this age was delayed for any reason, she wouldn't have to tell him. He would see her condition for himself. Yet she didn't want to postpone the trip any longer than necessary because of the danger to her parents.

Consternation tugged at her. There was so much to consider. She was certain Joshua was aware of all the possible obstacles. Telling him she may be carrying his babe would only add another worry, and she certainly didn't want to do that.

How she wanted her impending motherhood to be true! She loved Joshua so much and felt nothing would make him happier.

His love made her whole. But even with that love she wouldn't be content without her parents and Aida. Nor would she be content if she couldn't know for certain who Aimon's mother was. With that thought came a more frightening and chilling one.

Aimon's mother had died giving birth to him.

Stephen's voice broke into her thoughts.

"The important thing is to get the orb to work, Joshua. Then we can proceed to plan our trip from there."

"Darling," Joshua said, "directly after our wedding supper we'll go to the Hilton Riverside. I've booked a suite for the night. We'll go to Gene's on Sunday evening to see if he can decode or define the orb's symbols."

Ailith smiled at Joshua, knowing he was unaware of her turmoil and the fear suddenly engulfing her. Her most fervent wish was to see her parents again, but if it was really accomplished, how safe would they be? Indeed, what would become of her?

"I am looking forward to meeting the professor," she mumbled without enthusiasm.

Joshua frowned. Remaining motionless for a second, he studied her carefully, then, still looking intently at her, imparted, "If he can indeed solve the mystery of the symbols, our next concern would be to prepare for our journey back in time."

Stephen, who was lounging in a leather recliner across from them, let out a deep breath. "And if we're lucky, you'll get to see your parents again," he declared. "But if we're *reeeaaallly* lucky, we'll get to see *ours* again."

Joshua laughed and looked at Stephen. "Do you doubt it?"

Stephen swallowed the contents from his glass. "Which part?" he asked as he retrieved the bottle of champagne from the floor and refilled his glass. "Getting there or getting back?"

"Both," Joshua replied.

"Well, frankly I still can't grasp that Ailith is from another era." He shrugged. "It's hard for me to put much credence in traveling through time either way."

Joshua eyed him with interest. "I thought you were convinced of Ailith's plight."

"It seems it took *you* a while to accept her situation," Stephen muttered.

"Yeah, it did. But then I realized a misguided point-of-view wouldn't advance the cause of science and time travel," Joshua reasoned, in defense of his earlier skepticism.

"Well, be that as it may, pal, if the professor can solve the orb's mystery and we are jettisoned back through time, the skepticism and wondering will be moot." Draining his glass again, he set it down on the table next to him and stood. "The proof of the medieval pudding would be there for the asking—"

"Eating," Joshua corrected.

"As if I'd eat it," Stephen countered.

He started for the door to the entrance hall. Reaching it, he placed his hand on the knob, then stopped and turned to face them again.

"Anyway, you two, I'm looking forward to the ultimate adventure. I'm doubtful that it can ever happen, but am rather apprehensive that it will."

He stared at Joshua's face, and Joshua knew the uncertainty he felt was there for Stephen to see, but Stephen didn't comment on it.

"Good night, my friends," he said instead. With that, he opened the door and let himself out.

Joshua turned to Ailith, holding out his arms to her. "Is something bothering you?" he asked as she stepped into his embrace.

"Not really," Ailith responded. "I'm merely wondering whether we can actually breach the time barrier again."

"We'll know in a few short days," Joshua said softly, stroking her silky hair. "Are you ready to go upstairs, sweetheart?" His question was seductive and inviting.

Ailith hugged him tightly. "Yes, my love," she whispered.

Chapter 24

THE WALKERS CAME to the wedding, including Cassidy Walker with her fiancé. Though Ailith mostly had eyes for her new husband, she did consider Cassidy long enough to conclude that she was quite pretty.

To Ailith's surprise, Melissa Devereaux and her friends, Myra and Emily, also attended. Quite polite, almost amiable, Melissa wished her and Joshua a long, happy union.

Joshua's look of surprise at seeing Melissa wasn't lost to Ailith. He obviously hadn't expected her, yet he accepted her congratulations with good grace.

Myra, on the other hand, proved a different story. She glared with open hostility at Ailith, who thought how close to accurate Joshua had come in his description of Myra as an aggravating, sexless, mean-spirited, fat, little troll. She, Ailith, had never intentionally cast aspersions on anyone before. It had never been in her character to be judgmental without just cause. But the nearest thing she could think of to compare Myra to was a bitch—a melancholy, fat little bitch.

She found Emily only as tolerable as Melissa. Still, neither of them bothered her in the least. After all, *she* was the one married to Joshua. With that conclusion, she proceeded to enjoy her wedding.

In Ailith's perception, her wedding was perfect. While the staff had prepared the food that wouldn't be catered, Ailith had lent her advice and opinions, which Connor, Loquisha, and Shawanda had graciously accepted, even telling her how helpful some of her suggestions were.

Including her and Joshua, twenty-four people attended the ceremony, just enough for the seating arrangement in his—their—dining room.

As always, the food was superb, and champagne was the only wine accompanying the meal. The sinfully scrumptious raspberry crepes flambé simply delighted Ailith, in addition to a small three-tiered wedding cake.

Toward the evening's conclusion, Stephen stood from his seat and tapped his glass for quiet.

"To the bride and groom," he declared, raising his glass in salute. "Ailith, Josh, I wish you health and prosperity." A sly grin curved his handsome features. "Now be fruitful and multiply."

"Hear, hear!" the guests chorused as they stood and raised their glasses.

Heat crept up her cheeks. It wasn't from the toast, but from the fact that she and Joshua had already begun to be fruitful, which was a secret she alone knew. The fallacy of not telling him stuck in her throat like a bitter herb. Her husband, her love. How could she go on deceiving him?

If they went back for her parents without her telling him about the baby, what would his reactions be? Would he hate her for putting their unborn child at risk? For not having enough faith in him, in his love, that he would understand her need to get her parents to this era as quickly as possible?

And what of the identity of Aimon's mother? What if she discovered that, indeed, it had been she?

While she and Frances had been shopping for her wedding dress, she'd questioned the Claybourne ancestry and information regarding Aimon's mother.

"She was a peasant girl, dear," Frances had responded. "But I never discovered her name."

Ailith's heart rate had sped up. *She* had been a peasant girl.

"D-did you know anything else about her?" she'd whispered through the bile in her throat.

Frances shook her head. "Not much. Merely that she was some years younger than Preston and she died giving birth to Aimon."

With a nod, Ailith digested that information. "And Aimon?" she'd questioned. "What became of him after 1435, the year he was knighted?"

Distaste registered in Frances's eyes.

"It is believed he was responsible for his father's death."

Ailith gasped. "B-but you wrote that Preston *expired*."

"It could never be proved, of course, that Aimon murdered Preston, however—"

"Ailith?" The sound of Joshua's voice brought Ailith out of her musings.

Joshua looked at his wife with concern. Her emotions, worry and confusion, were written on her face, a face that nearly took his breath away.

Her golden hair hung to her tiny waist. The cream-colored, form-fitting suit clung to her slender figure, revealing every perfect line from her proud, round breasts to her smooth shapely ankles, which the dress allowed to show. In spite of the look on her face, she was so very, very lovely.

"Darling, are you all right?" he asked, his own anxiety evident in his voice. Standing, he took her hand and gently tugged her from her seat.

Ailith released a little embarrassed laugh and gazed at everyone. Melissa stared at her coolly. Some sort of odd satisfaction joined the incipient hostility emanating from Myra. Stephen stared at her with encouragement.

She had been so deep in thought that she had blocked out everyone there. Although Joshua was indeed her main concern, for a brief moment she'd blocked out his presence, too.

"Can't you see she's been embarrassed?" Frances

snapped. "Ailith is very old-fashioned." She glared at Stephen. "Speaking of being fruitful and multiplying can be mortifying to someone with her sensibilities."

Ailith could've kissed Frances, because there was no way she could have explained the sudden change in her demeanor. As a bride, she was supposed to be happy! All things considered, she was ecstatic to be Joshua's wife. It was just that the things she had been considering were daunting and frightening.

She smiled at her new mother-in-law. "Joshua warned me about keeping my expression bland," she inserted smoothly. "You and Jonathan can read me as well as he can."

"Being fruitful shouldn't matter to you now that you're married, darling," Frances drawled. "But I do understand how you feel."

Joshua hugged Ailith close to his chest. "Someday I'll explain Mother's Claybourne Doctrine to you," he said with a laugh.

Frances grinned good-naturedly. "Never mind my doctrine."

Joshua winked at his mother before focusing on Ailith once again. "Mrs. Kenley," he began, "can you think of any reason why we should remain in the company of these peasants any longer?"

"Joshua!" Ailith said with mock severity, giving him a playful smack on his arm. "How rude. They brought us presents."

"And I'm sure they must be very nice presents, too," Joshua said teasingly.

Slipping his arm around her waist, he guided her away from the table.

"Well," Stephen remarked loudly, "looks like we've all overstayed our welcome."

"Nonsense," Joshua replied. "You are all welcome to stay as long as you like. There's a honeymoon suite waiting for me and my bride that would be criminal to keep on hold much longer."

"You're right," Frances interjected. "This has been an exhausting day. I'm sure Ailith must be tired."

"As if she has rest on her mind," Myra huffed.

"Oh, do hush, Myra," Frances chastised.

"Well, Josh," Melissa piped up in that cool, clear voice of hers. "I'm sure you'll be very happy. Again, I wish you and Ailith the best."

Joshua nodded. "Thank you again, Mel."

"Yes, thank you, Melissa," Ailith said in a soft, shy voice. "You're very kind."

Melissa gave a short laugh. "Do me a favor, you two. When you open your gifts, open mine first."

"Oh, of course, Melissa," Ailith said with a sure voice. "That was very generous of you."

"Think nothing of it." Melissa glided away with Emily and Myra in her wake. "Good night, everyone," she said when they reached the door.

Frances captured Joshua's attention again. "Joshua, your overnight bags have been brought to your car, so you and your bride can leave whenever you're ready."

"We're ready now, Mother." Joshua studied her, then turned a glare on her. "May I see you a moment in private?"

Frances sighed. "Of course, dear."

He watched as she departed the room, then turned to his friends. "Thanks for coming, gang. Ailith and I are very happy that you did. There's still plenty to eat and drink if you care to indulge further. Good night, everyone."

He took Ailith's arm and steered her to the door with salutations echoing in his ears. Stopping at the entrance where Frances stood, he turned a furious glower on his mother.

"How dare you take it upon yourself to invite Melissa Devereaux to *my* wedding?" he snarled between clenched teeth. "Do you realize what an embarrassing, awkward situation you could have created for Ailith? Mother, this time you went to far."

Frances shifted her weight from one foot to the other.

"Joshua," she whispered imploringly, "I had no choice. Melissa dropped by this afternoon with a beautifully wrapped gift. She said she wanted to extend congratulations to you and Ailith. And I, fool that I am, fell into her trap. I told her to drop by later. She misunderstood and said she would be delighted to attend the wedding with her two friends."

Joshua's frown faded, and he shook his head, a slow grin starting across his face. "You're losing it, Frances," he declared. "There was once a time no one could pull the wool over your eyes." His anger fully dissipated, he kissed her on the cheek. "Forget it, Mother. I'm sorry I reacted the way I did. It wasn't exactly your fault."

"I will *not* forget Melissa Devereaux," Frances scoffed. "If I have to, I will use armed guards to keep her away from your formal wedding." She turned to Ailith. "Forgive me, darling. Sometimes I act like an old fool. I meant no disrespect to you. Besides"—she winked at Joshua as she embraced Ailith—"I have no doubt that this delicate little flower could have handled Melissa with ease."

"No doubt she could have, Mother," Joshua said with complete confidence.

Not long afterward, he and Ailith went through the door to the waiting limousine that would bring them to the honeymoon suite.

Joshua carried Ailith into one of the loveliest sitting rooms she'd ever seen. White damask rose draperies adorned floor-to-ceiling windows. Elegant rosewood furniture stood on plush gray carpeting. Filled with a bottle of chilled champagne, a crystal champagne bucket sat on a round table, which was located in front of one of the windows. Matching flutes sat next to this. Joshua padded over to the sofa, which matched the curtains, and placed her there. On the sofa table was a large bowl of fresh fruit as well as a box of fine chocolates and fresh strawberries and cream. Curious to know what other amenities the bedroom held, Ailith stood and went to the adjoining door.

Opening it, she found a huge sleigh bed and a beautifully carved teakwood nightstand, graced by a crystal vase filled with long-stemmed coral roses.

She felt Joshua's nearness and turned to face him.

"Hello, Mrs. Kenley, my love," he said softly.

"Hello, Mr. Kenley, my life," she whispered in return.

"I love you, Ailith," Joshua said, hoarse with emotion.

He lifted her and brought her to the bed, kissing her full on the mouth as he carried her. She drew in a ragged sigh when he deposited her on the bed. Keeping her arms around his neck, she returned his kiss.

"I-I do love you so, Joshua," she said breathlessly, breaking the contact of their lips.

"Ailith, my exquisite, captivating alien," he whispered against her lips. "Let me show you how much I love you."

"Yes, Joshua, show me," she responded in a quivering voice, her body beginning to heat.

Joshua rested his hand at the top button of her jacket. Maintaining his control, with shaking hands, he began slowly unbuttoning it. His need for her wasn't evident by only his arousal, but his intensity. When he'd bared her lovely body to the waist, he began kissing every inch of her exposed, velvety skin.

Joshua's sensual caresses and kisses fueled the heat coursing through Ailith, prickling feverishly along her nerve endings. When his mouth found her breasts, she trembled with the intensity of excitement surging through her.

"Please, Joshua," she said with a gasp. "I need you so."

"Yes, darling, yes," he responded hoarsely. He removed the rest of her clothing, worshipping her, devouring her with his eyes. Drawing in a ragged breath, he stood and stripped off his own clothes. His task complete, he rejoined her on the bed to resume his tortuous seduction, bringing them both to the brink of madness.

"Joshua, Joshua," Ailith murmured in a heated whisper as he tenderly caressed and suckled her breasts, making her nipples as hard as pebbles. When his hand slid slowly down her belly to the triangled treasure between her thighs, she whimpered.

He drew her closer and titillated her center with his fingers, stroking, massaging. His arousal, hot and hard, pressed into her thigh.

Her blood rushed through her veins in a fiery maelstrom, and she writhed in sweet agony. He kissed her fiercely, ravenously, taking away her breath. She tasted wonder and magic in his kiss. And love, the love she would desperately need to see her through the predicament she faced. Joshua shifted, and she felt the length of his body press against hers. When his rigid manhood entered her, she moaned with elation.

Joshua's passion blazed. Tenderly stroking in and out, he thought he would die from the sheer wonder of Ailith. He gazed down into her exquisite face, almost consumed by the love he bore her.

"I never knew how wonderful life could be," he whispered in ragged tones. "Or that this kind of love was possible. I am awed by you, my medieval princess."

Ailith couldn't answer. With closed eyes, she smiled and brought her head back. As Joshua drove deeper and his thrusts became more powerful, the tumultuous force absorbed her, and she cried out in sweet surrender.

Joshua enfolded her to his body in a crushing embrace, giving one last, furious thrust, molding them as one. His heart pounding a mad rhythm, he lay atop her, gulping great drafts of air.

"All right, my love?" he asked when his breathing returned to normal.

Without waiting for her answer, he withdrew from her and rolled over, pulling her into his embrace and kissing her forehead.

Ailith rested her hand on his bare chest. She looked up, meeting his golden gaze, and smiled.

"Yes, my love. I'll always be all right with you at my side."

Joshua drew in a contented sigh. "Would you like to give me a child, my darling?"

Ailith hoped he didn't feel the unconscious stiffening of her body. Perhaps he didn't, for he didn't respond.

"Giving you a child is my fondest wish," she softly replied, successfully keeping the tension out of her tone.

"Wouldn't it be wonderful if we've already created a new life?" Joshua whispered. "To me it would simply be mind-boggling. A woman from the distant past would actually give birth to my child, a child of the present and of the future."

Making a tired little sound, Ailith laughed, the hope filling his voice inducing guilt. "Are you still grasping with the reality of my existence in your time, Joshua?"

Pondering her question, Joshua remained silent for a moment. "It's still awe-inspiring," he admitted, "but I know every inch of your loveliness. The green of your eyes. The softness of your skin. The silkiness of your beautiful hair." He paused to drop a kiss on her head. "I know the touch of your hand and the rapture of your body clinging to me when I'm inside you. Your existence in my world may indeed be awe-inspiring, my love. But I have long ago come to grips with the reality of that existence.

"You are very real to me. You've become a part of me." He smiled. "No matter that you could be someone's grandmother, one hundred times great. You're *my* old lady, and I adore you."

"Oh, Joshua!" Ailith's arm went as far around his waist as she could stretch it, and she clung to him. "I find such comfort with you," she murmured tearily. "You've brought me so much joy. I love you."

He slid his hand over her satiny skin in response and he felt her shiver. He chuckled. "Well, we were like two sex maniacs. We didn't even turn down the covers. Are you cold?"

"A little."

He untangled himself from her, and Ailith rolled away from him to turn the covers down on her side of the bed.

He did the same to his before they scrambled beneath the blankets, laughing joyfully.

Joshua turned on his side, bringing her into the crook of his bended knees, snuggling close with her against his chest. Ailith sighed in contentment.

Running his hand across her belly, Joshua laughed roguishly. "Are you warm now, my darling?"

"Umm, almost hot."

"I could toss the covers aside again, but I have a more pleasant way to cool you off," he said.

As he began kissing her, the flames of her passion sparked once again.

Plunged into a whirlwind of desire, Joshua's lovemaking brought them to the brink of eternity, to sweet, sweet, tender gratification.

Afterwards, exhausted and content, she laid awake as Joshua slept peacefully next to her, her happiness marred by the uncertainty of the days to come.

Chapter 25

TWO DAYS LATER Ailith sat in Professor Gene Callenberg's library with Joshua and Stephen, watching intently as the professor examined the orb.

He reminded her of the mad professor from cable television. Gene had long, unkempt white hair, a robust girth, and an annoying habit of unconsciously tapping his quill-tipped pen when he sat behind his desk.

Occasionally Ailith's gaze would stray to the hordes of books on the shelves. Joshua had told her the professor had books dealing with past histories on a score of nations and subjects. Some of the cultures were so old they were extinct. These were called antiques, and because of Professor Callenberg's work in old and extinct cultures, he was deemed an antiquarian.

The interest showing on Gene's face lapsed into a frown, catching Ailith's attention. Her eyes widened at the look, and she grew anxious. Was the orb broken?

Since everyone was watching him, she assumed they'd all seen the look. Joshua stood from his seat and went to the huge, crowded oak desk where the professor sat.

"Is there a problem, Gene?" he asked, tension knotting his brow.

The professor scrutinized the orb further before pausing to gaze with pale blue eyes over his wire-rimmed glasses at Joshua. His bushy white eyebrows came together without a break in one straight line across his ruddy forehead.

"This is amazing, Joshua," he remarked excitedly, rising from his chair and walking from behind his desk. "Truly amazing. This object is more than twelve hundred years old! Have you found an archeological dig? Where on earth did you get it?"

Joshua exchanged quick glances with Stephen and Ailith, and she noted the flicker of doubt in his eyes.

"W-why . . . um . . . I don't exactly remember," he said with discomfort.

She realized Joshua was at a crossroads. He didn't know which course to take. Perhaps he didn't want to reveal any more of her origin than was necessary. Or maybe he thought Stephen should be the only other person who knew the truth. She would readily agree with that notion if Joshua and Stephen were as knowledgeable a historian as the professor was. But she knew they were not.

"Professor Callenberg," she began hesitantly, garnering the men's attention, "*I* brought the orb with me."

"Yes, that's right," Joshua quickly said. "She's from England."

He stung Ailith with a warning look. She noted that it wasn't lost to the professor, and a moment of embarrassed silence ensued.

Gene pierced Joshua with an accusing glare. "There's something you haven't told me, isn't there?" he asked, his tone matching his look.

Running his hand through his hair, Joshua sighed. He glanced at Stephen, who sat passive and restrained. He knew Stephen was wise enough to hold his peace. But why should he? After all, he would make the trip back in time with him and Ailith—if they could get the orb in working order again.

He looked again at Ailith, her eyes dark and challenging. Why, she looked angry! Recalling the other times she'd gotten angry, he almost laughed out loud. Who said women were passive and submissive in the Middle Ages?

Ailith had certainly been born way ahead of her time in the fifteenth century. Perhaps her assent here was meant to happen, because she was definitely a nineties kind of woman.

His gaze roamed back to the professor, who stood patiently waiting for his question to be answered. Stephen's look held neither approval nor disapproval, and for that Joshua was grateful. But Ailith's censorious glare both amused him and gave him reason to pause.

They hadn't discussed *not* telling Gene how she came to be in this time and place. Only he had thought of possible repercussions if their revelation turned out to be folly. Gene, after all, was an antiquarian. Would he be able to contain that information within the confines of his library? Joshua didn't want Ailith turned into a media freak.

His regard met the professor's now-staid glance.

"Yes," he said finally. "There is something I'm not telling you."

Gene nodded as he digested the information. "About how you acquired the orb?"

"Actually it does belong to Ailith."

"Ailith, huh?" With a glance in her direction, Gene rested on the edge of his desk. "I see."

"Gene," Joshua said, "I know you're a man of your word but I need further assurance that if I reveal anything to you, it will go no farther than these walls."

His pale blue eyes alert and curious, Professor Callenberg surveyed Joshua sharply. "Whatever it is, Joshua," he imparted, "you, *all* of you, have my solemn oath. Your secret will go no farther than this room."

Joshua released a sigh of relief, feeling a weight lift from his shoulders. "Thank you, Gene. I can reveal nothing, however, without the consent of my wife." His regard went in Ailith's direction.

She beamed a smile at him. "I would have it no other

way," she said. "I have put my trust in you, Josh, and I know you trust the prof . . . Gene."

Joshua shrugged. "Very well then. Stephen?"

His friend nodded his consent.

"Darling," Joshua continued, "it's your story. You do the honors and tell Gene."

Ailith hesitated only a moment before lapsing into the incredible story of her journey through history to this time and place.

As he listened to her tale, Gene reseated himself behind his desk.

Never before had Ailith seen such intense emotions on anyone's face. When she told of her father's invention, the eagerness on Gene's face was a pleasure to see.

With each different occurrence she revealed, he commented with words such as "remarkable," "beyond belief," "God-inspired," and "mystifying."

When she finished relating her story, it pleased her to note that the one thing she didn't see on his face was skepticism. He'd *believed* her from the start.

With her hand in Joshua's, she sat silent, watching as the beaming professor quietly observed her. Joshua gave her hand a gentle, reassuring squeeze.

Several minutes passed, and the man remained quiet.

"Well, Gene?" Joshua prodded. "I don't need to ask your opinion. I can tell by your reaction that you're astounded by this bit of news."

Gene drew in an excited breath. "I can only remember one other time I was so speechless, Josh. That was when I became a father for the first time. I thought I was awed by that experience. But this . . . this is spellbinding. This is beyond my wildest and most ardent wishes."

He stood from his chair and went to Ailith, taking her hands into his liver-spotted, work-roughened ones.

"Let me look at you, my dear," he murmured in a reverent whisper. "My, but you are exquisite." He smiled reassuringly. "Of course we'll find a way to bring you and your parents together in this time. Have no doubt about that.''

"Oh!" Ailith could only manage with grateful excitement.

Joshua put his arm around her waist and chuckled as Stephen spoke for the first time that evening.

"When will you know, Gene?"

"It's hard to tell, but Joshua was right, Stephen," Gene answered. "The markings are indeed ancient Hindu-Arabic symbols." He released Ailith's hand. "Since I'll be doing this without help from the Antiquarian Society, it'll take some time to translate."

Joshua frowned. "How much time?"

"I can't accurately say, Josh. Two days to two months, depending on the availability of the material I need to define the symbols."

"Oh!" Ailith said again, this time with apprehension.

Two months was too long. Joshua would surely find out about the baby by then. And her parents. What would have happened to them? Through her musings, she heard Gene's deep chuckle.

"Don't worry, Ailith my dear. You'll find your parents safe," he offered.

Apparently he thought her cry of distress had been from worry for only her mother and father. "That much I promise you."

Stephen snorted. "How can you be so sure?"

"Once I get the hang of the workings of the orb, I'm sure it can be set to go as far back in time as the symbols allow."

"Of course!" Joshua agreed with enthusiasm. "We can set it to the day *before* Ailith got into the black tent."

"That way we know her parents are safe," Stephen put in.

"How wonderful!" Ailith chimed.

"Not so fast, you three," Gene warned. "I can understand your enthusiasm, but the orb may not be what brought

Ailith to us. If indeed it *is* what brought her to us, it may not ever work again.''

Ailith's hand flew to her mouth, stifling the low cry before it escaped. Joshua gathered her in his arms.

''Ailith,'' Gene continued, ''I have no doubt that the orb *is* what brought you here and that I'll find out how it operates. But you *must* be prepared for all possibilities, including the orb's failure.''

''Of course, Gene,'' Ailith responded in a deflated voice. ''I-I do understand.'' She leaned her head on Joshua's chest.

Joshua's arm tightened around her. ''Don't worry, darling, it'll work.''

Gene smiled. ''Just keep the faith. The orb's rim seems to have some kind of gems embedded into it. They look like diamond chips.''

''I noticed that, Gene,'' Joshua said, ''but I didn't comment on it because I didn't think they were real.''

''Oh, they're real, all right,'' Gene answered. ''This orb is probably worth a small fortune.''

Releasing his hold on Ailith, Joshua looked expectantly at her.

''The dagger, Ailith. The hilt was covered with jewels. Were they real?''

Ailith gave him a ''surely-you-must-be-joking'' look.

''Why, yes, Joshua. Lord Preston would never give me anything less. Why do you ask?''

A spurt of jealousy went through him at her look as well as her tone, but he pushed it aside. ''Because it's too valuable to be where it is.'' He paused in puzzlement. ''Where exactly is it?''

''In a shoebox,'' she answered as she stood and walked away from him to look at the books on the shelves.

''Well,'' Gene chortled, ''it seems Ailith didn't come to you emptyhanded. She could be almost as rich as you are, Josh. Her dagger and the orb combined could bring in a pretty penny.''

"Neither is for sale, Gene." Joshua's tone had a ring of finality to it.

"I didn't expect they were, Josh," Gene said without rancor. He went to the door and called his housekeeper to bring in some refreshments.

For the rest of the evening Gene enraptured Ailith. His sense of wonder at the circumstances surrounding her arrival matched her own sense of enchantment. By the time they left the professor's home, she was thoroughly infatuated with him.

Chapter 26

THEY'D ONLY BEEN married four days.

Since they hadn't had their formal wedding yet, they decided against waiting on the Southern tradition of eight days before opening their gifts, which some couples chose to ignore anyway. Ailith requested it to be a private affair in their bedroom, with just her and Joshua present.

They only had twenty gifts, although they hadn't expected *any* at this wedding ceremony. When Ailith finally remembered Melissa's request to open her gift first, she and Joshua had already opened half their presents. She was a little chagrined that she had forgotten, but Joshua merely laughed and hugged her tightly to him.

"Who's going to tell her?"

Ailith giggled. "You'd certainly better not." She stared at the gold-papered box. "Oh, Joshua, it's so beautifully wrapped, I hate to disturb it."

"You'd better," Joshua imparted. "How would you know what to thank her for if you don't?"

"Good point." Ailith laughed. "But I will be careful with the wrapping."

Which she was. Carefully untying the gold and white ribbon, she set it aside, then proceeded to unwrap the package with the utmost care.

Joshua rolled his eyes heavenward. "Ailith!" he shouted with impatience.

She smiled at him. "Just a little more, darling." Mischief filled her voice. "There."

She placed the wrapping aside, lifted the top off the box, and stared. Inside lay several pairs of jockey shorts with a note attached to one.

Thought you'd be needing these, darling. I hope your new bride has as much fun taking them off you as I did. Much happiness to you both. Mellie.

Throwing the box aside, Joshua reached for Ailith, but she turned away from him, her body quivering. His jaw tautened.

"Vindictive bitch!" he said through clenched teeth. "Ailith, please, my darling, don't cry. I'm so sorry about this."

He turned her around to face him, and her laughter rang in his ears.

"Ailith?"

"Oh, Joshua," she said, gasping between peals of merriment. "You said she wasn't angry with you. You said you two made better friends than you did lovers." She indicated the gift with a wave of her hand. "What do you think of your friend now?"

Joshua turned a black frown on her. "Control yourself, woman!" he snapped. "I fail to see the humor in it. Here I thought you were crying because another woman sent reminders of our past affair. Instead, you're collapsing in merriment at *my* humiliation."

"But, darling, would you prefer it caused me pain?" Ailith asked as innocently as possible.

Joshua stood up, folding his arms across his chest. He looked down at her and grinned. "I see that I am married to a little tease." Reaching for her hand, he brought her to her feet and pulled her into his embrace. "What do you think of the note?" he muttered.

"Tell me what it said. I couldn't understand the way she wrote some of the alphabets."

"That's something else we'll have to take care of. I'll have you privately tutored starting tomorrow."

"The note, my love."

Joshua told her what was on it and had to further explain that their sexual encounters weren't that frequent. As proof he took four pairs of brand-new jockeys out of the box, just planted there to give credence to Melissa's story. And, in truth, he always undressed himself.

Ailith wasn't sure she believed his impassioned plea, but loved his confusion anyway. "She can't possibly have had as much fun as we have undressing each other," she said, unbuttoning the top button of his pajama shirt.

"Not in a million years, sweet brat," Joshua assured her.

He kissed her so passionately she swayed in his arms.

"I'm glad Melissa's meanness didn't hurt you," he whispered against her lips. "She shouldn't be allowed to get away with such viciousness." He kissed her eyelids.

Ailith sighed, kissing him on his firm jaw. "I think we should send her a thank-you note."

Allowing her to remove his pajama top, Joshua looked at her in surprise. "Surely you're not serious?" he asked, slipping out of his bottoms.

"Very," came the heated reply.

Totally undressed now, he slipped her arms out of her sleeves. "But why?"

"Darling, where are your manners?" Ailith smiled. "Your mother wouldn't want you to omit an acknowledgment of a gift. Neither would I. I can tell by the contents that Melissa put a lot of thought into it."

Joshua eyed her suspiciously. "And you're going to put a lot of thought into that thank-you note, aren't you? I don't think she deserves that satisfaction."

Ailith kissed him in the hollow of his neck, going down to his chest and flicking her tongue over his nipple, causing him to draw in a quick breath.

"I would agree," she cooed in a seductive tone, "if it was anyone but Melissa. Failure to reply would make her think she succeeded in hurting me."

"Ailith," Joshua groaned as she brought her kisses to his other nipple. "You little temptress." He flipped her beneath him on the soft, cushiony carpet and kissed her hungrily, deeply, before pulling his lips away. "What are you proposing?"

His kiss left her breathless. "N-nothing. I'll tell her how much we both appreciated her thoughtfulness in returning your underwear."

Joshua caressed her soft breasts, peaking the buds.

"God, you're so beautiful," he whispered, kissing each one, blocking thoughts of Melissa from his mind.

Ailith gasped. "I-I can't think when you do that, my love." She felt his hands caressing her body, sliding down between her thighs before his fingers entered her.

She vaguely knew she had been discussing Melissa, trying at the same time to seduce Joshua into agreeing with her idea to respond to her gift. But as she felt his first thrust inside her, she realized she had been the one seduced. Thoughts of anything else, except the man causing such sweet ecstasy, shut down.

At the moment all her senses focused on Joshua and his lovemaking, torturously slow and agonizingly tender. And so sweet, so very, very sweet.

She whispered his name, feeling overwhelming waves of sheer rapture. Joshua's thrusts became more demanding, and she lost control over the vortex, over the web of magic enveloping her. She swirled into a whirlpool of tingles and shivers, of feelings so intense she questioned her survival.

Feeling her quivers, Joshua surrendered his love inside her, his release crumbling around him like the walls of Jericho. He shuddered and clung to her.

"Ailith, my sweet love," he whispered between breaths.

A sense of boneless weightlessness overtook Ailith. Tears streaked the sides of her face, her emotions so powerful they rendered her speechless. Never before had she felt so cherished. For long moments they lay together on the carpet.

When Joshua slowly withdrew from her, the sensation

caused a slight rush of heat to course through her. Then she trembled at the complete loss of him inside her.

He leaned over her and caressed her cheek.

"I love you."

She smiled at him.

"Before we were sidetracked from our discussion," he continued with a roguish grin, "as we sometimes are, I was going to tell you to do as you see fit where Melissa is concerned."

"Oh," Ailith began with a laugh, "I am merely going to tell her you stopped wearing underwear and that we'll put those aside in case you change your mind again."

A wide grin split Joshua's face. "I don't think she'll like that, sweetheart."

"I know," Ailith agreed with a smirk.

She sat up, unashamedly stretching her arms above her exquisite form. Joshua groaned.

She smiled, then stood up. "I'm going to start the spray under the shower. Care to join me?"

Joshua laid on his back, watching her glide to the bathroom. He chuckled, knowing how they would end up. Her effect on him was so strong, sometimes the mere thought of her excited him to arousal.

He rolled over onto his stomach, just in time to see her slide the shower doors open, reach inside, and start the water flow going. She turned and looked at him. His loins stirred.

Her hair, golden with yellow streaks, the color of cornsilk, flowed in glorious disarray down her back and over her shoulders. By far, she was the loveliest woman he had ever seen.

A sudden ache to feel her pressed against his body shot through him, and he got up to join her in the bathroom.

Chapter 27

THE VERY NEXT day as Joshua promised, he hired a tutor for Ailith.

In the ensuing weeks, Ailith discovered it wasn't as hard as she thought it would be. Or as easy, for that matter. As generous as Joshua's ancestor had been in educating her, that education proved completely useless in Joshua's time, unless, of course, someone wanted information about the time she'd ascended from.

There was so much to learn, and she was indeed eager to do so. She had to learn reading, math, and writing. She also had to learn the correct way to spell the words she would write—words with the same sounds but different meanings.

"You're already up to an eighth-grade level, Mrs. Kenley," Mrs. Frazier, Ailith's instructor, said, encouragement sparkling in her eyes.

As they had every evening since the lessons began, they sat in Joshua's comfortable office at Kenley Manor, listening to Mrs. Frazier's assessment of Ailith's progress.

Ailith smiled with satisfaction, and Joshua leaned over, rewarding her with a passionate kiss on the lips, then curved his mouth into a heartstopping grin.

"I'm very proud of you, darling," he told her.

"At least you haven't forgotten how to respond to the sensual side of life," Mrs. Frazier observed.

Joshua winked at Ailith, still grinning. She stifled a laugh, wondering how long the amnesia story would hold up.

Later that evening as they lay on their bed, settled in for the night, she asked Joshua about the continued credibility of the tale.

"The story is foolproof," he reassured her. "It's obvious to anyone watching that you're not familiar with the subjects you're being taught, darling. Or at the very least, the way they're being instructed. Since you have no knowledge of what's being taught, it's not hard to believe you've probably forgotten any previous lessons you may have learned."

Ailith snuggled closer to him as he gently stroked her hair.

"Mrs. Frazier thinks my quick positive responses are due to the fact that I haven't completely forgotten everything I've learned in school," she explained. "That, and maybe my memory is returning."

"I know better," Joshua said with pride. "You *don't* have amnesia. You border on genius. I'm sure your IQ is very high, because your intelligence is so far above average. I promise as soon as time permits, I'll have you tested."

"Okay," Ailith murmured sleepily. "I hope you won't be disappointed if I only turn out to be average."

"Never," Joshua answered without hesitation. "I'll only be disappointed if you don't keep our dinner date with me and Stephen tomorrow."

Ailith yawned. "Trust me," she mumbled. "I'll be there. I canceled last week because of an unexpected test Mrs. Frazier gave me."

Joshua leaned over and kissed her on her forehead, before turning out the light.

* * *

The next afternoon Ailith sat waiting for Stephen and Joshua at the Palace Café on Canal Street, thinking how proud she was of herself for what she'd accomplished in so short a period.

If only Gene would get back to them with word on *his* accomplishments. Five weeks had passed since Gene Callenberg had taken the orb to penetrate its secrets. And more than six weeks had gone by since she first suspected she was carrying Joshua's babe—baby. Morning sickness had begun to besiege her. Yet Joshua was still unaware of her condition because she never got out of bed until long after he left for work. She usually felt better by evening.

In all that time, she hadn't discovered any more about the identity of Aimon's mother. She had learned that Preston had *expired* due to poisoning, however. The night before his death, he and Aimon had an awful disagreement. About what, no one was ever sure, but supposedly Aimon had vowed vengeance.

Frances insisted that Preston had always held the boy in the highest esteem and her illustrious ancestor—with whom she held some great fascination—was a good man and undeserving of Aimon's treatment.

Joshua was a good man, warm, loving, and kind—traits Ailith had once attributed to Preston Claybourne. But without her cooperation, his kindness ceased, putting her and her parents at his mercy.

In some respects, their personalities were similar, and their resemblance was uncanny. Further comparison, however, showed her Preston was a ruthless, unyielding man who used others for his own gain. And he was very vengeful.

Yet it was hard for Ailith to accept that Preston's son had murdered him. If indeed she had borne Aimon—and apparently wouldn't do so now—then she had altered history. She had prevented Preston's murder, that is, if Aimon had actually killed him.

Ailith shivered. If only she knew Aimon's fate. Would some great catastrophe take place because Aimon hadn't been born? She supposed she would discover her answers once they returned to her time, because Frances had told her all she knew.

She looked around the restaurant, not sure she'd make it through the early dinner they'd planned. The combined smells of various foods made her queasy. She had eaten a very light lunch, and it had stayed down. When she'd first come in, she could have sworn she was hungry enough to eat a horse. But now she was so nauseated she feared even water would cause her to regurgitate.

Taking deep, calming breaths, she gazed out the window next to her, and saw Joshua and Stephen crossing the wide street. As they drew nearer, she caught Joshua's eyes and smiled tremulously at him and waved. Another few minutes and they were in the restaurant, pulling out the chairs at her table to sit.

Joshua leaned down and kissed her tenderly on her mouth, not hurrying to end it until Stephen cleared his throat.

"Umm, delicious." Joshua seated himself. "Remind me to take this up again when we get home."

Ailith forced a smile. "My pleasure, milord." *God! She was going to be sick!* She swallowed convulsively, then bounded out of her chair. "Excuse me," she mumbled and rushed toward the ladies' room.

Giving the female attendant a cursory glance, she went straight to an empty stall, where she immediately heaved into the commode. After a few horrible minutes in there, she emerged red-faced with embarrassment, but feeling a little better. She returned the attendant's disapproving stare with a haughty one of her own, and the woman made a snorting sound in her throat.

"Are you all right, miss?" she said.

Apparently she finally remembered what she was being paid to do, though her censorious look remained.

"Y-yes, thank you," Ailith replied, wondering if the woman thought she'd had too much drink in her . . . if she thought she was drunk. In this time, Ailith reminded herself, people preferred the word *drunk*.

Irrelevantly the woman brought to mind a cross between *I Love Lucy*'s Lucy and the Beave and Wally's mother.

"Would you like some water?" the woman asked. "Or perhaps a mint candy?"

"Perhaps a mint, thank you," Ailith said, thinking to settle her stomach with the candy. She popped it into her mouth before leaving the attendant to her duty in the ladies' room.

When Ailith returned to the table, she found an anxious Joshua and a concerned Stephen, who both stood at her approach.

"Sweetheart, are you all right?" Joshua asked in worried tones as he pulled out her chair.

Ailith smiled at him and sat down. "I'm just fine, darling," she responded.

"You were as pale as a ghost when you left," Stephen put in.

Ailith swallowed some of the essence from the candy melting in her mouth and working to balance the upset inside her. She bestowed her most beaming smile on her husband and his friend.

"I hope that's not still the case."

Raising his brow in skepticism, Joshua reseated himself. "That's certainly not the case. But you gave me reason to pause just now."

"I am sorry, Joshua. I had a-a feminine problem," Ailith barely whispered the words.

She lowered her head, blushing furiously, both from the intimacy of her statement and the lie she had to tell. A quick assessment of what she'd just said made her realize she really *did* have a female problem. For God's sake, she was pregnant!

Nevertheless, she *had* to stop using her gender's unique difference to thwart the Kenley slash—she chuckled to herself at that—Claybourne men. Both past and present.

Joshua's look told her he was ready to take her to the

nearest doctor's office. She couldn't let that happen, not just yet! She drew in a breath.

"I'm famished," she said with a forced chuckle. "Shall we order?"

Ailith ordered light, chicken broth with crackers and a green salad. The suspicion in Joshua's eyes throughout the meal made her groan silently. He knew of her penchant for modern-day food and was probably wondering why she didn't order something exotic, as was her wont most of the time.

"Are you absolutely sure you're all right?" he asked again for the tenth time in as many minutes.

"Perfect," she answered again. "But I'd go beyond perfect if I knew what Gene is up to with the orb. Neither of you have said anything since the night in his library, other than he's still working on it," she added.

"And so he is," Stephen said. "We believe he may be getting close to a solution." A mischievous light entered his eyes. "He said we should start picking out the latest fashions of the day for the year 1413."

Ailith gasped. "Joshua!" she exclaimed in a loud whisper. "Why didn't you tell me?"

"I fully intended to, sweetheart, but I wanted to be sure there were no glitches or unforeseen delays to disappoint you." He sighed and gestured to Stephen. "Unfortunately Motormouth here didn't give me a chance."

Stephen snickered with humor. "Forewarned is forearmed. You should have told me of your plans not to mention anything to her just yet. Anyway, what's the harm? As far as we know, everything is going great."

"That's true."

Joshua sipped his coffee, then turned in concern to Ailith.

Just as Ailith desperately wanted information about the orb, she desperately wanted to steer her husband's attention away from thinking she needed medical attention. She thought she'd done that when she'd broached the subject of Professor Callenberg. But she'd refused dessert because she couldn't tolerate it. And now Joshua was looking at her like a prized falcon eyeing his prey.

Ailith glanced at Stephen. "So, what does that mean?"

"We'll find out tomorrow, darling," Joshua said.

"Tomorrow," she echoed.

Because he was still giving her *that* look, she picked up his spoon and tasted the caramel custard he had before him. Forcing the sweet dessert down her throat, she smiled. "Ummm, yum!" She hoped this worked to stem Joshua's suspicions. "Delicious."

"I'll order some for you," Stephen volunteered, attempting to garner the waiter's attention. "I was beginning to worry about you. I've never seen you eat so little."

"No, you won't order anything for me!" Ailith declared in alarm.

"Why not, sweetheart?" Joshua asked. He drew his mouth into a thin line. "Are you hiding something from me? Are you ill and not telling me? You can't be worrying about your figure. As much as you like to eat you haven't gained a pound. You're probably the envy of most women. So what, my love, are you hiding?"

Ailith let forth a little high-pitched laugh, the sound so out of character to her, she swallowed back a string of Joshua's favorite curses. "Joshua, why would I want to hide anything from you?" She patted his hand. "Please, darling, be at ease. I promise you I'm fine."

As fine as I can be for the condition I'm in.

Except for the miserable hours she experienced until the early evenings, she really felt quite well.

"Maybe she's just a bit under the weather," Stephen suggested. "Stop acting like her mother, Josh. Or like *your* mother!"

Letting out a hoarse moan and clutching his chest, Joshua grimaced. "Please, no! I can't be that bad," he said, feigning outrage. Looking up, he beseeched some unseen benefactor. "The woman has me coming unhinged. She's played havoc with my senses since the day I met her. And now she's turning me into my mother!"

Ailith smiled at him, attempting to upset his senses even more.

"Tell me I haven't really been that bad," he implored.

Ailith and Stephen burst out laughing.

"He's losing it, Ailith," Stephen said gleefully. "And if he goes completely over the edge, his mother will have to help nurse him back to health."

When Joshua gave a dejected shake of his head, Ailith laughed harder.

"That's a real sobering thought," he muttered. "To be forced to abide my mother's care." He grasped Ailith's hand. "Darling, have I really been that bad?"

"Of course not," Ailith said, giving his hand a gentle squeeze. "Today is the first time you seemed so overly concerned with my well-being." She paused to grin at Stephen. "But you needn't fear, Mother Kenley. I'm in the best of health."

"That's right, Frances," Stephen chortled with delight. "All you have to do is look at Ailith to see that."

A stricken look settled in Joshua's face. "How could you, Ailith?" he asked in the best hurt tones he could muster. "My concern was for you. For *your* good health. And you called me M-Mother K-Kenley! I thought you loved me!"

Giggles convulsed Ailith, and Stephen wasn't much better.

"And you, Stephen!" Joshua continued, trying to control his own laughter. He ignored the tight-lipped glares of the other patrons. "You called me a-a-a *Frances*!" He shivered dramatically. "Yuck! I thought you were my friend."

"All right, Josh," Stephen said, guffawing uncontrollably. "I take it back. There's not enough room on the planet, in the universe, for two Franceses." He frowned. "Did I say that right? Frances . . . sis?"

Ailith gasped. "Stop! Have you two been drinking? Joshua, your mother is a *lovely* woman!"

Joshua nodded his agreement. "Of course she is, Ailith. But I don't want to *be* her!"

They got the sillies all over again and didn't regain control for a full five minutes.

Finally when the tab was paid, Stephen rose. "Bless Frances's bossy little heart. We wouldn't love her so much if she were any different." He leaned down and kissed Ailith on her cheek. "Good night, you two. I'll see you at Gene's tomorrow night."

"Sure thing, Stevie." Joshua watched his friend stroll toward the door before turning to Ailith and smiling. "How about it, sweetheart, are you about ready to leave?"

"Yes," she answered.

Joshua drew in a breath, gazing intensely at her. She gave him a curious look.

"There's something about you, darling," he said. "Something different. I just can't put my finger on it."

Ailith giggled nervously, gathering her purse, then pushing herself away from the table. Joshua was up immediately, helping her on with her coat. His hands lingered on her shoulders a moment, and he leaned close to her ear.

"What the hell are you keeping from me, Ailith?" he asked in a hoarse whisper. "Are you going to have our baby?"

Chapter 28

AILITH NEARLY BLANCHED, but quickly gained control and gave Joshua a vacuous look. With a nonchalance she didn't feel, she allowed her gaze to survey the room.

"What a question to ask, my love, in a room full of people."

She turned from the table, and Joshua took her arm, steering her out of the restaurant.

Not speaking again until they were settled inside the car on the way home, Ailith hoped to take the conversation in another direction.

"Did Stephen have a late date, Joshua?" Amusement laced her voice. "He left rather abruptly."

Joshua grinned at her, but tension still hung between them.

"Was he that transparent? You remember Kayla, don't you? His flight attendant girlfriend?"

When she nodded affirmatively, he continued.

"Well, he has to meet her flight this evening."

"Oh. Is it serious between them?"

"Who knows?" came the reply. "It may be for Kayla. I'm sure Stephen is fighting it, though."

Making her expression as bland as possible, Ailith turned her attention to the windshield, but didn't really notice the scenery as the car whizzed by.

God forbid he brings up the baby again.

Joshua's question had been direct, and a yes or no answer would have sufficed. She wouldn't volunteer any information until it became absolutely necessary, but she couldn't lie to Joshua either. The way his question had been posed, she had to be just as exact with her answer, aye or nay.

Could she delay her response if he asked the question again? Should she? She pondered these heavily weighing queries as they reached Kenley Manor.

In silence Joshua parked the car in the driveway, and, not waiting for him to open her door as she usually did, she got out of the car while Joshua redirected his steps to the kitchen and unlocked the door. Stepping in, he grasped her hand tightly, took her through the dimly lit hallway to the winding staircase and up to their bedroom, where he finally released her.

Presenting Joshua with a happy, devil-may-care facade, Ailith fell backward on the bed, in the manner she'd seen him do many times.

"Oh, I can't believe it!" she gushed. "We'll soon be traveling back to my time to get my parents and Aida."

"Believe it, baby." Joshua fell beside her. "Just have faith that Gene will make it happen."

He slipped his arm around her waist, pulling her close to kiss her cheek and then bury his face in her hair. Taking in a deep sigh, he snuggled up to her throat, kissing her there. Sitting up, he pulled her with him and stood, then began fidgeting with the fasteners on the back of her dress.

Ailith moaned softly. Every time she tried to reason her problems to a logical conclusion, it seemed Joshua robbed her of her thinking capacity. She responded with all the need inside her to his hot, demanding kisses, which he stopped only long enough to remove their clothing.

Starting his torturous assault on her once again, he lifted

her up and tenderly placed her back on the bed. Soon he locked his body with hers, inflicting breath-stealing sensations on her whole being. She uttered soft little sounds, vaguely recalling assisting in the removal of their clothes.

Joshua held Ailith to him with both arms enfolded around her. Each gentle thrust inside her swelled his heart to near bursting. Indeed, he thought it would explode from the powerful love he felt for her. He murmured sweet things in her ears, saying her name over and over. His thrusts became demanding, faster, his release gripping him in a surrender that overwhelmed him. He shuddered and clung to the woman who was now so much a part of him.

Yielding to the spasms of bliss that seized her, Ailith raked her nails across Joshua's broad back. Utterly enraptured, she trembled in her ecstasy, feeling extremely weightless. She clung to him a heartbeat longer before letting him withdraw from her completely. Without a sound, she went into his arms, laying her head on his chest.

He kissed her on her soft, flushed cheek. "I love you. I will never tire of telling you that." Tightening his arm around her, he drew her closer. "Good night, sweetheart."

When Ailith muttered something in response, he smiled. He felt sure she was tired and *knew* she wasn't feeling well. He wondered what was truly ailing her. It dawned on him that she hadn't answered his question about the baby.

Perhaps she had in a way. Surely he wouldn't have to *ask* her if she was pregnant. She would probably be so enchanted with the knowledge, she wouldn't wait to tell him. He decided not to mention the subject again. If she *was* pregnant, she surely wouldn't hesitate to tell him.

It was as shiny and bright as it was the day she first laid eyes on it. Joshua had cleaned it weeks ago, but somehow tonight the orb looked brand new—that instrument of mystery and magic.

She'd heard Gene explain to them—Joshua, Stephen, and herself—that he had figured out the meaning of the symbols. Now they all gave him their undivided attention.

Gene studied each one of them, then kept his gaze on her.

"It's going to be a hell of a ride. Wish I could join the three of you."

Ailith released a breathless gasp, the words he'd spoken nearly sending her reeling.

"Then you've not only figured out the meaning of the symbols, but also how to get us back in time?" Joshua asked in wonder.

"I hope so," Gene answered.

"What do you mean you hope so?" Stephen snapped. "I thought it was a foregone conclusion."

Unperturbed by Stephen's aggravation, Gene replied, "So far it is, Stephen." Holding out the orb for all to see, he indicated some markings on it. "These numbers represent years," he continued.

He pointed to what Ailith perceived to be tiny dots.

"They go as far back as the eighth century. Perhaps to the time of Charlemagne." He paused to allow his gaping friends to absorb his words and their meaning. "They end in the year 2000."

"My God," Joshua imparted, "Ailith could have gone *back* in time just as easily as she came forward." That thought made him cringe. He again surveyed the orb the professor still held up. "How did she end up here?"

Gene slid his hand across his chin. "She set the date," he replied.

Ailith straightened in her seat. "Set the date?" she echoed. "B-but how? I merely laid down to take a nap and *woke up* in this time period."

"Ailith," Gene said soothingly, "when you were telling your story, you said you twisted the handle." He looked at her over his glasses. "Or was it the dial? But you had to have done it with some effort. It's hard to turn."

"I-I don't recall," Ailith responded, her knees suddenly feeling like rubber. It dawned on her that she *had* turned the dial. But she hadn't known it *was* a dial. In her anxious state she'd turned the handle on the orb, thus setting the dial to this year and time.

Her knees buckled. Joshua was instantly beside her, slipping his arms around her waist, pressing her close. The same thought seemed to occur to everyone at the same time.

"Don't think about it, my love," Joshua commanded, leading her to the nearest chair. "Fate and the orb brought you to me."

"My God!" Stephen exclaimed in a ragged whisper. "As if the fifteenth century wasn't barbaric enough. She could have been even more at risk had she landed in the eighth century."

Joshua squeezed Ailith's hand, which was clammy and cold. Pulling her up out of the chair he'd so recently deposited her in, he drew her close, caressing her shoulders and back soothingly. He lifted her chin with his forefinger and placed a gentle kiss on her trembling soft lips.

"What is it, darling?" he murmured.

"I can't bear the thought of never having met you," she whispered, tears gathering in her eyes. "And from the history I've learned of those times, even horses were prized above women—"

"It's all right, Ailith," Gene soothed. "You must have been predestined to live in this century. Otherwise you would have turned the dial the other way, perhaps going from one hundred to seven hundred years back from your time. The difference certainly would have been noticeable, but not as shocking as your ascension to this modern world."

"You said the numbers on the orb represent years," Ailith said timidly.

Gene nodded. "That's correct, Ailith."

"What about months? Will we not be able to go back to the day *before* I went to the black tent as you suggested on our first visit?"

"I'm sorry, Ailith," Gene murmured. "But the hours move steadily forward in your time period, just as they do in this present time."

"I see," Ailith said in a choked voice. "So, even as we plan to go back, my parents may be living out their days in Lord Preston's dungeon."

A long silence followed Ailith's broken statement. The only sounds that could be heard were the ticking of the grandfather clock just outside Gene's library in the entrance hall and Ailith's soft sobs.

Finally Joshua asked, "Precisely how did she get here?" Still holding Ailith, he felt her start to relax in his arms.

"Well," Gene began, ambling around his desk to take a seat, "the orb works in conjunction with something else."

"What else?" Stephen inquired impatiently.

"I haven't figured that out yet," Gene admitted.

"Shit!" Joshua scoffed, seeing the same dismay he felt written in everyone else's features.

"Ailith," Gene said, "go over the part of your story again from where you entered the magician's tent to waking up in Josh's tent. Something besides just setting the dial to this date triggered the time warp."

Tiredly Ailith went over her story once again.

The three men, as if on cue, blurted in unison, "It was the black tent!"

"W-what?" she asked in astonishment. "How have you concluded that?"

"Because," Stephen began, then stopped to ask his companions with a sheepish grin, "May I?"

They nodded, and he proceeded to answer Ailith's question.

"Well, there was no natural light inside the tent. From what you said, even the flap was secured against the light."

"B-but there were lighted tapers in sconces," Ailith remembered.

"Yes, darling," Joshua said, "but their light wasn't natural."

"And," Gene added, "despite all that, it was the mysterious black tent. The fabric of the tent which, from the way you described it, didn't allow any sunlight to penetrate it."

"But, Gene," Ailith protested, "there was no natural light in Joshua's closet. It was very dark in there, and sometimes the orb would glow dimly. Then, just as suddenly, it would grow cold and dark. I wished to be in my own time then, but, of course, nothing happened. Why?"

"Because the dial is still set for this time period. 1998," Gene answered. "You apparently weren't fiddling with it this time."

"Goddammit!" Joshua flared. "That goddamn orb is dangerous! She could have just disappeared again into oblivion."

"Take it easy, Joshua," Gene said. "We don't want your temper surfacing. I'm convinced the orb only works in a black tent. Besides, light probably does filter into your closet from under the door crack. I'm sure Ailith was safe enough."

"But you wouldn't bet on it," Joshua grumbled.

Hunching his sagging shoulders, Gene threw up his hands.

"No, I wouldn't," he admitted. "But knowing what we know now, she certainly is safe at the moment."

Joshua drew in a breath. "What have we got facing us, Gene?"

Ailith marveled at the amount of preparation that would be involved for their journey back in time as Gene advised them to get authentic and exact replicas of garments worn in that time period.

No reflection on Ailith, he said, since, after all, she'd lived back then.

During the course of the conversation, Stephen sat and folded his hands behind his head, sprawling his long legs carelessly in front of him, anticipation lighting his cobalt eyes.

"How will we all be transferred at once, since there is only one orb?" he asked.

"Good question." Gene picked up a pen, only to begin absently tapping it against his desk. "I think holding hands or some physical contact with one another, while one of you holds the orb, will be sufficient.''

Stephen nodded and shifted in his seat. ''Shouldn't we be on horses or something? Wouldn't want to arrive there without transportation.''

Joshua rolled his eyes heavenward. ''If we are on horses, how will they be transported?''

''The same way you will be,'' Gene responded. ''You will be in the same physical contact with the horses, as with each other. You will each be astride a horse, holding one another's hand, or whatever. Just don't lose touch—physical touch—with one another during the transportation process.''

Ailith thought she'd better ask the all-important question. ''When do we leave?''

''As soon as everything is set in place,'' Gene assured her.

''Okay,'' Joshua said. ''What do we need?''

''First and foremost, you need to construct a black tent, large enough to accommodate three people sitting on three large horses,'' Gene explained. ''By the time that's completed, everything else should be in readiness.''

''And when everything is finally set, then what do we do?'' Ailith asked.

''You go inside the tent and set the dial to 1413,'' Gene replied. ''That should breach the time barrier again.''

''Sounds good,'' Joshua said. ''If everything goes well, how do we get back? We'll have three extra people coming back to this time period.''

''Sit one each on a horse behind each of you. You'll be holding on to one another to get back here, the same way you leave. Your three passengers will, of course, be holding onto you.''

''Looks good on paper,'' Stephen muttered. ''But a niggling question: How is it the cot Ailith went to sleep on didn't leave with her?''

Gene reared back and took a hearty stretch. ''It would have,'' he answered afterward. ''If she were actually on it.

In spite of what she said, I'm convinced she must have rolled off somehow at the last crucial minute.''

The explanation was logical enough, so Ailith didn't argue with that. As it was, it was hard enough for her to make sense out of the situation. She shuddered sometimes to think it might all be a dream. But for her parents and the question of Aimon, she wouldn't call it a nightmare because of all the magical inventions. And because of Joshua, her wonderful love.

If it *was* a dream, she never wanted to awaken.

When Gene offered her a drink, her thoughts snapped back to the matter at hand. Having heard on television about the bad effect alcohol had on unborn babies, she declined the wine, but raised a glass of 7UP instead, ignoring Joshua's predatory stare.

They toasted the successful translation of the symbols on the orb, then left an excited, well-satisfied Gene to further amuse himself.

Chapter 29

THE EXCITEMENT WAS palpable.

With progress delayed by rainy weather, it took three days to complete the construction of the tent. It loomed large, taking up nearly three times the amount of space one tent usually did.

Ailith stood outside with Joshua, looking at it. Neighbors and passers-by stopped to inquire about the reason for having the tent there so soon after the Medieval Faire had ended. Was another fair on the horizon?

"My fairs are held only once a year," Joshua assured them. "This tent is only a salesman's demonstration and will come down in a week."

The kindly old woman who lived next door with three cats, a parakeet, and two dogs, inquired, "A salesman's demonstration? Whatever for?"

Ailith shifted her weight. "They would like Joshua to purchase one of these for next year's fair, Mrs. Lee."

The explanation proved satisfactory, although some others grouched that since the tent was already erected, Joshua could have been gracious enough to have a party for at least one day—a point he ignored.

Back inside the house, they were joined by Stephen and

Connor. A week ago Joshua had told her Connor should be informed of her true origins. She and Connor had become fast friends, and she genuinely liked him, so she didn't object to Joshua's suggestion.

At the news Connor at first had displayed disbelief, then awe, and finally acceptance. He had always been attentive to her, but since the revelation, Connor's devotion was inspiring and quite amusing. Ailith would have been flattered if he hadn't made her feel like a lackwit all over again just when she was beginning to overcome that particular sentiment about herself.

She was proud—no, ecstatic—about her accomplishments. She could read and write and had begun to acquire a basic understanding of the twentieth century. And now there was Connor? Connor, who felt the need to explain something to her every time he spoke around her.

True, all things modern awed her. And she hadn't given much thought to the mechanism of a manure spreader or the workings of a lightbulb. One was supposed to make things grow, and a flick of a switch lit things up with the other. How these things were accomplished were certainly interesting, but not necessarily imperative to know.

If Connor continued with his relentless teachings, she would surely end up being the smartest person in Kenley Manor.

She took a bite of the sandwich she'd retrieved from the tray Connor placed on the table in the breakfast room.

"I fixed the sandwich the way you like it, Miss Ailith," Connor explained. "With mayonnaise, pickle, and lettuce. The mayonnaise, of course, was made from eggs and lemon juice and perhaps another ingredient or two. The pickle was once a cucumber just pickled in brine. Did you have pickling way back then?"

Taking another bite of her sandwich, Ailith gave Connor an exasperated look.

Joshua laughed. "Connor?"

"Yes, Mr. J?"

"Do you really feel it's necessary to explain the ingredients of the food we eat?"

Connor drew his eyebrows together. "Not to you, Mr. J, but Miss Ailith might be interested."

"Darling, as long as it tastes good, do you really give a damn about what's in it?" Joshua asked.

"Of course not," Ailith replied with a chuckle. "I really don't."

"Well," Stephen boomed, "I'm convinced no one *really* gives a damn about what they're eating, Connor. If you'd stop making an ass of yourself because of Ailith, you'd be convinced, too."

"Stephen!" Ailith said with reproof. "I'm sure Connor thought he was being helpful. I appreciate it, Connor, I really do, but I would also appreciate going back to the way we were, before you learned of my true origins."

"Of course, Miss Ailith," Connor agreed, unperturbed. "But if you need to know something, I'll be happy to explain it to you."

"Thank you."

"Now that that's settled," Stephen said, "did you fill my duffel bags with the things I listed, Connor, my good man?"

"Yes, I did, Mr. Steve. Everyone's bag is ready for transport."

"Good," Joshua put in. "When there aren't so many prying eyes, we'll get the horses here tonight. We leave sometime after midnight. Connor, you know to tell my parents that I've taken a short vacation. Tell Mother she's still welcome for her daily visit." His parents had moved to their condo several weeks ago, but his mother made it a point to stop over every day. "My assistant will take over my galleries until I return. Any questions?"

"None that I can think of, Mr. J."

"Good," Stephen responded. "Let's all synchronize our watches."

Joshua frowned. "Why?"

Stephen shrugged. "I don't know. Seems like the thing

to do,'' he speculated. "Everyone else does it when they're about to do something significant.''

Joshua snickered. "*Significant* doesn't seem a strong enough word for what we're about to undertake.''

Two hours later, Ailith's heart nearly rose to her throat. She didn't quite know how to feel. The excitement inside her ran rampant, as did the fear. What they planned was indeed significant and so much, much more. She had excused herself nearly an hour ago to lie down and try to nap, but she couldn't relax.

It had been nearly three months since she'd come here, and she didn't know what she would face when she returned home. She *should* know. The quality of life hadn't changed one whit in her absence. Neither had the circumstances surrounding her parents' imprisonment.

Perhaps she knew after all what she would face.

She rested her hands across her stomach. "Joshua,'' she murmured softly.

He'd never asked again if she was pregnant. He trusted her implicitly, and she was betraying that trust. She had to tell him, for she could betray him no longer.

Briefly she wondered if Preston Claybourne would have been as charitable in his assumption of her pregnancy. Would he have accepted her evasive answer without further question? She doubted it.

Ailith knew Joshua wouldn't be pleased at her revelation, because she'd hidden it from him for so long, but would he become angry? Suppose he refused to go back in time and wouldn't allow her to go back either?

She wanted to weep—a malady that affected her with increasing fervor of late. If Joshua did get angry, he would be justified in doing so. The longer she delayed telling him, the harder it would be to do so. She lifted the receiver on the phone and pressed the number for the breakfast nook. When Connor answered, she told him she needed to see Joshua right away.

She was standing at the window, looking out at the black

tent when, after five minutes, Joshua appeared. Walking up behind her, he slipped his strong arms around her thankfully-still-slim waist. He kissed her behind her neck and nibbled at her earlobe.

"You summoned me, Lady Ailith?"

He sniffed the freshness of her hair.

Ailith placed her hand over his. "Yes," she whispered tremulously as he blew into her ear.

He turned her around to face him. "What is it, Ailith? Are you afraid of what will happen tonight?"

"How can I possibly be afraid, knowing you'll be at my side?" she replied with a show of bravado. But in spite of her brave words, sudden dread shrouded her, a portent of danger that she ignored.

Joshua chuckled. "I'm flattered, my love, for your confidence in me. Even if I don't share that view."

He led her away from the window to a chair. Sitting down, he pulled her into his lap.

"There's something bothering you, darling. I want to know what it is."

"Oh, Joshua!" Ailith nearly strangled on the sob she swallowed back. "I'm afraid what I have to tell you will make you angry."

"Unless you tell me everything I know about you is some elaborate hoax perpetrated by some scheming promotor, there's nothing you can say that will anger me."

Ailith released a short, quick breath. Her eyes met and held Joshua's golden ones.

"Joshua," she said, so softly it almost came out as a whisper, "we're going to have a baby."

A look of astonishment passed over his face, which in a heartbeat was split by a wide grin. Then he bent her backward across his lap, far enough to reach her mouth and give her a passionate kiss.

"Oh, Joshua!" Ailith said breathlessly when the kiss ended. "I thought you would be angry with me."

"Angry?" Joshua replied with amazement. "My sweet

love, I couldn't be happier. Why would I be angry with you?''

''Well, because of tonight. . . .'' Ailith began, but halted when she felt his body tense.

''How long have you known about this?'' he asked in a low, dangerous tone. He narrowed his eyes, fury hardening his features as comprehension dawned on him. ''You knew when I asked you about it, didn't you?''

Ailith swallowed convulsively. ''Y-yes.''

''Goddammit, Ailith!'' He pushed her aside and stood up. ''You've obviously known for quite some time. Shit!'' He stomped to the other side of the room. ''Why the hell didn't you tell me?''

''B-because I-I didn't want you to cancel our plans—''

''Well, they're certainly out,'' he interrupted with a snarl. ''Unless I go without you, there's no way I am going to risk you and our child to some time-warp fate!''

Ailith felt the color drain from her face. Clutching her hands to her breasts, she stood, raising pleading eyes to Joshua.

''Please don't say that, Joshua. You must let me go. I am to be your guide. And there's no way you would be able to identify my parents. Or convince them of who you are or why you're there.''

Anger and the feeling of betrayal slowly simmering, Joshua stared coldly at his wife. ''How could you, Ailith? You knew exactly what you were doing by telling me this at the eleventh hour,'' he stated with bitterness, ''when indeed there's no turning back at this juncture. You've put our baby at risk in more ways than one.''

''I-I have not, Joshua!'' Ailith said, trying to defend herself and fighting back tears.

''Yes, you have,'' Joshua insisted angrily. ''You should have an obstetrician to insure you'll have a healthy baby.'' He paused then continued. ''If my baby is injured, or worse, in any way, I'll never forgive you.''

Joshua's words fell on her ears like ice chips. She loved their unborn child as much as he did, but felt defenseless against his anger. It cut deeply that he thought she would put the baby in peril. All she wanted was to have her parents and friend live in the twentieth century. And, except to satisfy her curiosity, she no longer cared about the identity of Aimon's mother. But her obsession might have lost her Joshua's love.

"I'm so sorry you feel that way, Joshua," she said in a shaky voice. "Nothing would wound me more than to lose your love or to be beyond your power of forgiveness. I would never again be happy without seeing the faces of the three people I so dearly love. But I know I wouldn't want to survive if I've lost your love."

After imparting that, she looked at him briefly, then went into the bathroom and closed the door.

Joshua scowled at the door, too angry to care about the hurt and remorse in Ailith's eyes when she'd looked at him. Women were the same in any time period—fallacious and cunning. They used any means available to them to get what they wanted. And the prettier they were, the more guileful they were.

How could she even think of exposing his unborn baby to the hellish dangers of the fifteenth century just to get her parents?

He paused in his thinking. He would walk through the fires of hell if he had to for his parents. Why should Ailith be any different?

Well, *he* wasn't pregnant! *She* was.

He frowned at the closed bathroom door again. It seemed as if she wasn't coming out of there soon. How dare she get angry enough at him and lock herself behind closed doors? He should be the one sulking in a locked room. She'd wronged him, after all. But you'd think by her actions she was justified in shutting him out.

Maybe he had been harsh and hasty with her. But it wasn't every day that a man learned he was to become a father for the first time. He should have never learned under the circumstances in which he'd found out—on the verge of a journey through time to save his in-laws from his belligerent ancestor.

The scheming witch!

Since he'd promised her he would, he'd get her parents here, but she'd still have hell to pay when they got safely back to the present.

Once again he glanced at the closed door before going downstairs to await delivery of the horses and complete final preparations for the journey back in time.

Chapter 30

NEAR MIDNIGHT AILITH stood in the tent listening to Gene's last minute instructions, grouching to herself. If she had been in possession of the orb, she would have gone to the tent and sent *herself* back in time. No words, other than what was necessary for the sake of a safe journey, passed between her and Joshua.

She was willing to overlook *his* autocracy. *His* unwillingness to understand her need to have her parents with her was what had changed her weepy mood to a murderous one.

Why was he being so stubborn? She did comprehend that his anger was due to his fear for their unborn baby, but why couldn't he get past that and be civil to her? He could have at least let her try to assure him that she would be extra careful. Annoyed at his obstinacy, she vowed to avoid even looking at him if possible.

Her medieval attire made her profoundly uncomfortable. Having become used to modern-day dress, she wondered how she had ever tolerated long, multilayered garments.

"Is everyone ready?" Gene called, excitement and anticipation written in his features.

"We're all properly clothed and properly advised," Stephen assured him. "And anxious to fly."

"This can't be the same man who not so long ago feared the unknown?" Joshua teased.

"I'm scared shitless," Stephen admitted. "And, in all honesty, even now I don't think it will happen."

Gene's bushy white eyebrows straightened, forming an even more indistinguishable line.

"So, peasant," he said with mock severity, "you doubt me? Mount up, ye of little faith, and let me prove you wrong."

Joshua sniggered at Gene's bold confidence and went to secure Ailith's wool mantle around her.

"Do I have to wear this now?" she asked, stiffening to ward off the delicious feel of his hands on her.

"Yes!" Joshua snapped in a tone that brooked no further argument. "Back then there was no pollution to obscure the atmosphere. It's probably cold enough there to freeze a well digger's ass right now."

Well, it wasn't that cold here, Ailith thought with resentment. It wasn't cold at all! No matter that it was the last week of November. With the heavy mantle fastened so tightly around her, she swore she would faint from the heat. But she dared not complain. She wouldn't give Joshua further reason to gripe that she wasn't taking care of herself and *his* baby.

"I'm not so sure you should be straddling that horse in your condition," he declared.

Stephen narrowed his eyes, overhearing the comment. "What condition?"

Joshua gazed at Ailith a long while before answering.

"She's pregnant," he finally grumbled.

"What!" Stephen bellowed.

"Is she really?" Gene inquired.

Joshua gave a curt nod. "Yes."

"Wonderful!" Gene exclaimed. "What's your problem, Joshua? I should think you'd be very happy. As far as riding a horse is concerned, that can't be anything but helpful. Strengthens her pelvic muscles for natural delivery."

"Right," Joshua growled. "Natural birth in a barbaric, hostile world."

When Gene grinned and ignored Joshua's testiness, Ailith sincerely wished she could learn how to do that.

"Which century are you describing? Hers or ours?" Joshua glowered at Gene.

"Joshua," Gene said mildly, "you should be gone only two days at the most. Follow all the instructions I've given you, and you'll get back home in no time, safe and sound. Then you can pamper your wife throughout her pregnancy. And where she can give birth securely. In *our* nonhostile, nonbarbaric time."

"Well, it's too late to debate the issue now," Stephen stated. "All systems are set to go."

"We're not in a frigging spaceship, Stephen," Joshua grouched.

Stephen merely laughed. "No, we're going to be on frigging space horses."

"Enough of this," Gene chastised. "It's time to get moving. Joshua, help Ailith onto her horse."

Grumbling, Joshua complied.

Ailith had never sat on a horse before. Had Joshua considered that? She and Aida traveled about mostly on foot. And if the distance proved too far, they were allowed to journey around in a horse-pulled cart. In the *cart*, not on the *horse*.

This horse looked especially big and wide. And tall. What if she fell off? The horse whinnied, shaking its head up and down, and Ailith sat in the saddle as stiff as a board.

"Oh, no!" Joshua said through clenched teeth. Threading his fingers through his hair, he frowned at Ailith. "You're afraid of that horse, aren't you?"

"Y-yes," she whispered, clinging to the saddlehorn.

"Shit! And I thought I knew everything about you," he snapped, reaching for her. "What other surprises do you have in store for me?"

He set her on her feet.

"So she's afraid of a horse," Stephen said with ire, glaring at Joshua. "That's no reason to snap at her. What's the matter with you, Joshua?"

"This doesn't concern you, Stephen, so stay the hell out of it," Joshua ordered.

"May I suggest, Josh," Gene began, unperturbed, "that you sit Ailith across your lap and secure all the duffel bags to her horse?"

Joshua's face heated with agitation. He loved Ailith so. But as much as he loved her, he wanted to stay angry with her. She had deceived him, after all. Yet he couldn't stay angry if she was snuggled up against him, where he could feel her sweet softness. She would probably have him aroused the whole damn trip.

That made him even angrier. The seductive, little medieval witch. Unfortunately he knew he had to bow to circumstances.

"Yes, Gene, that's an excellent idea," he replied stiffly.

After several more minutes of unnecessary arguing, everything was finally in readiness. Ailith's heart pounded in her bosom in anticipation of what was to come. She leaned her head against Joshua's chest and found his heart was beating just as fast.

She felt safe with him, although she knew he was apprehensive. Despite his anger at her, she knew how much he loved her. It was solely for her that he was making this dangerous trip. Somehow she would convince him that she wasn't the devious woman he thought her to be. She would make him realize that if the orb had been decoded sooner, they would have made the trip and returned before even her suspicions regarding her pregnancy had been confirmed. Mostly, however, she would make him realize just how much she loved him.

She looked down from the security of Joshua's lap to see Connor rush through the flap.

"Connor!" Gene yelled. "You know better than to open that flap now!"

That was the first time Ailith had ever seen Gene perturbed.

"I'm sorry, Professor Callenberg," Connor said apologetically, "but I couldn't let them go without saying good-bye."

His voice quavered, and his features showed the fear he was feeling.

"It's going to be all right, Connor," Joshua reassured him. "You're a good friend, and I appreciate your concern. Just hold down the fort until we get back."

"Sure thing, Mr. J.," Connor drawled. "So long, sir. Good-bye, Mr. Steve." He gave Ailith a gentle smile. "And you, Miss Ailith, take care of yourself."

"See you soon, my good man," Stephen told him.

"Good-bye, Connor," Ailith said as Joshua drew her closer to his body.

Blood pounding in her head, she watched Stephen slip his hand through the curve of her husband's elbow. The horses stood stock still, and she wondered if they had been trained to do that. She saw Joshua turn the dial on the orb and heard Gene's voice from a vast distance yelling something that sounded like "Wait! The black tent for your return!" But she couldn't be sure.

Her mind was as foggy as the mist that suddenly enveloped her, and, despite her best effort, she couldn't stop herself from sinking into a deep sleep.

Chapter 31

AILITH'S EYES FLEW open abruptly at the sound of Stephen's voice.

"Well, damn me!" he expelled in astonishment. "I can't believe we did it!"

Still seated on Joshua's lap as he sat on the horse, Ailith looked around. It was pitch dark and damned cold. Where were they?

"Ailith?" Joshua murmured. "Are you doing okay?"

"I . . . yes," she responded nervously. "I could have sworn I had fallen asleep."

"You did," Joshua told her. "We all did." He glanced at his watch with the luminous dial. "But it was only for a few minutes. Probably just long enough for the transporting to take place."

"Well, I'm grateful it was that gentle," Stephen put in. "Considering the number of centuries breached, we're lucky we didn't arrive here all bruised and bloodied. Just where the hell *is* here anyway?"

"Ailith?" Joshua questioned, looking down at her.

She sat up straight and surveyed her surroundings, what she could see of them, which wasn't very much in view of the fact that there was no moonlight to illuminate the area.

"Why," she declared in a small voice, "I haven't the faintest notion."

"What?" chorused two very annoyed male voices.

"Joshua," she said imploringly, "I do not travel these parts at night. Or *any* part at night, for that matter. These parts ain't fit for man or beasts at night, partners!" She stopped and giggled, realizing how modern she sounded.

Joshua laughed. "No more television for you, young lady, especially westerns."

Ailith chuckled, loving the rumbling sound he made when he laughed. She scrutinized the area more closely to try to get her bearings. They stood on the precipice of the forest she'd left so many weeks ago. Eerie night sounds reached her ears.

"I'm certain we're near the spot that held the black tent. It's too dark to be absolute about it, though."

As he had during the breach through time, Stephen tightly gripped the reins of the two nervously prancing horses, his and the one they were using as a packhorse.

"Why is it so hard for you to be sure, Ailith?"

"Well, Stephen, when I was here last, there was a bazaar going on. But the forest where DeLepee Rouge hides out is behind us and—"

"What's a DeLepee Rouge?" Stephen interrupted.

"An outlaw," Ailith answered. "And I fear we could be in danger of an attack if we tarry here any longer."

"Then by all means show us the way out, Ailith," Joshua commanded. "These swords we're wearing are no more than props."

"Yeah," Stephen agreed. "The only thing we've ever skewered were sirloins on the grill. And for that we used forks. Besides, it's cold out here. Before we go, Josh, tell me the plan again if the real Preston returns?"

"We won't be there long enough for the real Preston to return," Joshua said with calm assurance. "At most three or four hours, only long enough for Ailith to explain everything to her parents, find Aida, and make our escape. Since I've decided the best way to get into the keep with the least possible explanations is if I pose as Lord Radford, I can't foresee any other problems.''

Stephen snorted.

"Don't fret, Stephen," Ailith reassured him. " 'Tis the beginning of December in this time, and Lord Radford always travels to Essex to visit Lady Glenna for the Christmas season. Although the festivities don't begin until December twenty-fourth, he likes to go fox hunting. However, 'tis doubtful he has finished with King Hal in Dover.''

When no one responded, she once again looked behind her at the forest, then at the three pathways that led in different directions. She urged Joshua west, in the direction she perceived the castle to be.

Going through pastures and fields, they passed wattle-and-daub huts, some with thatched roofs. Here and there, light from a tallow or hearth fire could be seen through a crack in a loosely hinged window.

When they came to the apple orchards, Ailith knew they were no more than ten kilometers away from His Lordship's keep. The level terrain they'd been traversing abruptly changed, and the horses seemed to strain with their burdens as they crested a steep bluff. Even in the dark Ailith saw their breath plumming, circling their heads like white smoke. Elation filled her when, directly in their path in the near distance, the sprawling stone structure came into view.

"There it is!" she exclaimed.

"It looks like a solid fortress," Joshua said in awe, taking in as much as he could with the help of the many lighted torches along the curtained walls.

"Very impressive," Stephen commented. "But how do we get in?"

"That shouldn't be a problem," Joshua said. "Ailith is known. She used to live here, remember?"

Stephen nodded. "All right, let's get going then so we can accomplish our impossible mission and get the hell out of Dodge."

They trotted their horses to the entrance of the bailey, stopping in front of the drawbridge.

"Hark!" a masculine voice called from the gatehouse. "What matters concern you with Greyhawke Keep at this hour?"

"It's Neville," Ailith whispered in relief to Joshua.

"Neville?" he responded.

"Yes, one of His Lordship's knights. I think he's smitten with me."

Joshua scowled. "Will I have to fight a duel with this Neville person to keep you?" he asked, his tone tinged with jealousy.

Ailith smiled serenely. "I never said *I* was smitten with *him*, did I?"

"*You* would hardly have a say in the matter—" Joshua began.

"Dammit!" Stephen barked, maneuvering his horse and the packhorse closer to Joshua's. "Would you two stop bickering and answer the man before he pours a caldron of hot oil or something equally damaging and painful down on us?"

"Good point," Joshua agreed. "Make yourself known, Ailith."

"No, Joshua, it's best . . . I mean *'tis* best you make yourself known. You are the lord of the keep. Only please remember to speak the medieval language. I fear by the time this is all over, I will be so thoroughly confused I will not want to speak at all."

"Well, you're doing enough speaking *now* to compensate for a lifetime of silence," Stephen chastised. "I am getting the willies out here. One of you better damn well make yourself known, and now!"

"I guess I'm it," Joshua grumbled. "Here goes nothing." He lifted his gaze toward the gatehouse. " 'Tis I, Neville," he announced in a deep, commanding voice, imitating, as much as possible, the way Ailith had described Preston's voice. "Open the gate. I and my companions seek the shelter of my solar."

"Lord Radford!" Neville shouted in surprise. "We had word that the king sent you to Essex to be at the side of your lady wife who is near her time of—"

Neville's voice trailed off at Joshua's stern, "Neville!"

"F-forgive me, Your Lordship. I'm but a fool to listen to such gossip. Raise the portal!" he called.

In a few minutes the gate was raised high enough for them to enter the bailey. Soldiers who were part of the permanent castle guard rushed out of their sleeping quarters, swords at the ready.

"Be at ease, men," Joshua called out with all the authority he could muster.

" 'Tis His Lordship!" someone remarked, sheathing his sword.

Ailith sat erect as they made their way across the bailey to the thick gray stone steps of the keep, which led to the Great Hall.

Joshua slid off his horse, then reached up and helped her down. The hood of the scarlet mantle that covered her head and part of her face slipped backwards.

"Why, it's Lady Ailith!" Neville declared in astonishment. "Saints and angels be praised. His Lordship delivered her from the clutches of DeLepee Rouge!"

"Aye, Neville, saints be praised indeed," Ailith said. "But we are weary, for we have traveled long and far. Have someone start a fire in the hearth in His Lordship's solar, then summon my parents and Brint Pfiester to his presence."

"Oh, my lady, I will gladly have someone fire up the hearth. But I am afraid I cannot summon your parents or the magician."

Ailith's heart slammed against her chest, taking away her breath so she couldn't speak. She had arrived too late. Lord Radford had done away with her parents. She swayed against Joshua, and he slipped his arm around her waist to steady her.

"Why can't they be summoned?" he snapped.

Disapproval flickered in Neville's features as he observed Joshua holding Ailith possessively. "Because they are not here, my lord," he answered, a distinct chill in his voice.

"Goddammit!" Stephen muttered under his breath.

Joshua took a menacing step closer to Neville. "Where in bloody hell are they?" he asked, his tone leaving no doubt to his annoyance.

Neville paled considerably. "Lady Ailith's parents journeyed to the shire of Cleveland a fortnight ago, my lord."

"Why?" came Joshua's icy response.

"For the burial of Aida's last living relative," Neville answered. "Her uncle succumbed to a fever. Galen and Meghanne thought they had lost their daughter, Lady Ailith, to the outlaw, my lord. They have taken Aida as their own. Their grief has been great."

"Oh," Ailith whimpered, unable to stop the tears that began streaming down her cheeks at the relief she felt that her parents were safe. "W-when will they return?"

"Any day, my lady," Neville assured in a husky voice, giving her a gentle smile.

Not liking Neville's tone, Joshua narrowed his eyes and pulled Ailith a little closer to him.

Seeing the look, Neville cleared his throat and explained, "We all anxiously await them. Meghanne left Rufus to rule as the keep's steward until her return, but Rufus fell ill two days after their departure."

"And the magician?" Joshua asked.

"No one is sure where he has gone, my lord. He left two moons past."

Joshua posed his features into a ferocious frown, and Neville took a step back. The man couldn't know that Joshua's feral glare was due as much to his disappointment at not finding the deCotmers there as it was to the admiring look he'd given Ailith.

"Th-the Great Hall is not as t-tidy as it could be, my lord, since Rufus fell ill," Neville said in a nervous rush.

"Enough!" Joshua roared. "I'll hear no excuses. Rouse

a servant and have my chambers prepared for my habitancy. I will see your face no more this night!''

"Aye, Lord Radford,'' Neville intoned frostily, hurrying away to do Joshua's bidding.

Two stablehands rushed forward to take the duffel bags off the horses, placing them on the steps and leading the horses to the stable. Stephen watched them disappear in the stable then cleared his throat. He laughed, the sound full of mischief and boyishness.

"I will see your face no more this night? Way to go, Josh! Quite an impressive performance. Just don't push it. Your enthusiasm might blow your cover.'' He picked up a duffle bag and started up the steps. "By the way, Your Lordship, who's guarding the gate?''

Joshua glanced at Ailith.

"It's all right, Joshua,'' she murmured in a reassuring voice. "There are others on the wall.''

He reached for the other two duffel bags. One he lifted with a little effort, but the other wouldn't budge.

"What the hell's in there?'' he growled, pointing at the overstuffed bag.

Stephen skidded back down the stairs. "You take one handle, I'll take the other one.''

"What the hell good are the servants?'' Joshua grouched.

"This stuff is too valuable to trust to lowly medieval servants, Josh,'' Stephen admonished. "Quit grumbling and help me bring this stuff to our suite.''

Ailith giggled. "I won't tell you about our *suite*, Stephen,'' she mocked. "I'll just let you see for yourself.''

She led the way into the Great Hall and stopped just inside the doorway. The sight, as well as the foul odor that greeted them, stung her senses.

Dogs slept in rotting, withered rushes, which she was sure hadn't been changed in days. The scent of sooty smoke from the vast central hearth filtered in the air, but couldn't disguise the smell of sour, greasy food, still left on the trestle tables from the last evening's meal. To top all that, not only did she get a whiff of the dogs' calling cards, she was sure she stepped in their generous contribution to the rushes as well. Her stomach lurched, and her anger simmered. How dare they treat His Lordship's keep in this manner?

Stephen wrinkled his nose, his face mirroring the distaste she felt as he gawked around.

"What a garbage dump. What a field day environmentalists would have with this. Even skunks would detour this pigsty."

"To some it's a garbage dump and environmental nightmare, Stephen," Joshua remarked wryly. "But to the antique connoisseur, it's old world charm."

"Joshua! Stephen! This is nothing to joke about," Ailith whispered in outrage. "*Look* at this place!"

"*Smell* this place," Stephen added.

Neville came down the stairs and walked, rather gingerly, through the rushes toward them. " 'Tis truly sorry I am, milord," he blurted to Joshua.

Joshua blazed a withering stare in Neville's direction. "You will have this corrected before I break my fast on the morrow!" he commanded angrily. "You'd best see that the scullery wenches are set to work at first light. Now. Lady Ailith and Sir Stephen and I will retire to my quarters. Disturb me at your own peril."

"Your privacy will be assured, milord," Neville called over his shoulder as he rushed out the doors of the Great Hall.

"Lead the way to the master's chambers, milady," Joshua whispered to her.

Oh, yes—aye—Ailith thought, she needed to get out of there before she retched out her insides, thereby reminding Joshua that she was pregnant.

"Follow me," she said with a sigh, starting for the stairs.

Chapter 32

REACHING THE SOLAR with Joshua and Stephen, Ailith found it infinitely more appealing. Tapers along the walls gave light to the room. But despite the several logs burning in the hooded fireplace, she still felt an uncomfortable chill.

"What a dump," Stephen said, mimicking Bette Davis.

He and Joshua dropped their bags on the stone floor.

Ailith sat on the settle, which was covered with animal pelts. Leaning back, she took in calming breaths.

Joshua sat next to her. "Are you feeling all right, sweetheart?"

The concern in his voice nearly undid her. She wanted to cry. Why had she insisted on taking the journey back here? Her parents were not even at the keep. The longer they stayed to wait for them, the more peril they would be in. She hadn't long known Neville before she'd left, but she knew he was crafty and sly.

Her eyes feeling misty with lurking tears, she sighed and looked at Joshua to answer his question.

"Yes, Josh. Now I am," she murmured. "I was just a little repulsed by the stench in the Great Hall, that's all."

"Good. I don't want you ill."

He paused and swung his gaze to Stephen, who stood looking like he shared Joshua's sentiment of wanting to be someplace else.

"Grab a chair or a bench or whatever, Stephen," he encouraged. "We have to decide our next move."

"I suggest we move on over to the twentieth century," Stephen conveyed. He sauntered to the glowing fireplace and held out his hands, absorbing the warmth. "It's colder than a witch's tit in here."

"And you can't get much colder than that," Joshua said in an attempt at humor.

They faced an unexpected dilemma, one they hadn't thought of—not finding the deCotmers at the keep. He hoped the delay in waiting for them wouldn't cause Ailith any major problems. Certainly he hadn't planned on bringing his pregnant wife back to this century. Though he wanted to stay angry with her, his heart melted at her forlorn look.

It was as much his fault as hers that they were here. He could have refused to come. Or destroyed that goddamned orb to keep her from making the attempt herself. But without knowing her parents' fate, her heart would have shattered. Besides, he wanted to give her everything he could to make her happy. Wanting to see her parents again was all she asked for. As stupendous as that request was, he loved her too much to deny her anything.

They'd *both* put their unborn child at risk. But had Ailith told him sooner, they most definitely would've delayed this trip of a lifetime.

"We're here now," Stephen was saying, going toward the duffel bags. "We might as well make the best of it until your in-laws arrive."

Ailith got up from the settle and went to her duffel bag, unzipping it. Stephen smiled at her in friendly challenge and unzipped his.

"Me first," Ailith said with a laugh.

She began emptying her bag. First she took out a loaf of sliced white bread and placed it beside the box of soda

crackers she'd already retrieved. Next came three thermoses, several cans of meat, chicken breast, smoked oysters, Cheez Whiz, liverwurst, and tuna. Wrapped in foil and
covered in dry ice and wineskins were several cans of 7UP,
three bottles of champagne, and a carton of orange juice.

While Ailith was unloading her horde, Stephen was doing likewise with his.

Joshua stared as Stephen pulled out a nine millimeter
pistol with extra clips and a silencer accompanied by a .357
magnum.

"Shit!"

Ignoring Joshua's angry expletive, Stephen continued un-
packing and also took out three large thermoses, a battery-
powered one-hundred-fifty-watt light, which he immediately switched on, and two flashlights. Another retrieval
yielded a large bag of mint candy, another large thermos,
and some plastic eating utensils. Finally he pulled out a
first-aid kit the size of a briefcase. Checking the inside, he
found a small box of plastic bandages, a bottle of rubbing
alcohol, a small bottle of tincture of iodine, a one-hundred-
count bottle each of extra-strength aspirin and Tylenol, a
box of Alka-Seltzer, a packet of Rolaids, tissues, presoaked
towelettes, and sterile, rolled bandages.

Stephen straightened himself and sighed with satisfaction. "Ahh, twentieth-century perks. I feel so much better
now."

Positively incredulous at what he saw, Joshua looked
from his wife to his friend. "Are you two mad?" he gritted.
"Guns and cans and thermoses? And whatever the hell else
you're *not* supposed to have in this time?" He scowled at
Ailith. "I'll deal with you later," he said, then turned back
to Stephen. "You must have a damn good reason for doing
this, since you do know better. Care to explain it?"

As usual Stephen was unaffected by Joshua's temper and
merely nodded.

"I do have a reason, pal," he said with a nonchalant
shrug. "It's called survival. A bullet flies faster than an
arrow every time."

"Stephen!" Joshua growled.

"Come on, Josh," Stephen interjected, impatient. "What's the harm? Nothing brought from the twentieth century stays here. I'll see to that. In the meantime, one of us may cut a finger or get a headache." He gave Ailith's belly a pointed look. "Or an upset stomach. And without proper attention we could get an infection or something. I promise you, the guns will not even be brought out unless we're in danger of losing our very lives."

Joshua glared at Stephen, then shucked off his black velvet cloak. It had suddenly become very warm in there. In truth, he did feel better knowing they had twentieth-century protection with them. They were all very much at risk, and he would die himself before letting harm come to Ailith. He grudgingly conceded Stephen's forethought was indeed a wise one.

"All right, Stephen. I guess there's no harm. As long as we don't interfere with the natural order of the way history is supposed to proceed."

He looked at Ailith, who was scrambling for something inside her duffel bag. With a triumphant smile, she lifted out a can opener.

Joshua shook his head. "Geez," he snorted, "it's a conspiracy."

"Blame Connor."

Ailith unscrewed a thermos and poured steaming hot clam chowder into the cup that also served as the cover, then passed it over to Joshua.

"Bon appétit, my love."

Unscrewing the tops from the other two thermoses, she filled one for herself and one for Stephen.

"I have an idea," Stephen said.

He went to the settle and removed the animal skins, placing them on the floor in front of the fireplace.

Joshua steered Ailith in front of the fire. "Well, one couldn't ask for a better picnic spot."

They all sat down and dined on clam chowder, soda crackers, smoked oysters, Spam sandwiches, and Cheez Whiz. Having forgotten to put in glasses for the champagne, they each took turns drinking out of the bottle. Each time they raised the bottle to their lips, the bubbles overflowed.

Not wanting to harm the baby, Ailith had only two sips of her favorite beverage, before settling for a can of 7UP, shaking the can, and spraying all three of them. By the time they decided to lie down, they were more than a little relaxed as well as damp and sticky from champagne and 7UP, having been overtaken by the sillies again.

Standing up and bringing Ailith to her feet along with him, Joshua then pushed the long sleeve of his houppelande back from his wrist and looked at his digital watch.

"It's three-thirty," he drawled. "Time for all little girls and boys to wipe the beverages from their bodies and go to bed."

Stephen remained on the skins before the fireplace, stretching his length out fully. "I guess I'm already in my bed and I refuse to move just to dry myself. That can wait until my return home. After all, how long can Ailith's parents be away?" Not awaiting an answer, he said, "Good night, you two. We must do this again sometime."

Joshua nodded and went to the door of Preston's bedchamber. Pushing it open, he stepped aside to allow Ailith to go in before him, then surveyed the room.

A large bed stood in the middle of the floor. Its size, he surmised, must be what was the king size of the era. Animal skins topped red velvet for warmth but had been turned down halfway to reveal the white linen covering the mattress and pillows. Curtains bearing the Radford coat-of-arms surrounded the great bed. A clothes chest with a cushion on top made of the same red velvet material covering the bed sat at its foot. Two benches and a small table stood against the wall, but there was no hearth or fireplace in here, and a severe chill hung in the air.

Ailith shivered, and Joshua folded her in his arms.

"Oh, Joshua," she whispered miserably. "I want to go home."

She could hardly believe her own words. When had she
learned to disdain all things medieval?

But it was cold here, and she knew how hard life was in
comparison with the one she had been—and would be—
leading in Joshua's time. And so little value was placed on
life in her day and age.

With a sigh of resignation, she quickly stepped away
from Joshua and removed her own houppelande, then her
pointed-toed shoes. Next she ungartered her silk stockings
and threw them aside, but left on her linen chemise and
scrambled into bed, under the weight of the heavy animal
skins.

After removing his long hose, Joshua immediately joined
her and drew her close. "We'll get through this, darling,"
he murmured hoarsely. "Just have faith." He kissed her
then, stirring her to passion. "What do you suppose it
would be like to make love in my ancestor's uncomfortable
bed?" he asked in a teasing voice, laving her throat with
his tongue.

"What you don't know won't hurt you!" Stephen yelled.
"For God's sake, close the door, Josh. What do you think
I'm made of, stone?"

"Shit!" Joshua said under his breath. "No, Stephen,"
he grouched. "I just thought you were asleep. But nooo!
Instead, I find you eavesdropping, you pervert."

Stephen chuckled as he came to the chamber door. "It
doesn't look like you're going to get up to close the door,
pal."

"Are you kidding?" Joshua replied seriously. "I just got
warm."

"I'll just bet you did," Stephen snickered. "Although I
would use the word *hot*." With that, he slammed the door.

"Now where was I?" Joshua murmured, giving his attention back to his wife.

Ailith kissed him hungrily. "I believe we were about
here," she whispered, burying her face in his chest.

They soon came together as one. Achingly slow, insidi-
ously tender, they made love on the great bed, ignoring its

lumpy, uncomfortable surface. Afterward, Joshua held Ailith in his arms as she slept. But sleep didn't come as easily for him. He thought about Connor and Gene, safe in 1998.

He smiled at the thought of Connor's consideration of them. He'd packed three thermoses of spring water, a thermos of coffee, and the soup and chowder. He hadn't opened his own duffel bag for fear of what twentieth century no-no he would find in it. Gratefulness for all that Connor had packed settled in him, and he silently promised to give Connor a huge bonus upon their return.

Sighing, Joshua shifted his weight slightly, bringing Ailith closer to his chest, his heart. His fear for her safety was palpable. But as much as he feared for her comfort and safety, his fear for a safe transport back to their own time nearly suffocated him. Just as sure that he'd heard Gene yell, "Wait! The black tent for your return!" he was sure that in all of England, Brint Pfiester was the only one in possession of a black tent—a black tent in which the orb would only work.

How could Gene, or himself for that matter, have overlooked something as important as their gateway back to 1998? After all the focus they'd put on it?

A sense of impending doom hit him, and he suddenly felt it had nothing to do with his sinking feeling that Brint Pfiester would be harder to find than a needle in a haystack.

Joshua held on to Ailith just a little tighter.

Chapter 33

"HELP!" STEPHEN SHOUTED. "I've been attacked by cooties, or whatever the hell they're called in this time."

Hearing Stephen's call, Joshua rushed out of Preston's bedchamber with Ailith close behind, holding her mantle against her bosom.

"They're not cooties, Stephen," she clarified. "They're fleas."

Joshua spun around to face her.

"Fleas! You packed everything else—why didn't you throw in some flea spray?" he admonished. "Do you know the disease fleas carry?"

"Check your bags, Josh," Ailith said soothingly, wrapping the mantle about her to ward off the chill. "Connor may have put the flea spray there."

Why hadn't the cold killed the fleas? she wondered. She and Joshua passed the night practically unscathed, although she had felt a bite now and then.

Joshua snatched open his bag. He pulled out a change of clothes for each of them, a tube of toothpaste, three toothbrushes, deodorant, a four-pack roll of toilet paper, a bar of bath soap, and a can of Off insect repellent.

"Shit!" He stared at the items before him, rummaging through them again. "As soon as humanly possible, I'm going to fire Connor," he stormed. "How could the man *not* put flea spray in my bag? After all, he thought of everything else!" He turned to a squirming Stephen. "Take it easy," he advised. "Maybe some of the rubbing alcohol will help you."

Stephen stood from his bed of animal pelt in front of the fireplace, where the flames—due to his stoking the fire throughout the night—still flickered. "Why aren't you guys scratching?" he asked irritably. "Are we dealing with fleas with discriminating tastes here?"

"Precisely," Joshua answered smugly. "The heat from the fireplace stirred them out of their lethargy. Ailith and I slept in cold storage. The fleas were too cold even to open their mouths in there!"

"So where did the fleas come from?" Stephen snapped in vexation. He patted his bare arms with the alcohol, then turned a horrified expression to Joshua and Ailith. "Is this the year fleas caused the Black Death?" he gasped.

Ailith yelped in surprise. "*Fleas* cause the plague?"

"Yes," Joshua explained softly. "Rat fleas, but it won't be proved until 1907 by the Second Indian Plague Commission of the British government."

He enfolded her in his arms and placed a gentle kiss on her forehead.

"Even though 1413 wasn't a particularly bad year for it, I would still like to get the hell back home so I can get you to safety."

"*Particularly bad*," Stephen grouched. "Those are the key words."

Ailith trembled in Joshua's embrace. What great harm had she done in insisting they return here? Knowing what she did about fleas and the advanced technology of Joshua's time, how could she stay here without altering history, intentionally or not?

Yet even as those thoughts skitted through her mind, Ailith couldn't leave without her parents or without discovering what she could about the identity of Aimon's mother. Although the return to the relative safety of 1998 lay within the turn of a dial, she had come too far to retreat now. A sense of impending disaster struck her, and she prayed the feeling had come about because of her heightened imagination.

She noticed that Stephen now stood before them, properly attired in tall black boots, which were buckled on the outside, black hose, and a blue houppelande.

Since she was determined to stay, she had to make Joshua and Stephen conform to the strictures of the day.

"Joshua," she said with a sigh, disentangling herself from his embrace, "what time is it?"

"Nearly ten," came the reply.

"No one in this age stays in bed, I mean *abed*, so late in the day," she warned. "Not even the lord of the keep. The light must be taken advantage of."

"I know, darling," Joshua reassured her. "Why don't you get dressed and do whatever it is you normally did before you escaped from here?"

"Escaped?" Ailith murmured, turning a rueful smile on him. "That's a unique way of putting it." She retrieved the thermos containing the coffee and poured out a cup for each of them before handing Joshua one. "But most appropriate. I'll see to the cleaning of the hall." Looking at Joshua, she released a mischievous laugh, forced though it was given her tormented thoughts. "What is your choice for breakfast, my lord? And you, Sir Stephen?" She handed Stephen a cup of coffee. "Do you have a preference?"

"Yeah, I mean, *aye*, milady," Stephen replied. "How's about a couple of Egg McMuffins?"

Ailith chuckled, sipping from her own cup. "Coming right up, Sir Stephen. Although it will, *'twill*, probably be in the form of boiled beef or boiled mutton, along with ale and wine."

She smiled at the stricken looks on Joshua's and Stephen's faces.

"It won't be that bad. I'll substitute milk for the ale and wine," she reassured Joshua.

"No!" Joshua snapped in firm denial. "No milk, Ailith. It's not pasteurized. I don't want you getting sick."

She knew her look conveyed the odd feeling that passed through her. After all, she had drank milk on occasion before she went into his time, and it hadn't been pasteurized, whatever *that* meant. But she wouldn't drink it now if he insisted. She made that promise to him before they'd finished drinking their coffee, thoroughly enjoying the strong brew. Once she and Joshua were dressed in medieval fashion, she tucked some mint candies under her sleeve in anticipation of her morning sickness. Then they started down the small stairwell, which led to the Great Hall. As they did so, she noticed Joshua had stuffed the orb inside his waistband under his tunic, but she didn't remark upon it.

Reaching the Great Hall, the change from the night before astonished her. The rotted rushes had been replaced by fresh ones sprinkled with peppermint and wintergreen leaves. Apparently, the soldiers had already eaten and returned to their stations because the scullery maids were busy cleaning up their leavings.

"Remember the difference in speech," she reminded Joshua and Stephen in a conspiratorial whisper, walking behind them toward the high table.

When they sat upon the dias, two serving girls rushed to the table, going first to Joshua. One of the girls started to place a hunk of stewed meat in a bread trencher before him, but Ailith halted her.

"Nay, Lizbeth," she commanded. "Bring His Lordship some cheese and fresh-baked bread. 'Twill be sufficient for this meal for the three of us."

Ailith retrieved one of her mints and placed it in her mouth. Just the sight of the meat and grease-soaked bread trencher nauseated her. Trying to stave off the feeling, she drew in a breath. "Please remove this at once."

Lizbeth gave Ailith a confused look. Ailith knew Lord Preston rarely sent food back, if ever, and apparently Lizbeth remembered this as well, but without delay she deemed to do as she was bade.

Joshua stared at Ailith in concern. "Are you feeling ill, darling?"

"A-a little," Ailith managed weakly, feeling the revolt in her insides.

"Then maybe you should go up . . . *above*stairs and stay there until this morning thing is under control," Stephen suggested with sympathy.

Ailith laughed nervously. "I've discovered that this 'morning thing' has a way of occurring at any time of the day."

"After what they placed in front of us to eat," Joshua complained, "I was about to develop a 'morning thing' myself. Maybe"—he noticed Ailith's pointed look—"may*hap* we should skip this meal altogether."

"I agree!" Stephen interjected instantly.

"Later we can eat the food we brought from home," Ailith told them. "There's enough left for at least two good meals for each of us."

"Smart girl."

Joshua leaned over and kissed her leisurely.

When someone cleared his throat, Joshua raised his head, allowing Ailith full view of Neville. The look he gave Joshua—one of pure hatred—nearly daunted her.

"Pardon the intrusion, milord," Neville emitted, strained cordiality in his tone.

Joshua noted the menacing look the man gave him and decided it was best to watch his back around the young knight. He damned himself for momentarily forgetting the name of the man before him.

"Speak, Sir knight," he demanded.

"There has been word, milord, that Galen and Meghanne deCotmer and the girl, Aida, will arrive late on the morrow."

Joshua drew in a sigh of profound relief. "Thank you"— he searched his mind—"Neville. And may I commend you on the efficiency and speed in which you handled the matter of restoring the hall to rights?''

Neville gave him a brittle smile.

"Though 'twas not *my* duty, Lord Radford, 'twas certainly my duty to see that His Lordship's orders were carried out,'' he responded with barely disguised insolence. "If His Lordship has no further need of my services in here, I will see to the duties for which I was hired.''

"You have leave to do so, Neville,'' Joshua imparted in frosty tones.

He watched him stalk the length of the hall and out the door. Bringing his regard to Stephen, he saw a wary expression on his friend's face.

"Rather arrogant jerk,'' Stephen commented.

Just as he rose from his seat, Lizbeth returned with a tray of food.

"We've decided against eating anything, Lizbeth,'' Ailith said, rising with Joshua.

She said a silent prayer, thanking God that her parents were returning. Neville was trouble, and the foreboding she had been beset with earlier returned as dread tugged at her heart.

'' 'Twould be nice,'' she continued, "to have potpies for midmeal along with the usual.''

Now looking thoroughly confused, Lizbeth replied, "Of course, Lady Ailith,'' and went back in the direction of the kitchens.

Ailith looked at Joshua. "Mayhap the pies will be more pleasing.'' She shifted her weight from foot to foot. "Joshua, there's something I haven't told you.''

She saw him stiffen and knew he was remembering her last deception when she hadn't told him of the baby.

"What now, Lady Ailith?'' he murmured in a silky tone.

"Preston Claybourne had a son who was rumored to have murdered him,'' she expelled in a rush.

Perhaps . . . mayhap if she shared some of her burdens with Joshua, she could make some sense of them.

Relief flooded Joshua's face, surprising her as much as his next words did.

"Aimon?" he asked.

She didn't think Joshua had such a vested interest in his ancestors. But apparently he did, otherwise he wouldn't have known of whom she spoke.

She nodded. "Yes, Aimon." She bowed her head in misery. "I think he was my son as well."

Joshua hooted with laughter. She raised her narrowed gaze to him.

"Sweetheart," he soothed, "Preston had a penchant for pretty peasant maids. You apparently were not the first or the last beautiful maiden he dallied with. It seems he became smitten with his steward's daughter, and on July 30, 1415, she bore him a son, then died in childbirth."

"Truly, Joshua?" Ailith whispered, her relief evident.

"Truly, my love."

Ailith frowned. "1415? The book Frances gave me shows the date as—"

"1414," Joshua finished for her. "The actual year was always in dispute. But Preston is away on campaign. For the girl to give birth in seven months, he would had to have been here in October."

"Which he was not," Ailith responded. "Then Preston wasn't murdered as Frances believed?"

Joshua shrugged. "So far as history states, he was. How accurate *that* tale is, is anyone's guess."

"B-but by his own son?" Ailith asked with incredulity.

"By one of his own knights, darling," Joshua clarified. "You see, he took the maiden from this knight and forced her to his bed."

"F-Frances seemed so sure of her facts," Ailith argued.

"In most of the recording of our family history, she's quite accurate but has always held a strange fascination with Preston and romanticized his life as much as she could. She wouldn't have it that during the time the steward's daughter became pregnant Preston was more than likely away on campaign. Nor would she have it that he stole the girl away from his knight and forced her to his bed. She wants it that Preston was murdered due to Aimon's greed, instead of his own callousness.''

Ailith gulped, and a dizzying array of emotions assaulted her. She could breathe easier knowing she hadn't altered history by not carrying Preston's child. Still, sorrow that Preston met with such an end crept into her. He was a harsh, hard man, who had once been her hero. Yet his demeanor, she surmised, was due more to the edicts of the era.

''D-do you know the name of the knight who murdered him?'' Ailith continued, in control of her thoughts again.

Joshua shook his head. ''No, sweetheart, I don't.''

''How do you know all this, Joshua?'' she asked.

''Mother has almost the entire history of both the Claybournes and the Kenleys, Ailith, as far back as recording was possible.''

''B-but she only gave me one book and—''

''Stay calm, love. Mother has other things on her mind— our wedding, their condo, and everyone else's business. I assure you what she showed you about the Claybournes isn't all she has. Mother has the history of the very first Claybourne knight.''

''Oh,'' Ailith responded in a small voice. ''W-what became of Aimon upon his father's death?''

''He avenged his father's death and became landed in his own right. You see, Preston's eldest legitimate son by Lady Glenna assumed the earldom and inherited the keep.''

A hazy memory of catching Neville in the stables embracing a petite red-head named Salinde—the steward's daughter—flared in Ailith's brain.

''Oh, Joshua!'' she blurted. ''I just had a horrible thought.''

''What?''

''Suppose the knight who killed Preston was Neville?''

''Even if he was, Ailith, we mustn't alter coming events.''

''Shit, Josh,'' Stephen said. ''Think of the repercussions.

Neville is glaring at you like he wishes to murder you the first chance he gets.''

Joshua threw his friend an unconcerned smile. ''Preston wasn't murdered until 1437,'' he reassured him. ''So don't go pull out your nine millimeter and blast him away.''

''But—''

''Enough, Stephen! I don't like the bastard any more than you do. And judging by the leers he gives to Ailith, he is probably as free with his 'charms' as Preston is with his. But as long as he believes I'm Preston, my life isn't in danger. Now let's just drop the goddamned subject.''

Ailith and Stephen nodded in compliance.

Wanting to get the hell back to 1998, Joshua gazed at Ailith a long moment. God, she was lovely in any century, and her brilliant medieval finery added to her golden beauty. Of course, he'd noticed her beauty the first time he'd laid eyes on her. Her face and clothing smudged, she'd worn medieval garments even then, though not as fine. He remembered her saying they would have potpies for lunch— midmeal, he corrected himself—because they might have been more pleasing. But how could pies, or anything else, be more pleasing to him than Ailith? Never could they be. Not in a million years. He smiled at her.

''My lady Ailith, would you care to show Sir Stephen and me around the keep?''

Ailith returned his smile.

''As much as I would like to, my love, I must decline,'' she answered. ''These people are my friends, whom I will never see again after tomorrow. I want to gaze upon their faces one last time. Would you mind very much if I went alone?''

Joshua kissed her on the cheek. ''Not at all, darling.''

''Looks like we're on our own,'' Stephen said. ''Shall we explore?''

Joshua nodded in approval, and Ailith watched them depart the hall.

She followed the routine she once had, the routine she'd known so well. Often she had gone with Meghanne as

Meghanne went about His Lordship's business. Like her mother, Ailith had been extremely well liked by everyone from the village priest to the lowly groom and sweeper.

Since she'd staved off her nausea with the mint candy, and knowing a visit to the kitchens would bring it back, she decided to go there last. With that in mind, she made her rounds to most of the castle's staff, including the pantler, the butler, and the spinners. Everyone she came in contact with expressed surprise and delight at her return to Greyhawke Keep. They all thought she had met with a grisly fate at the hands of DeLepee Rouge.

Yet she suspected most of the staff didn't express their true thoughts, which was that she'd ceded to their lord's demands and went willingly to his bed. Though she was sure they were sincerely glad of her return, she'd also become a lesser person in their eyes.

She hated that, but she couldn't rectify it. Her satisfaction was in knowing the truth and realizing in her heart *nothing* would have made her yield to Preston Claybourne. Before she would have allowed him to imprison her parents, she would've thrown herself from the castle's tower. Not only was it not possible for her to become his leman, but it wasn't possible for her to love anyone as much as she loved Joshua.

Presently she found herself in the bailey. Profound loss tugged at her heart as her gaze slowly swept across the courtyard. She saw changes, though to some they were probably hardly important and not particularly noticeable. The storeroom seemed slightly enlarged. A fence stood around the herb garden. New faces in the persons of additional knights walked around.

Folding her arms, she watched some of them stir up dust in mock battle. She thought she'd felt relatively safe knowing the Castle Guard was always there, but she knew she wouldn't miss them. Until her ascent into the future, she'd never known what it was like to go to bed anytime of the night or get up any time of the day and not worry about daylight. Or wonder if the guard would be forced to defend the castle while she slept.

One knight, on horseback, broke rank and trotted his horse toward her. As he neared her, he took off his helmet, and she immediately recognized Neville.

"A pleasant morn to you, Lady Ailith," he said, looking down from his mount.

Though a chill persisted in the air, the sun shone bright and high in the azure sky, and she squinted up at him, shading her eyes with her hand.

Neville continued, not allowing her to respond to his greeting.

"It was quite a surprise to find you with His Lordship at the gate last night. Quite surprising indeed!" he finished with a sneer.

Ailith's temper rose, and she glared at him. "What exactly do you mean, Neville?" she snapped. "Am I to understand your surprise resulted not from my safe return, but with whom I returned?"

Familiar with Ailith's temper, but even more familiar with the formidable temper of his liege, Neville thought to curb his total distaste for the attention Lord Preston forced on Lady Ailith. Besides, 'twas of no concern of his. He had Salinde and, although Lord Preston had shown interest in her, mayhap Lady Ailith could keep their lord amused enough to stay away from the steward's daughter. He wished to marry Salinde on St. Swithin's Day next.

When he spoke again it was with deference. "I meant no disrespect, Lady Ailith," he assured her. "And I am certainly happy for your safe return. 'Tis certainly true your presence once again will bring great joy to Galen and Meghanne."

His features a mixture of puzzlement and pity, he stared at her momentarily, then smiled with cordiality.

"By your leave, milady." He thumped his chest with his fist and trotted back to his men.

Ailith stared after him, sure of his insincerity. Only fear of Joshua, the man he thought to be Lord Preston, put a rein on his scurrilous tongue. Neville commanded the garrison, and she realized they were at his mercy. He couldn't hide his disdain for her husband.

Would he dare attempt to dislodge the lord of the keep? The king's own vassal? Although Joshua had assured her Preston hadn't been murdered until 1437, Neville's attitude sent a growing force of unease quaking through her.

She went back inside the castle, instinct telling her she, Joshua, and Stephen were in mortal dread.

Chapter 34

AILITH'S DISPIRITING THOUGHTS fled after the evening meal when she'd settled once again in Preston's solar with Joshua and Stephen. She laughed with glee when they recounted their odyssey to the village, and the surprise of the peasants upon seeing their lord in their midst.

"You should have seen him, Ailith," Stephen said merrily.

He had sprayed himself thoroughly with the insect repellent and now sat with confidence on the animal skins. A cozy fire blazed in the fireplace, where flames danced and wood crackled.

"He thought he had center stage at one of his fairs. I was surprised at what a ham he is."

"He's just jealous because no one called *him* milord. . . ." Joshua began, stopping when he noticed Ailith staring up at the top of the chest in the corner. His gaze fell on what had caught her attention, as did Stephen's.

As if on cue, they gasped in unison, "The vase!"

"I knew that vase in your hallway looked familiar," Ailith blurted from the bare settle, where she and Joshua sat wrapped in their cloaks to ward off the cold since the only part of the chamber that was warm was in front of the fireplace. "It's the very same one!"

"Let's bring that one back with us, and you'll have a pair," Stephen suggested. Confusion knitted his brow. "Or will you? Think about it! How many of your illustrious ancestors did that vase pass down to before you came to have it?"

"Stephen!" Joshua scoffed. "I don't care. The vase stays *here*."

"I was just kidding. I won't do anything to upset history's delicate balance."

Joshua drew in an exasperated breath. "Well, knock it off!" he sneered. "Nothing from the twentieth century stays here, and nothing from this century leaves here."

"Meaning we can't take Ailith and her parents back with us," Stephen jibed.

Ailith looked at Joshua. "He's something of a lackwit," she noted.

"Yeah," Joshua agreed. "But in modern times that translates to butthole!"

Stephen laughed. "Two against one. I haven't got a chance."

Ailith smiled at him. She'd become quite fond of her husband's roguish friend and was thoroughly enjoying the moment with them.

"Well, my fellow conspirators," Stephen went on, "what's on the agenda for tonight? Since we've already dined—and I use the word loosely—shall we take in a movie?"

"Ailith and I would like to stay and watch the flea feast, if you don't mind, Stevie," Joshua commented.

"Flea feast indeed. If the Off doesn't repulse them, the one-hundred-fifty-watt light will probably render them too blind to see what they're eating," he said, evoking laughter from all of them.

"I suggest," Joshua began, "that we get everything in order. We should repack our bags and make sure we have everything, including our twentieth-century trash. Of course, we'll leave out what's necessary until our departure."

"Good man," Stephen said, placing his hands behind his head and reclining back on the pelts. "And very bossy."

Ailith's heartbeat quickened. Tomorrow. Tomorrow she would be back in New Orleans, in America the United States. That's the United States of America, she corrected herself.

Father will love it!

She couldn't wait to see her parents and Aida. A comparison between Frances and Meghanne flashed through her mind. Perhaps Frances would overwhelm her mother with her assertiveness. Well, she decided, her mother would just have to learn how to live in the twentieth century. So would Aida, for that matter.

Every now and then, Ailith allowed herself to listen to bits and pieces of Joshua's and Stephen's conversation. At the moment Stephen was being adamant about keeping at least one of the guns he'd brought within quick grasp. Although Joshua insisted it was against his better judgment, he finally capitulated.

Ailith smiled at Joshua and with a puzzled look he kissed her on the cheek. His look told her he wondered exactly why she was smiling. He couldn't know that she was making another comparison, once again between Joshua and Lord Preston.

The Earl of Radford would never capitulate, not for anyone. He wasn't too arrogant to consider wise advice, such as her father's, but his word was law. It was also final. He never would have allowed one of his knights to gainsay him.

Joshua would make a wonderful liege. Although he *was* somewhat arrogant himself, he wasn't supremely so. At least not to the point of vaingloriousness, as was Preston. Ailith recalled her infatuation with the Lord of Greyhawke. Those traits in him then, though always outstanding in her mind, hadn't seemed so important. Joshua's fair-minded personality brought their differences into sharp focus. Lord Preston was a-a-a *butthole*!

She must remember to ask Joshua what that meant. If it

meant what she thought it did, Joshua should be ashamed of himself for comparing people to such a body part. She giggled. As she should, except in the case of the erstwhile Lord of Greyhawke.

"Have a 7UP, sweetheart."

Joshua cut into her seemingly constant musings. He had already opened the can, and she took it from him. She found it still cold, and she marveled again at the simple magic of the substance called dry ice.

"Thank you, Lord Joshua," she said with a chuckle.

"You are most welcome, my lady," Joshua replied. "We're toasting our imminent escape from Dump City."

"What's the first thing you're going to do when you get home, Ailith?" Stephen asked, taking a swig of champagne from the bottle before passing it over to Joshua.

Ailith laughed, yearning for a taste of the bubbly wine. "You two are impossible. Let me see," she continued thoughtfully. "This really is quite simple. The first thing I'm going to do is take a long leisurely bath."

"Good woman!" Stephen boomed. "Those are *my* sentiments exactly."

Joshua held out the now half-full bottle to Stephen.

"To the future," Stephen said. He took another drink, then passed the bottle back to Joshua.

"Yes," Joshua intoned, "to the future." He took a long swallow.

Ailith sipped from her can. "I thought everyone drank at the same time when toasting?"

"Yes, but sometimes you have to improvise," Joshua explained.

"We could all hold our drinks in our mouths and then *swallow* at the same time," Stephen suggested with a chuckle.

Ailith laughed. "Never mind. To the future, and to my beautiful clothes, and wonderful hot dogs, and—"

"My kind of nineties woman," Joshua interrupted with pride. "Except for the hot dogs."

Ailith's mind whirled. Hot dogs, ice cream, tacos, *beig-*

nets, crawfish. She would have such fun introducing her new world to Aida. Ailith was sure Aida would become as enchanted as she was.

Unsure of the time, she felt herself becoming weary. Though truly tired and ready for sleep, she expected to lie awake all night in anticipation of many things. First and foremost, fear that Lord Preston would for some reason return unexpectedly. He had done so two winters past because of a quarrel with Lady Glenna.

If he did, then what would they do? At the moment no one dared question Joshua's presence as the Earl of Radford. But that wasn't to say they didn't wonder at his mysterious return with herself and an unknown knight at his side. And Joshua hadn't once approached "his" knights in command with so much as a greeting. No matter how powerful the lord of the keep was, he didn't snub the men hired to protect him.

Preston was wise enough to know this. Why didn't Joshua? Joshua, who was supposedly founder and president of a medievalist club. And why hadn't *she* thought of it before now? She sat straighter in her seat, sure now that Joshua's snub was part of the reason for Neville's impertinence.

"Joshua," she said, her voice reflecting her anxiety.

"Yes, darling?"

"Why haven't you visited the garrison and talked to the knights in command?"

Joshua slid his hand across her back. "Don't be uneasy, sweetheart. I am well aware of the lord's responsibilities to his soldiers. But I hadn't expected to be here this long. We'll leave tomorrow, within the hour of your parents' return once you've explained everything to them. If we don't, we have a problem."

He paused and drew her into his arms.

"I don't know one knight from the other," he explained. "I barely remembered Neville's name. I certainly won't know what to *say* to them. Try not to worry, darling," he whispered. "We should be safe at home by this time to-morrow."

He gently pushed her to her feet, then took her hand and brought her to the bedchamber.

"Why don't you lie down and try to sleep? I'll join you after a while."

Ailith almost protested his condescending dismissal of her, but decided against it. Too tired to do anything more, she meekly obeyed, discarding her outer garments and, in her chemise, snuggling beneath the tons of covers.

Joshua left the door to the bedchamber slightly ajar, then crossed the solar to sit beside Stephen on the pelts in front of the fireplace. Resting his elbows on his raised knees, he drew in a tormented breath. Stephen got up to put another log on the dying flame.

"You shouldn't do that, if you don't want to get eaten alive again tonight," Joshua advised quietly. "You'll want it cold in here."

"Quite right." Stephen placed the log back beside the fireplace and sat down again. He gave Joshua a piercing look. "Okay, Josh. Spit it out. What's eating you?"

Joshua sighed. "I thought you would have realized the obvious by now."

"And that is?"

"Have you noticed that we're one black tent short unless we find Brint?"

"So we're a black tent short. What's that got to do with any . . ."

The significance of that dawned on him.

"Holy shit! We're a black tent short! How in hell are we going to get out of here?"

"Keep your voice down," Joshua warned. "I don't want to cause Ailith undue alarm."

"Undue alarm?" Stephen snarled, shooting to his feet. "Undue alarm, Joshua? Believe me, alarm was never more *due*. I ought to punch your stupid lights out! How could you overlook that one important thing?"

Joshua stood up. "I doubt you could punch my lights

out, you supercilious bastard. I didn't have exclusive rights to remembering the goddamn tent. You were free to exercise that option.''

''*You* were supposed to be our leader,'' Stephen taunted. ''You couldn't lead a goddamn horse to a wagon, even if you carried the beast on your back!''

In spite of his vexation at his friend, Joshua laughed. ''Good one, Stephen,'' he told him silkily. ''Now apologize to me, or I'll let your ass rot here.''

Stephen threaded his hand through his hair and chuckled. ''Well, giving it more thought, we *don't* want to alarm Ailith. And it certainly wouldn't do for us to try to beat each other's brains out, no matter how much the situation sucks. I'll apologize now, but I want the option of rescinding that apology the minute we hit 1998 New Orleans. Deal?''

Joshua nodded curtly. ''Deal,'' he agreed. ''Your decision. Your brain. If you're not satisfied with the way it is, I'll be glad to scramble it for you.''

Stephen glared at him. ''Do we have any other options at all to get back?'' he asked. ''Or should we plan to set up housekeeping in this lousy time?''

''We'll just have to find a black tent and erect it at the edge of the village.''

''Suppose that outlaw attacks, or worse, Neville tries to overthrow you while we're putting up the tent?'' Stephen asked, hands on hips, his voice laced with consternation.

''Then be grateful you had the forethought to bring those guns, my friend,'' Joshua responded wearily. ''Because I'll change history if I have to, to bring Ailith safely back to the future!'' He walked to the bedchamber, then gave Stephen a spartan look. ''Rest well. You may need all your strength and faculties to deal with what tomorrow holds for us.''

Chapter 35

THE NEXT MORNING Ailith threw up intermittently for a full half hour, which left her drained.

Joshua fussed over her, demanding she stay in bed, only allowing her to venture down for the midday meal. The menu consisted of baked spiced apples and pears, accompanied with cheese and fresh-baked bread, roasted veal, and roasted rabbits. Though she found the meal amazingly tolerable, she didn't touch the rabbit, she ate very little veal, and nothing of the customary other fare of stews, greasy sauces and porridges.

Ailith could hardly contain her excitement. After midmeal she wanted to linger in the Great Hall to await her parents, but Joshua wouldn't allow it because of her particularly bad morning. At her forlorn look, Joshua relented and permitted her to see to the cleanup of the hall, but then ushered her back above . . . hell, *up*stairs, she thought defiantly. Who was to know what she was thinking?

When he and Stephen left to look over the spot at the edge of the forest, she knew something was amiss . . . wrong, something was wrong. Though she didn't know what, she realized both Joshua and Stephen had been subdued this morning with not even a hint of the carefree silliness between them that she'd come to expect and adore. In fact, their expressions had been dark and somber. Whatever the problem, she knew it was serious. As a result, when Joshua again ordered her to wait for her parents in the solar, she hadn't protested.

Now, several hours later, she stood at the window looking out and saw Joshua and Stephen return, riding their horses inside the bailey.

What handsome knights they would make. Joshua is a born leader. He looks every bit the part of a nobleman.

They trotted the beasts across the courtyard to the steps of the keep, then dismounted. For a moment, they conversed before Stephen took the horses's reins and, along with the groom, went in the direction of the stable. She wondered why Stephen hadn't relinquished the horses to the groom and come up with Joshua.

A few minutes later Ailith started for the door in anticipation of Joshua's arrival, but it swung open just as she reached it.

Folding her in his arms, Joshua lifted her off her feet.

"Your lord issued an order," he murmured against her cheek. "You're supposed to be in bed. You're supposed to be *a*bed," he joked, sliding her down his body, setting her back on her feet.

Her arms around his neck, Ailith's eyes met his golden gaze. She saw none of the unease she'd seen there this morning. What she did see was the love she knew he felt for her—and his innate confidence once again. She smiled, then slid her hands across his broad chest.

"I pray thee, milord, indulge my foolish whims," she whispered coyly. "I ask of thee but this one boon."

Joshua chuckled and nibbled at her ear. "And what might that be, you saucy wench?"

Ailith sighed dramatically. "That I might be allowed to greet my parents here in milord's solar."

Pushing her a little apart from him, Joshua said softly, "Boon granted. But you mustn't get overly excited. Remember you're carrying our baby and . . .'' He stopped at the horrified look on Ailith's face.

Turning to see what terrible thing had caused the wide-eyed terror in her features, he felt the point of cold steel pierce the right side of his lower back. The shock of the sudden pain astounded him, nearly stealing his very breath away. It robbed him of his ability to stand, and he sank, as if in slow motion, to the cold, stone floor.

His capability to think had been taken away by the excruciating ache. Yet, just before he slipped into blessed, painless oblivion, he thought he felt the weight of his wife on his body.

Too stunned to utter a word, no sound came out of Ailith. She should have been screaming her lungs out. Instead, she stood there in horrified fascination, as things unfolded in dreamlike sequence.

Galen, without speaking a word, had lifted Preston's lance off the wall and, with malicious purpose, thrust it into Joshua's back. Had Joshua not turned at the exact moment of impact, he would have taken the thrust full force into his spine.

''I would gladly give my life in exchange for my lord's dishonor of my daughter,'' he snarled, poising his lance to strike once again.

Ailith flung herself across Joshua's prone figure. ''No! Father, no!'' she screamed, finding her voice. '' 'Tis not what you think!''

Contorted rage masked Galen's face.

''My eyes do not deceive me, daughter!'' he snapped, still holding the lance. ''Nor do my ears. That he has sorely used you is disgrace enough, but you have willingly gone to his bed. I will not abide that. I am already as good as dead, Ailith, for I have wounded our liege. But I will not go to my grave without knowing he lies dead at my feet. Remove your person from this man!''

''Mister, if you don't drop that stick right now, I'm going to send you to the great beyond with your goddamn head missing,'' Stephen promised viciously, his pistol pointed at Galen's head.

Galen turned in alarm.

"Now!'' Stephen barked.

"Stephen, don't!'' Ailith cried, hysteria bursting within her. "Please! He's my father!'' Quickly she turned her attention to Galen. "Father, he means it. Please do as he says.''

Staring at his daughter in puzzlement, he let the lance slowly drop from his hand.

Closing the door and stuffing the gun under his houppelande, Stephen rushed to Joshua's side.

His face was ashen, and blood from his wound had pooled on the floor under his back.

"If we don't stop the bleeding, he may bleed to death,'' Stephen croaked.

Fear coiled within Ailith, and at Stephen's words her heart splintered. "H-how can we stop it?''

"How the hell should I know?'' Stephen snapped, giving her a furiously cold look. "But I can tell you what I *do* know. If Joshua dies, so will Galen. That's a promise. Now tell him to help me get Joshua into bed.''

Without protest or hesitation, Galen helped bring Joshua into Preston's bedchamber, laying him gently on the bed, where Stephen dug inside his duffel bag for the alcohol and bandages. Finding what he needed, he went to Joshua, rolled him on his stomach, and doused the wound with alcohol, then packed it with the sterilized gauze. Miraculously the bleeding stopped, and Ailith said a silent prayer of thanks.

"We need to cover the packing, Ailith, to keep it from slipping out or getting germs,'' Stephen commanded in a toneless voice.

Ailith searched through their duffel bags, but could come up with nothing large enough for what Stephen needed to do.

Hoping the use of any linen from this time didn't harm Joshua more so and ordering herself not to faint, she whispered in a strained voice, "We can tear the bed cover."

She couldn't allow vapors to overtake her. Joshua needed her. Dear Mother of God, he looked so pale.

Knowing of the lack of modern washing facilities to clean bedding on a regular basis, Ailith watched in dread as Stephen cut a large square of material from the opposite side from where Joshua lay. Folding it to fit over the wound, he secured it with a number of plastic Band-Aids.

He turned to Galen. "You're a barbaric fool!" His voice was low and concise. "Without giving him a chance to defend himself, you plunged a spear into my friend's back. A man who risked his own life by coming back to this time to get you and your wife. To make your daughter happy because of his love for her. And you, you sonofabitch, tried to kill him!"

Galen turned a look of remorse on Ailith, which she responded with a penetrating glare.

"You have probably given my husband a mortal wound, Father," she asserted. "And—"

Galen gasped. "Y-your husband?"

"Yes!" Ailith answered, deliberately using the modern word of affirmation. "My husband!"

"Forgive me, daughter," Galen lamented. "I am confused. I meant to cause you no harm." He frowned. "You appear different somehow." Looking at Joshua, his frown deepened. "How could Lord Preston marry you without first setting aside Lady Glenna?"

"This man isn't your frigging Lord Preston!" Stephen gritted through clenched teeth. "But he is indeed married to Ailith."

"God's justice, you say!" Galen exclaimed.

"Sit down, Father. I have something to tell you," Ailith said, feeling strangely calm again. "But first I want you to get Mother and Aida. I want them to hear this, too. Why didn't they come up with you?"

Galen looked at Ailith with amazement, and she sensed the awe and mystery enveloping him.

"They did not know of your presence. They were weary

from the journey, and I sent them to their chambers to rest. 'Twas after their departure that Neville informed me that you had returned.''

"I see," Ailith responded. "Go, Father. Bring Mother and Aida here." It was more in the form of a command than a request, which he instantly heeded.

She wanted to rail at her father. Dear God, he had done the unthinkable. How could her father run Joshua through when he was unarmed? She had worried about trouble from some other source. *Never* had she thought her own father would harm Joshua. Was Galen as barbaric as Preston?

Woodenly she sat on the side of the bed. His face turned toward her, Joshua lay on his stomach.

"Oh, my love, my love!" she cried, her voice trembling. "What have I done to you? Please forgive me!" She placed her hand on his hot cheek. "I love you so, Joshua, please don't leave me!"

Ailith's torment broke through Stephen's icy rage, and he walked over to her and patted her gently on the back.

"Stop it, Ailith," he soothed. "You didn't do anything. This was unforeseen."

Ailith shook her head fiercely. "No, Stephen," she insisted. "It's my fault. He's here because of me."

"All right, Ailith," Stephen admonished, "that's enough! You must be strong. You not only have Joshua to think about, but also the baby. You *must* believe that he'll be all right."

"Do you believe it, Stephen?" Ailith sniffled.

"With all my heart," came the quiet reply.

"Th-then I believe it, too," she whispered miserably. Gently, tenderly, she stroked Joshua's silky black hair before asking Stephen, "Do you think he's in pain?"

"Not at the moment," Stephen reassured her.

They fell silent, and Ailith stayed with Stephen at Joshua's side until her parents and Aida came in. Then she went into the solar, while Stephen stayed with Joshua, placing both the .357 magnum and the nine millimeter within immediate grasp.

Ailith collapsed into the arms of her mother as her friend stood tearily by, not saying a word.

This should have been a day of triumph. Instead, despair racked her. And though she was angry with her father, she also understood his reasoning. Still, she couldn't reconcile that with her gravely wounded husband. Finally Ailith pushed her frayed emotions aside and explained, as best she could, what had happened to her.

Her family listened in baffled wonderment as she told of the orb and how it had brought her nearly six hundred years into the future.

Galen expressed his enthrallment to her. He attempted to express his sorrow at what he had done to Joshua, but Ailith silenced him every time.

Meghanne embraced her once again. " 'Tis hard to believe the thing was accomplished, even according to our own hopes, Ailith," her mother said. "But 'tis as you have said. Middlesbrough is barbaric and dangerous. Yet you risked your life for your father, Aida, and me. Nowhere in this realm could a better daughter be found. 'Tis most sorry I am for this grievous deed your father committed against your brave husband."

"He didn't know then what he knows now, Mother," Ailith mumbled, trying to make sense of the act with some justification.

She turned to Aida, who still sat in rapt silence.

"My friend," she said quietly. "I must know what happened in the tent the day I disappeared. What was your reaction?"

"Oh, Ailith," Aida answered softly. "I thought you had slipped under the tent and been captured by DeLepee Rouge. I-I slept and when I awakened you were gone."

"But what of the magician?" Ailith questioned. "Brint Pfiester?"

"Brint Pfiester was sore of heart by your disappearance, my child," Galen answered. "He even rode with me and the Castle Guard against the Red Sword. But you seemed lost to us forever."

"W-what happened to Brint Pfiester?" Ailith asked, her mouth suddenly dry.

"He'd urged you into his tent and his protection. When you disappeared, he blamed himself. He went on an odyssey, promising to find a way to bring you back." Galen paused. "Now I understand his despair. He knew the orb had caused your disappearance and he couldn't tell me."

Ailith glanced into the bedchamber and found Stephen sitting on a clothes chest, watching Joshua. She stood up from the settle and went back to sit on the side of the bed. She couldn't listen to any more of what her father was saying. Now that they understood her reasons for coming back, she *wouldn't* listen anymore. Only wanting to be at her husband's side, she could no longer focus on her parents.

"What can we do, Stephen?" she whispered.

"Nothing at the moment, honey," Stephen answered with sympathy. "He seems to be resting comfortably."

"W-why doesn't he wake up?"

"I heard somewhere that the mind is a wonderful thing. When something happens to us that's too great for our consciousness to handle, it shuts off until things improve."

Ailith turned to him in skepticism.

Stephen smiled. "I might not have explained exactly how it works, sweetheart, but I came close enough. Quit worrying. He'll be all right."

"Thank you, Stephen. You're a good friend."

By nightfall Ailith turned frantic. It became obvious that Joshua's wound had become infected. It was discolored, and he had developed a burning fever. At two different times he'd awakened, only to drift back into unconsciousness again.

"You said he would be all right, Stephen!" Ailith raged. "What's happening to him?"

"It's the infection," Stephen answered, his voice low and angry. "We've got to get him back to 1998 and a hospital before it spreads. He needs antibiotics. He could die without it.''

When Stephen uttered the last statement with matter-of-fact precision, Ailith's despair deepened, and she thought she would strangle on her fear.

Chapter 36

SOMETIME LATER AILITH redressed the wound. After cleansing it with alcohol, she swabbed it with the tincture of iodine. Because the profuse bleeding had stopped, she didn't have to use the bedcover again, for which she was grateful, so she recovered the incision with sterile gauze from Stephen's first-aid kit.

"Stephen," she wearily called over her shoulder, "he's resting more comfortably."

Joshua groaned and, without warning, opened his eyes, his pain-filled gaze falling on her.

"A-Ai-lith," he whispered in ragged tones.

She placed her hand on his jaw, finding it still abnormally hot. "Yes, my love, I'm here." She took his hand in hers.

Hearing Joshua's voice, Stephen pulled the chest closer to the bed and sat on it. Not quite eye level with Joshua, Stephen seemed satisfied not to be standing over him.

"How do you feel, Josh?" he asked.

"I-I have a searing pain in my back," Joshua muttered hoarsely. "A-and I feel like an incendiary bomb about to explode. What the hell happened to me?"

When he tried to turn over, he moaned loudly at the pain his movements caused him.

"Oh, no, darling!" Ailith said in alarm. "You mustn't move. You may cause bleeding. You . . . you've been stabbed—"

"Stabbed?" Stephen sneered, anger at the pain Joshua experienced boiling in him. "I'm not so sure that's an accurate definition. Perhaps if the man had used a kitchen knife, even a *butcher* knife! But he ran through him, Ailith, with a goddamn lance! He put a hole in him the size of a silver dollar!" His voice rose to an angry pitch, and he stood from the chest. Going to the window, he took in deep, calming breaths.

Joshua grimaced, but raised his head to her tear-stained face. "Who stabbed me, Ailith?" he asked weakly.

"M-my father," she murmured, feeling suddenly ill. "He thought you were Lord Preston. Oh, my love, I'm so sorry. Please forgive me for making you come here and jeopardizing your safety."

"My sweet medieval lady," Joshua croaked, "I would give my life in exchange for your happiness. Never think you're to blame for anything that has happened or will happen. I love you, Ailith."

She placed her trembling lips on Joshua's warm, dry ones. She tasted fever and her own salty tears. "Don't die, Joshua," she wept. "We'll find a way to get back home."

Home. The twentieth century, where Kenley Manor beckoned, safe and sound. Home. They *had* to get back. Maybe her father could help.

"Ailith," Joshua began, "may I have some water?"

She raised her tear-glistened eyes to his face. "We used all the water already."

"How about a 7UP?" Stephen suggested.

"F-fine," Joshua answered. Lying on his side, he eased himself on his back and winced.

"Be careful," Ailith advised him.

She poured the drink into a tankard and put it into his hand. The dry ice had dissolved, but the room temperature was such that the 7UP remained somewhat cool.

Joshua drank deeply, then looked at Ailith and Stephen.

"How bad is it?" he asked through clenched teeth.

"You've developed an infection, Josh," Stephen stated quietly.

"I see." Joshua sighed. "Ailith, promise me you'll go back to the future with Stephen as soon as he finds a way home."

"N-no, Joshua!" Ailith's voice faltered as she realized Joshua seemed to consider his life already at an end. "You will be with us." She swallowed the sob lodged in her throat.

"I want to be, darling," Joshua answered, "but the wound has become infected. Without antibiotics I may not have a snowball's chance in hell to survive."

"We'll get you back, Josh," Stephen declared. "Somehow we'll get you back."

"Maybe I can help," Galen stated from the doorway.

"Father!" Ailith cried, whirling around to face him.

"What the hell are you doing here?" Stephen snarled.

"Lamenting my foul, cowardly deed, Sir knight," Galen answered, stepping fully into the chamber and walking to the foot of the bed. "But my remorse does not change it. I will go in search of the magician, Brint Pfiester."

"Brint Pfiester?" Ailith asked in surprise. "But you said he was gone. Nowhere to be found," she reminded him.

"You departed before I had concluded my explanation, daughter," Galen said. "Brint Pfiester is in Middlesbrough again. 'Twas rumored he had been here for a sennight. If 'tis true, I will find him this eventide and bring him to the bedside of your husband."

"Oh, Father, I pray you are successful."

Galen patted Ailith on her shoulder, then tried to move closer to Joshua's side, but Stephen immediately placed himself between Galen and Joshua.

"It's all right, Stephen," Joshua said. "Let him come forward."

Glowering at Galen, Stephen reluctantly stepped aside.

Reaching the bed, Galen said, "Thank you, husband of my daughter. If 'tis within my power, I will rectify my folly. My sorrow is great for the harm I have caused you, Joshua. If forgiveness is in your heart, I most humbly beseech it.''

''Oh, Father!'' Ailith said with a sob.

''Don't cry, darling,'' Joshua soothed. ''It was a natural mistake. After all, I could be Preston's twin.'' He tried to smile, but he only succeeded in grimacing with pain. ''You're forgiven, Galen,'' he continued. ''I probably would've reacted the same way if she were my daughter.''

''All right, Galen,'' Stephen said in frosty tones. ''Joshua has forgiven you, but I haven't, no matter what the circumstances were. Bring that so-called magician here to help him. If you do that, *then* we'll talk forgiveness. Until then, I'll hold my benevolence in reserve.''

Galen held Stephen's gaze momentarily. ''Fair enough, Sir knight,'' he finally said. With a parting glance to Ailith, he quit the room.

As the day wore on, Ailith sat without speaking on the chest Stephen had brought into the bedchamber. She had given Joshua Tylenol for his pain, and he slept fitfully. Though he still had a fever, he didn't seem any hotter than before, for which she was grateful. All the while, Meghanne and Aida sat in the solar, wanting to be of some comfort to her.

Since no one went down to partake of it, Meghanne had portions of the midday meal brought to them. Ailith thought tiredly that it could have stayed where it was since no one partook of it anyway. Stephen refused to leave Preston's quarters, but instead paced the length and breadth of the solar and bedchamber in nervous agitation.

Ailith knew of the camaraderie between Joshua and Stephen but until now she hadn't realized how deeply rooted that friendship was. She also knew without a doubt that if Joshua died, Stephen would kill Galen.

Her heart cried out *no!* She wouldn't lose her husband and father in one day. She stifled a sob. As guilty as it made her feel, she could survive Galen's death, but if she lost Joshua she too would surely die.

In lieu of those torturous—and in her mind traitorous—thoughts, she tried to focus on Neville and the castle's servants. What must their thoughts be at not seeing their liege make his customary appearance? Would his knights demand an audience with him? She sighed, cursing her thoughts, which went from one dangerous situation to another.

Again she refocused her thinking and recalled some of the history she'd learned about her time, occurrences that hadn't even happened yet.

Prince Hal . . . King Henry would defeat the French in the Battle of Agincourt in 1415. He married the daughter of Charles VI, the King of France, in a few years.

But other than what Frances told her, Ailith had read nothing of Preston Claybourne. Where was his place in the scheme of history? Once Frances had said Preston had been regaled as a knight among knights, and he remained a loyal and trusted friend to King Henry until Henry's death in 1422. When she returned home, she would ask Frances for the other family history books on the Claybournes and Kenleys. Who knew what other interesting tidbit she would discover?

Ailith gasped, suddenly feeling like a . . . a sorceress. She knew what no one else in this time period knew, and it frightened her. She didn't want to know what she did and still live here.

She stood and went to Joshua's side, placing her hand on his forehead. Still hot.

He opened his eyes. "I'm not sleeping, darling," he whispered, swallowing hard.

"Are you in pain, my love?" Ailith asked.

"Not too bad," Joshua lied.

In truth, he was in agony, but he didn't want to cause Ailith more worry than she was already going through. He was in such pain, he was barely able to think clearly. Yet when he did, all his thoughts were of Ailith and their baby.

He had already accepted that he wouldn't survive, but he wouldn't relinquish his last breath until he was assured that

Stephen had found a way to take Ailith back to Kenley Manor.

"Lie down beside me, sweetheart," he croaked. "You need to get off your feet."

In compliance Ailith stretched next to him and gently laid her head on his chest.

"I love you," he murmured, resting his chin on her silken mane.

Ailith closed her eyes, refusing to think of Joshua lying so helpless, nor would she think of Neville or of Preston. Instead, she would think of Connor and Shawanda and Loquisha. Not of the past, but of the future.

When she thought of Frances, she managed a smile. Frances had told her how the Claybournes had come to America. In the early nineteenth century, Joshua's great-grandfather's grandfather came to America as a young man on a lark, but with every intention of returning to England. He fell in love with and married an American girl and settled in Jamestown, however. He hadn't been penniless and he acquired vast amounts of land, thus starting the Claybourne dynasty of America. From what Frances said of her husband's ancestors, it seemed the Kenleys had settled in the Deep South.

Ailith lifted her head off Joshua's chest. His steady breathing told her he slept again. Though she didn't want to think of the past, it kept invading her mind. Oh, where was Galen?

As if in answer to her question, the solar door burst open, and Galen and Brint Pfiester rushed inside, breathing rapidly.

"We must make haste to leave this place," Galen warned. "A messenger has reported that Lord Preston is journeying with Lady Glenna and their infant son to Greyhawke Keep. 'Tis with the king's permission that he travels here. His journey is but a few hours from an end. The message was given to Neville in the village. Now he knows that Joshua is an imposter. Even as we speak, Neville hastens to rouse Lord Preston."

Chapter 37

AILITH'S HANDS FLEW to her breast. "We can't let that happen," she said with a gasp. "Neville will surely kill him."

"Not if I can help it," Stephen vowed, fingering the pistol in his waistband.

"They are too many, even with your awesome weapons," Brint Pfiester declared. "Gather your things, Sir knight. Galen has spoken of a secret room we must all retreat to swiftly."

Quickly Ailith helped secure their things as Aida rushed down to see if the Great Hall was empty. No one wanted to explain why the "liege" was wounded.

Thinking of the dank stone floor in her father's hidden room, she implored everyone to take as much bed covering and animal pelts as they could carry. Knowing Joshua had to lie on the floor, she wanted him to be as comfortable as possible under the circumstances.

When Aida returned minutes later, she declared the Great Hall safely unoccupied.

"As well you know, that could change at any time," Meghanne said to Ailith.

Ailith nodded. "I know, but it's a chance we must take,"

she said breathlessly, her fear and hurried movements beginning to take their toll. "I don't wish to think of the consequences if Lord Preston reaches us."

"Sir knight, is there anything we can do to hasten our retreat?" Brint asked calmly.

"I'm called Stephen," he responded. "And yes, support one side of Joshua while I hold up his other side." He turned to Ailith and found her attempting to lift one of the duffel bags. "No, honey, that's too heavy for you. Let the others carry the bags. Is everyone ready?"

After Meghanne, Galen, and Aida each lifted a bag, Stephen stuck his gun in his waistband, then he and Brint supported each side of Joshua.

Galen led the way down the small stairwell, which led directly to the Great Hall.

"Wait, Father!" Ailith called in a loud whisper. "See if the room is still empty."

Peeking around the corner, Galen raised his hand for them to halt. He straightened himself and murmured, "Saints preserve us!"

Before Ailith could question what was wrong, a voice belonging to an unseen soldier cried, "Rouse the Castle Guard! Sir Neville has sent a messenger informing us there are imposters in our midst!"

"Damn that bastard!" Joshua moaned weakly, attempting to straighten himself.

"What do you want us to do, Josh?" Stephen asked, swiping at his brow.

"G-Galen, how many are out there?" Joshua asked.

"Two."

"Are they still there, Father?"

Without a sound, Galen glanced around the corner again, then turned back with a curt nod.

The oppressiveness of the small area suddenly weighing her down, Ailith leaned against the cold, stone wall and closed her eyes in defeat. Sweat beaded her body, and her mouth had gone dry. They were trapped, destined to die here. Through her misery, she vaguely heard Galen say the soldiers had departed.

" 'Twill only be for a moment," Aida said, her voice trembling.

Stephen jerked Ailith from against the wall. "Come on, honey. We have to move."

Joshua gave her a wan smile, and it took every bit of the willpower she possessed not to cry out at his pale countenance.

"Go!" Brint commanded her.

Ailith rushed behind her parents and Aida as they rounded the corner into the Great Hall. Though no one was near the dogs that usually lazed about, they seemed to sense something amiss and sat alert. Once she had crossed the room, Ailith looked over her shoulder and found Stephen and Brint, supporting a now-unconscious Joshua, right behind her. Just as she breathed a sigh of relief, she heard the heavy wooden entrance door being thrown open.

"Go!" Stephen cried, pulling out his gun, though they hadn't been spotted yet.

"This way," Galen said, his breath coming in heavy pants. "The room is not much farther."

He led them down the narrow corridor to a door at the extreme end. Opening it and hurrying through, they found a short stairwell, which led down to another corridor.

Rats scurried across their feet; a rank odor filled the area; water dripped from an unknown location onto the floor; and except for a lone torch looming at the far end, darkness surrounded them.

Ailith tempered the nausea rising within her and followed her father. Finally they reached the torch, and she realized another door stood beside it. As Galen lifted the torch out of its holder, she remembered with unerring clarity the exact location of their whereabouts. No one would discover them as long as they remained in her father's secret room, because it was housed in the bowels of the castle. Indeed, she wondered how Galen had discovered it.

Pulling open the door, Ailith cringed as the hinges made

a loud creaking noise, groaning against the invasion. A narrow stairway stood on the other side. Going down and opening one last door, they finally reached the safety of the secret room.

Inside she spread out one of the pelts on the floor, and Stephen and Brint gently placed Joshua down. She sat beside him and found him half-conscious.

Guilt descended on her because they were trapped like rats in a pit, not only in this room, but in this time period. Her Joshua was dying, and there was nothing she could do about it.

If only she hadn't insisted they return for her parents . . .

She drew in a breath, hopelessness pervading her. Tears cascaded down her cheeks.

His eyes on her, Stephen went from where he stood against the wall and sat on the pelt next to her and Joshua. Angrily she brushed her tears away.

"I wouldn't blame you if you hated me, Stephen," she said miserably. "How could I have caused such harm to befall you and Joshua?"

Stephen smiled sadly, hugging her around her shoulders. "I could never hate you, honey. Not in . . . what . . . ? . . . five-hundred eighty-five years?" he said, attempting to lighten the mood. "I don't know how, but I know we'll *all* get safely out of here. So take heart, sweetheart."

"Your friend speaks wisely," Brint Pfiester said. "You must take heart, Lady Ailith."

He gave her a liquid mixture he'd started blending together just after they reached the room.

"Your husband must drink all of it," he instructed. " 'Twill clear his thoughts and lessen the hold the fever has on his body for a spell."

"Oh, Brint!" Ailith exclaimed. "Thank you."

Calling his name softly, Stephen had already lifted Joshua's head, while Ailith urged him to drink the mixture. He drank it all, making a disgusted face.

He grimaced. "I think I've been poisoned."

" 'Twill help you, Joshua Kenley," Brint Pfiester said, "for a short time."

"Thank you, Brint Pfiester." Joshua's voice seemed somehow stronger already. "I assume you have figured a way to get us there?"

"There's no way other than the way you came," Brint answered. "Through the black tent."

"*Your* black tent," Stephen said.

"Aye," Brint responded. "To assure you'll return to the same spot you left from, you have to leave from the same spot you arrived at."

"Meaning?" Joshua asked.

"Meaning the tent must be pitched at the exact spot of your appearance," Brint answered.

Stephen threw up his hands in frustration. "Well, we've had it. With Preston, or should I say, Lord Attila and his Huns lurking about, they'll grab us the minute we show our faces."

"Brint and myself are not being hunted," Galen informed him. "We will raise the tent ourselves."

Meghanne spoke for the first time since coming to the secret room. " 'Twould still be much danger. Does not Neville know Galen has spent time in Lord Preston's chambers with a man claiming to be our liege?"

Ailith knew her father would be much at risk, which seemed, by the look on her mother's face to be Meghanne's greatest fear. Although she had come back, she knew her mother had thought her lost to them forever. And if an arrow pierced his heart, her father would be lost, too, lost with no hope of ever returning. The thought chilled her.

"Why can't the deed be done from here?" Meghanne asked.

"Because we would not land back at the place we started from, Meghanne," Stephen said with impatience. "Haven't you been listening to the magician?"

"Have patience, Stephen," Ailith admonished. "My mother fears for us all."

"Aye, Sir Stephen," Galen said. "We will get the tent

ready, then figure a way out of here undetected."

Stephen nodded curtly.

"Then let us depart," Brint said.

"Just a minute," Stephen called, halting them. "Have you any more of that stuff you gave Joshua? It helped him a lot."

"Nay," Brint answered. "I do not have all of the ingredients on hand to prepare more. That is why we must make haste to leave here. When the potion wears off, the infection will spread rapidly. Without the immediate help from his time . . ." His voice tailed off.

Stephen swallowed. "Then make haste, man, make haste!"

Brint and Galen departed without further words, then Stephen went back and sank down beside Ailith. He looked at Joshua, who lay with his eyes closed. He knew Joshua as well as everyone else had heard Brint's dooming words, but no one said anything. They all seemed lost in their own thoughts, lost in fear and in hope.

He gave Meghanne a cursory glance, then his gaze fell on Aida. He had been so absorbed in Joshua's well-being, he'd hardly been aware of her existence. For the first time, he really looked at her.

Long waves of rich, brown hair tumbled down her back, past her waist. When he'd first seen her, she had been wearing a wimple, as Meghanne was at the moment.

Stephen studied Aida further. God, she was almost as beautiful as Ailith! As large as a doe's, her eyes were as blue as the sea and seemed almost too big for her elfin face, with eyelashes that wouldn't quit. She had a perfectly beautiful face. Oh, yes, he *had* to know her better. They *must* reach home safely.

He glanced at Ailith, who sat hovering over the sleeping Joshua like a mother bird.

Feeling Stephen's gaze on her, Ailith smiled at him, who nodded with encouragement. Why didn't this end? *Now* was her time, but she felt suspended between the old and the new. She realized now *was* her time. Past tense, and she hated the now.

An eternity passed before her father and the magician returned with conflicting news. Neville and his men were everywhere, they claimed, but they still were able to erect the tent at the edge of the forest. They had to wait until the soldiers gave up the search for them before they could leave.

Joshua had awakened again.

Despite the effort and pain, he raised himself to a sitting position. "We will not be defeated!" he commanded. "I've decided I want to live to see my child born in the twentieth century."

Everyone looked at him in amazement.

"Yeah," Stephen grouched. "So what's *your* plan to leave this hell hole?"

"Is there another way out of this room?" Joshua asked.

"Aye," Galen answered quickly. "Next to the cistern there's a stone that can be rolled back. Inside there's a narrow passageway that leads to the outside. The way out is blocked by a stone barrier, which in turn, is covered over by natural barriers of brush and thistle."

"Father," Ailith whispered, "have you ever left this chamber by that exit?"

"Many times," came the reply.

"So you were obviously not discovered," Stephen pointed out.

"They'll give up their search when it gets dark," Joshua speculated. "We'll leave then, but we'll need the horses. I won't make it on foot."

"Then we'll get the horses," Stephen assured him. "We'll all go together or we won't go at all. So let's synchronize our—"

"Our what?" Ailith asked, feeling some oppression lift from her spirits for the first time since they'd come there.

"Synchronize our thoughts," Stephen chortled.

Joshua chuckled, and Ailith wanted to kiss Stephen for bringing *that* sound out of him.

Everyone's mood was markedly changed this time, Ailith noted, as they waited for the full blackness of night to descend.

Stephen left with Galen and Brint when they thought the soldiers were asleep.

Meghanne warned that not all the soldiers were heavy sleepers, especially if they didn't have drink in them.

Stephen promised to heed the warning and took both guns along in case someone woke up and objected to their taking the horses.

Ailith, Joshua, Meghanne, and Aida set forth out of the relative safety of the chamber immediately after Stephen and the others left. While Joshua leaned heavily on Ailith, the other two women struggled with the duffel bags. Silently Ailith prayed Stephen would succeed with her father and Brint and get the horses.

The journey through the passageway took what seemed like an hour. When they reached the exit, Joshua, nearly fainting from exhaustion, was breathing heavily and beset with fever once again. Although Ailith could barely discern his features, she knew he was flushed. The potion Brint had given him was beginning to wear off!

She struggled with Meghanne and Aida to push away the stone barrier, and they in turn helped her bring Joshua out. They stayed close against the wall, Ailith's heart sinking.

It was bitterly cold outside, but worse than that, it wasn't a dark night. The full moon shone its light as bright as early dawn, casting shadows on everything that moved.

Joshua groaned and sank to the ground.

"Hold on, my love," Ailith sobbed, fighting to keep from giving in to her fear. "Please hold on. It'll soon be over." She prayed to God and to all the saints she could think of.

"Ailith, where are they?" Joshua asked in a hoarse voice.

"They'll be here any minute, darling. Stephen promised."

She pressed her cheek against the hot flesh of his jaw.

The pounding cadence of hoofbeats, galloping in their direction, reached her ears, and she tensed. The sound grew ominously louder. Within moments Stephen and the others emerged through the clearing, and she released her breath in relief.

But her peace didn't last long, for she heard more distant hoofbeats, still too far away to cause undue alarm.

Stephen leaped off his stallion and rushed to where Joshua sat. "We are being pursued. Neville and Preston are not far behind us! Give me a hand quickly, Galen," he ordered. "We must get him on the horse and get the hell out of here. I'll saddle up behind him."

Hurriedly they placed Joshua astride Stephen's horse. Ailith noticed only three horses stood in the clearing—three horses that seven people had to ride! Before she had time to truly become hysterical, Joshua was ordering her up behind Stephen.

The others rode double, carrying the duffel bags. As they lit out for the tent, an arrow flew harmlessly above their heads.

Ailith turned and discovered Preston was fast gaining on them.

"Halt," he boomed, "in the name of the king!"

Once they left the cover of the brush behind, the other soldiers were alerted to their whereabouts, and they were quickly closing the gap.

More arrows flew past them, missing them by mere inches. Metal grated against metal as Preston unsheathed his sword and Ailith screamed, clutching Stephen tighter.

"Stephen, do something!" she cried. "Preston has his sword drawn!"

Without turning around, Stephen said, his voice quavering from the wild ride, "Hang on, Ailith." Holding the reins with one hand, he reached for the pistol in his waistband with the other. "I may have to shoot in the air, Joshua."

"What the hell for?" Joshua demanded in an agonized tone.

"To scare them," Stephen replied.

"Scare them, my ass!" Joshua snarled in a voice suddenly wrought with strength and authority. "They're aiming at us, Stephen, and trying their best to hit us!"

"I can't shoot at them, Joshua," Stephen snapped. "Your illustrious, bloodthirsty ancestor is riding with that posse of clowns! I wouldn't want to upset the course of history by blowing him away."

"Then shoot in the air," Joshua urged, "before one of the goddamn arrows hits Ailith in the back!"

"Try not to fall off, pal," Stephen instructed.

The horse carrying Preston was only one length away. But when Stephen held the gun high above his head and fired off several rounds into the air, it neighed in fear. Ailith knew Preston's horse had been seasoned for battle, but it careened to a stop, unseating Preston in the process. For a few precious minutes, the roaring din of an army of pursuing horses ceased.

"Yahoo!" Stephen yelled in cowboy fashion. "Did you hear that sound? Preston and his heroes just dumped in their armor. We scared the shit out of them!"

As abruptly as they had stopped, the ominous hoofbeats started again, making relief short-lived.

"Shit!" Joshua growled. "He's a persistent, stubborn bastard."

"Reminds me of someone *I* know," Stephen grumbled.

"I thought Lord Preston wouldn't reach Middlesbrough for some time," Ailith squeaked in panic.

"With this demented bunch, you never know," Stephen said.

As if Divinity had intervened if their favor, the black tent suddenly came into view, and Ailith made the sign of the cross.

With a relief-filled shout, Stephen trotted the horse inside the tent, the others hot on his heels.

"May I accompany you, Joshua Kenley?" Brint asked quietly.

"I expect you to," Joshua replied in a considerably

weakened tone. "For assisting us in our escape, you've jeopardized your own safety—"

"Whatever, dammit!" Stephen interrupted impatiently. "We're not saved yet. Hurry and get each horse on either side of mine."

Without delay, everyone did as they were ordered.

"Do not lose physical contact with me, Josh, Ailith, or this horse. Now, who has the orb?"

A collective, disbelieving chorus of "*what?*" echoed through the tent.

"Just kidding," Stephen snickered, pulling the orb from under his houppelande. He set the dial to 1998. The soldiers crashed through the tent, but luckily the mist had already began to surround Ailith and the others.

Chapter 38

WHEN THE MIST disappeared, Ailith found herself and the others inside Joshua's tent on his property on the lakefront.

"Goddammit! We made it!" Stephen shouted joyfully. "I'll never doubt again."

"Is Ailith all right?" Joshua asked, his voice weak and tired.

Ailith reached around Stephen's body to touch Joshua on his arm. "Yes, my love," she reassured him softly.

"Galen, help Ailith off this horse," Joshua commanded. "I have to get to a hospital."

Galen hurriedly complied, and Ailith rushed to where Joshua leaned heavily against Stephen as they still sat on the spent horse.

"He's right," Stephen said, his tone serious now. Holding on to Joshua to keep him from falling off the horse, he slid down. "Galen, give me a hand."

Without hesitation, Galen rushed to Stephen's side.

Once they'd gotten Joshua down, Ailith took his hand into her own.

"Just a little while longer, my love," she soothed.

"I'll be all right, sweetheart," Joshua responded. "See

to our guests, darling. They must be in shock.''

''Oh! Of course,'' Ailith said, remembering the rest of her family. ''Mother, Aida, Stephen and I have to bring Joshua to the hospital—''

''H-hospital?'' Aida interrupted timidly.

''Yes, Aida. Don't you remember we talked about it at the keep?''

When Aida only stared blankly at her, Ailith continued.

''Never mind. Mother, I know everything is going to be strange to you and Aida, but please don't be frightened. It's all so wonderful! You'll wait for me in Joshua's manor. Connor will take care of you.''

''Of course, daughter,'' Meghanne declared bravely, the slight quivering in her voice betraying her fear. ''You must see to your husband.''

''Come, then,'' Ailith instructed.

She went outside in the wake of her husband and the other men, including Brint Pfiester. A gentle rain was falling, and no one knew whether it was dusk or dawn, but Ailith was grateful for the rain and the clouds because no one was lurking about. Her motley medieval crew must have presented a strange spectacle, which would have required lots of answers and explanations.

Connor greeted them at the entrance. ''Miss Ailith, welcome home. I have to tether the horses. I'll be right back inside,'' he said.

Rushing past her, he headed in the direction of the tent.

Ailith took her mother and Aida into the warmth of the house, where Gene Callenberg stood conversing with Stephen.

''Where's Joshua?'' she asked when she didn't see him.

Gene came to her and embraced her happily.

''Ailith, my dear.''

''Oh, Gene, it's wonderful to be back,'' Ailith responded, not wanting to be rude in her haste to find Joshua. ''I won't ask what you're doing here at this hour. Not now, anyway. We must get Joshua to the hospital. Where is he?'' she asked again, this time more firmly.

"Lying on the sofa in the living room," Stephen answered.

"We must make haste, Stephen." With everyone following her, she hurried from the kitchen toward the living room.

"It's all right, Ailith," Stephen told her. "I called 911. An ambulance is on its way here."

He had no sooner made that statement than Connor, back from securing the horses, informed him the medical unit had arrived.

Ailith watched in fascination as the attendants took Joshua's vital signs, then checked the wound. Without further adieu, they transferred him from the sofa to a stretcher and wheeled him to the waiting vehicle, where an IV was immediately started.

Ailith rode with Joshua inside the ambulance while Stephen followed in his own car.

"You're going to be all right, my love," Ailith said, looking worriedly at the paleness of Joshua's complexion.

"Y-you b-bet I am, angel," Joshua croaked.

The medical attendant radioed in information regarding Joshua, then listened for a moment, to whom Ailith wasn't sure. All she heard was an awful crackling sound. She guessed that he had received all of the instructions he needed when he laid the radio aside. Seated across from Joshua, he had a clipboard on his lap, holding a pen in his hand and monitoring a strange machine attached to Joshua's chest.

Finally he looked at her and asked, "Can you tell me exactly how he attained his wound?"

Fear and uncertainty swirled in Ailith. "Why . . . he . . . I—" she began.

"It w-was an accident," Joshua interrupted. "I was jousting a-at a f-friend's medieval costume party and . . . and this happened. Since I know it w-was an accident, I . . . the name of the person is . . . is unimportant."

"It's all right, Mr. Kenley," the attendant said. "The lady can answer other questions."

"N-no. S-she's not familiar with . . . with. . . ." Joshua's voice trailed off.

"My husband's friend is following us, sir," Ailith said, the strength in her voice surprising her. "He'll respond to any questions you need answers to."

"We can wait for answers until we get to our destination," the attendant said kindly.

The loud wail of the siren and the incredible speed of the ambulance played havoc with Ailith's aplomb, but they arrived at Ochsner Foundation in record time.

Stephen took over answering all pertinent questions, while the hospital staff took over Joshua's care.

Though the medical staff eyed the three of them curiously because of their attire, Ailith didn't feel at all out of place staying at Joshua's side dressed in her medieval garb. She would have stayed with him wearing nothing at all. She was ordered to wait in the family room, however, until they cleansed and prepped Joshua's wound, preparing him for a few days in the hospital.

"Ailith?" Stephen murmured when he caught sight of her entering the waiting room.

"Oh, Stephen!" she wailed, and rushed into his arms.

"What is it, Ailith?" Stephen asked in alarm, gently caressing her back. "Is Joshua worse?"

"N-no! I . . . they said they needed to work on his wound and get him ready for a private room."

Stephen sighed. "Well, I guess that means he'll be in here for a while."

Ailith nodded. "They said he'll be here about three days."

"Then maybe I should go to Kenley Manor and bring you back a change of clothes?"

"Oh, would you?

Stephen laughed, and Ailith pushed herself out of his embrace.

" 'Twould be my pleasure, Lady Ailith," he said, "but on one condition."

"And what's that?"

"That you tell me everything you know about Aida."

"Aida?" Ailith asked in surprise. "My friend?"

At Stephen's sheepish look, she giggled.

"Why, Stephen Edwards, have you become smitten with her?"

"I'm just blown away by her, Ailith," Stephen admitted wistfully. "I've just got to know her better."

"Stephen," Ailith responded, close to tears, "nothing would make me happier."

"Er . . . excuse me," a male voice interrupted, and they turned to find a tall, gangly man standing there. "I'm Dr. Barnes. Are you Mrs. Kenley?"

"Yes," Ailith answered expectantly.

Dr. Barnes smiled. Judging by the laugh lines around his mouth and the compassionate expression in his eyes, she knew his smiles were common occurrences.

"Your husband said you wouldn't be hard to find. He told me to look for a couple dressed as if they'd just left the Middle Ages in a mad dash."

Ailith looked at Stephen, and he winked at her.

"What's the story, Doc?" Stephen asked.

"So far Mister Kenley is responding well to the antibiotics. Strong doses are being fed directly into his veins. He should show a marked improvement in the next twenty-four hours."

"Oh, that's wonderful!" Ailith exclaimed, the tears that had been lurking in her eyes now cascading down her cheeks. "May we see him?"

"Of course," Dr. Barnes answered with another smile curving his mouth. "He has been transferred to his room. I've left instructions for his care with the nurse and I'll see him again tomorrow. Pleasure to meet you two."

He shook their hands, then gave them Joshua's room number and took his leave.

Ailith sat watching Joshua. A full day had passed, and his color had returned; he now slept peacefully. She had no intention of leaving the hospital until he was well enough to be released and could leave with her.

"Knock, knock," Stephen said as he opened the door and walked in. "How's the patient?"

"Trying to sleep," Joshua said in a weak but teasing tone. "But nooo, you won't let me."

Stephen laughed, and they slapped each other with a high-five handshake.

"I want out of here," Joshua complained.

"Patience, patient," Stephen said. "You'll be outta here in due time."

"I thought you were asleep, Joshua Kenley," Ailith said, feigning hurt tones.

"No, my angel," Joshua replied. "I wasn't asleep. I was just thinking, and I'll let you know exactly *what* I was thinking as soon as we can get rid of the pest here."

"Why don't you just ask me to leave?" Stephen said in challenge.

"Get the hell out of here, Stephen," Joshua ordered.

"See," Stephen responded.

He sat in the chair Ailith had vacated to sit next to Joshua on the side of the bed.

"That's all you had to say. Now, would you two care to hear about the four fugitives from Fiefdom?"

"I assume you mean Ailith's parents and friends?" Joshua asked in exasperation.

"Affirmative."

"Where do you come up with these ridiculous titles, Stephen?"

Stephen shrugged. "You're just jealous, Josh, because you can't think of them. Now, shut up and listen."

Describing the wonderment a new discovery incited from the "four fugitives from Fiefdom," Stephen evoked laughter from Joshua and Ailith.

Her sense of relief was great at learning of the care Connor and Gene Callenberg had taken to insure her parents' and friends' comfort. They would be eased into the twentieth century, thus giving them more benefit than she'd had.

She realized, too, the fun she was going to have helping them to overcome their culture shock.

Before Stephen left, he generously offered to take over Aida's enlightenment of the twentieth century. Ailith knew that that magnanimous gesture was due solely to his attraction to her friend.

"So," Joshua said when they were alone once again. "I've always known Stephen and I were alike in that we're both attracted to old-fashioned girls."

Ailith laid her head on his chest. "Old-fashioned indeed."

"Only in certain instances, my love," Joshua whispered, stroking her hair. "You have truly become very modern. I think I have the best of both worlds in you."

Lifting her head, she caressed his stubbly cheek.

"My handsome, magnificent Joshua. I do love you so."

Easing her mouth down to meet his, Joshua kissed her tenderly at first, then with passion. The fires she knew were consuming him caught Ailith. Their words of love made her long to express the sentiment in a more intimate way, but they couldn't.

"Ailith, I need you, darling," Joshua rasped.

It seemed as if he had read her mind.

"J-Joshua, your wound. You must be careful."

"Let me worry about my wound, angel," Joshua said between kisses.

"But someone may come in."

Ailith gulped in a breath, feeling Joshua's tongue sliding over the breast she only then realized he had bared.

"Close the curtain," he demanded in a passionate murmur.

Ailith complied, leaving him long enough to do his bidding and then slip out of her jeans. Returning to him, he positioned her on top of him and gently slipped his aroused manhood inside her. He groaned in both pain and pleasure.

Not wanting to hurt him, Ailith tried to control the sensations spurting through her and robbing her of all breath, but she lost the battle. As Joshua shivered with his release, she moaned in ecstasy and gave in to her own feverish thrills that were almost rendering her mindless.

"Ahh, my sweet love," Joshua said, stroking her hair when she rested her head on his chest once again. "You're all the medicine I need."

Ailith smiled, very happy to be the cure he needed. She would lie on him a few minutes more before getting dressed again. No matter how much she relished the feel of his bare flesh next to hers, they were, after all, lying naked together in a hospital room.

She sighed in contentment at their daring, then got up and reached for her clothes.

Had it really been just two months since that dreadful ordeal? Joshua had recovered so quickly, Ailith hardly remembered he had been so ill.

Her mind filled with sheer happiness as she sat gazing at her reflection in the vanity mirror, adjusting her veil while photographers snapped away.

Her wedding day. Again. The day Joshua had promised her. Though she'd closed her mind to all the chattering going on around her, she knew the sound of every person's voice.

Pamela, Joshua's sister and her matron of honor, had much of Frances's mannerisms, but not all of her personality.

For that she thanked all things holy. As she had suspected from their telephone conversation, Ailith liked Pam immediately when they met in person and knew they would become fast friends.

She wondered how Aida was faring. Ailith had asked her to be a bridesmaid and was nearly floored when Aida told her she was to marry Stephen and had to plan her own wedding. Now she sat across the hall in one of the guest bedrooms being subjected to the same wonderful torture as herself.

They were being married in a double ceremony, and she couldn't have wished a better fate for her friend. Stephen was smitten out of his mind with Aida. Everyone was finding their niche. Her parents lived at Kenley Manor on a permanent basis. Or at least until Meghanne overcame her fear of twentieth-century technology.

Brint had found a friend in Gene Callenberg. They shared common interests, which Galen also shared, with his sharp mind and curious intelligence.

Dubbed by Stephen as the "three Einsteins," they all became active in science projects for the future.

Brint liked the present so much, he even made up a birth-date to match his current age, which, Ailith realized, they all had to do.

They'd offered to give the orb back to Brint, but he insisted they keep it, after somehow rendering it useless and never explaining how he'd come to have it in the first place. It was just as well it no longer carried the power to breach the time barrier. She and Joshua had no plans to travel backward again.

The door suddenly swung opened for the hundredth time, and Frances glided in.

By the time Frances had gotten wind of Joshua's "accident," he was already out of the hospital. Ailith suspected Frances didn't believe Joshua's story of jousting at a friend's medieval party. But beyond wanting to know who had hosted the party and where it had been held, she hadn't pursued any more questioning. She had hugged him fiercely, announced she was going to stay at the manor for a week or two, and changed the subject.

Now she cut into Ailith's calm musings and, with the autocracy of a drill sergeant, chased everyone out, including Meghanne and Pamela.

When they were alone, Frances closed the door and faced Ailith.

"I was just in with your friend, Aida," she began. "She makes a lovely bride."

"Romance seems to be in the air," Ailith responded happily. "I'm overjoyed that we're having a double wedding ceremony. Stephen really swept Aida off her feet."

"No offense, dear, but that doesn't seem like the only thing off on her," Frances commented. "She's a very strange little creature. I had no idea Stephen was attracted to that sort of girl."

"Well," Ailith replied, momentarily at a loss for words. "Um . . . Aida is just a little bit shy. I'm sure she'll overcome that in time."

Frances shrugged. "If you say so, darling. Your parents, especially your mother, also seem a bit shy and out of place. Don't they like New Orleans?"

Ailith laughed, knowing what her mother and Aida were experiencing because she'd been there. In time they would indeed adjust.

"They *love* New Orleans, Frances. Take my word for it."

"I hope I didn't offend, dear."

"Of course not. Why don't you take Mother under your wing and show her the ropes?" Ailith suggested.

There was no better way for Meghanne to learn anything than through Frances's harmless but autocratic ideas. She herself had learned simply to get away from Frances's irritating ways when they became too much for her.

"You know I'll do what I can, Ailith," Frances gushed with anticipation. "It would be my extreme pleasure." She paused then continued. "Ailith, I want to tell you how glad I am that you're marrying my son. Joshua is very happy, and he loves you very much. I want to officially welcome you to the family, dear."

"Thank you, Frances," Ailith responded, fighting back tears.

A knock sounded on the door, quelling any response from Frances.

"Come in," Ailith called, and Joshua opened the door.

Stepping inside, he strode to where she sat and she stood up, spreading her gown around her. She'd never seen him look more handsome, as he did now, wearing his tuxedo.

Frances glowered at Joshua. "You know it's bad luck to see the bride before the wedding."

"But we're already married, Mother," Joshua emphasized.

"For that we can all be grateful," Frances retorted with a pointed look at Ailith's belly. "That gown is fitting her a bit snug."

Joshua smiled indulgently. "Yes, Mother. Ailith's three and a half months pregnant, but why do I get the feeling you already knew that?" He didn't wait for a reply. "Please close the door on your way out. I'd like a moment alone with my bride."

Frances smiled and winked at him. "I can't wait for the blessed event, darling," she drawled before walking to the door. Stepping into the hall, she closed the door behind her.

Shaking his head ruefully at the closed door, he then turned to Ailith. "We may have to leave the planet to keep her away from our child."

"I think by then Meghanne deCotmer may also have a thing or two to say," she reassured him.

"God, but you're beautiful, Ailith," Joshua murmured and gulped in a breath. "Stephen and Aida are ready."

When Ailith slid her arms around his neck, he croaked, "Don't start what you can't finish, Mrs. Kenley. If I kiss you now, I won't be able to stop. I'll probably ruin your beautiful makeup." He planted a feather-light kiss on her cheek. "I love you so, Ailith. I've always dreamed of having an old-fashioned wife, but you've exceeded all my expectations. You have brought me such joy. I adore you, my lady, my wife, my love."

Joshua kissed her again with a whispery touch to her mouth and, at the gentle contact of his lips on hers, Ailith sighed. She had leaped across time for his kiss, for his love.

Stepping away from her, Joshua held out his arm to her. "Time to go, darling."

Ailith beamed as Joshua led her to the door and into a future of married . . . nay, wedded bliss. Patting her stomach, she smiled to herself. All was right with her world, and a great sense of peace descended on her.

For the love she and Joshua shared cemented them to each other, to this time, to this place, and to eternity.

TIME PASSAGES

_CRYSTAL MEMORIES   Ginny Aiken   0-515-12159-2

_A DANCE THROUGH TIME   Lynn Kurland

                                    0-515-11927-X

_ECHOES OF TOMORROW   Jenny Lykins   0-515-12079-0

_LOST YESTERDAY   Jenny Lykins   0-515-12013-8

_MY LADY IN TIME   Angie Ray   0-515-12227-0

_NICK OF TIME   Casey Claybourne   0-515-12189-4

_REMEMBER LOVE   Susan Plunkett   0-515-11980-6

_SILVER TOMORROWS   Susan Plunkett 0-515-12047-2

_THIS TIME TOGETHER   Susan Leslie Liepitz

                                    0-515-11981-4

_WAITING FOR YESTERDAY   Jenny Lykins

                                    0-515-12129-0

_HEAVEN'S TIME   Susan Plunkett   0-515-12287-4

_THE LAST HIGHLANDER   Claire Cross 0-515-12337-4

_A TIME FOR US   Christine Holden   0-515-12375-7

All books $5.99

VISIT PENGUIN PUTNAM ONLINE ON THE INTERNET:
http://www.penguinputnam.com

Our Town ...where love is always right around the corner!

■ ■